CONDOR

THE SHORT TAKES

CONDOR
THE SHORT TAKES

JAMES GRADY

MYSTERIOUSPRESS.COM

OPEN ROAD
INTEGRATED MEDIA
NEW YORK

Copyright © 2019 by James Grady

Cover design by Mauricio Díaz

ISBN: 978-1-5040-5650-2

Published in 2019 by MysteriousPress.com/Open Road Integrated Media, Inc.
180 Maiden Lane
New York, NY 10038
www.openroadmedia.com

for Robert Redford

CONTENTS

INTRODUCTION:
OUR CONDOR SKY

In 1975, generals in the KGB—the Soviet Union's chief spy agency—got their Russian hands on a new Robert Redford movie: *Three Days of the Condor*.

In that movie—produced by Dino DeLaurentiis, directed by Sidney Pollack, also starring Faye Dunaway, Cliff Robertson, Max Von Sydow, and Tina Chen—screenwriters Lorezno Semple Jr. and David Rayfiel adapted a slim first novel by a twenty-four-year-old unknown dreamer into a ticking-clock masterpiece propelled by Redford's character, a bookish intelligence analyst who comes back from lunch to the New York office for his obscure secret CIA research department and finds his coworkers murdered.

Redford's CIA codename was Condor.

As Redford/Condor insists to the Faye Dunaway character he kidnaps:

"Listen, I work for the CIA. I'm not a spy. I just read books. We read everything published in the world, and we . . . we feed the plots—dirty tricks, codes—into a computer, and the computer checks against actual CIA plans and operations. I look for leaks, I

*look for new ideas. We read adventures and novels and journals
... I ... I ... Who'd invent a job like that?"*

In 2008, Pulitzer Prize–nominated Pete Earley revealed that
the movie stunned Russia's KGB generals and convinced them
they had fallen behind their CIA foes in a critical espionage
endeavor: the work they saw Redford/Condor doing.

So the KGB created their own top-secret unit inspired by
Condor.

Like in the movie and novel, the KGB headquartered their new
secret division in a quiet neighborhood—Flotskaya Street in Moscow—and stuck a phony brass plaque by its front door proclaiming
that place to be the "All-Union Scientific Research Institute of Systems Analysis"—a nonsense name instead of the *real* title of the "Scientific Research Institute of Intelligence Problems of the First Chief
Directorate of the KGB"—known by its Russian initials of NIIRP.

Both the movie and the novel projected Condor's secret
department as a small bureaucratic entity with fewer employees
than the fingers of your two hands.

The KGB's Condor-inspired NIIRP employed 2,000 Soviet
citizens.

Picture a snow-dusted night in January 2008, inside Washington,
DC's Beltway.

Our dog Jack and *not-quite-sixty* me are shuffling downhill, back toward my middle class, two-kids-launched suburban
home and author's lair, when through the darkness, I hear my
wife, Bonnie Goldstein, shouting: "You've got a phone call!"

That call came from Jeff Stein, a former Vietnam War undercover spy, then a journalist for *Congressional Quarterly* covering
espionage. Jeff had Earley's book and barely contained his excitement as he interviewed me about Condor and the KGB.

I was blown away.

As crime author Mark Terry noted in his 2010 essay about *Six
Days of the Condor* for *Thrillers: 100 Must Reads*, master novelist

John Le Carré says: "If you write one book that, for whatever reason, becomes iconic, it's an extraordinary blessing."

Call me blessed.

And come with me to that lucky blessing's beginning in Washington's blustery January of 1971, long before my Condor soared in a now—*so far*—forty-four years' flight that's become three novels, a handful of novellas and short stories, a globally famous movie, a TV series—and a template for a fundamentalist assassin and Russian spies.

In 1971, I was a senior at the University of Montana, a Congressional Journalism Intern, one of twenty *Woodstock* (generation) *warriors* brought from America's colleges to Washington to work on Congressional staffs and be night-schooled by a scrappy genre of journalists called *investigative reporters*. I lived on A Street, Southeast, six blocks from the white icing Capitol Dome in a rented third-floor garret.

Every weekday, I brushed my recently barbered hair, put on my only suit, struggled into a boxy tan overcoat, and walked through winter residential streets to my internship on the staff of a United States senator.

And every workday, I walked past a white stucco townhouse set back from the corner of A and Fourth Street, Southeast. A short, black-iron fence marked the border between the public sidewalk and that building's domain. Shades obscured the windows. A bronze plaque by the solid black door proclaimed the building as the headquarters of the American Historical Association.

But I never saw anyone go in or out of that building.

Fiction creates alternative realities.

And most fiction is born from a *what-if* question.

Two history-altering *what-if* questions hit me as I walked past that townhouse:

What if it's a CIA front?

What if I came back to work from lunch and everybody in my office was dead?

Logical questions considering those times.

The Cold War ruled. Kim Philby haunted Britain while ghosts of JFK, RFK, MLK, and Lee Harvey Oswald made America tremble. *Dr. Strangelove* caressed Doomsday weapons. The Soviet Union sprawled as an evil Gulag wasteland behind an Iron Curtain, while Communist China coiled like an invisible dragon behind a Bamboo Wall. J. Edgar Hoover's FBI knew everything about everybody. Israeli avengers stalked the globe: they got Eichmann, they could get anybody. Apartheid bedeviled South Africa. South American drug dealers were still "small-time," but America's Mafia had a French connection for heroin. "Terrorists" were often called "revolutionaries," whether they wore KKK robes, counterfeit Black Panther berets, the PLO's *kufiah*, or the Weather Underground long hair and love beads stolen from *the rainbow daze* of the Sixties. Cults like the murderous Manson family stalked our streets. Something enshrouding and protecting our globe called the ozone layer was in jeopardy because of deodorant we sprayed in our armpits. Not far from my rented garret, President Nixon's White House henchmen were formalizing "dirty tricks" into thuggish crews called "plumbers" created for truth suppression, burglaries, and murder. In Vietnam, my generation was in that war's twelfth year of Americans killing and dying.

Only the ignorant weren't paranoid.

My what-if fantasy about a covert CIA office on Capitol Hill had a visible counterpart. A flat-faced, masked-windowed, gray concrete building with an always-lowered garage door and an unlabeled slab of gray wood entrance crouched on Pennsylvania Avenue amidst restaurants, bookstores, and bars just three blocks from the Capitol Dome. Hill staffers shared the common knowledge "secret" that the building belonged to the FBI, one of their "translation centers."

Sure, but what do they really do?

Within pistol range of that secretive FBI fortress sat the townhouse headquarters for Liberty Lobby, an ultra-right-wing political sect that in coming years would with impunity advertise and sell illegal drugs through the mail—Laetrile, a compound its salesmen claim cures cancer that the great actor Steve McQueen decamped to Mexico to use in the days before cancer killed him.

The last lecturer to my class of interns was Les Whitten, a novelist, translator of French poetry, and partner to Jack Anderson, whose syndicated investigative reporting column ran in almost a thousand newspapers. Unbeknownst to them, Jack and Les were under surveillance by the CIA. Les was the epitome of a muckraker—a term of honor.

I stayed after class that night in a Congressional office to persuade Les to tell me the "great story" about the CIA he'd told the class he would break the next week.

Allen Ginsberg is *the* Beat poet. He'd seen the best minds of his generation destroyed by madness, dragging themselves through America's streets is search of an angry fix. The horrors of heroin screamed too loudly for the man inside the poet to ignore. Cherubic, bald, bearded, homosexual, *Om*-chanting Ginsberg, hated by conservative cheerleaders of "law and order," did what his critics didn't dare: he declared a personal war on heroin. Les's "great story" concerned Ginsberg's investigations into the CIA's allies in our Southeast Asian war and their ties to the heroin business.

As Les stood in the nighttime halls of a Congressional office building and whispered his news to me, the world trembled.

But I was just a college kid headed back to my hometown of Shelby, Montana, sixty miles east of the Rocky Mountains, thirty miles south of Canada, and a million miles from "real world" places like New York and London.

My grandfather had been a cowboy and card shark for saloons, my grandmother was a polio-crippled midwife who'd seen eight of her own children survive, including my mother and her four sisters who all lived in our hometown and who helped raise me like a pack of fun-loving coyotes. My Sicilian uncle had a still-unclear-to-me management role in our local red stucco two-story brothel that was protected by the cops and county health officials, a . . . *confusing* civic attitude toward law and morality that also manifested in our frontier doctor/former mayor performing often tragically botched illegal abortions in his office above Main Street, a reality that, judging from his steady stream of out-of-town patients, everyone west of the Mississippi River knew.

You know the kid I was.

Coke-bottle-thick eyeglasses. Off in the clouds. The son of loving, respectable middle class parents who did their best. My workaholic father managed movie theaters, which meant I grew up seeing thousands of Grade B movies. My mother was a county librarian, which meant I didn't need to worry about how long I kept the thousands of crime and adventure novels I devoured. I'd worked since grade school: theater ticket taker, motion picture projectionist, janitor, hay bale bucker, rock picker, tractor jockey, gravedigger. I put myself through my state university shoveling for the city road crew.

When I went to the University of Montana, I was so naïve I thought that the Journalism Department included my passion: writing fiction.

I'd started spinning fictional tales before I could write, dictating stories to my patient mother (she threw them away). By my high school graduation, I'd written my senior class play and had dozens of short stories rejected by magazines. I was seven weeks into my university studies before I realized that the Journalism major I'd chosen did not cover fiction. But the J School gave me scholarships the fiction writing department couldn't—though that department did have novelist professors James Lee Burke and James Crumley, plus poet Richard Hugo, the only one of that illustrious American literary trio whose classes I took. Yeah, *dumb me.* My journalism major trained me in tight prose, let me review movies for the student newspaper—coolest gig *ever* for a cinema and writing nut. I got to cover *the times a'changing* in the streets. And staying in journalism landed me the gig in Washington.

When I came back from my DC internship, I had no idea how to make my dreams work. All I wanted to do—well, not *all*—was write fiction. In the autumn of 1971, I began an "independent undergraduate studies" fifth year to give me what I thought was a necessary academic umbrella to write fiction . . .

. . . only to be saved—*dazzled*, actually—by another dose of great luck.

Montana was re-writing its outdated, robber-baron-bred state constitution—Dashiell Hammett created *noir* fiction with *Red Harvest*, his debut novel of crime and corruption set in the old constitution's Montana. The staff of the new constitutional effort needed an emergency replacement who could write fast and had a résumé involving government (*say*, interning for a US senator). They picked me.

After the convention, spring of 1972, I disappeared on the road for a few months, came back to Helena, Montana, and after a brief foray as a laborer/fire hydrant inspector, took a *feed-me* job in government bureaucracy.

The rage to write burned in me like a heroin addiction welded to sex.

I'd decided that the only way to learn how to write a novel . . . was to write a novel.

And that the only way to be a writer . . . was to write.

I lived in a second-story apartment above a cottage not far from the state capitol building in Helena. For a while, my roommate was Rick Applegate, one of America's smartest Baby Boomers. Often, I stole my fictional characters' names from the spines of Rick's nonfiction books (*Condor's* Heidegger). Our neighbors were a *so cool* couple: he was an affable whip-smart lawyer, she was that tawny-haired artsy woman so many of us *Sixties soldiers* wanted to be or wed. I lived in that apartment long enough to meet their first born, a baby girl named Maile Meloy who grew up to be a major American author, but I moved out of town before they brought home their second child, a son Colin Meloy, leader and chief writer for the famous twenty-first-century indie-folk-rock band The Decemberists. I labored in a bureaucracy, jogged and studied judo, saw my girlfriend when I could, soared in AM radio rock 'n' roll, read hundreds of novels, went to movies, saved my pennies, and spent hours at the kitchen table hunkered over a battered green manual typewriter.

And felt two *what-if* questions from my Washington, DC, days come to life.

In those days, James Bond, *super spy*, dominated espionage fiction. Despite fine movies having been made from their excellent books, John Le Carré and Len Deighton were overshadowed by 007. Eric Ambler, Josef Conrad, and Graham Greene could be found on library shelves, but at bookstores, they were blanked out by the glitz of *Dr. No*, *Goldfinger*, and *From Russia With Love* (the best Bonds)—Sean Connery and Ursula Andress, sex and a Walther PPK.

As much as I love *"Bond, James Bond,"* I didn't want to write about a superhero. I wanted my imaginary hero to feel real, even though he worked for the CIA.

The Central Intelligence Agency, America's best-known spy shop. In that fearful post–Joe McCarthy era, when assassinated JFK had publicly loved James Bond and secretly been entangled in covert intrigues like assassination plots against Cuba's Fidel Castro outsourced to the Mafia by our spies, the CIA was invisible.

When I researched Condor, I found only three credible books on the CIA, two by David Wise and Thomas Ross (*The Invisible Government* and *The Espionage Establishment*) and one by Andrew Tully (*CIA: The Inside Story*). I stumbled across a book by historian Alfred W. McCoy, who braved the wrath of the US government, French intelligence agencies, the Mafia, the *Union*

Corse (the major French criminal syndicate), the Chinese Triads, and our exiled *Kuomitang* Chinese allies to write *The Politics of Heroin in Southeast Asia.* McCoy tramped the mountains of Laos, air-conditioned government corridors of Saigon (now Ho Chi Minh City), and along the *klongs* of Bangkok to show how, in our crusade against communism, America's government had *in the least* embraced ignorance about the gangsterism of those we called our allies. Allen Ginsberg *redeemed.*

Those works plus a few columns by muckraker Jack Anderson constituted the only "reporting" I did on the CIA.

My imagination was thus unencumbered by much reality.

Prose fiction in that era treated the CIA like a phantom. CIA agents made appearances in hundreds of novels, but they were inscrutable.

Three notable exceptions were *Richard Condon,* whose *Manchurian Candidate* military intelligence nightmare blew me away in adolescence as both a novel and a movie; a cynical novel by *Noel Behn* and its John Huston–directed movie *The Kremlin Letter* ("off the books" spy groups, not the CIA); and great novels by *Charles McCarry,* who worked as a deep cover CIA operative.

Another CIA agent named *Victor Marchetti*—who post-*Condor* 1974 coauthored *The CIA and the Cult of Intelligence,* an exposé censored word-by-word—first wrote a 1971 novel that followed a then-common practice: he changed the name of the CIA, further distancing fiction from reality.

Hollywood treated the CIA with a Tinkerbell touch: the CIA meant fancy gadgets, trenchcoated knights in righteous pursuit of *truth, justice, and the American way.*

An engrossing exception that few people saw was the 1972 movie *Scorpio,* starring Burt Lancaster as a CIA executive who may or may not deserve the French assassin the Agency forces to hunt him. During its Washington filming, the cast for that movie stayed in the same hotel that Nixon's Plumbers used as a base of operations to burgle the Watergate complex across the street. Nixon burglar and *former* CIA agent E. Howard Hunt even spy-trick "coincidentally" rode the elevator with the movie's co-star Alain Delon and tried to impress the actor by speaking French.

I was a fan of my high school days TV show *I Spy* starring Bill Cosby and Robert Culp, but TV in the Sixties broadcast in the shackles of censorious "standards," and those two American agents too often came off like super spies. Over-the-top "spy" TV shows like *Mission: Impossible, The Avengers,* and *The Man from Uncle* were addictively entertaining, but TV's most realistic "spy show" was the Patrick McGoohan drama called *Secret Agent* in the US (with a great Johnny Rivers rock 'n' roll theme song) and *Danger Man* in Britain.

Of course, there was Alfred Hitchcock. *The King.* His movies often unfolded in worlds of espionage and international intrigue. But for Hitchcock, spies were merely agents of *the MacGuffin*—that force that throws often-innocent characters together, the "what it's about" for suspense and action.

For my novel, I "invented" a CIA job I'd love if I couldn't be a writer: reading novels for espionage hints.

After my experiences in the US Senate, working on Montana road crews, and for a federally funded state office, I decided that even a secret agency was still a government bureaucracy powered by the same forces and foibles I witnessed every day.

So, I thought, knowing all that, how would I organize the CIA?

And I "projected" the answers to my questions in my fiction, including creating such (to me) obvious things as a "panic line" for agents in trouble, because whatever my plot was, my hero had to panic and had to need all the help he could get. I chose his name to reflect what twenty-first-century slang refers to as "a nerd." No cool Hemingway "Nick" or TV *Hawaii Five-O* "Steve" for my guy: he became *Ronald Malcolm.* Like me, even his friends called him by his last name.

And like me, my hero had to be young, fresh out of college, a Sixties Citizen who was definitely *not* from the generations still in charge.

Hollywood had capitalized on youth's "counter-culture" with movies like James Dean's *Rebel Without a Cause*, Arlo Guthrie's multimedia saga *Alice's Restaurant*, and *Easy Rider*'s motorcycle outlaws.

But Sixties souls were still rare in prose fiction, with wonderful exceptions like Evan Hunter's *Blackboard Jungle*, Charles Webb's *The Graduate*, Richard Farina's *I've Been Down So Long It Looks Like Up To Me*. Young protagonists were particularly rare in *noir thriller* fiction—

—except for the sagas of hyper-cool British author Adam Diment, who'd scored a publishing deal at twenty-three, launched his first novel in 1967, and then vanished in 1973 like a Tom Pynchon–Alfred Hitchcock hero.

Diment showed that a hero could be *talking 'bout my generation*, not some never-ages hero like Bond or some mysterious uncle like George Smiley.

Nights and weekends for four months, I sat in that yellow kitchen nook in Helena, Montana, and let my imagination command my fingertips on that green typewriter. I had no idea what I was going to call the book until I finished it, realized I had a chronology that fit into six days: our culture already had a thriller titled "*seven* days" (*in May*). I spent a Saturday lunch coming up with Malcolm's codename, settled on "condor" because it connoted death and sounded cooler than "vulture."

Of course, I was a nobody living thousands of miles from the publishing world of New York. I had no one to advise me, make a phone call, write a letter, knock on a door.

I searched the library for publishers of fiction akin to my manuscript. Found thirty. I used my work's "high tech" IBM Selectric typewriter and Xerox machine, crafted a synopsis that did not reveal the novel's ending, a sample chapter, and a biography that while true, hinted at mystery in my life: *Could he be . . . ?* Dropped thirty packets of hope in the US mail. Of the thirty publishers, half responded in my pitch packet's self-addressed, stamped envelopes; of that half, six said they'd consider my book. I picked one at random, sent the manuscript off.

Four months later, still having heard nothing, I was about to leave my job in Helena for a starving-author's life in Missoula, then a more "cosmopolitan" Montana city. I called publisher number one, got through to the editor, who politely told me they were rejecting my novel. I waited until I had my new address and phone number in Missoula, then dropped the manuscript in the mail to W. W. Norton, and moved.

My parents and friends were terrified: nobody we knew made a living writing fiction. I didn't care. In 1973, I was twenty-four living in a shack in a Missoula. Subsisting off my savings. Hustling less than a month's rent worth of freelance journalism. Sneaking showers in my *alma mater* university dorms. Spending only what I had to—I rationed Cokes I drank to nights my karate club practiced. Excitedly pounding out fiction on that green machine, including one twelve-plus-hour marathon session that ended only when my typing fingers began to bleed—call that chapter of my life *Blood On The Keys.*

That period's output included a "college awakening" novel hopefully no one else will ever read and one comic caper novel called *The Great Pebble Affair,* published under a pseudonym in America, under my name in Britain, France, and Italy.

But before then, back in the real world, my bank account was dwindling. The news increasingly focused on scandals of crime and intrigue coming out of the Nixon White House. Washington sounded much more exciting than starvation row. My former boss, Senator Lee Metcalf, had a year-long fellowship open to Montana applicants who were journalists—a stretch for me, but the Missoula paper had published my freelance work and the national magazine *Sport* was about to run my three paragraph story about a prairie dog (*aka* 'gopher') racing stunt back in my hometown. I applied for that fellowship, started thinking about road crew jobs or white collar bureaucracy work that wouldn't sap my creativity for my *real* work.

When the phone rang.

The man on the call introduced himself as Starling Lawrence, an eventual novelist but then an editor from W. W. Norton, who said they wanted to publish *Condor* and would pay me $1,000— more than 10 percent of the annual yearly salary I'd made as a bureaucrat. Of course I said *yes*, and he said: "We think we can sell it as a movie, too."

Doesn't he know that kind of thing only happens in *movies?* I thought, but said nothing and refrained from laughing: he was going to publish my novel.

Two weeks later, as I stood in my empty bathtub, trying to use duct tape to rig a shower out of some stranger's discarded plumbing parts, again the phone rang.

Starling Lawrence and a pack of Norton staffers were on the line, telling me that famed movie producer Dino DeLaurentiis had read *Condor* in manuscript and wanted to make it a movie. Dino later told me he knew after reading the first four pages. He bought the book outright, and my share of the sale would be $81,000.

I stood there holding the spool of gray duct tape, listened while Starling excitedly rehashed what he'd told me, then I said: "You'll have to excuse me, I need to go back to fixing my shower and I haven't heard a word you've said after $81,000."

I could subsist writing fiction for *years* on that!

A week later, Senator Metcalf gave me a new fellowship to work in Washington.

I was twenty-four years old.

Every novel is two books: the manuscript the author writes, and the product that publishers, editors, and the author carve out for readers. In the process of creating that second book, the author is both beef and butcher.

My manuscript Condor is as he's become in legend, but the novel published in 1974 is not quite the story I first created.

The manuscript is a *noir* spy story propelling Condor through my *what-ifs* with a plot about rogue CIA operatives smuggling heroin out of the Vietnam War. That MacGuffin races Condor through his six days of life-changing peril during which the woman he dragoons into being his lover and co-target (Faye Dunaway) is killed by an assassin, an act that transforms Condor from *victim and prey* to *hunter and killer*.

A prologue and epilogue set in Vietnam bookended my DC spy-slaughtering saga. The manuscript also set the story in rock 'n' roll, from the silky Temptations singing "Just My Imagination" on the radio as we meet Condor "girl watching" to the climax when, call it *assassination* or call it *justice*, Condor murders the villain in the men's room at National (now Reagan National) Airport while the piped-in lavatory-bland instrumental music plays four quoted lines from the Beatles: "With A Little Help From My Friends."

Those Beatles lines were first to go: what I saw as literary journalism, the song rights holders saw as a necessary fee. I was too nervous about my economic future to risk that in-hindsight paltry sum. My editor thought the Temptations playing on the radio as Condor stole time from his work to sit at the window and watch for a certain unknown girl to walk by seemed too *obvious*. While the girl stayed—how often had I sat at that window, plus that girl is a diversionary red-herring for Faye Dunaway's character—the radio and song got red-lined.

But I was proud of how little editing the book seemed to need from Starling and the hardback publisher, though he did have me drop my Vietnam prologue and epilogue.

Then, after the Hollywood sale, the paperback publisher's editorial committee asked Norton if I would make two "small" changes.

First, change heroin into something else: "Could it be some kind of super drug?" With the movie *The French Connection* having been a hit, "the feeling is, heroin's been done."

Second, let the Faye Dunaway heroine live: "Killing her is so dark."

Losing the rock 'n' roll made me sad. Dropping the epilogue and prologue in favor of faster, more immediate plot development made sense.

But changing heroin into "some kind of super drug" was ludicrous.

And letting the heroine live meant Condor had no trigger to transform into the kind of assassin he'd been fleeing.

So I came up with Condor only *thinking* she'd been killed on the theory that was "good enough" for his homicidal revenge motivation.

As for heroin, this rube from Montana ran a Trojan horse past the "sophisticated" New York City paperback editors: instead of heroin, have the bad guys smuggling bricks of morphine. "Wonderful!" was the response. I realized those faceless gatekeepers knew next to nothing about our world's narcotics scourge. Nobody smuggles morphine bricks into America, it's not worth it. Morphine is an early manufactured stage of . . . heroin. But at least morphine was real, not some committee-hallucinated "super drug" that would have made Condor a parody of truth.

Still, I was only a twenty-four-year-old first time novelist. I was lucky to get off with the light editing *Condor* received. Hell, I was lucky to be published at all.

Some lucky novels are three books: the author's original work, the edited published volume, and the story Hollywood projects onto the silver screen.

Casting for *Condor* locked up Robert Redford before I'd even met my editor in the *going up* elevator of his New York skyscraper.

And history exploding in our streets after the manuscript's acceptance inspired changes for the movie's creative team.

Already the plot had been shifted from Washington to New York because Redford had to shoot two movies that year: *Condor* and *All the President's Men*. His family lived in New York and he didn't want to move to Washington for a year. Of the two movies' plots, only *Condor* could be moved to New York.

More importantly came the MacGuffin.

Just after *Condor* sold, the United States got hit with its first oil embargo. Petroleum Politics suddenly ruled. That change was too powerful to ignore, so the MacGuffin went from *drugs* to *oil*. And instead of my *noir* dark ending, the brilliant screenwriters came up with a chilling, culturally impactful *Lady Or The Tiger?* climax.

There's no way to describe what it's like for a novelist to walk onto a movie set created from a vision born in the writer's fevered dreams.

Director Sydney Pollack showed me around, letting me see the exacting detail with which he approached his art, right down to hand-selecting the assassins' never-filmed-before guns. I listened in awe as he described how to create tension in a scene by having nothing happen—except, of course, that the ruthless killer and his prey ride the same elevator surrounded by innocent witnesses. Sydney explained that in film, telling a chronological chase story meant he couldn't show an increasingly scruffy Redford on the run for six days and night, so everything compressed into . . . three days.

Redford went out of his way to be gracious, stood outside with me one wintry Manhattan morning on the front steps of the set's secret CIA office and talked about "our" work while we ignored two mink-coated high society women who'd imperiously breezed through the police lines only to look up and see who was standing there. Those two *oh-so-sophisticated* Manhattan matrons . . . clutched each other like schoolgirls, hip-hopped past us in gasping glee.

I've often wondered if Redford has that effect on women, too.

Hollywood took my slim first novel, elevated and enhanced it into a cinematic masterpiece. My whole life has been blessed by the shadow of *Condor*.

But until the KGB story broke, who knew that shadow was so huge?

In the same year that the great American author of my generation, Bruce Springsteen, released his seminal *Born to Run* album, "my" movie had come out, Nixon had resigned, my Senate fellowship had ended, I had two more novels about to be published, and I'd jumped at a chance to join Jack Anderson's muckrakers. After all, Nixon's thugs had plotted to murder Jack, and Les Whitten, the man who'd helped lead me to Condor, was one of my bosses.

And though I'd rushed a sequel into another bestseller, I realized that the quintet of Condor novels I envisioned would crash into the image created by Robert Redford.

I let Condor fly away.

Vanish.

Until 9/11.

As that smoke cleared, Condor flew back.

His return was influenced by a claim Watergate burglar Frank Sturgis made to me after "my" movie hit theater screens. Sturgis said the CIA rotated codenames, and that briefly, before my novel was even written, he'd been codenamed Condor. Frank was a crook, a liar, and a spy—charming though thuggish—but this may have been true.

I'd published a novel about spies and an attack on the World Trade Towers seven years before 9/11 (*Thunder*), but that infamy compelled me to write about our new world of spies. I realized that the best way to do so would be to bring back Condor.

Both practically and out of respect for readers and movie goers, I couldn't violate the legend or images Robert Redford gave the world. I had to merge Redford with my original—and on-going—vision of Condor.

The result was a 2005 novella called *condor.net*, where a young CIA cyber intelligence analyst with the recycled codename of Condor finds himself slammed into the same but post-9/11 slaughterhouse of intrigue and corruption as my first Condor.

What I realized after that "short fiction" experience was that in Condor, I had a perfect character to shine light on the challenges and arenas of intrigue emerging after the fall of the Twin Towers. And I could use "short fiction" to do so. After all, many of my literary inspirations and instructions came out of great short fiction by such authors as Shirley Jackson, Ring Lardner, Harlan Ellison, Jim Harrison, and volumes of genre-lumped stories published in *Alfred Hitchcock's Mystery Magazine*, *Analog*, and other pulp sci-fi, noir, crime, and mystery treasures sold cheap at the newsstands and drugstore racks that once populated America.

Five other Condor short fictions flew from me, two novellas and three short stories published in magazines and as standalones in the US, England, and France—all of the stories dealing with my original, aged-with-our-times Condor as he survives where I'd slyly locked him up in my 2006 novel *Mad Dogs*: the CIA's secret insane asylum.

Then came the Russian cyber attacks on America in 2016 and a political scandal that will rock our country for generations to come. The plan for publishing an anthology of the first five "Condor shorts" was already underway. And I wanted to include a new never-before-published novella in this anthology to make it "six" short fictions—as in "six days of" (and eventually, as in the six chambers of a revolver used for Russian roulette). The biggest spy war attack in history had just hit my country: Condor had to be there.

And now that sixth and brand new novella waits for you at the end of this volume.

The anthology before your eyes now contains those Condor short fictions, and that it exists and you are reading these words brings me great happiness.

And Condor kept on soaring in my skies.

One night I swirled awake with a novel that my wife, Bonnie, nailed with the perfect title over our morning coffee: *Last Days of the Condor.*

I had to do it *true.*

Write a novel true to my original character fused with Redford. Write the story true to his literary history my short tales had created. Write a novel true to my belief that "literary franchise" characters should age as they would in our reality. Write a novel as true to its times—our times now—as I could.

Plus, Condor had become a cultural force—including in 1980, inspiring a hired American assassin to disguise himself as a Washington, DC, mailman to gun down the exiled diplomat target of his fundamentalist puppet masters in Iran.

Condor inspired parodies on the TV shows *Seinfeld, The Simpsons, Frasier, King of the Hill,* and cultural chatter references on shows like *NCIS* and *Breaking Bad.* The avant-garde rock group Radiohead samples the movie's dialogue on a song.

In his January 2000 *Washington Post* essay on films of the preceding century, Pulitzer Prize–winning movie reviewer and renowned novelist Stephen Hunter picked *Three Days of the Condor* as the movie most emblematic of the 1970s, the film typical of its paranoid times. Also, wrote Hunter: "This marks the globalization of the cinema as Tinseltown has surrendered its own natural mantle of world centrality."

And on that morning when my wife and I shared coffee and smiles over the *Last Days* title of my novel a-borning, Condor was back in the sky over our brave new world where spies target all of us—the secrets in our cell phones, the power in our elections, what happens when we sit on a park bench in Salisbury, England.

Now more than ever before, we all live in Condor's world.

Listen.

You can hear his wings.

CONDOR.NET

First published in *Perfect 10*, 2005

"Do you know who you are?" said steel-haired boss Richard Dray from behind his Washington, DC, desk in a closed door office that smelled of hot chocolate. Bifocals hung from a shoelace looped around Dray's neck.

The younger man on the other side of the desk that spring Monday morning said: "Aren't I the guy in my mirror?"

"No. You're Condor. Our new Condor. A South American assassination consortium and two previous shadow operatives for Uncle Sam had that code name."

"What happened to those other two guys?"

"One became a Watergate burglar. The other had . . . odd luck."

"I can imagine."

"That's not your job."

"Sure it is," said Condor. "I'm a cyber spy. I troll the world-wide web. If I find something hinky, I zap a report into our secret network. Mark Twain said history doesn't repeat itself, though it might rhyme. I try to imagine those rhymes."

"You *imagine* rhymes." Repeated. Rhetorical. Reproachful. Rebuking.

Condor shrugged: "It's a gift."

"A gift? From the CIA? *Ha!*"

"Ha?" said Condor.

"You think I trust the CIA? We held onto this open source cyber section here at Homeland Security because they lost out when we all got shoved under the Director of National Intelligence umbrella. Then last week, they dumped you here. Now I'm getting complaints about you using your Top Secret clearance to track a Pentagon mission called . . ." Dray consulted his computer monitor: ". . . called Rising Thunder."

"Why are you stepping outside your job description?" asked his boss.

"I see our guys' faces," said Condor, as his imagination ran a movie of twelve Rising Thunder Delta Force commandos in a musty Pakistani barracks.

Condor became obsessed with the dozen American soldiers through video and photos in secret data streams he surfed. Twelve flesh-and-blood men, their destiny shaped by the CIA's discovery of an al Qaeda base infecting an Afghan village, a threat that with slam dunk certainty fit every prediction, every electronic intercept from terrorist-friendly TV journalists to cell phone chatter in Malaysia. Condor knew every informant's whisper, every NSA satellite photo of bearded "villagers" carrying AK-47s.

Rising Thunder was a *surgical strike.* Twelve American RT/Delta commandos would insert into the village via a stealth helicopter chopping through cold night, covertly slam the al Qaeda command hut, *wet work* authorized, *secure* until a cavalry wave of Army Rangers helicoptered over the mountains' dawn horizon to liberate the rest of the village and harvest fanatic foes from amidst the innocents.

"I know what's there," Condor told boss Richard Dray that Monday morning. "I know they're GO in 31 hours. But I don't know what's bothering me."

"Doesn't matter. Rising Thunder is covered and you're not the blanket."

"If not me, who?"

"*Who?* You're Condor, not an owl. No more . . . unauthorized imagining!"

"I'll do my best." Condor left his boss's private lair to walk out to the maze.

Condor looked around that second-floor cavern in a mixed business and residential neighborhood thirty-one blocks north- west of the National Zoo's tigers. Security engineers had bricked- over the cavern's windows to enclose a chessboard maze of cubicles. Jacobs Ladders atop each heart-high green plastic par- tition rippled waves of blue electric bolts. Those electric bolts countered any snooping microwaves and made this second-story spy factory crackle like Dr. Frankenstein's laboratory.

Color printouts taped up inside Condor's cubicle made kalei- doscopic murals. Classified reports and home pages of terrorist websites hung beside downloaded scenes from movies like *Fight Club, The Magnificent Seven, noir* crime flicks from the preceding century that none of his coworkers knew, plus office favorites *The Matrix* and *The Social Network.* A color photo of 9/11's smoking World Trade Center clung to one green plastic partition beside the all-black *New Yorker* silhouette cover memorializing the twin towers. A cell phone snap of Condor maneuvering up a gym's climbing wall was his only personal photo.

Instead of going to his cubicle, Condor walked to the coffee machine where he thought no one would overhear him, snuck his cell phone out of his gray sports jacket.

The woman who answered his phone call said: "Now what?"

Condor whispered into his cell phone: "You've got to get me out of here!"

"I pulled strings to get you *in* there. One week, and you already want to leave! There's no coming back across the river. Not now. The politics— *Are you in trouble?*"

"Not exactly."

"Not again! Say it's not the same thing!"

"Like I told you ten days ago, something about that Afghan op . . ."

"Bugs you. Your snooping on that triggered paranoids in our Firm. I had to promise you'd stop, that you were a smart trade to Homeland, that . . ."

"Hey, this morning I almost figured out what's bothering me!" He smelled burnt coffee. *If I'd texted her, I couldn't have heard her voice.* "I just want to do my job."

"No. Do the job *they* want. I'm not your boss anymore."

"But you know me. And I'm not going to stop, so . . . Where are you now?"

"In my car by the White House."

"Meet me. Twenty minutes. Where I spilled on you."

He heard the hum of traffic. Angry honks. Her mental wheels whirling.

"Come on, Renee," said Condor. "Help me figure this out."

Renee Lake sighed. "Give me twenty-five minutes."

Condor put his cell phone away. Saw none of the other five on-duty analysts watching. The boss's door was closed. Condor dumped the hot mud in the coffee machine's glass pot down the drain. He switched the machine off, swung it open. Pulled a red wire loose. Closed the machine. Flipped the power switch.

The power light stayed unlit.

He sighed guilt but walked to an intercom on a wall, pushed the call button.

"Yes?" Boss Dray's voice boomed through the speaker.

"The coffee machine's dead," Condor told the intercom box. "I'm making a Starbucks run. Do you want a café mocha?"

A voice yelled from the maze of cubicles: "Not fair!"

The other five analysts popped their head above their green cubicle walls.

Juan loomed like a thoughtful NFL tackle: "We should all get to go."

The boss's disembodied voice boomed: "Non-task departures of personnel . . ."

"Staff motivation meeting!" ad-libbed Sarita. Officially, the Jacobs Ladder electric surges were bio-benign, but Condor worried every time he saw static frame Sarita's beautiful Bombay face with a floating black fan of her electro-charged hair.

"No!" he yelled to the intercom box and his colleagues: "I want to go alone!"

The disembodied voice boomed: "It is inappropriate for a supervisor to request personal favors from subordinate personnel. No whipped cream."

The Beatles—two analysts with self-inflicted shaggy retro haircuts—high-fived through an electric blue bolt undulating up from the partition between their cubicles.

"I'll go on ahead!" Condor hurried away from his five gathering colleagues. At the top of the stairs, his eyes filled with sunlight streaming into the first floor entryway through the glass door that could withstand a burst from an AK-47.

Clumping down the stairs, he fumbled for his cell phone to call Renee.

Saw a mailman walking up the outside stairs toward the glass door.

Saw the leather pouch the blue-uniformed mailman clutched to his chest.

Condor opened the door.

"Thanks." The postal carrier stepped into the entryway. His nametag read Burt. The mailman put envelopes into the postal box that hid chemical sensors in its walls.

"And thanks again for pickin' me up yesterday in the rain. Most people never see us. It's like mailmen are invisible."

"I see ghosts." Condor anxiously fingered his cell phone.

"That's not the line from the movie."

"You work with what you got."

"True that," said the mailman. "Which reminds me . . ."

Burt nodded toward the plaque mounted by the door buzzer.

". . . Feenix Data Systems, Inc. What do you guys do?"

His fellow analysts maneuvered past Condor and the mail-man—except for Juan, who stood still as a mountain, blocking the stairs up.

Condor diverted the mailman out to the stoop: "We work with what they give us."

"I hear you." The mailman walked to the next door.

"Let's go," said Juan, directing Condor to join their crew walking the other way.

"Nerds on parade!" joked Sarita as the six coworkers strolled up the sidewalk.

Condor sighed. *Can't call to cancel now.* "Not what I planned."

"Life happens." Sarita wrinkled her brow. "Is this about more than coffee?"

Sarita smelled like oranges. She set her eyes on Condor as he walked beside her. Asked *the new guy,* a single guy her age: "So what else did you have in mind?"

"Dudes!" interrupted the chubby analyst named Hershel. He wore classic black and white sneakers. "You won't believe what I popped onto last Friday!"

Juan lowered his voice: "We don't talk about work."

"Then what else can we talk about except movies?" said Hershel as they neared the neighborhood's Starbucks. "Everything else we can say is on Facebook!"

"Facebook is so over," said Sarita. "Unless you're trying to overthrow the government and, *hey*, people, we *are* the government."

"We're regular people," said the short Beatle as he held open the Starbucks door for his colleagues. "We got a lot to say."

"Nobody listens," said the tall Beatle as the secret agents entered Starbucks.

Condor scanned the coffee-scented chamber: *No Renee*. An old man in the corner nursed a cup of wake-up as he fed memories into a laptop. A *Mommy and Me* quartet devoured adult conversation while three mommies rolled strollers with sleeping babies back and forth. Mom number four rocked her baby in a shoulder snuggly while she texted in her way-too-smart phone. Steam hissed. Two green-aproned baristas worked behind the brown wooden counter. The sound system played Muddy Waters growling "Mannish Boy" blues. The phone in Condor's pocket felt like a boulder.

"Order for me, OK?" he asked Juan. Condor hurried down a dead-end hall.

"You're supposed to need to go *after* coffee!" teased Hershel.

"Grow up," said Sarita.

Condor entered the men's room where all he heard through the closed door was Muddy Waters thumping blues. Condor grabbed his phone. Punched re-dial.

One ring.

The bathroom sink glistened white. He saw himself in the mirror. Gray blazer, blue shirt, no tie, cell phone pressed to his ear as Muddy Waters proclaimed himself "a full grown man." Condor stared at his own mirrored reflection.

Two rings.

A stroller-rolling mom glanced at the Starbucks door as a man wearing a face-covering hoodie entered the ordinary coffee shop. His left hand pulled off the hood, freeing his optics and revealing his bald head as he thrust his right arm into the partially zipped garment. The mom thought: *Hope he's not having a heart attack.* She turned to her laughing friends. Didn't see that man's surgeon-gloved left hand lock the café door.

Three rings.

The bald man swung a silencer-equipped Uzi out from under his hoodie: *Cough!* The woman barista wore a new red earring as she fell. *Cough!* A heart shot knocked the male barista into the pastry case.

Four rings.

The bald man thumbed the Uzi to full auto and sprayed the huddle of just-beginning-to-realize coworkers. Juan. Hershel. Sarita. The Beatles. They all crashed in bloody heaps. Ejected brass shell casings tinkled on the coffee shop's floor. The old man in the corner ducked behind his laptop's screen. *Cough!* One bullet punched a hole through that plastic and crimson flecked the keyboard.

In the bathroom, Condor heard weird noises. *What the Hell?*

The bald man *cough*ed a bullet into a mother's screaming mouth. Babies wailed. Muddy Waters growled. One mom shoved her stroller away—*cough*—she sprawled across the table, knocking over paper cups of coffee to add to the liquid mess.

The third stroller mom sprang like a lioness toward the killer and he *coughed* a red line across her white blouse.

The mom with the snuggly cupped her hands over her baby's head. "Please, no!"

In the bathroom, Condor heard the woman's plea as a warning of *threat! Danger!* Dropped his phone in his pocket and grabbed the only thing he could find to weaponize.

Baldy zeroed his Uzi on snuggly mom's forehead, pulled the trigger. Click.

Hope flickered in her eyes.

His left hand drew the 9mm Glock pistol holstered on his belt.

Motion erupted behind snuggly mom.

Condor charged from the bathroom, his arm cocked to throw what he'd grabbed. He saw lumpy clothes heaped on the floor. Saw a bald man holding two guns. Leapt over the counter toward cover as he threw—

A toilet paper roll, its white paper chain unspooling toward the startled killer.

Off her funeral pyre rose Sarita. Shoulder shot. Rib shot.

Refusing death. She charged the bald man who dared presume to be her assassin.

Three targets distracted the bald killer:

A mom.

The Indian bitch who—*damn it!*—wouldn't just *die.*

The flying-through-the-air dork who'd thrown a fucking roll of toilet paper.

Bam! A bullet drilled through Sarita's chest missing her lungs, heart, aorta and spine as it ripped from her back. Stumbling, she kept going.

Bam! Bam! Bullets zinged past Condor as he fell behind the counter.

Bam! Snuggly mom's left eye flowed like a red fountain.

The crazy shot-to-Hell spy woman flopped toward the killer. He shoved her away with the empty Uzi, leveled his Glock at her face and *Bam!* A red dot blossomed right smack where American-born her never thought to wear a caste mark.

Condor threw a giant cappuccino off the serving bar and hit the Glock.

Scalding liquid splashed the killer's face. Wincing, he closed his eyes.

Condor vaulted the counter, wrestled the killer for the Uzi and Glock.

The killer let Condor have both guns, grabbed his jacket lapels, and windmilled Condor through the air with the *tomo-nage* foot-in-the-stomach judo throw.

Condor flew shoes-first into the Starbucks plate glass window.

Bustin' glass exploded him outside, inertia tumbled him to his feet, bounced him off a parked car, his cell phone flipping from his pocket—skidding into the sewer slit. Condor still clung to both guns. Looked through the shattered window. Saw the bald man clawing his pants leg up.

Ankle holster!

Condor threw the Uzi through the broken window and missed hitting the killer.

Got a pistol in my other hand! Bam! Condor blasted a Glock slug at the killer. The bullet ripped through the Starbuck's bathroom wall and shattered the mirror.

Condor heard a voice behind him yell: ". . . shoot!"

Whirl aim at murder sound/man with gun— Bam!

Middle of the street, a blue-shirted cop spun a pirouette—fell beside his cruiser.

Bam!

A bullet zinged past Condor from inside the Starbucks and he ducked, ran in the opposite direction of the quickly parked police cruiser. Ran fast. Ran hard.

Ran knowing: *The killer's shooting at me!*

Ran knowing: *I shot a cop!*

He darted around the first corner—dress shop, card shop, blocks of houses.

"*Aaaah!*" screamed a woman with puffy dyed blond hair at *man with a gun*.

Condor waved his arms: "No! I'm the good guy!"

The woman screamed again as he ran.

Look back—nothing at the corner—*but the killer must be coming!* Condor stuck the pistol in his belt under his jacket, ran down an alley. Sirens wailed.

Four blocks later, he stood in the middle of a commercial strip. Sirens filled the blue sky cupping the upscale neighborhood. Pedestrians scanned the streets as Condor caught his breath. Grabbed for his cell phone—gone.

Retroville read a pink neon sign over a store. A bell tinkled as Condor raced into that jumble of disco jackets, lava lamps, Elvis busts, rubber Halloween masks—JFK, Nixon, Reagan, Clinton, the first Bush, the second Bush, Obama. No mask for President Gerald Ford who a Charles-Manson-cult-follower named

Squeaky tried to assassinate. In Retroville, a shop chick with tattoo sleeves leaned against the glass counter.

Condor rushed to her: "Phone!"

"Like, *what*?"

"A pay phone! Do you have a pay phone?"

"Hate to break it to you, but it's a world of cells."

"Where can I find one? A pay phone! A phone booth!"

"Like," she said, "that changing into Superman thing is *so* over."

Condor was so jangled he didn't realize he should have demanded her cell or the store phone until after he heard the bell ding as he hurried out.

Cars and minivans slowed to a traffic jam in this neighborhood where expensive homes waited two blocks off the street of shops. Regular people, like he'd been just minutes ago, frowned toward where the wailing sirens seemed to converge. An ambulance whooshed past.

"Go!" whispered Condor. But he knew they were too late.

A sad and lonely pay phone clung to a drugstore's brick wall near an alley blocked by a delivery truck with blinking flashers. Condor grabbed the silver corded receiver—heard *dial tone.* Tapped in the toll-free CIA Panic Line number.

A woman's voice answered his call after the second ring: "Hello?"

"They're—we got— This is Condor. I'm detached to Homeland Sec'; I'm— Their Section Gamma Six Seven. We got hit!"

"Say again."

"Condor! It's me! In Starbucks . . . with a machine gun . . . and everybody . . ."

"Stay calm. Report."

"We can't just talk on the damn phone!"

"It's OK. We'll take care of you. Where are you?"

"What?"

"What's your location? How can we help you if we don't know where you are?"

He frowned. "You popped my location on the first ring! Target on my back and you tell me to stay calm!"

Warning lights blinked on the truck in the nearby mouth of an alley.

"Condor, you called the right number. Now stay put."

"Out here in the open? With a killer loose? What sense does that make?"

"Are you armed?"

"Yeah, but I'm—I'm not a real spy! I just imagine things!"

"Talk to me. Everything's . . ."

Car brakes squeal!

Condor whirled. A black sedan shuddered to a halt crossways in this side street. The driver ducked below the steering wheel, the passenger—*man, black leather jacket*—

Black Leather Jacket leapt out of the sedan, slammed his hands on its roof, his double-grip aiming a pistol.

At me! Condor dropped the phone, jerked the Glock from his belt and jumped toward the truck-filled alley.

Bam! A bullet splattered the brick wall beside Condor. Metal fragments sliced his sports jacket as he dodged down the alley alongside the delivery truck.

Behind him a man bellowed: "Fucker!"

Black Leather Jacket charged the alley. Hugged the edge of the drugstore wall. Sirens filled the city air. He crouched low—whirled into the gap between the drugstore bricks and the delivery truck. Saw *empty alley*. Gun thrust in front of him, he scurried toward a gold SUV idling where the alley met the next street.

The driver of the super-sized SUV never turned her face toward the gun-waving black-jacketed man as he surged toward her driver's side window. A National Public Radio report on the plight of women in the Arab world's wave of revolutions vibrated her gigantic hippopotamus vehicle's rolled-up windows. Regular glasses saddled her head while prescription sunglasses covered her eyes. Her left hand pressed a cell phone to that ear. Her right hand held the steering wheel as the traffic light two cars ahead of her turned green.

The SUV lurched forward as Black Leather Jacket ran from the alley. He saw only the driver's side. The SUV's departure cleared his view of the next section of alley's dumpsters and parked cars. The SUV lumbered through a left turn. Neither its multi-tasking driver nor Black Leather Jacket saw a man clinging to the SUV'S door handles as he huddled on the passenger side running board. The SUV slowed for the traffic jam. Condor flopped off the running board—

And ran until he spotted a brown kiosk pole painted with a white "M"—Metro, Washington's subway. He stumbled down escalator stairs.

Underground in the enormous gray cave, Condor caught his breath. Subway tracks bordered each side of the red-tiled platform where he stood. A nursery school group trundled past him. A curly haired girl smiled at Condor: "Where are you going?"

An electronic sign above the platform glowed computer letters: *10:41 a.m. Terrorist Threat Level Yellow. Two trains arriving.*

A train roared into the station on the tracks behind him. Brakes squealed. Strangers' eyes shot bullets at him.

Ding-dong! chimed the train stopped behind Condor as its doors sprang open. People hurried out of the cars. The school kids lined up on the other edge of the platform.

Wait. Wait. He glanced at the computer letters sliding through the electric sign: *10:42 a.m. Terrorist Threat Level Elevated to Level Orange.*

Ding-dong! Condor jumped into the car a beat before the doors clunked shut. The train surged. Out the window, he saw that little girl wave *good-bye.*

Where are you going? Condor roared into a world of flashes. *Flash* and he's sitting on an orange plastic bench in a rocketing subway train. *Flash* that man in the tan windbreaker avoids his gaze. *Flash* that blonde putting on red lipstick watches him in her compact's makeup mirror. *Flash* a teenager nails him with disdainful eyes. *Flash* and Condor's changing trains once, twice, three times. *Flash* he stands holding on to a subway car's bright silver pole that traps his curved reflection. *Flash* and he's back on another train's orange seat, shaking, soundlessly screaming for the whole world to see.

Who he saw coming toward him was Crazy Guy—wild hair above wilder eyes. He plopped on the seat beside Condor and filled the subway car with sour body odor.

Crazy Guy muttered: "They're everywhere! They can see you!"

"Yeah," said Condor.

Crazy Guy bathed Condor with rancid breath, whispered: "I'm invisible!"

"True that," said Condor.

Then he blinked. Remembered.

Gently, firmly, Condor worked his way up from the seat and past Crazy Guy, saying: "This is where I get off."

"But nothing's gone *ding-dong!*" said Crazy Guy.

"I hear things," said Condor as he walked to the doors of the slowing train.

A slanting subway shaft telescoped into an ever-bigger, ever-brighter circle of sunlight as its escalator carried Condor up from underground darkness to the street of an ordinary high noon Monday in the capital of the new American empire.

He hiked six blocks to the huge postal service building he'd been to yesterday in the rain. Condor walked around to the parking yard of red, white, and blue vehicles. He waved at the pensioner in the guard booth who didn't look up from his newspaper.

Condor hopped onto the loading dock, took the hall to the locker room and, when three mailmen in the corner spotted him, said: "You guys seen Burt?"

"Ain't he still out on his route?" One man checked his watch.

"Told him not to make me wait," lied Condor, walking away. Two aisles over, he heard them resume *back in the day* chatter, and knew, to them, he was not even there.

He worked his way along the aisle of green lockers. Stole a mailman uniform, a blue cap. The second mail carrier jacket he found hung loose on him but covered the Glock in his belt. Condor spotted a bin of leather mail pouches, grabbed one, stuffed it with his stolen gear and joined a group of off-shift personnel strolling past the pensioner security guard.

The metro bus he took rumbled through DC. Reflections of the skull-like Capitol Dome shimmered in the bus window glass. He covered his face as the bus rolled past swiveling video cameras perched on poles. He left the bus two blocks from an address he'd driven by a dozen times purely out of convenience or coincidence—*not like some teen Romeo*—went behind a green dumpster, changed into the postal jacket and cap, put his gray jacket in the pouch, and stepped out from behind the dumpster as a mailman.

Invisible.

The Cairo Arms is an eleven-story apartment complex by a park. Condor took a deep breath, walked toward its glass front doors like he knew what he was doing.

In the lobby, an old woman harangued the desk clerk. Neither of them noticed the mailman get in an elevator that whisked him up, up and away.

Seventh floor, on the side where the apartment balconies faced the park. Condor stood in the empty hall outside the door labeled 722. Reached his hand up to knock— Stopped. Inspiration lit his face. He rode the elevator up one floor.

Standing outside Apartment 822 he heard that door vibrating Bruce Springsteen.

He sang that song before I was born and he's still around. Will I last that long?

Rode up one more floor. Standing outside Apartment 922 he

heard nothing. He pressed his ear against the wooden door. Still nothing. Knocked. No one responded. Condor pulled the Glock from his belt. Hands out for balance, he raised his right foot to kick in the door—froze. Put his foot down. Wrapped his hand around 922's doorknob, turned his wrist—

And the neglected door swung open.

Condor scurried into the apartment, the unlocked door shutting behind him.

Like a SWAT warrior on TV, Condor darted from room to room and found no one in the apartment with its jumble of law school books. In the bedroom, he stepped over a white bra and crumpled blue jeans, went to the balcony's sliding glass door and peered down to treetops of the park.

Muttered: "*Like*, that changing into Superman thing is *so* over."

He slid open the glass door. White curtains billowed around him.

Condor stood nine stories above the ground, far above the tallest trees in the park. Nobody else was on a balcony to admire his view or the long fall to earth.

"It's only a movie," Condor mumbled as he unsnapped the leather shoulder strap from the mailbag, clipped the bag onto his belt. Condor looped the strap around the black iron railing post at the balcony floor concrete. He swung his legs over the balcony, his toes pressing concrete, his heels resting on nine stories of empty air.

And lowered himself—*fell*, swinging, dangling above the long drop by holding the mail pouch strap with both hands. He swung back and forth until one swing put his shoes above the next balcony down—and he let go of the strap in his left hand.

Flew/crashed onto the concrete balcony below him. Because he still grasped the strap in one hand, it came with him. He bounced to his feet and pressed against the wall.

Saw no witnesses on the other eighth floor balconies.

The Springsteen rock 'n' roll he'd heard in the hall outside door of 822 vibrated that apartment balcony's glass door.

Condor edged along the glass door, peered around the open curtains. Saw a bedroom. Saw a mirror reflecting the living room where a gray-haired grandfather wearing black jeans and a polo shirt rocked out to the soundtrack of his life.

"You go, man," whispered Condor.

He looped the pouch strap around the eighth floor railing post, swung to the balcony below. He glanced around the curtains over the seventh floor balcony's glass door, cracked open for the lilac scented spring air: bedroom, bureau, bed, door to the living room.

Condor left the mailbag and strap on the balcony's chaise lounge. Gripped the Glock, slid the glass door open, and stepped into the bedroom. Glanced into the bathroom: shower tub, toilet, sink. He eased toward the angled-open bedroom door . . .

Jumped into the living room, Glock aiming—

"*Fuck you!*"

Startled, Condor swung Glock to shoot or—

"*Awack! Fuck you!*" said the green parrot in a black cage.

Condor scanned the apartment living room beyond his gunsight: glass coffee table, black leather sofa, easy chair, TV, the front door, kitchen nook.

A red On light glowed in an alarm box mounted by the front door.

He ran to the alarm box, read its LCD screen: Motion Detector Off.

The parrot hopped around in the black steel cage.

Condor slumped into the black leather chair. He put the Glock on the coffee table. Books and good art filled the walls. A wine rack stood near the kitchen.

The flat screen TV stared at Condor. Its screen played muted visions: A bald man machinegunned a Starbucks ballet. A baby stroller rolled through a hail of bullets. The TiVo clock read 1:32.

The TV screen showed an imagined movie of RT/Delta finishing breakfast in Pakistan.

"Awk! Fuck you!" cawed the parrot.

"Somebody beat you to it," whispered Condor.

The universe spun—he jerked alert. His watch read 2:25. *Shock, it's making me fall through time, lose my grasp on where and when. And what.* In the TV, Condor saw RT/Delta cleaning assault rifles. They'd smell like gun oil. Like gunsmoke. *Like me.*

Condor left the black Glock on the coffee table.

The fridge held orange juice, carry out boxes, one apple. *How can I be hungry?* But he was. He microwaved white cardboard boxes of Chinese food that tasted like a golden goop of soy oil, white rice and limp broccoli. He slumped in the leather chair. His watch read 3:42. A mirage in the TV showed an RT/Delta intel officer use a red-beamed laser pointer on a satellite photo of the al Qaeda-held village. The TV scene changed to Juan blocking the stairs that morning. Chubby Hershel told a story as he walked toward Starbucks. Sarita smiled as a blue lightning bolt crackled behind her face and floated her long black hair.

Click—door lock!

Condor whirled, saw the handle of the deadbolt on the apartment door turning . . .

He grabbed the Glock and ran into the bedroom. The parrot cursed. Condor heard the front door swing open. Beeps shut off the alarm and a man's raspy voice said: "We're checking your place."

"Awwk! Fuck you!"

Condor scurried to the bedroom balcony's glass door.

"Nice pet," said a second man's voice.

Renee said: "He suits me."

"Take long to train him?" said a third man, a sneer in his voice.

"No longer than any other male."

Condor slipped out to the balcony, left the glass door open an inch. The curtains blocked a view of him from anyone who didn't step onto the balcony.

Twenty heartbeats later, fingers gripped the glass door, slowly slid it open . . .

"Look under the bed!" yelled a man's voice from deep in the apartment.

"Like I'd forget?" The man inside the bedroom saw a balcony only birds could get to and left the glass door open.

Condor counted to thirty. Peered cautiously into the empty bedroom: empty. The door to the living room still gaped open. *Risk it*: he slipped inside the bedroom.

A giant framed sepia art photo of wild horses running through a blizzard hung above the bed's brass-poled headboard. The photo glass reflected Condor as he sneaked behind the angled-open bedroom door to listen to the voices in the living room.

Where Renee Lake sat on her couch. She wore a jacket and slacks, a chic brown shag cut above a bold face with eyes like comets and lips set in a grim line she gave the man in her leather chair and the five thugs fanned out behind him.

Renee said: "Don't bother bugging my place. I wired it with countermeasures."

"Are you that paranoid?" The man in the leather chair had the raspy voice.

"I'm that professional."

"We're all on the same team."

"You mean the team that just lost five dead plus *beaucoup* collateral KIA's?"

"But not your Condor. Tell me about him."

"I've done my de-brief."

"And I still think you should be stashed with his boss Dray in the bowels of the Graylin, but I'm just a brick agent, not a suite star. But when we leave, there'll be a team on your door, one in the stairwell, one in the garage, one in the lobby."

"Leave my door and hallway clean. We can't spook any citizens, especially my neighbors. I need to maintain cover. Buck me on this and you'll answer to my Deputy Director. He doesn't have my sense of humor."

"Is that what Condor likes? Word is, he has a monster crush on you."

"I don't know about that."

"He even hacked into your personnel file."

"So have you."

"I do my job. Condor's renegade snoop gave him this address."

"I've never seen him around here."

"What are you to each other?"

"He's an intuitive savant. A dreamer. After 9/11, he had the weird desire to do something more than make money. He signed up, passed clearance and analyst training, got attached to my section of the CIA Counter-Terrorism Center. I was his boss—only his boss. Nothing inappropriate materialized between us."

"Materialized is such a . . . *careful* word."

"You want sloppy, interrogate somebody else."

"If the massacre was so sloppy that Condor survived, why is he still in the wind?"

"Beats me. Shock. Or good sense. When he called our Panic Line, two gunmen jumped him, and of course they *absolutely* identified themselves as jacked-up undercover cops responding to the wounded patrolman's *Officer Shot!* call."

In the bedroom, Condor grimaced: *Shit!*

The man in the living room said: "You think Condor just over-reacted?"

"I think he stayed alive in streets gone crazy with guns."

"So you trust him?"

Hesitation. Then Renee said: "As I know him, he's a good man."

"Just before we drove you over here, your people uncovered a

Cayman Island bank account for him. With fifty grand in it. How did your good man earn that?"

"What? What are you . . ."

"The cop he shot in the street made a positive I.D. on your 'good man.' The analyst Sarita got hit by a bullet from a gun like he's shooting. His fingerprints are on the Uzi recovered at the scene—only his."

"I can't figure that."

The man stood. "We've come up with three scenarios: Your Condor is crazy, confused, or crooked. When we figure out which, we might look hard at you."

"What you see is what you get."

The raspy voiced man said: "Really?"

Hiding behind the bedroom door, Condor heard men leave the apartment. Heard the locks click. Heard Renee say: "Asshole."

"Bwack!"

Footsteps entered the bedroom beyond the door he hid behind. Shoes kicked off. Bare feet padded into the bathroom. A light switch clicked. The tinkle of urine. Toilet paper unspooled. Toilet flushed. Sink water ran, stopped. A jacket got tossed onto the bed. Followed by a holstered gun.

Renee walked past his view. Didn't look at the door that hid Condor. Why would she? Her home had been *secured.* Her pants were undone from the bathroom. She shut the drapes. Snapped on the bed table lamp. Her back stayed to him. Condor pushed the door away. Watched her work her slacks down, off sleek white thighs. She wore black bikini panties. Renee unbuttoned her blouse, tossed it to the bed. Condor's gun rose as she unhooked her black bra, tossed it behind her onto the bed.

He yelled: "Stop!"

And she whirled, hands up—*kung fu* fighter. Saw him in the mailman's jacket, gun locked on her. Her eyes flicked to the bed. To her holstered pistol.

"Freeze!" he said. "You were a field agent before you were

a boss. I'm just an analyst, but don't make me show you I can shoot."

"How'd you get in here?"

"I rose to the occasion."

Her eyes focused on the stolen uniform he wore: "Have you gone postal?"

"Yeah," he said, "and here's your mail: I didn't kill anybody!"

"Let's keep it that way."

Suddenly he realized Renee wore black panties and no bra. Her breasts were swollen teardrops. His gun trembled.

And she blushed. Pulled her hands from their martial pose to cover herself. She looked past the black bore of his gun to his eyes. Said, "What now?"

"You can put your shirt back on."

"Don't watch."

"We're not there yet."

He kept his gun on her as she grabbed the blouse, used her other arm to cover her breasts. She gave him her naked spine as she put on the blouse. She turned around.

Found he'd clipped her gun on his belt. He sent her to the living room couch. He took the chair opposite her long bare legs and buttoned blouse. Kept his gun in his hand.

The parrot hopped wildly in his cage.

"So," said Condor: "How was your day?"

"Same old, same old." Renee glanced at the glass coffee table between them. An art deco ashtray with swooping naked beauties sat out of plumb with the table edges. She casually leaned forward to adjust the heavy glass object.

"Stop!" She froze at Condor's order, flicked her gaze toward his alert pistol as he said: "You don't need to straighten anything."

Renee shrugged. "Whatever you want. You got the gun."

"Let me tell you about my day." And he did.

Sunset streamed through the windows when he finished.

She stared at him through the crimson light. Said, "Why?"

"Why what? Why kill us? *Why* equals *who*. Not a berserker nut or a gangbanger, it was too . . . polished. But all the superpowers are gone; now it's just us."

"Plus some slice of a few billion people who think we're the new evil empire."

"Yeah, but, al Qaeda, they . . ." Condor blinked. "*It's a world of cells.* 'Cells' is what we call secret teams of terrorists or spies. But even if CIA and FBI are right about al Qaeda cells operating inside our country, why all this?"

"Why come to me?" Renee shifted.

Even distracted as he was, Condor's gun bore shifted with her like a watchful eye.

The parrot squawked.

"You're who I've got left," said Condor. "Plus somebody's framed me with an offshore account. Plus I put my fingerprints on the Uzi. Plus I shot a cop. Accidentally, but you're the pro, you add up my score."

Her eyes pulled him like gravity. "What do you really want me to do?"

"Believe me. Believe *in* me."

"You've got the gun."

"And if I put it down?"

"I believe you're in trouble."

"Hey, I *am* trouble." Wasn't a laugh he made. "And I'm not a trouble guy. Not a gunner like the Delta guys in Rising Thunder. Maybe, what I was doing, all this is linked to Dray, my boss. He talked about getting complaints about me, but . . ."

Condor's blink keyed Renee to unfold and spread her legs, her black bikinied half moon facing him as her bare feet gripped the floor. Condor seemed not to care.

"But it was *all* of us who got killed," he said, his eyes floating back to the Starbucks. "Not just me. So if it wasn't about me or Rising Thunder . . . *Hershel!*"

Condor's shout startled Renee, but she used that natural

reaction to disguise her hands finding a grip on the edge of the couch.

"Hershel! He was wild about something he popped onto last Friday! He would have run straight to our boss, Dray! But forget Hershel. Home Sec' and the Agency will have my boss and every-body else focused on me because of the frame job and . . ."

Renee's bare thighs squeaked on the black leather couch.

Condor's Glock zeroed her heart: *"No!"*

"I was just . . ."

"No," he said. Saw the way her jaw set and knew he'd been right.

"Do you have any rope?" he said.

She blinked. "I've got twine in the utility drawer in the kitchen, I'll go get . . ."

"Don't!" Condor rocketed out of the chair and away from her as she *naturally* started to rise with her suggestion. "You're not the helpful kind."

He made her kneel on the hard wooden floor. He backed into the kitchen, gun on her the whole time, aiming over the open counter. His free hand groped in the counter's utility drawer, lifted out a sheathed throwing knife.

"So much for your domestic side," he told her.

Renee watched his eyes float around her home while keeping her kneeling form in his gaze—and in the aim of his gun. His gaze locked on a P.C. in the corner. He ordered her to unplug and gather up all the P.C.'s cords, then march into the bedroom.

"What are you doing?" she said, as he made her sit in the middle of the bed.

"I have to get Dray to see everything, not just the frame trap-ping me. Together we can focus Home Sec' and the Agency, the FBI on the truth. If nobody kills me first."

He made her tie one chord to her right wrist, tie the other end to the headboard's same side brass corner pole. Made her lie down, her right arm lashed up behind her. He made a loop of a chord, cinched it around her left ankle.

"You can't get to Dray!" She raised her head off the bed while he lashed her left leg to that bottom corner pole. "They've got a team securing him at the Graylin Hotel!"

"How's our whole intelligence community done with security so far?" He shook his head. "I never thought I'd be standing here."

He pulled her right leg wide and apart from its mate, lashed it to the other corner post. Her spread-wide legs exposed her bikini panties' dark crescent.

"Watchers are on all my exits! You can't get out of here!"

"I'll do my best to disappoint you," he told her.

And grabbed her left wrist. Tied her to the headboard.

"Don't leave me like this!" He went into the bathroom. Came out with a wide spool of white medical tape. "What if you don't come back?"

"Don't worry." He stared at her spread-eagled body. "Somebody will find you. You're the lucky kind."

Then he pressed a strip of white tape over her beautiful mouth, left.

The elevator dropped him down to the subbasement. He found a laundry room, storage bins, the furnace room jammed with a giant aluminum Christmas tree and a matching Star of David, strings of lights and ornaments. But no door out.

He rode the elevator up to One. The elevator door slid open. He saw the reception desk, two men sitting in the lobby, watching the building entrance. The elevator door closed. Condor pushed the button marked Roof.

He stood beneath the night sky of Washington, DC—not the artistic rooftops of Paris, or the pigeon-cooped roofs of New York, but neither of those skylines hold the glow of the Capitol Dome, the blinking red light atop the Washington Monument.

On the rear of Renee's building, the park side, Condor found steel rungs—and a plaque reading: Warning—Ladder Rungs End with Forty Foot Drop.

Pollution covered the stars. He spun in a frustrated circle

under that lost light. The red eye atop the Washington Monument winked at him.

Condor blinked.

He found it back in the subbasement amidst the Christmas decorations: a thick snow-proof orange extension cord; had to be 100 feet long. Rode the elevator back to the roof. He cinched one end of the cord around his chest, tied it to the other end. Dumped the orange loop off the roof by the steel rungs. Condor grabbed steel rungs . . .

And climbed down the back of the eleven-story building.

He lost count of the rungs, his arms and legs aching, his heart pounding, his shoe—stepping down to find nothing. Four stories of nothing. The big drop.

Condor untied one end of the extension cord, fed it over a rung until *whoosh*: gravity sucked the long cord down into darkness.

"Bad idea," he whispered.

Hand-over-hand, working the thick rubber extension cord like a pulley, Condor lowered himself down four stories of brick wall. The loop cinched around his chest dug into him, but pain meant he was still alive. On the ground, he had to tie the cord looped on the rungs where it could be found by any midnight rambler. He ran into the park. Trees leapt out of the darkness. He swatted them away, got to a main street, caught a cab.

"You hear the news?" asked the cabby.

Condor found the cabby's eyes in the rearview mirror. "What news?"

"Them massacre shootings. Like a dozen dead. But you know the good thing?"

"No."

"TV says it's them Russian mafias dusting each other. 'Means they ain't gonna be locking up more Black men."

The yellow cab rolled through the dark night.

"What am I doing here?" whispered Condor as the cab stopped near a cheap hotel.

"—where you told me to take you," said the cabby.

Condor paid, sent the taxi on its way. Watched the twin red tail lights disappear in the night of the city street. Condor unbuttoned his filthy gray sports jacket.

In the bowels of the Graylin. A no-registration hole to hide a potential witness. Condor circled the block until he stared at the alley behind his target zone.

Coming up on midnight, his watch told him. An indigo city night, USA.

In daylight Pakistan, RT/Delta techs would be prepping the stealth helicopter.

He ran to the mouth of the Graylin alley. Nothing moved. He checked his back, his sides; saw only a laughing trio of club hoppers getting into a car a block away.

"Hell," muttered Condor. "I should have been dead this morning."

He walked into the alley, the Glock in his hand. He eased along the back of a building. Closed doors. Fire escapes overhead. A blue neon sign above a door by a foul-smelling dumpster read: Grayl n. A rat scurried past him.

Condor noticed the dumpster lid was wedged open—by a shoe.

He eased the lid up . . .

The shoe was on a dead man—atop another dead man.

The dumpster lid crashed down. *Bang!*

Condor threw open the hotel's backdoor and jumped inside to a dank concrete maze of air ducts and cluttered corridors and throbbing machinery.

He thrust the Glock in front of him. Jumped around a corner: long corridor, service carts, overhead pipes, and a shaft of yellow light spilling out an open door.

Condor eased toward the light—stepped on a brass cartridge

case. Stumbled into a serving cart piled high with dirty dishes. The cart slammed the wall. Plates crashed and shattered on the corridor floor.

A dead man flopped from behind the rolling cart.

Face-shot corpse! Black man with a badge on his belt. Condor swung the Glock away from the corpse, aimed down the corridor. A dead white male lay by a metal cabinet twenty feet further up the hall. *Partners.*

Condor leapt into the glowing yellow room.

Over the Glock sight, he saw a closet and a cot, a TV, a table against the far wall with a chair where his boss Dray slumped, the eyeglasses dangling from a shoelace around his neck getting smeared by blood streaming from his slashed throat.

Bleeding, he's still . . .

The closet burst open. The bald killer slammed a palm strike into Condor's back. The Glock flew from Condor's hand, hit a cinderblock wall, bounced back on the gray-tiled floor as Condor's feet swept out from under him. Sprawled on the floor, Condor grabbed for the Glock. The killer kicked Condor's head. *White flash* burned his vision, but he saw a flutter near the killer, white paper scrap floating . . .

"Freeze!" yelled someone else.

Looking from the floor between the bald man's legs, Condor saw a third man in the hall—a third man aiming a pistol into this yellow room.

Third man jerked/crumpled, his gun stabbing toward the ceiling firing *Bang!* The bald killer ran from the room.

Condor scrambled to his feet. Grabbed the Glock. Stuffed the paper scrap in his pants pocket. Stepped into the hall.

The third man lay back-shot, conscious, his eyes turning up to Condor.

"Halt!" yelled a voice from the corner of the corridor where Condor had come.

Condor ran the other way. A gun roared. A bullet splattered the wall near him. He ran through a yellow maze of pipes and locked doors.

Saw a giant open gap in the wall to his left. The sign above the gap read: Laundry Bundles Only.

Feet first, he plunged into the dark chute. Slid to the basement laundry room. A conveyer belt angled up to a barred door. Condor scrambled up the conveyer belt, threw the bar off the door, leapt outside, ran through the city night as sirens wailed.

Two taxis and a half-mile walk later, he stood behind Renee's building. The orange extension cord loop dangled from the iron rungs four stories up. Condor envisioned RT/Delta training, those men using a rope loop to pulley and walk up an obstacle course wall. Knew he had to will himself into a Delta superman. Or die.

Renee heard her locks click. Her front door open and close. *"Squawk! Fuck you!"* Condor stood staring down at her on the bed. He looked terrible. Smeared filthy. Flecked with red. Trembling. He tried to speak, shook his head. Left her tied to the bed and went into the bathroom. Shut the door.

Took himself down to naked. Let the shower rain on his still-alive flesh. He didn't know if she could hear him gasping, sobbing in the steam. He dried off. Couldn't put his bloody shirt on again. Spotted a huge maroon Harvard sweatshirt she slept in, pulled it on. Wore his modesty-protecting filthy trousers. Opened the bathroom door.

She stared at him with her brown eyes, hands and legs tied spread on the bed. Tape covered her mouth. He slumped beside her. The guns were on the bathroom floor.

He said: "I don't want any more killing."

Gently as he could, he pulled the tape off her mouth. She licked her lips, and he held her head so she could drink from the nightstand bottle of water.

Words flowed from him, babble summed up with: "They got there first."

"*They*? Who are *they*?" she said.

"Bald guy and his buddy who shot the man in the hall. Plus that shot man and his crew. So many *theys*, and I got trapped between them."

"The hit squad. And the good guys."

"How can you tell the difference?" asked Condor.

"That's your problem. How did bald guy know about the Graylin? Unless his cell is hooked into the good guys. Which means we can't trust anybody."

"*We?* You believe me?"

"The verdict on you is crazy, corrupt or confused. I've never seen a more confused man."

"That's what I've got going for me?" He stared at her. "Why do you believe me?"

"Because you came back."

"That's all?"

"That's enough. For a start. For you."

"For me?" Condor shook his head. "I'm some guy running in the night. I don't even know who or what I'm running from."

"You're staying alive."

Condor stared at the woman he'd tied to the bed. "I have to trust you."

She shrugged. "Makes sense."

He untied her right hand. She lowered it to her side to let the blood flow back into it as he untied her left hand. She sat up, her legs still tied spread wide.

Exhausted, Condor told her: "You could beat the hell out of me tonight."

"I could beat the hell out of you tomorrow." She smiled. "Might as well wait. Plus, if you're right, the bad guys are where they can watch us. Me. If I break my pattern they'll move on us before we're ready. So everything has to wait."

He untied first one of her legs, then the other. She flexed them. Stayed on the bed and didn't kill him or knock him down or go for the guns on the bathroom floor.

He blushed. "What that security guy told you. About me having a monster crush on you. I didn't . . . want you to find out like that."

"I already knew." She looked away. "Why do you think I transferred you out of my section—beside your annoying tendency to poke around and make trouble?"

"Sorry."

"I'm not. At least, I'm not sorry about your monster crush."

He blinked.

She said: "I didn't want you to die feeling sorry for liking me."

"You're too romantic."

"Yeah, that's my problem."

His hand floated up to her face. His thumb rubbed off tape adhesive stuck to her lower lip. Her face stayed held by him. She saw his eyes close as he leaned in for a kiss. Mission accomplished, he pulled back, saw his reflection fill her gaze.

Then her hands cupped his face. Her thumbs lay along his cheekbones. She whispered: "I could gouge out your eyes."

Condor blinked. "Don't stop there."

She pulled him in to kiss. Put him on his back. Straddled him, long white legs and black bikini pinning him to the mattress. She stared down at him, ripped open her blouse and let it fall. He imagined her nakedness mirrored in the glass of the picture above the bed, superimposed over a sepia scene of wild horses in a blizzard as Renee picked up his trembling hands, filled them with her teardrops of flesh.

Later. Under the covers of her bed. Lying face to face.

He whispered: "This isn't what I imagined."

"Never is," said Renee.

"Yeah, well the *how* and the *why* of this *us* never figured into my dreams." He kissed her. "You have no idea how glad I am to be here. But . . ."

"No buts until after tomorrow."

He absolutely knew what she meant. Nodded. Said, "What time is it?"

"Right now." Then she smiled. Gave him the situational answer: "Near 3 a.m."

"Noon for RT/Delta. Nine hours and counting. Will you stop them?"

"How? Why? Besides, they—*we*—still have time."

Condor shook his head. "Feels like I'm trapped in some net."

Her bare leg rose over him, her hand soothed his cheek. "You're here now."

He shook his head. "I was a regular guy, looking for a real life."

"Congratulations, you found it." Her fingers brushed his lids. "But now close your eyes. Even if you can't sleep, I'm all that's here to see."

She reached across him, snapped out the bed lamp.

Dawn found Condor standing in Renee's kitchen nook staring into the black coffee in his mug, smelling Starbucks and seeing Sarita and the slaughter café, dead men in the bowels of a hotel, RT/Delta gearing up for their raid. His coffee swirled.

He wore his filthy pants. Her Harvard sweatshirt. He needed a shave.

The Glock waited on the counter. He pushed the button on the handle to release the ammo magazine. He thumbed two bullets free and it was empty.

"Plus one in the barrel," he muttered. Reloaded, set the Glock on the counter.

His eyes roamed around her home.

Memory made him open a counter drawer. Find the sheathed throwing knife. He pushed up the sweatshirt's left sleeve, strapped the knife to his arm, pulled the sleeve down, made sure his right hand could slide up under the sleeve to unsnap and draw the knife. He hung his arms naturally and the knife stayed hidden, as like a boy playing gunslinger, he checked his blurry image in the mirror of the aluminum refrigerator.

Shook his head, whispered to his reflection: "My name is Condor."

Renee walked out of the bedroom and tossed him a Steve McQueen green nylon jacket, saying: "See how you look in this."

She wore pants, a red bra that pulled at his eyes, her gun clipped on her belt.

He grinned: "Yeah, you'll get the stairwell guards to walk you to your car."

"After the Graylin, they'll want to make sure the basement garage guards haven't been ambushed. That should let you to slip out the fire exit."

Renee pulled on a sweater, scrutinized him in the Steve McQueen jacket, said: "It fits, but you're lucky I like my things big."

She crossed to a desk, pulled out a cell phone with its number taped on it. Memorized the number, gave it to Condor and put a spare cell phone battery in her pocket. The paper scrap from the hotel crime scene was still in the plastic baggy where he'd sealed it. She put the baggy in her pocket, tossed him a set of car keys.

"Remember, it's a brown Ford, DC tags with a dented rear left door. Space 363. Just sign in as Parnell Jones and act like you have the right to be who you are."

"Who *I* am?" Condor smiled. "Spare cell phones, spare car stashed a few blocks away—Parnell—it could be a man or a woman, right? Are you always so . . . prepared?"

"A street dog keeps her bite," she told him. "Agency policies encourage that. But I'm going to violate the Hell out of policy this morning to forensic that scrap of paper."

"Do you think . . ."

"Evidence like that paper is sacred to the Agency. Believe me, we know how to create a whole scenario from one scrap."

She slipped it into her jacket, beckoned him to follow her to the door, saying: "Remember, I call you. Don't get stopped for a traffic ticket. Park at some mall away from the light poles and mounted cameras. Stay in the car. Shouldn't take more than an hour or so to get what's gettable."

"Then what?"

She nodded toward the counter: "Don't forget your gun."

Renee was wrong: she called him in 137 minutes later, an eternity he agonized through in a mall parking lot on the fuzzy line between DC and Maryland.

"Took me this long to shake my security," she said in his new cell phone. "I'm in the car now, almost across the river."

The scrap of paper was a torn electric bill for a suburban house. "Easy Beltway access, quick shot to three airports, Amtrak, Capitol Hill and the White House."

He rendezvoused with her BMW. Electric signs on the road flashed Terrorist Threat Level Orange. No one followed them into an ordinary neighborhood.

She pulled to the curb. He parked behind her. No one moved on the sidewalks. No one watched out any house windows. No cars rolled by them as she climbed in his car, nodded to a white frame dwelling set back from the street. The house was bordered by one neighbor's man-high hedge and another neighbor's tall wooden plank fence.

He looked at his watch: Nearly sunset for RT/Delta. Last gear check before quarantine and their rendezvous with fate. Condor stared at the suspect house.

No one stopped them as they walked to the front door. They saw no one.

"Remember," said Renee: "Don't shoot if you don't have to."

She kicked in the front door. Condor raced behind her

through a living room with a TV and boxes of clothes, through to the tiny dining room with two cots.

And a green stuffed chair that enthroned the bald man.

Who blinked at them, his empty hands in his lap.

"Cover him!" yelled Renee.

She stepped out of Condor's way as he eased forward, gun leveled at the bald man. Renee backed toward Condor and the front room with its *what's-up-there* staircase. As she stepped beside Condor, the bald man . . . smiled.

Fast, so fast that Condor didn't know what was happening, Renee locked his gun hand in an *aikido* grasp, flipped him head over heels. His back slammed on the wooden floor. Breath blew out of him and he felt the Glock slide from his grasp to hers.

Bam! Bam!

The bald man in the green stuffed chair jerked with an astonished look on his face as two red flowers blossomed on his chest.

Condor gasped. On his back, he saw Renee with her arms spread like soaring wings with her right hand pointing her smoking pistol at the shot man as her left hand aimed Condor's Glock at the wall by the front door: *Bam!*

The Glock's slide blew back and locked after firing its last round. She set the Glock on the floor, used a two-handed grip on her own gun to zero Condor. "The irony is that *you* were supposed to die first."

Condor stared at the dead man in the green chair.

Renee said: "He's a CIA outsource contractor, always in it for money. He and I found the al Qaeda cell based in this ordinary house. But instead of busting them, he sold himself. Of course, I pulled all his strings, but I'm invisible. The terrorists don't know I exist. Baldy bought my strategy because al Qaeda won't deal with a woman.

"Now he can't demand his share." She smiled. "He was an

easier hook than you, though, originally, neither of you were supposed to die until . . ."

She checked her watch: ". . . a few hours from now. After Rising Thunder."

"You sold out the Delta team! They're heading into an ambush! How much did you get out of al Qeada for killing our own guys?"

"Money makes the world go round. I want my turns."

"How much?"

She shrugged. "Five million. But don't worry; our guys won't die. Get up."

And he did, slowly, his back to her, saying: "But if our guys won't die . . ."

"Death is a commodity. If innocent Afghanis are slaughtered by an American raid caught on TV for the world . . . that's a bonanza for al Qaeda."

Condor saw the TV behind her. Envisioned its dead green screen showing images of AK47-toting terrorists in a village. Saw those images blur, morph, mutate into a young girl, a frightened mother, an old man, a father and his baby.

"You're creating a My Lai massacre! You'll make our real terrorist war rhyme with the worst of Vietnam!

"You two and al Qaeda created perfect fake intelligence!" Excitement rang through Condor's fear. "That's what bugged me! Everything fit with absolute certainty!"

"People who are absolutely certain they're right are ripe to be absolutely wrong."

He shook his head. "Won't work. Our Delta boys are the best gunners in the world. Savvy. Been there, done that. They won't massacre innocent civilians."

"They won't have to," said Renee. "Al Qaeda martyrs will kill the villagers with American guns. The al Qaeda guys will fire on RT/Delta. Shoot at our guys, they shoot back. Imagine two, three minutes at full auto fire. Foreign TV cameras are camped close enough to arrive at the same time as the Rangers' helicopters. And in the glare of TV lights, who can prove it wasn't America that massacred some mother and child?

"No one will buy America's denials," she said. "How many times has the world found out we fibbed? But the Agency will look for a plot. Hunt for villains. Won't stop until they find something. So to cover my ass, I had to give them a fall guy.

"You. *Condor*. Framed as a traitor for al Qaeda. You spied on Rising Thunder because I kept steering you to it until you got hooked. I transferred you away from me to Homeland Security. I set up your Cayman account. We were going to kill you after Rising Thunder to make it look like al Qaeda was covering its tracks.

"But then yesterday morning, you called me. Said you were close to figuring out what was bugging you. We couldn't take a chance. Plus we didn't know what you'd told your coworkers. They weren't even factored into our yesterday *scrambled on-the-fly* plan Version Two Point Zero to kill you and make it look like you heroically had gotten too close to the terrorists. We were going to deal with whatever you'd told your coworkers later but, hey, *bonus*: thanks for bunching them all in the Starbucks kill zone."

"That's not my fault!"

"Maybe not, but now here's how it looks in my new Version Three Point Zero: your Homeland Security team suspected you, so you had to kill them all—including your boss—before they could interfere with your betrayal of Rising Thunder.

"And here you are, caught dead to rights with Baldy who helped you betray America, kill your coworkers, and hunt down your boss. Al Qaeda fingerprints are everywhere in this safe house and at the Graylin where they backed up Baldy. You checked their car out of the parking lot, put your fingerprints on the steering wheel. A wounded Homeland Security guy saw you at the Graylin. My planting that electric bill in your car just now was a nice touch. It was going to be found dropped at the Graylin to lead the Agency here, but then you grabbed it and put your DNA on it. Thanks."

"You've been working me and the CIA, Baldy, and al Qaeda for months!"

"I'm an industrious girl."

"Is that what you call it?" Condor swallowed. "How am I supposed to die?"

"Resisting capture. I spotted you in my car mirrors. Maybe you were after me, too, who knows? I flipped your tail job. But, gosh, my cell phone battery died. Shit happens. I couldn't call for back-up.

"So I dogged you here. Exercised justifiable initiative. Kicked the door. You popped a round at me but I nailed you. Baldy went for his gun. I had to drill him. Trust me, the forensics will line up: it's not an exact science. While the CIA is busy sorting out this mess . . . Rising Thunder explodes in global primetime."

"You think that will work?" said Condor.

"So do you. TV and computers create reality."

"Truth in a box." Condor shook his head. "Like a coffin."

"Pick up your empty gun," she told him. "Move over to the other side of Baldy."

"Why?"

She smiled. "So you can live longer."

Condor felt the weight of the dingy room. A dead man slumped in a green chair. The trash of an al Qaeda sleeper cell lay scattered everywhere. He smelled a banana peel. The woman he'd trusted—adored!—stood behind him preparing his murder.

"Living is all I've got," muttered Condor. He dropped his eyes. Slumped.

She saw him bend toward the Glock to pick it up with both hands.

Blast toward her like an uncoiling wrestler. She clubbed his left elbow with her gun. He yelled, hooked his right hand at her and she snapped her left arm up to block . . .

Lightning ripped her forearm. Renee screamed. *Knife, where did he get? . . . Oh!* She deflected his next stab, chopped his knife wrist. His blade flew across the room.

But the knife surprise unbalanced her. Condor grabbed her gun, felt . . .

Renee thrust her gun arm straight up. Condor clung to her. His body pressed against hers as if they were ballet dancers. She pivoted into a hip throw. But as she curled into him, his free hand punched her bloody gash. Pain made her wince. That flinch meant that throwing him unbalanced her. They tumbled together.

Crashed with him on top of her, both of them face down.

She rolled him onto his back, her spine pressed his chest, her skull alongside his cheek. He'd gained control of her pistol. Stabbed the bore of her gun under her jaw.

Renee lay on top of him.

They lay there.

Staring up at the white ceiling.

Until she said: "*Gotcha.*"

"What?" yelled Condor.

Her hair tickled his left cheek. Smelled like coconut shampoo.

The gun under her jaw made Renee grimace her words: "You're not a killer."

"I almost got you with your knife! And . . . I'll shoot you now!"

"No. Self-defense, sure. Combat, only if you're lucky. But now you'd have to do it stone cold, and that's not you. You're no executioner."

She flicked her left shoe off so that one bare foot kissed the wooden floor.

He pushed the gun barrel into her: "Don't!"

"OK," she said. "You're the one with the big hard gun."

"Yes, I am. And you're going to . . . to . . ." Her weight pressed down on him.

"To what?"

"I'm not going to stay trapped on this floor"

"You're trapped on more than this floor," said Renee. "Officially, you're either corrupt, crazy, or confused. The Agency doesn't forgive any of those. So let me help you out. After all, we're in this together."

Condor said: "I didn't kill anybody. Or betray my country."

"Countries aren't what they used to be. And everybody dies sometime."

"There's freedom. There's justice."

"Justice. What is going to happen to *just us*?" Renee shifted.

Condor pushed the gun tighter under her jaw.

"You won't execute me. So it's my word against yours. Home Sec', the CIA—they won't know who to believe. They're stuck with their cover lies about the murders. CYA is their first and their second rule. So admitting they lied and got tricked by me? They'll flush us both down some black hole. I'll be guilty, but you'll be a chump."

She maneuvered her knees higher so her hips rubbed his groin, so they were almost cheek to cheek. Said, "Is that better for you?"

"You don't care."

"Actually, I do. A girl should always respect a monster crush."

"You're the monster."

"But you're the one who's caught."

"No."

"Yes." He felt her smile. "Unless we become partners. We can stop the Rising Thunder disaster. Create Version Four Point Zero. Pin all the sins on Baldy and al Qaeda. Bust this al Qaeda cell—they've got other big, nasty plans. We'll come out of this as heroes—or at least free and clear. You won't want to ride off into the sunset with me, but we can share a goodbye kiss."

"Are you crazy?"

"Crazy doesn't mean much anymore."

"They'll get you!"

"Even if you convince them I'm guilty, even if you can move

the system in time to save Rising Thunder, only I can rat out this al Qaeda cell. Stop their next *kill-a-few-thousand-Americans* mission. Nobody can torture or drug it out of me, so our bosses will have to deal. Yesterday's gone and today is on its way out the door. I'm selling a safer tomorrow for a guarantee that takes me off the hook. If you rebel against all that, then *you* become a national security problem."

"They're better than that!"

"*They*? Who is *they*? They are us, us is you, and look where you are."

"You can't win!" He felt his heart slamming under hers.

"I won't lose," said Renee. "How about you?"

He felt her smile. "Who are you going to be? A killer, a chump, or a hero?"

They lay on their backs, she on top of him, his gun pressing under her jaw.

"Fuck your labels, I decide who I am," said Condor. "Put the gun in your mouth. Hold it tight. If you *kung fu*, I pull the trigger. We're getting off this floor."

He eased the pistol's bore up over her chin until it rested lightly on her lips.

She whispered into that black hole, "Then what?"

"Then I prove you wrong. The Agency and Home Sec' won't buy your lies. They won't plea-bargain your treason and murders. All this, *us*—we're about more than what works. They'll give you what you deserve, and they'll let me be me."

Renee smiled. Said. "Really?"

And slowly slid her lips around the steel barrel of his gun.

CAGED DAZE OF THE CONDOR

First published in *The Red Bulletin*, 2014

Blink, you're trapped in the CIA's secret insane asylum.

No one knows your real name.

They call you Condor.

Only you know that locked up in here with all the crazy spies is an *activated agent* who's busting some move today, *now*, and it's not you because, *let's face it*, you're one of the crazy ones, so no one will believe you about the phone you spotted five days ago in the fire extinguisher cabinet when you were patrolling for homicidal mice.

Cell phone. Stashed in a dead drop. Forbidden in this Maine woods castle containing NATIONAL SECURITY SECRETS.

Now this morning: cell phone *gone*.

MICE: Menace In Confining Environment.

And, *Condor*: crazy *sure*, but you're still a sworn soldier of National Security.

So *sorry Nurse Nora*, who's the fierce side of forty, white uniform curves, lips the color of blood.

Alone with you in this 9:47 a.m. locked third floor lemon ammonia corridor.

Push her to the wall. Nora gasps.

Drop to your knees. Your unworthy hands circle her ankles. Slide up her calves, her white slacks. Her thighs tense like a mare. Caresses her crotch. Cup the moon of her hips. Your hands travel her spine to heaving shoulders, the front of her uniform, down and *oh!* Your grasps fill with her heavy *now*, better than any dream and *Yes!* she's concealing no phone, no weapon. *Let go* and where you touched *burns.*

Nora hisses: "Ten minutes until Half 'n' Half. And that's the last time you ever touch me like that!"

Tell a truth. Tell a lie. "I hope so."

She makes you lead the way, buzzed into the Dayroom ruled by orderlies with barbell muscles. *Hope none of them are the spy.* Two orderlies unfold chairs in a circle for Group as five of your fellow whackos and psychiatrist Dr. Cohn watch. Nora heads to that shrink. *Will she rat you out?* You walk to the duty desk where Administrator Josh flashes a *what's-up?* smile.

Tell him: "Nora sent me to get you."

"Thanks, man." Josh. Mr. Friendly. Mr. *pictures of my kids* Guy. Who saunters from behind the desk toward his colleagues.

Quick! Pull the pink messages pad from down your pants where you shoved it after you pickpocketed it from groping-shocked Nora. Use a blue crayon stolen from Art Therapy—*writes*, but can't be sharpened into a weapon beyond what you scrawl on the pink message slip you stick under the lock-secured desk phone.

Join the group settling in the folding chairs' circle.

Half 'n' Half:

Half short-timers pulled from meltdowns in today's cloisters of national security.

Half longtime lock-ups like white-haired Green Beret Zane whose sanity never came back from Saigon and CIA Victor who blew preventing 9/11 while getting his lover butchered.

And you. Condor. *What happened to you?*

Theory is, mix still potentially productive superstars of spook world with brilliant burnouts who are never going home and the Group Therapy will help the short-timers see that they don't have it so bad, make them want to get better.

Three short-timers.

There's mangy-haired, scab-picker Clare, a legendary CIA analyst who wakes up screaming that Osama bin Laden isn't *he isn't!* dead.

And got-the-shakes Paul, Chief of Station Kiev, who had to keep smiling at a cocktail party as he realized the infilt' team of Ukrainians he'd Green Lit into Russia were sneaking straight into a Putin ambush.

The last short-timer is the only one besides frisked Nora who you know is not the spy: pudgy Weston who wrangled Big Data for the NSA until he started seeing human ears crawling on the floor.

He's not the spy because he's the spy's target.

Because in yesterday's Group, Dr. Cohn said: "Next time, Weston, you share."

Then the cell phone disappeared.

To report whatever Weston will say today, now.

Count the suspects: Josh. Four muscled orderlies. Dr. Cohn. Scab-picker Clare. Got-the-shakes Paul. Even white-haired vet Zane or 9/11 haunted Victor: Weston's NSA secrets share might be worth more than money, might negotiate a way out of here.

"Weston," says Dr. Cohn: "Go."

That NSA genius whispers: "There are ears everywhere!"

Victor says: "Tell us what we don't know."

Is it him?

By the wall with four orderlies and Josh: Nora, sad eyes. *Did she tell?*

Weston whispers: "I'm not here because the ears listen."

Josh drifts back toward the control desk.

"I freaked out because it only takes three steps to make the ears talk."

Josh reaches the control desk. Spots that pink message slip.

"Trick the ears, an easy three step hack, then any villain knows corporate plans, billionaires' bank accounts, presidents' scams, that website you visited!"

Josh frantically unlocks the desk's phone, punches in the number blue crayoned on the pink message slip above: "yr kids' school, active shooter rampage"

"First hijacking step: get a great laptop."

Watch the orderlies. The shrink. Your fellow whackos circled with you on folding chairs. Not pawed and cleared Nora. Or tricked and thus eliminated Josh listening to the buzz from calling the *this-device* number you sneaked off the stashed phone.

"Second step: transmit something the ears hunger to hear."

Vibration.

Coming from suddenly pale CIA exec Paul getting a surprise call.

We are what we do.

Your only play is crazy.

Charge across the circle. Palm-strike Paul's forehead. Screaming *not just you two screaming.* Paul grabs you—backwards-somersault judo foot in his stomach. He whirls over you. Paul crashes through panic-abandoned chairs, hits the tiles and skids over them as you yell: "Did you betray your infilt' team, too?"

Orderlies swarm and pin you.

Rip the shirtsleeve off your trapped left arm.

Nora points: "On the floor!"

A cell phone trailing a gray duct tape strip stuck to Paul's combat-bared stomach.

Weston screams as he runs in circles: "Ears! Ears!"

Two orderlies roll off you to chase him.

Victor, *not going to blow it again*, chops Paul's neck as that traitor tries to rise.

Prick burns your left arm. Hypodermic needle. No matter what, rules send you to padded cell lockdown for violence, minimum a month, and as you melt into a drugged blur, your last conscious *maybe crazy* vision is of smiling ruby lips.

JASMINE DAZE
OF THE CONDOR

First published in *Playboy*, 2015

You're crammed into the backseat of a banana-scented Toyota rumbling through a battered city's night. Riding shotgun is the cleric Ahmed. He holds a cellphone: its glow shows you've got just 47 minutes to make it to the Exfilt.

So abort trying to identify the Firm's target amidst the six people jammed into this car with you. Otherwise, if the bad guy doesn't get you, then your crazy will.

Streetlights work but darkness fills the flat glass buildings and shuttered stores streaming past the car windows. A trash barrel burns on a street corner. A white dog trots through the head-lights 45 minutes before your only chance for rescue.

Mashed beside Ahmed in the front seat is Travua, he claims to be a geek. Nour drives, her college coed hair flying wild. On your left sits Skander, says he's a mortician. On your right, Renee strobes she hates your guts. Silver threads lace her black hair. Then comes Zied who smells of goats as he says: "We thought you were dead."

Answer: "Just locked up."

"Guantanamo?" asks cleric Ahmed.

"No. The CIA's secret insane asylum."

Maine forest, bare trees swaying like skeletons. A castle.
Hypodermics.

"How'd you get out?" asks geek Travua.

"Broke the rules."

Six days ago. A suit from Langley sends the white coats out of
your padded cell. Says: "You're our optimal chance."

Because of 1989. Berlin Wall falls. The Soviet-Afghan war
you've been helping fuel ends. You leave Paris. Leave Renee.

But she's still a street dreamer. Now helping invent Arab
Spring. And NSA ears have discovered her local Council On
Freedom has been infiltrated by a gunner from the band of terrorists who killed fifty-eight people when they attacked a Catho-
lic church in Baghdad four months ago on Halloween, 2010:

"... and so our soldier will steer those unenlightened rebels to
jihad."

In your padded cell, you tell the CIA suit: "You're optimally
screwed because I'm fucking nuts."

"The docs can shoot you full of meds, *functionalize* you. This
is a bad group aborning. Breaking off from al Qaeda Iraq because
they're too soft. Us on their hate list. We got no shoes in those
protest streets. White House rules say *hands off*, so we've got to
be cleverer, so you're our only spy shot even if. . . ."

"Even if *what*?"

"You'll only have six days to actualize the target and exfil-
trate before your meds wear off. Then your . . . your *crazy* will
escape, probably get you killed, definitely lost to us. Plus, even
when you're medically stoned enough to hold it together, you're
so wacko you'll only be able to tell the truth."

No one in your padded cell comments on such a concept.

"And this gig is my ticket out of here?"

"Sure," lies the suit.

What the Hell. No ride lasts forever.

Now in the backseat of the Toyota, mortician Skander gestures toward streets sparkling with shattered glass. "Breaking rules is what this is all about."

"No!" Driver Nour fingers hair off her face. "This is about making rules!"

Goat-stench Zied says: "After centuries of dictators, we don't know how to do that."

"All is written," intones Ahmed. "The tyrants crushing us have got to go."

Old enough to be these rebels' mother Renee says: "Our Council must help make this revolution work for love, not hate."

Travua mumbles: "I just want a job."

Too many names. Too many faces. Can't keep them straight.

Remember who you are.

Travua shakes his head at *you* being crammed into the car he chose. "Gotta admit this is cool. I mean, you're a legend. You're Condor."

A codename. A face in your mirror. Some *him* in a movie called your life.

"*Ha!*" snaps Renee.

Four days ago, she opened the door to her mouse hole office, saw *him* standing there. Pounded his chest like she was stabbing his heart. "You should be dead!"

"Yes."

Tears oceaned her blue eyes. "Why did you do that to me? I believed in you!"

"Me, too." Condor shrugged.

"I help you rescue mountains from communists, you give them to monsters who turn girls into slaves. The Russians slink away and so do you, you leave, *leave me!*"

"I wasn't all there and you were all too much."

She slapped him. "Twenty years I've wanted to do that!"

"Then do it again."

Renee blinked. Slapped him, *slapped him*, hammered his ribs—crumpled. Condor held her on her feet. Buried his face in her silver-laced long black hair that smelled of jasmine, the official flower of this rebellion. Her flowers-and-flesh musk filled his skull. Her eyes fluttered, those full lips parted and he risked/won *that* kiss.

Outside, 100,000 men and women pack the city square. Helicopters *whump-whump* above the crowd. Army soldiers stare down black uniformed secret police thugs. Banners flap. Signs, some in English: *Don't bomb us. Democracy like USA. Facebook.* Laptops YouTube global rock 'n' roll. Chants echo: *"Lib-er-te! Lib-er-te!"*

Renee pulls off his jacket. His shirt. Pushes his pants down. Then hers. Their trembling hands unbutton her blouse, she shrugs it off, turns to offer him her bra clasp—*undone*. His hands slide over her woman warm smooth back. Follow the forward curve of her ribs. Fill with thick flesh, feel her swellings. *Oui!* Tears slick her cheeks, slick on her thighs. She folds across the political posters-cluttered desk, raises her round hips to him and *yes* he can he does *yes* then *no*, turning her so her spine presses on slogan signs as he says: "I want you to see me." Her legs scissor him *yes* and *oui* and *YES.*

Draped over her, panting, heart slowing, Condor heard Renee say: "Lay here with me for a moment before you tell me what you really want."

She said *no.*

"But you know who the infiltrator is," said Condor.

"We're all infiltrators. All voices must be heard to make this movement work."

"My target hates every voice except his own. He—"

Renee snapped: "Why must a *man* be who you fear?"

"Not my rules," said Condor. "The bad guys are too afraid of women to let them do any more than work, weep, and die. Their

name keeps changing but not who they are. Now they call themselves ISIS. And they'll steal your movement."

"If no one can trust me, then *you* have stolen *me* from the
movement." She shook her head. "Doesn't matter what we say.
What we do is our real politics. If I serve you and not the movement . . ."

"You don't want them stealing this show either. I understand
being cautious about helping us. No one will know."

"Except me. You. Your masters. The wind, the stars. If I betray
what I believe—"

"—to keep it from being betrayed . . ."

"If everything is treachery, we've already lost. I will at least
keep my soul clean."

But she let him stay. Slept naked beside him. Stuck to his legend: introduced him to the rebels who came 'round her office as
the whistleblower from *Way Back When*, the notorious man in
the newspapers who opposed the CIA in the name of truth—and
so, he saw in the eyes of those he met, was someone *they* could
use for their own . . . truths.

Now your eyes ride trapped in the rearview mirror of a
banana-stinking Toyota rumbling through the sixth night since
national security sprang you from its nuthouse.

This morning, this convulsing country's top general resigned
rather than order troops to shoot the protestors. Cell phones and
laptops played his speech as you stood in the city square surrounded by thousands of jubilant rebels. The North African air
shook as if it were a fruit bowl held by a Godzilla-sized monkey
who's laughing at you as his hairy finger *fire graffitis* the blue sky:

FUNCTIONALIZATION FADES!

Uh-oh.

Still, you convinced Renee and all five of her group to

ride with you to the drop site. No one hangs back, becomes innocent.

You can do this. Maintain or at least fake it. Finish the mission. Get out alive.

Thirty-seven minutes until Go or Gone Forever.

"Are you sure crates of first aid kits will be in that building?" Nour steers the Toyota around the blackened metal skeleton of a burned-out car.

"All the right bribes were paid." Don't say *by who.*

"How will we know who to bribe after the revolution?" asks geek Travua.

"The revolution means no more bribes," says goat-smelling Zied.

"Things will be as they say they are," says Skander.

"The law will be the law," says cleric Ahmed.

Renee's words agree with them, target you: "No buying and selling of right and wrong."

"We will choose what's right and what's wrong!" yells the college coed.

Answer her with words for Renee: "Free to choose doesn't make choices free."

Headlights blast the Toyota's windshield.

A pickup truck converted into an ambulance races past, another mission in the revolution's night.

Your mission.

Priority Option means "actualize" the target from UNKNOWN to secretly photographed, videoed and recorded by your *next generation* CIA cell phone. Call his phone so NSA web spinners can reveal his links, follow his phone, turn it on for their ears. Reconfigure him as an unaware vessel for your not-so-crazy colleagues to use to penetrate an emerging empire of terror.

Fallback Option puts the target's name on the Authorized Kill List the moment *after* he's, *say,* fallen from some roof.

Failure is everything else, even if Condor gets out alive and back to the nuthouse.

Exfilt launches in thirty-one minutes. You still don't know which rebel is your target. Worse, Day Six is bleeding *what's real* from *what you see.*

"Can't be Nour," slips from your lips.

"No," says mortician Skander as the car swerves, "she's really doing quite good."

Skander tells the woman working the steering wheel: "We're proud of you."

Nour brakes. Turns to ask you: "This is where, *oui?*"

A nine-story white stone and black glass monolith pierces the night sky.

Your eyes are wide open. See yourself answer: "OK."

Exfilt in twenty-one minutes.

Everyone climbs out of the parked Toyota like clowns in an amateur circus.

"Look!" Zied points down the urban canyon to the city square built by French colonists who ruled here in the black and white TV days before the last revolution. A pulsating rainbow fills the end of that canyon from cell phones and laptops and lanterns, from security spotlights brought by the secret police on trucks bought before the current regime's love affair with torture turned off foreign aid faucets.

Rene's swollen lips whisper: "That glow never goes out."

You hear yourself say: "—hope not."

"*Insha'Allah,*" whispers Ahmed.

Renee's blue eyes press on you.

"Condor," says Zied: "We love what America says it is, but why does your country do such stupid things?"

"I don't know." *Is he the fanatic who wants to blow up the Statue of Liberty or is he just like the fifty-year-old white guy in an Iowa City Starbucks who votes red-white-and-blue conservative and says the same thing?* Shrug. "We're just people."

Zied who smells of goats wrinkles his nose: "Politics."

"Politics is the *how*, not the *why*."

"We must be better than that," says geek Travua.

"*Insha'Allah*," intones Ahmed.

Is one of you two the CIA target?

Nineteen minutes until Exfilt.

Zied points: "What's in your jeans' pocket?"

Next thing you know, in your hand is a gray metal, spring blade knife. Your palm obeys invisible stars, offers *what you were issued* to Goat-guy.

Who takes it, shoves the gray sword into crack above the building's door lock, wiggles the thin blade—

Snap!

Geek Travua stares at Condor. "Do you have any more lethal devices?"

"No. And now that doesn't seem like such a great idea."

Nour frowns at the silver-haired American: "What's wrong with you?"

"We don't have enough time for that answer."

Ahmed says: "How are we going to get in to get the first aid kits?"

"I've got a key."

"Why didn't you say so?" Skander grabs the key.

Nour shakes her head: "Why did you have a knife?"

Open your mouth and quote the woman you wish you could love forever: "What we do is our real politics."

Renee's blink vibrates the air.

You've got seventeen minutes.

Skander yells: "We're in!"

Flow with your crew into the hollow echo that haunts modern structures.

"*Waves of hallucinogenic perception by the patient mark psychotic breaks with diminished competencies in reality,*" said a shrink's memo in your file you hacked one night from the rec room back at the CIA's secret insane asylum.

Hell, if all you've got is reality, you're already fucked.

Nour says: "Now what?"

Skander tells that coed: "You'll know when it's time."

Shadows and substance in the building lobby swirl into *there stands Renee.*

She stares at Skander. "What did you mean back there in the car?"

Far bigger than you Skander, whose cheeks sport regularly shaved stubble, says: "What do you mean, what do I mean?"

"When you said you were proud of Nour's driving," says Renee.

Skander shrugs: "She did a good job for a woman."

Renee's smile is a curved saber. "What jobs are for a woman?"

"Don't be silly," says Skander. "We have more important things to decide now."

"No!" yells Renee. "Now is about deciding *exactly* that!"

Skander proclaims: "Everyone has a place in our glory."

Born during the Paris barricades of 1968, clubbed by the goons of power in dozens of cities, alive every day Renee raises her shoulders to the wind, the stars, shouts: "And you claim the right to decide everyone's place! Leave me the hell out of your *glory!*"

Then she spits at Skander.

And as her disgust hits its target, you realize that for Renee, helping Condor is the lesser betrayal.

Skander lunges at *who dared to.*

Grab him, whisper: "Forget it. We need her. Come, back me up."

"What?"

"The last bribe has to be paid after we confirm we got the goods. My guy is in the building and on the clock. If we don't pay him, there's no pipeline."

"You want me to meet your source? Back you up because he's not trustworthy? Could betray you—I mean *betray us*?" Wheels turn in Skander's brown eyes. "Of course I'll help you."

Of course you will.

Whirl so you're looking at the others as you say: "You all go check to be sure our delivery is in the basement. Everyone give me your cell phone numbers."

Eyes on the five innocent rebels and Renee—*oh, Renee!*—you miss the blur that is Skander until he's grabbed your right hand, stopped it from reaching inside your black leather jacket to the pocket over your heart that holds the CIA's cell phone.

"I have all their numbers," snaps Skander. "Let's go."

No way to defy him and not make it a big deal, maybe blow your cover.

Lead him toward the bank of elevators, push the summons button, fixate on the glowing skyward arrow until the elevator's *Ding!* breaks you free.

With eleven minutes until Exfilt.

Mirror steel elevator doors slide open and release a blast of light.

Like a northern desert wind carries you into the elevator cage. Spins you around dizzy. The flat gray metal wall braces your back as your stomach pulls reality's breath into your lungs. Skanders' hands . . . steady you. You both pretend you don't feel him pick-pocket your CIA cell phone.

He says: "Are you OK?"

"I am how I am."

Skander's stare drills your bones. "You need to push the right button."

"Don't we all."

A steel plate on the wall displays all the levels this cage can take you to. You're free to choose whatever button you're shown. But they're labeled in languages you never mastered. Run your finger to the top of the list—can't remember what the word is in the French written there or those swooping Arabic symbols. . . . *So fuck it*, push that button.

"We're going to the roof?" says Skander.

"Guess so."

Inertia from the rocketing up cage sinks you in your shoes.

Out of your mouth comes: "You could kill me up there."

"What a crazy thing to say."

"Really."

There's a familiar bulge in Skander's shirt pocket. The CIA phone. A grab away. Or manipulate him into giving it to you. Trick him into letting you photograph, video, call him, compromise him.

Or use the roof.

Seven minutes to Exfilt.

Fight the feeling that the elevator's gray steel walls are really water.

"I wonder," says Skander as the metal cage carrying you two hums upward: "Is this how it feels to ascend to what you infidels call heaven?

"Of course," he adds, "this could also be how it feels to fall into damnation."

"Either way, life's about flying."

"No. The end justifies the trip, not the other way around."

"Ah," you say. "Justice."

Ding! The elevator doors slide open to the night.

"After you," says the man whose eyes are measuring your murder.

Step out onto the tarred roof.

As behind you, where he can not see as much of this realm in the sky and so logically, strategically should wait to strike, Skander says: "I wonder who's here for us."

"Maybe it just looks like we're alone," is the worthless truth you say.

What it looks like is a long way down.

Nine stories up from the sidewalk, this flat roof stretches out under a star-shotgunned black umbrella. The moon grows brighter with every slamming beat of your heart. The hard surface beneath your shoes is a rectangular domain where strategically placed industrial air-conditioning units loom like hulking chess pieces. Out beyond the edge of where you can stand and not fall through the night, most of the buildings and neighborhoods show no lights as citizens hope that hiding in darkness will keep them safe. At this distance it's impossible to tell if those huddled masses are staring at screens streaming data, images, sounds. Up here, you hear the faint *whump-whump* of TV and police helicopters hovering over the protestors occupying the distant glowing city square. Somewhere a siren *wee-oo*'s away into *gone*. Overhead, perhaps that's the flapping of a bat. You breathe deep, the air is cool, and you smell old tar, your sweat and fear.

The dark breeze is soft.

Not enough to blow a steady man off his feet and over the edge.

Don't let Skander see you wobble with whispers from the ghosts of who you loved, who you fooled, who you killed. Hold on as you walk to the center of the roof.

Walking behind you comes a bear of a man.

Who says: "I don't see anyone who wanted us to come up here."

"My whole life I've been told where to go by people I can't see."

"And they call you Condor."

Turn. Face him.

Blinking red aviation warning lights on the edges of the roof mark how far you can run. Their scarlet hue helps the moon let you see and be seen.

The bear man says: "Do people believe you are who you say you are?"

"Do you?"

He shakes his head of black hair shorn too short for an easy grab.

Says: "Yes."

Says: "No."

Says: "You are Condor, but you are not the enemy of the CIA or America."

Behind him stand ghosts. They're laughing.

This man you were supposed to unmask says: "In fact, you are the CIA."

"Everybody's gotta be somebody."

That bear man slides left, puts you between him and the closest edge of the roof.

You say: "Why don't we call the others and let them decide who's who?"

"Democracy is a terrible system."

"Works better than what you've got in mind."

"Not if you are among the faithful," he says.

"Faithful *to you.* Everybody else is fucked."

Shrug, stay loose, ready.

Say: "Let's call the others, see what they think."

"Call?" Skander boxer-shuffles you toward the edge of the roof. "On this?"

Your cell phone jiggles in his hand.

"This is fancy." He taunts you with it like a playground bully. "Brand new—newer than new, yes? Probably tells the CIA right where it is—where *you* are."

Maybe he's trained in Afghanistan's mountains, in secret camps in Iraq—hell, maybe he paid for *Krav Maga* lessons in Berlin or Beirut, *whatever*: you sense skill in his stance, know he's bigger, younger, stronger, able to do more these last few years than solo *T'ai chi* and pushups in a padded cell.

The phone, that *rescue me* lifeline and mission *actualizer*, that phone they gave you wiggles gripped in the leading left hand of he who would kill you as he says: "You will get the phone tossed to you, but not . . . Not yet. Not . . . *up here.*"

He's backing you closer to the edge of the roof.

"There is only one freedom for the likes of you," says the man who would be a caliph of the kind despised by cleric Ahmed. "You may have the freedom to scream."

You whirl and curl, yell: "Siri— *Flash bang!*"

That phone in that killer's hand, that phone with its souped-up battery not yet seen outside of Silicone Valley or secret corridors inside the Beltway, that phone upgraded with software that will go on sale in TV commercials to your fellow Americans in a few months, that phone hears your command.

White light FLASH blinds your killer.

The *bang* bloodies his hand, not fatal (next year's upgrade), but he's blinking—

Snap-kick your right foot high and hard into his groin. He jackknifes, exposes his temples to your double palm-heel strikes, drops like a stone.

Ninety seconds to Exfilt.

He's out, drag him to the edge of the roof and the only other sanctioned option.

Or . . .

Sanctions are for the sane.

Be sure he stays out: kick him in the head.

Run down the ranks of the A.C. hulks until you find the unit painted 9.

Slam your shoulder into that steel wall—*BAM!* it clatters away. Grab what's cached in the A.C.

Get back to where the bad guy lays moaning.

Pull off his pants.

He's one of those guys who goes commando.

Takes you twenty seconds to gear up.

Whump-whump-whump from a helicopter chopping closer in the night.

He's too heavy for you to pick up.

Lay on top of half-naked him. Wrap your arms around him.

Roll over so he's on top—so you can tie his pants around the two of you.

Whump-whump.

A spotlight drops from heaven, reveals your waving hand and the gear it holds.

Like a black mamba drops from the helicopter.

Lands on Skander's back, shocks him awake to see and feel you clicking the harness you're wearing to the cable and he *gets it*, struggles, yells: "You're insane!"

"Yeah."

Whump-whump revs up.

"I'm not the only one after you!" yells the warrior of what he calls holy.

"You're who I caught. And if your pants come loose, if you let go, you'll get your reward of virgins. Or not. But no matter what, here's the *free* you tossed me."

The cable snaps tight—the big jerk, *whoosh.*

Across that night sky comes a helicopter cabled to screams.

NEXT DAY OF
THE CONDOR

First published by No Exit Press, 2015

They led him out of the CIA's secret insane asylum as the sun set over autumn's forest there in Maine.

Brian and Doug walked on either side of him, Brian a half-step back on the right, the package's strong side, because even when there'll be no problem, it pays to be prepared beyond a government salary you can only collect if you're still alive.

Brian and Doug seemed pleasant. Younger, *of course*, with functional yet fashionable short hair. Doug sported stubble that tomorrow could let him blend into Kabul with little more than a *shemagh* head wrap and minor clothing adjustments from the American mall apparel he wore today. Brian and Doug introduced themselves to the package at the Maine castle's front security desk. He hoped their mission was to take him where they said he was supposed to go and not to some deserted ditch in the woods.

Two sets of footsteps walked behind him and his escorts, but in what passes for our reality, he could only hear the walker with the clunky shoes. The soundless steps made more powerful cosmic vibrations.

The clunky shoes belonged to Dr. Quinton, who'd succeeded the murdered Dr. Friedman and mandated Performance Protocols to replace the patient-centric approach of his predecessor, policies that hadn't gotten that psychiatrist ice picked through his ear, but why not use that tragic opportunity to institute a new approach of accountability?

After all, you can't be wrong if you've got the right numbers.

The soundless steps are the scruffy sneakers footfalls of blond nurse Vicki.

She wore electric red lipstick.

And her wedding band linked to her high school sweetheart who like every day for the last eight years lay in a Bangor Veterans Home bed tubed and cabled to beeping machines tracking the flatline of his brain waves and his heart that refused to surrender.

The beating of that heart haunts the soft steps of she who no one really knows.

Except for the silver-haired man walking ahead of her from this secret castle.

And he's nuts, so . . .

The dimming of the day activates sensors in the castle's walled parking lot where these five public servants emerge. Brian and Doug steer the parade toward a "van camper," gray metal and tinted black glass side windows, small enough to parallel park, big enough for "road living" behind two cushioned chairs facing the sloped windshield. Utah license plates lied with their implication of *not a government ride.*

Doug said: "October used to be colder."

Brian eyed the package's scruffy black leather jacket. "Seems like a nice enough guy, moves better than his silver hair might make you think."

Doug slid open the van's side rear door with a whirring

rumble. Lights came on in the rear interior with built-in beds on each side of a narrow aisle.

Brian said: "How we going to do this?"

Dr. Quinton took a step—

Stopped by Nurse Vicki, who thrust one hand at the psychiatrist's chest and used her other to pluck the purse-like black medical case from his grasp.

"Protocols dictate—"

"This is still America," said Vicki. "No dictators."

Dr. Quinton blinked but she was beyond that, standing in front of the package with the cobalt blue eyes, looking straight at him as she said: "Are you ready?"

"Does that matter?"

Her ruby smile said *yes*, said *no*.

He spoke to both her and the two *soft clothes* soldiers: "Where do you want me?"

"Like she said," answered Doug, "it's a free country. Pick either bed."

The package chose the slab on the shotgun seat's side of the van because it was less likely to catch a bullet crashing through the windshield to take out the driver.

Nurse Vicki entered the van behind him.

Said: "You need to take your jacket off."

"Might be more comfortable to stay that way," called Brian as he climbed behind the steering wheel and slammed the driver's door shut.

The black leather jacket had been his *before*, but *now* the inner pocket over his heart held a laboratory-aged wallet with never-used ID's and credit cards. Felt sad to take off his old friend the black leather jacket. Felt good to shed its weight of new lies.

He wore a long-sleeved, suitable for an office blue shirt over black long-sleeved, thermal underwear suitable for the autumn forest. Fumbled with the buttons on his shirt. Sensed the nurse resisting helping him pull off the thermal underwear.

He sat on the bed. Naked from the waist up. Shivered, maybe from the evening chill, maybe from the proximity of a red-lipped younger woman.

Who couldn't help herself, cared about who she was and was a nurse, stared at his scars but there was nothing she could do for them now, for him, she was not that able.

Or free.

She unzipped the medical bag that opened like the jaws of a trap: one side held hypodermic needles, alcohol and swabs, the other side held pill bottles.

"You already took your final dose of meds back in the ward," she said.

"I took what they gave me. Hope that's not *final*."

Crimson lips curled in a smile. Tears shimmered her green eyes.

He said: "I'm glad it's you giving me the needle."

"—had to be," she whispered.

Swabbed his bare left shoulder.

Slid the needle into his flesh.

Pushed the plunger.

Said: "Not long now."

He dressed, stood to tuck his shirts into his black jeans.

Nurse Vicki turned down the blanket on the rack he'd chosen.

"Might want to keep your shoes on," said Doug from outside the van.

The package stretched out on his back, pillow under his head.

"Just a tip," said Doug. "Straps *first* is more comfortable."

Vicki—*made it through night school working as a grocery checker and sitting vigil beside a hospital bed where the patient never stirred*—Vicki fastened Safety Straps across the prone man, tucked the blanket over him to his chin, knew he could have been her father, knew she could have made him one, knew that wasn't—*isn't*—what mattered or what decided what were never going to be more than stolen heartbeats of rebellion and escape, comfort and yearning, the fever of beasts.

Let it go. Let it go.

"Do you remember the new name you picked?" she asked him. "*Not* Condor."

"How can I not be who I am?"

"That's part of the deal to get you out of here. Back to the real world."

"So that's where I'm going." His smile was sly.

"So they tell me." Her smile was honest. "Who are you, Condor?"

"Vin."

"*V* for *Vicki*," she said, like it was nothing.

"Yes," he lied to let her have everything he could give.

She pressed her crimson lips to his mouth: *Last kiss.*

Floated out of the van, a blur of white, the night spinning as Doug whirred the side door closed, climbed into the shotgun seat, slammed his door *thunk*.

Condor, Vin, whoever he was dropped into a black hole.

Drugged sleep. Flashes of sight, of sound, dreams in a heartbeat rhythm.

. . . white stripes flick through a night road's headlights . . .

. . . Springsteen guitars *State Trooper* . . .

. . . beeping machines web a hollow Marine to a hospital bed . . .

. . . naked thighs straining *yes yes yes* . . .

. . . *snap-clack* of a chambering .45 . . .

. . . red lips . . .

. . . Arab Spring crowds: "*Lib-er-te! Lib-er-te!*" . . .

. . . footsteps behind you on Paris cobblestones . . .

. . . the mailman clings to his pouch . . .

. . . drone's view of a rushing closer city square . . .

. . . plopped on a closet toilet, no pants, some guy saying, "*OK, here you go*" . . .

. . . walk into the alley, a friend waves you forward . . .

JOLT. Awake. He felt himself . . . awake. Sunlight through black glass windows.

Blink and you're flat on your back on a bed in a van. That's stopped.

Coffee, that wondrous rich aroma.

"OK, man," said . . . *Doug*, his name is Doug. "Straps are off. Sit up, have a cup of the good stuff from inside."

Inside where? Where am I?

He sipped coffee cut with milk from a paper cup logoed 'bucks!

"You gotta go again?" said Brian from the behind the wheel of the parked van. "We took you in the middle of the night, but . . . *Hey*, you're a guy that age and your med' reports say—*score*, by the way! The daily use pill with the TV commercial of the man and woman sitting in side by side bathtubs."

"Let's get you together before we meet the world," said Doug.

The Special Ops guys let him cram himself into the closet bathroom.

"Remember," Doug said through the closed bathroom door: "Your name is Vin."

After he flushed the van toilet—*Such a weird concept!*—Doug met him in the cramped aisle between the beds. Passed him a paper cup of pills to help him forget what he wasn't supposed to remember and act like he believed what other people saw.

A plastic bag labeled "For Our Forgetful Guests!" that had been repurposed from a Los Angeles hotel waited beside the metal sink. The bag held a disposable toothbrush and a tiny tube of toothpaste trademarked with a notorious TV cartoon squirrel.

"We figured," said Doug, "feel fresh for a fresh start."

Brian called out from behind the van's steering wheel: "Don't be impressed, he's had the whole ride here to think of that one."

Mouthful of minty toothpaste.

The sink faucet worked— *Amazing!* He rinsed, spit.

Raised his eyes to the metal plate polished to reflect like a mirror.

Saw a silver-haired, craggy and scarred faced, blue-eyed man staring back at him.

Whispered: "Your name is Vin."

Thought: *"Condor."*

Radio Voice from the van's dashboard:

"—is it for this edition of Rush Hour Rundown on New Jersey Public Radio, but throughout the day, stories we'll be following include attempts to bring Occupy Wall Street movements to middle America, life after Gadhafi in war-torn Libya, the last days of that Ohio zookeeper who freed his wild animals and then killed himself, and the billionaire brothers who've bought a chunk of America's politics, plus the latest actor to play Superman talks about his divorce from the, *um*, generously proportioned socialite hired by reality TV to play someone like herself, and one of our only two surviving Beatles is getting married—again. Finally, *remember*: today we're supposed to be terrified. Go forth in fear."

WHAT?

"Coming up, the third in our six-part series on how climate change—"

Click, off went the radio as Brian turned: "Did you say something?"

Doug held out the black leather jacket to *Vin*, said: "You ready to go?"

Then slid open the van's rear compartment side door and with the nostalgia of a paratrooper, hopped out into the rush of cool gray sunshine.

The silver-haired man put on his black leather jacket.

Stepped out into the light.

I'm in a parking lot.

Low gray sky, cool sun glistening on rows of parked cars surrounding a tan cement, crouched dragon building. Waves of sound whooshing past.

Slouching from the dragon building came a trio of zombies.

"No fucking way!" muttered Vin, muttered Condor.

Zombies, but their make-up and costumes were so lame you could tell who they weren't.

"Happy Halloween," said Brian as he posted beside Vin.

The zombies climbed into a five-year-old car with New Jersey license plates.

Doug said: "Today, everybody else is in costume."

His partner shook his head: "Don't be impressed. He's had the whole ride to think of that one, too."

"Go figure," said Doug. "It's fucking 2011 and everywhere you look, zombies."

"If we've got zombies," said Condor, said Vin, "do you got guns?"

Call it a pause in the cool morning air.

Then Doug answered: "We're fully sanctioned."

Condor shrugged. "As long as what you're full of is sanction."

The Escort Operatives stared at him with eyes that were stone canyons.

"You expecting trouble?" said Brian.

"Always. Never." Condor shook his head. "My meds are supposed to suffocate expectations."

"You just need some breakfast," said Brian. "Stand here a minute, get your land legs under you, get your breath, then we'll get something to eat."

"Want to do *T'ai chi*?" Doug gestured to a white gazebo in the corner of the parking lot. "Get your Form on?"

"That's not low-profile," said Vin, said Condor. "Citizens might think I'm weird."

"Really," said Brain. "*That's* what would make you seem weird?"

"Remember, *Vin*," said Doug: "We can do anything we want as long as nobody ever knows who we are. You know that's the heart and hard of any Op', so play it cool. Low key. Absolutely normal."

"Normal has been a problem."

"You're past that now," said Brian. "Remember?"

"Meanwhile," said Doug, "welcome to the Nick Logar Rest Stop on the New Jersey Turnpike."

"Monday morning, Halloween, 2011," said Brian. "Zero-nine-three three."

Doug frowned. "Who was Nick Logar?"

"Who cares?" said Brian.

Condor surprised them: "Poet. Black and white movie days, tough times, people working hard to just hold on, rich guys on top even after the stock market crash, bad guys savaging the world. Kind of quirky getting a rest stop named after Nick Logar. Rebel politics, road crazy. But nobody likes to talk about that, just his Congressional Medal of Honor and Pulitzer Prize for poetry no one reads, except for that famous one that doesn't flap the flag like— *God, it feels good to just talk!*"

"And look at you!" said Doug. "Got a lot to say and up on literature and shit."

"My first spy job was to know things like that."

Brian shrugged. "My first was a take-out in Tehran. We're not talking dinner."

"Let's talk breakfast," said Doug.

"Fuck talking," said Brian. "Let's eat."

The silver-haired man brushed his hands down the front of his black leather jacket, amateurishly revealing worry over not finding a gun hidden under there and thus implying that years of confinement had succeeded in making him not *Condor* but *Vin*.

"Chill," said Brian. "Everything's normal and OK. Just look."

Condor didn't tell his Escort Operative that *normal* and *OK* are not the same.

But he did *look*.

The parked gray van faced a chain link fence that made the north boundary of the rest stop. Beyond the fence, a yellowed marsh filled the median between Northbound and Southbound lanes of the Turnpike. The van sat closer to the Southbound lane, and that route's exit into the rest stop made a sloping hill behind the white gazebo.

The van's rear bumper faced four rows of cars parked in white striped spaces on the side of the rest stop's crouching dragon "facility" building, tan cement walls and a New Mexico meets Hong Kong green roof. The facility sat on a raised knoll to stay above rainwater runoff. Glass doors front and centered the facility, a dragon's face where a protruding tongue of concrete steps led down to the pavement between a mustache of two sloped ramps. The glass doors reflected the nearly full front parking lot.

People. Lots and lots of people.

A squat bleached-blond woman in a pink mohair sweater rummaged in her car's open trunk with one hand while her other held a straining leash clipped to the collar of a yippy terrier. The dog's and the bleached blonde's pink sweaters matched.

A young guy wearing a padded black costume, hip or horror, Condor couldn't tell, carried a brown paper sack as he walked toward the facility's rear and waiting green dumpsters below circling seagulls, plus the entrance to the Northbound road, the direction a mouse named Stuart Little took looking for love and a life to call his own.

A smiling family of Japanese tourists clustered together in the parking lot for pictures one of them took with a cell phone.

Call him twenty-four looking nineteen, baseball cap on backwards, gray sweatshirt, low slung blue jeans, sneakers shuffling toward the facility.

Two men in suits parked their dark-colored car.

A married couple who'd seen fifty in their rearview mirrors stepped out of their parked Chevy, slammed its doors and sighed as they shuffled in to use the bathrooms.

My next is now, thought Condor.

Brian said: "Let's get something before."

"Before what?" said Condor as his escorts walked him toward the facility.

Doug said: "Before your transfer ride shows up. Should have been here already."

"What about you guys?"

"Places to go," said Brian, "people to see."

"Is this the time you're going to do more than just *see*?" said Doug.

"Shut the fuck up," said his partner. Lovingly.

Three soda machines selling bottles and cans of caffeine and sugar and chemical concoctions stood sentinel near the ramp Condor and his escorts took to the glass front doors, past a bench where three *probably* just graduated high school girls sat, two of them wearing *hajib* headresses, all of them smoking cigarettes.

What struck Condor inside the rest stop facility was its atmosphere of closeness, of containment. The densely packed air smelled of . . .

Of floor tiles. Crackling meat grease. Hot sugar. Lemon scented ammonia.

Ahead gaped entrances for MENS and LADIES rooms. The wall between the restrooms held a YOU ARE HERE map and a bronze plaque with lines of writing that travellers hurrying into the bathrooms only glanced at but Condor read:

Drive, drive on. These are the highways of our lives.
Dwell not on the sharp quiet madness of our collective soul.
Call us all New Jersey. Call us all Americans, as on we go
    alone together.
          Nick Logar

Off to Condor's left waited the gift shop, wall racks of celebrity magazines and candy, glass coolers with yet more cans of syrupy caffeine, displays of key chains dangling green plastic models of the Statue of Liberty, T-shirts and buttons that "hearted" New York, postcards that nobody mailed anymore.

He turned right, toward the food court, a long open corridor with garish neon signs above each stop where money could be exchange for sustenance.

There was 'bucks, the coffee-centered franchise intent on conquering the world.

DANDY DONUTS! came next in line, sold coffee, too, essentially the same concoctions as 'bucks but somehow not as costly.

The red, white, and green logo for SACCO'S ITALIA seen mostly in airports, train stations, or rest stops centered the food stops wall.

Italian green gave way to broccoli green letters on a white background: NATURAL EATS & FRO YO, where display cases held plastic sealed salads and silver machines hummed behind the counter.

Last in the line of eateries came BURGERS BONAZA, the third biggest chain of hamburger and fries and cola drive-ins of Condor's youth, still clinging to that national sales rank partially because a dozen years remained on the company's fifty-year exclusive lease for this state's Turnpike stops signed with an unindicted former governor.

"Come on," Brian told Condor.

Gray tables lined the red tiles between the wall of eateries and the not quite ceiling-to-floor windows. Travelers sat on hard-to-shoplift black metal chairs.

Brian took a chair facing those front windows. Condor sat where he could look down the food court to the main doors, or look left out to the front parking lot through the wall of windows, or look right and see Doug shuffling in service lines. Behind Condor, a door labeled OFFICE waited near a glass door under a red sign glowing FIRE EXIT.

"What time is it?" asked Condor.

"No worries," said Brian. "We're where we belong and when we should be."

Doug came to them balancing cardboard trays like a man who'd worked his way through college as a waiter. The trays held 'bucks cups, plastic glasses of white yogurt and strawberry chunks, containers of raisins and granola, bananas, spoons, napkins, a white plastic knife almost useless for cutting someone's throat.

"And six donuts?" said Brian.

"The secret to life is knowing how to mix and match," said his partner. "Evens out health-wise with the yogurt. Gives us some bulk and energy for the ride back. Three classic chocolate donuts, three seasonal special pumpkin maple donuts. In good conscience, how could we pass those up?"

"You guys are driving back to Maine?" said Condor.

"Brooklyn," said Brian as he sliced a banana into his yogurt.

"Somebody's insisting on an overnight there," explained his partner.

Two kindergarten-aged boys ran past the table trailed by their harried mother.

"You wouldn't believe Brooklyn now," Brian told Condor.

"I didn't believe it then."

Doug said: "There's this ultra-hip coffee shop not far from—"

"Hey!" said his partner.

"Come on," Doug told his partner. "You can't just show up hoping she will."

The silver-haired man who was old enough to be the two gunners' father smiled.

Said: "We've all done that."

"What's the worst that could happen if you finally talked to her?" said Doug.

Condor shrugged. "You could watch your dreams die in her eyes."

"Me," said Doug, "I was gonna say *alimony*, but troop, if you do not engage the enemy, you create no chance of success."

His partner whispered: "Who's the enemy?"

"Ourselves," said Condor.

Brian blinked at the silver-haired legend. "*My man*: Welcome back!"

Condor ate his pumpkin maple donut as he stared out the window at travelers walking to and from their steel rides. Saw the guy dressed in padded black close the door on . . . *yes*, it *was* an old black hearse, walking away carrying a gym bag toward the south end of the rest stop and the rows of gas pumps controlled by attendants whose jobs were protected by state law. A yellow rental truck drove through Condor's view.

Buzz went cell phones in his escorts' pockets.

Doug read the text message, said: "Link-up ETA twelve minutes."

Seven minutes later, these three men were at the facility's main doors, Doug going through first, Brian posting drag, and Condor—

Flash!

From a cell phone held by a curly-haired woman on the other side of a glass door from Condor: *blurry picture* at best, and *sure*, she appeared innocently overwhelmed by carrying her purse and a takeout tray with two coffees, probably just clumsy fingers on her device, plus she didn't seem to notice that Brian followed her to her car, cell phoned photos of her and her license plate and her driver who stereotyped *husband* as they drove to the South-bound exit just ahead of a rusty black hearse, while hundreds of miles away near Washington, DC, their metrics became an I&M (Investigate & Monitor) upload.

Doug and Condor posted near the parked van.

Forty feet away, an easy (for him) pistol shot, Brian drifted amidst parked cars.

Zen. They were here. They were now. Not waiting: *being*, *doing*. Ready *for*.

The red car drove around the dragon facility from the North-bound entrance. A Japanese brand built in Tennessee that glided ever closer to two men standing by a gray van near the white gazebo.

Where the red car parked.

She opened the driver's door. Let them see no one rode with her (*unless they were laying on the back seat floor or huddled in the trunk*). Kept her hands in sight as she walked toward them and *yes*, it was only a cell phone in her left hand.

Statistically, most people shoot right handed.

"Hey," she said: "Aren't you friends of Gary Pettigrew?"

"Don't know the guy," answered Doug. Said *guy* and not *him* or *man*.

"So where you from?"

"Where we're going," answered Doug, sounding ordinary enough for any eavesdropper (none around) but not a likely response from a random stranger.

"Then I'm in the right place." She grinned. "Sorry I'm late. Traffic."

Her left hand showed them the package's picture in her cell phone.

"You must be Condor," she said, extending her right hand to shake his.

"*Vin*," corrected Doug. "But yeah."

She was young. Short black hair. Clean caramel complexion and bright ebony eyes. Dark slacks and a white blouse under an unbuttoned navy blue jacket.

Said: "Want to see my credentials?"

"If you're bogus and got the recognition code, you'll pack fake flash," said Doug.

"*Damn it!* I've been dying for a chance to whip out my I.D.: *Homeland Security, up against the wall!*"

"Rookie," said Doug.

"Who else would get stuck with a one -day road trip up to here and back to DC?"

Her voice stayed easy. "I'm Malati Chavali, and is that guy walking this way one of us?"

Doug smiled: "Yeah, *Rook'*, he's with us."

Brian drifted to her red car, glanced in the back seat, turned and said like that was the reason for his detour: "Where do you want his two bags?"

"What do you think?" she said to Doug—looked at Condor. "*I'm sorry!* I should ask *you*, it's not like you're . . ."

"Just a package?" said the man who could technically *maybe* be her grandfather.

"And you want me to call you *Vin*, right?"

He shrugged. "Mission requirements."

"Speaking of," said Brian. "We gotta hit the road."

"Brooklyn calls," joked his partner.

Condor's suitcases went in the red car's trunk.

He and its driver Malati watched the gray van pull out of its parking space and drive onto the Northbound ramp . . . gone.

"Can I ask you a favor?" she said to the silver-haired man as they stood in the cool morning air. "I know you're probably anxious to get to your new apartment—row house, actually, on Capitol Hill—your Settlement Specialist will meet us there, we'll call her when we hit the Beltway and . . . The thing is, I'm dying for coffee."

"Wouldn't want you to die," said Condor. "How would I get where I'm going?"

"There is that," she said.

They walked toward the rest stop's facility.

"Before we get where there are ears," he said as they moved between parked cars lined in rows of shiny steel, "you're Home Sec', not CIA?"

"Actually, detailed to the National Resources Operations Division of the Office of the Director of National Intelligence—there's CIA on staff there, too, but me . . . Yeah, I'm in Home Sec'. For now. Grad school at Georgetown—"

"Don't vomit your whole cover story—first chance you get," said the silver-haired man as they neared the main doors. "Even if it's true. Maybe especially if it's true."

Laughing coworkers in Groucho Marx glasses strode past them.

Malati whispered: "Sorry."

He held the building door for her. "Shit happens. So far, ours works."

She smiled *thank you* as she stepped past that older gentleman.

Heard him say: "Should you have let me behind you?"

A chill claimed her amidst the thick air inside the rest stop facility.

She answered: "I don't know."

Condor shrugged. "Too late to think about it now.

"I'm going in there," he said, pointing to the MEN'S room. "Get your coffee and we'll meet at a table."

"I thought I was in charge."

"Good," he said. Walked into the bathroom, left her standing there. Alone.

Five minutes later, he spotted her sitting at a table in the food court facing the restrooms, the gift shop, and the main doors. Tactically acceptable. The wall of eateries waited to her right, the windows to the parking lot on her heartside. Her eyes locked on him as he walked toward where she sat with two cups from 'bucks on the table.

"Please," she said, "sit. We've got time."

"You sure?"

"No. But we can make it work."

He settled on the black steel chair facing her.

"Look around," she said. "Most people are tuned out. Plugged into their cells or tablets. Not really here. Plus there's nobody behind me, right? Nobody behind you. Nobody close enough to hear even if we're not careful what we say."

He gave her a nod and the smile that wanted to come.

"I'd like to start over," she said. "The coffee's a peace offering."

"OK. We're probably going to have to stop at least once before DC anyway."

"When you want, when we can." She took a sip from her cup, left no lip stain.

Don't think about red lipstick. Gone. That's the forever. This is now.

Malati said: "Somehow now I don't think you're just, *say*, a former asset or KGB defector who's been in a retirement program and needs routine relocation."

"What do you know?"

"The codename I'm now not supposed to use." Malati shrugged. "*Vin*. Weird first name, but *whatever*, Vin: I volunteered for this *nobody wanted it* gig. Extra duty. Trying to prove I'm competent, trustable, a team player with initiative."

"What do you want?" he said.

"To do more than earn a paycheck. Serve my country. Do some good."

"And under that essay answer?"

"I don't want to be somebody who doesn't know what's really going on."

"*Reality*," he said: "I've heard of that."

He sipped his coffee. She'd gotten black and a couple to-go creamers so he could decide. He popped the lid off the cup, poured in cream, thought: *Why not?*

"Yesterday, our bosses decided I was no longer crazy.

"Or," he added, "at least not so crazy that I couldn't be released to a kind of free."

Though most people would have seen nothing, Condor sensed her tense up, but she sat there and *took it*.

Malati said: "Are you?"

"*Not so crazy* or *kind of free*?"

"It's your answer."

And *that* made him like her. Told him she might be worth it.

"Guess we'll see," he said. "You're my driver."

"Just for this road trip." She blurted: "I want to learn."

Motion outside pulled his eyes from her to look out the window.

A school bus: classic yellow, slowing down out front. The school bus seemed to wobble, stopped haphazardly near the rows of citizens' parked vehicles.

He nodded toward the school bus. "Did you ever ride one of those?"

"I'm not supposed to vomit my cover story. Even if it's true."

"Lesson one," he told her. "Give trust to get trust."

"That's not my first lesson from you." That acknowledgment made him like her even more as she added: "Yeah, I did bus time in Kansas City."

"We're not in Kansas anymore," he quoted.

"*Hey!*" she said. "We're talking Kansas City, *Missouri*. Whole different place."

They laughed together and as she relaxed into *this is where I'm from* stories, he looked around at where they were.

Sitting at a table by himself was a forty-ish man munching a morning cheeseburger, tie loosened over a cheap shirt already straining against too many such meals, a franchise manager who couldn't figure out why his boss hated him. Two tables away sat a thirty-ish mom leaning her forehead into one hand while the other held the cell phone against her ear for the report from the school on her daughter who'd been the teenage pregnancy that ended in getting out of what was now both their hometown. Two male medical techs in green scrubs munched on fried chicken, one was white, one was black, neither wanted to get back to the hospital where they could only give morphine and more bills to a cancer warrior. There sat a down vest over a white sweater blond beauty, *like*, OMG machinegun texting her cell phone and being *super careful* to not say she was scared to death because she had *no clue* about what came after nineteen. The gray-haired couple barely older than Condor sat staring everywhere but at each other and seeing nowhere better they could go. The two years out of college man who worked the night shift at a factory job one level above the summer work he'd done to help him pay for school sat drinking Diet Coke against the yawns, dreading tomorrow with its first of the month loan bills coming to the clapboard house where he lived in the basement below his working parents who loved him so much. Like Malati noted, many of the road-dazed travelers seemed hypnotized by screens.

We're all packages transporting from some there to another where.

And yet, thought Condor, we find the hope or the dreams or the responsibility, the dignity and courage to push ourselves away from the tables at this nowhere transit zone, get up, get up *again*, go outside, get in our cars and go, *go on*, get to where we can, tears *yes*, but laughter at it all and at ourselves, because if nothing else, this is the ride we got and we refuse to just surrender.

The Nick Logar Rest Stop.

These are the highways of our lives.

". . . so my parents wanted me to go into business, *but*," Malati shrugged, "profit doesn't turn me on as much as purpose."

Children. Chattering. Squealing. Half a dozen of them running through the main doors *TO THE BATHROOMS!* ahead of a woman teacher shouting: *"Stay together!"*

Condor and Malati looked out the window.

Saw a straggling line of second graders, marching across the parking lot from the school bus. Some kids wore Halloween glory—a witch, a fairy tale princess, a ghost, a cowboy, Saturday morning cartoon costumes. All the kids carried an orange "Trick or Treat!" plastic bucket in the shape of a pumpkin stenciled with black eyes, a toothy grin, and a corporate logo from the chain drugstore that accidentally ordered too many of the buckets to sell but cleverly recouped a tax donation to their local elementary school. As the children marched, those pumpkin heads swung wildly on wire loop handles gripped in their tiny hands.

"Time for us to go," said Condor.

Didn't matter who was in charge, they both knew he was right.

At the main entrance, Condor—*no*: Vin, his name is Vin—*the package* brushed her out of the way as he held a door for a man not much older than Malati, a guy in a wheelchair who was rolling himself up the ramp, a Philly vet named Warren Iverson who wore his Army jacket from the 10th Mountain Division and a smile on his boyish face.

Malati realized Vin didn't just notice the vet with wasted legs, Vin *saw* him.

Said: "Better hurry, man. A stampede of short stuffs is coming up behind you."

"Always." Warren rolled past the silver-haired man in a black leather jacket.

Malati leaned close to Vin as they stepped outside *and* aside to let the parade of costumed kids squeal their way into this wondrous rest stop oasis.

She whispered: "You keep doing stuff like that, you'll ruin your tough guy act."

"Be your cover," Vin told her. "Besides, looks like he's one of the men and women who pay when we fuck up our job. Or some politician fucks it up for us."

He shrugged.

"Do what should be done, nothing special about that," he told her sounding *so much* like her father.

But only he heard the *beep . . . beep . . . beep* of machines webbed to a hospital bed as he said: "Probably I owe guys like him something beyond *coulda* and *shoulda*."

She understood what he said but not what he meant.

Just walk beside him. Figure out what you can.

"My car's still there," she said as they started down one ramp to the parking lot.

The red Japanese motion machine, squatting *way over* by the north border fence and the white gazebo where exiting the Turnpike Southbound came a black hearse.

The black hearse parked in a row of cars near Malati's red ride. As the hearse glided to a stop, Condor envisioned the YOU ARE HERE map mounted on the wall between the bathrooms. Nick Logar was one of the few rest stops on the New Jersey Turnpike that serviced traffic going both directions. The padded black-clad driver got out of the hearse, opened its back door. If he'd forgotten something at this rest stop from when he left earlier behind the Southbound suspect cell phone photo couple, Mr. Black Costume would have had to drive about ten miles before he could exit, get back on the Turnpike north, then drive here, *but* . . . But then he would have needed to drive *past* this place or through it, go further north to another exit turnaround, again maybe ten miles away in order to come back and exit southbound back into the rest stop, *into here.*

Why make that long circle drive?

What's that sound? thought Condor as he and Malati neared the bottom of the ramp to the parking lot where two burly men stood with unlit cigarettes dangling from their lips. The man wearing the COUNTY SCHOOLS windbreaker pulled a silver lighter from his left front shirt pocket, clicked it open and thumbed its wheel to summon a flame and ignite the white papered cancer sticks, barely a pause as that bus driver said:

"Couldn't believe it, twenty minutes from the school if the traffic held, sure as shit ain't holding now, shut down and backed up behind me, so I got off lucky, *whump*—bus starts to shake, *what the fuck*, get it to this exit and wrestle it down over there, at least get the kids where they can pee, but my tires got four little black steel like . . . like stars or some other pointy things, and with three flats, we barely made it here."

Malati felt *Vin* drift her away from her waiting car, into the front parking lot.

"Listen!" he said. Made them stop and stand still, absolutely still.

"To what?"

"There's no whooshing."

He faced the unseen empty lanes of the expressway going south, turned to look past the hulk of the rest stop facility to the unseen empty expressway lanes going north.

Heard that silence.

Felt his own thundering heart.

From deep inside Malati came the whisper: *"We've got to go now."*

They looked across rows of parked vehicles toward her distant red car.

Saw ordinary human beings, everyday people strolling to and fro, the guy in black walking toward the facility from the hearse.

A honeymoon couple laughed.

The new husband aimed his cell phone camera.

The happy bride raised her face to the open sky.

Like a red mist flowered her skull as she flipped to the parking lot pavement.

The husband almost dropped his cell phone before a crimson fountain from his spine burst out of his blue-shirted chest.

Time became a child's clear marble dropped into a swimming pool . . .

. . . to slowly sink.

Not seeing what I'm seeing! Malati's mind registered her package, her responsibility, her . . . Condor *call him Vin*: he lunged before the second shot's *Crack!*

What she saw over rows of parked cars at an ordinary New Jersey Turnpike rest stop on an ordinary autumn Halloween was the not-so-far-away guy in black.

What she saw was that ordinary American boy face behind an assault rifle.

A gorilla roared from where the bus driver and the salesman were smoking.

The gunman sprayed bullets at what he heard.

The salesman and bus driver dropped twitching, bleeding, moaning, dying near the concrete ramp to where the children were.

Condor pulled the young fed' down between two parked cars. Yelled: "Can you get a good shot?"

"I don't have a gun! I'm not that kind of spy! And you're a crazy old man!"

Machinegun fire. Screams.

"Fucking Brooklyn." Condor waved her between two cars, stayed low as he scrambled two more cars over, eased his head above the hood of steel shelter.

The shooter looked like the robot of death. Padding under his black shirt and pants: *Had to be ballistic armor.* Working the assault rifle, thumbing the release to drop the spent magazine to the parking lot pavement, reaching in a pouch to pull out an expanded capacity mag' and slap it home: that movie star reload let Condor see a combat pump shotgun strapped across the robot's chest.

The robot stalked toward where Condor and Malati hid.

Gotchya! whirled the other way to *rat-a-tat-tat* a line of bullet holes through the food court's wall of windows. Condor spotted a pistol SWAT-style strapped to the shooter's right leg, a combat knife sheathed on his left ankle, strapped-on pouches. *Is that a computer tablet dangling from his belt?*

Condor dropped between the cars.

Malati said: "What's he doing?"

"Killing people."

"Why?"

"Because he can."

The machinegun buzzed like a monster's vibrating tongue.

"Did you see his hearse?" said Condor.

Malati started to rise—

Got jerked down. "You don't know where he's looking! You got no diversion!"

She shuddered in his grasp.

Condor said: "Shiny metal where the coffin should ride—Think they're bins."

"Bins?"

"The bus driver pulled black steel stars out of his tires. Caltrops. Tactical steel road tire spikes. State troopers and Army ambushers scatter them on the highway."

Somewhere in the parking lot a woman screamed like a fleeing banshee.

Malati shook her head. "What does that have to do with bins and where would—"

The machinegun roared.

No more banshee screaming.

"Maybe he got the spikes on Amazon," said Condor. "Get lots, rig metal bins in the coffin space. Cut holes in the back of the hearse, driver-controllable lids on the bins. He drove every stretch of road every direction out of here, probably weaving lane to lane to cover all drivable asphalt, picking his release spots just past or just before the rest stop exits and entrances, dropping, *what*, couple thousand of those things. A few flat tires, cars crashing into each other, stopped, and it's the mother of all backups every way in or out of here, walls of steel. He's isolated his kill zone. Stalled any rescue or escape."

BOOM! The robot switched to his shotgun.

Malati waved her arm: "When he's shooting the other way we can make it across the parking lot toward the Turnpike! Short fence, hop it, run, hide—"

She saw where Condor was looking.

The empty school bus.

She said: "All those kids."

He said: "All us everybody."

Machinegun bullets cut a line over their heads like the contrail of a jet on its way across this cool blue sky.

Her spine tensed. Her mind pushed against her forehead.

He said: "Cell phone!"

Pressed against her ear. "911 is . . . *Due to a high volume—*"

"Half the people here. Unless he's got a jammer."

"You can buy those?"

"You tell me, you're the one from the real world."

Car windows shatter. Bullets whine.

Why now? Why here? Why me?

Why not.

Her eyes were welded wide. "Where is he? Is he coming— Wait!"

Malati swooped the screen of her cell phone. Eased her cell above the car. Camera app, the phone like a periscope lens scanning the sounds of gunfire.

Like a movie.

"He's moving toward the main doors!"

Standing tall, *man*, striding toward the funnel for the fools— *Whoops*: fat guy in parking lot, *where'd he pop up from*, pulling at the passenger door on that green car *bullets' burst* and he's dancing and spraying red and sliding down to *dead, motherfucker*.

The side fire door of the rest stop facility flies open.

Half a dozen people charge out.

Crying tires as a silver SUV lunges out of its parking lot space.

Malati's cell phone showed the shooter drop flat on the pavement.

He fumbled with the book-sized computer thing lashed to his belt.

Silver SUV slows for six people running to its—

FLASH! by the green dumpsters *then* came the BOOM! of garage-mixed explosive gel shelled by ball bearings and old nails as the paper sack bomb exploded.

Take that, Columbine motherfuckers! The shooter keyboarded the tablet lashed to his waist so it was re-primed to send a wireless signal to any of his other planted bombs.

Windshield blasted glass slivers blinded the silver SUV's driver, an engaged office manager/volunteer at a Paterson, New Jersey, soup kitchen.

Bomb shrapnel hit three of the runners, bodies crashed to the pavement. The other three runners staggered—*arm*, the blast blew off the arm of a mother-of-two lawyer on her way to a deposition, she crumpled, bled out.

Like a cat person on TV, the shooter rocketed off the pavement.

Saw two targets staggering beside a drifting silver SUV.

Sprayed them with bullets. Nailed one, the other, *ah fuck him*, let him stagger away, maybe he's hit, certain he's damaged.

The shooter tossed like a rock toward the FIRE EXIT side of the facility.

Pop! Purple smoke grenade, *rescue me* surplus, that store off the Interstate.

"The grenade's to scare us," said Condor. "Keep the people inside."

Death's robot faced the stairs and ramps up to the main doors.

Malati stared at the huddled-beside-her silver-haired man in the black jacket who knew, who had to know: "What are we going to do?"

"Be crazier."

"—easy for you to say."

The robot of death. At the bottom of the ramp where the bus driver sprawled over another smoker's corpse.

Marching out of the main doors: Two women. Teachers. Marching down the ramp straight toward the shooter. Commanding: "Stop! Stop this!"

Behind them, running down the other concrete ramp:

Kids, scared, crying, stumbling down to the parking lot as the young man from Teach For America and some other citizen urge the twenty-one children forward, go, run, *run!*

The main doors whir open.

Out rolls Warren.

Wheelchair. Army jacket. *Fuck you* face.

Ready to charge. Ready to be *diversion*. Ready to take it to you, motherfucker.

Keep going kids! Run, run!

The shooter's stopped. Standing still. Assault rifle hanging on its sling.

Two teachers close on him, the *maybe maybe* prayer on their faces.

The robot drew his handgun *Bam! Bam-Bam!*

Schoolteachers collapsed in a heap atop a bus driver.

Tidy you want me to be *tidy* you want *tidy* I give you *tidy!*

Warren yelled and spun himself *charge* onto the ramp.

Bam! A third eye blasted into Warren.

The shooter aimed two-handed toward the main doors where Teach For America and some other guy lined up in the V front sight of a 15-shots semi-automatic pistol.

Count five blasted rounds into those two bodies, dropped them in a pile, *tidy.*

Wheelchair, carrying dead Warren, obeying inertia, rolling down the ramp—

Stopped as the shooter slammed his gun bore on the ribs under the Army jacket.

Why waste a bullet on this Army jacket guy with a red mush forehead?

He shoved the wheelchair. His force sent it freewheeling up to the flat landing outside the main doors. The burdened wheelchair spun sideways, stopped.

As twenty-one children stampede amidst parked cars.

The assault rifle sprayed zinging lead toward them.

But kids are short.

Bullets crashed through cars' windows, punched into steel chassis.

The shooter dropped to the ground.

Stared under rows of parked cars. Undercarriages of mufflers and pipes. Tires propped the cars at least six inches off the pavement and made a slit of scenery.

There—few rows away: running children's legs and feet.

The assault rifle fired a long sweep of bullets under the cars.

Zing ripped out from the under the metal that hid Condor and Malati, cut right between where they were crouched, right past the knocked-over 'bucks cup she'd *only God knows why* just let go of. Slugs slammed into another parked car, punched a hole in one door and out the other. A tire blew. Bullets ricocheted off parking lot asphalt.

Is that smell—

Two kids. Frozen in the lane between parked cars. Bullets zinged past their legs—one wore brown cords his mom picked out, one wore her favorite blue jeans.

The girl pushed her classmate away from the shooter: "Split up!"

She turned to run the other way than the boy so the bad guy couldn't—

Saw two crouching-down adults waving their hands.

Ran between the cars, into the arms of the Grampa guy.

"Got you!" he said as she burrowed her face into his leather jacket.

No wet no red she's not shot. Condor saw a Halloween pumpkin bucket looped through the belt on her blue jeans, a red jacket, white blouse. *"It's not a dorky costume!"* she'd insisted that morning as she did what she was 'posed to and ate her scrambled eggies: *"It's the idea of the flag and it's 'posed to make you think!"* But that glitter on her seven-year-old face? *That*, she said, *"that's me."* Didn't notice her mother not cry.

Machinegun roars sliced the air.

The second grader looked back to where she'd been.

Whispered: "Run, Johnny."

The shooter slapped fresh ammo into the assault rifle. *Seen it.* He'd seen running snot-nosed kids scramble onto the shutdown school bus across the parking lot. *You can't hide from me.* He machine-gunned the bus. Bullets banged through the yellow metal.

Malati held her cell phone above their parked cars cover.

"He's turning toward—I think he's going to go into the building, the food court!"

Risk it: Condor peeked over the car. Saw the black robot at the facility's main doors. Saw the dead vet in his wheelchair. Saw bodies heaped at the bottom of the ramp: bus driver who smoked, women. Saw the food court's bullet-holed tinted dark windows.

He glared at the little girl with the big brown eyes. "What's your name?"

"Phyllis Azar seven years old live at—"

Create focus.

"You're here. Now. With us."

The seven-year-old girl nodded: The silver-haired guy sounded like a principal!

Empower your asset to gain their trust.

Condor said: "What do you want me to call you?"

Bam! Bam! Bam! Paced steady rhythm shots hit the building.

Suppression fire as the black clad shooter neared the main doors.

"Daddy calls me *Punkin.*" She shrugged at the orange plastic pumpkin bucket she'd looped to herself with her belt *special* so *no way* would she lose it.

"Punkin, I'm—*Condor, Vin,* doesn't matter, she's *Malati.*"

A bullet ricocheted off a car roof.

Punkin said: "We going to be OK?"

The big girl woman nodded *yes* as Mr. Silver Hair said: "We might get hurt."

"Might get *dead.*" Punkin shook her head. "That would suck."

Malati watched her cell phone: "He's standing at the main doors!"

In the canyon of car metal next row over: a side mirror of an SUV dangled upside down, its cracked glass captured the reflection of a trapped man, woman, child.

Malati inhaled that sight of yesterday, today, tomorrow.

"Condor!" yelled Malati: "Smell that *oh my God!* Why didn't it it's going to—"

Like a piano chord exploded the meds' weight on his mind.

A lightning flash of seeing.

He grabbed the belt around the little girl NEVER NOBODY 'POSED TO and he's jerking it undone saying: "—fifty-fifty shot at next to no chance in Hell and *Punkin!*"

She locked on him as he said: "We got one chance to save anybody!"

Punkin gave him a nod from her bones.

"But you gotta do one thing you're not 'posed to."

Punkin didn't blink.

Condor told her: "You have to say a bad word."

The shooter paused outside the main doors. To his left were a heap of bodies he'd dropped with his pistol—*good fucking shots.* Behind him near the top of the ramp was the listless wheelchair full of some dead older guy wearing an Army jacket.

Crucial question: *Which gun?*

Level up *cool.* Now it's your game.

Nothing like a shotgun for close quarters tactical situations.

He let the black military-cool rifle dangle on its sling, wrapped his right hand around the pistol-grip of the black steel and plastic Italian-made shotgun manufactured after America's 1994 assault weapons ban expired.

And just for a moment, felt regret.

While he loved the high-tech look of his semi-automatic 12 gauge that fed new shells into the chamber after each shot, the *ratchet-clack* of pumping a fresh shell into an old-school "regular" shotgun was *epic.* But besides slowing his rate of fire, a pump shotgun made him clumsy, so as much as he appreciated cool, he knew he'd been smart to go semi-auto, out with the old, in with new. *Right tool, right job.*

Like he expected, he saw no one standing beyond the closed glass doors.

There's the wall with doors to the bathrooms. There's that stupid plaque.

—good as Bruce Lee, he stomped his discount store black sneaker out to his side, a kick that smacked the circular aluminum door opener pressure plate and like the yawn this place was—used to be, had been *until me*—the doors gaped open for him.

My turn.

He slid through the open doors like ninja. Blasted buckshot into the Gift Shop where the old Korean lady behind the counter, *yeah*, she'd ducked somewhere already. *Stay down, Honey, I'll be back.* Pirouetted a slo-mo circle until the food court filled his vision BOOM! Buckshot tore through air that smelled like coffee and burnt hamburgers. Like in *Slaughter Soldier 2* for Xbox, he grabbed a grenade from the pouch on his hip, pulled the pin with his teeth and made a left-handed throw, landed it on the tiles by the health food rip-off place BOOM! Purple smoke mushroomed through the food court.

Hope it won't hide too much from security cameras mounted in the ceiling.

He combat jumped into the MEN'S room—looked empty, closed aluminum stalls.

Can't fool me with that shit. He switched the shotgun for his pistol, punched two bullets through the wall of the nearest stall.

A man screamed and fell off the toilet where he'd been crouched.

WOMEN'S room. Suburban mom sobbing and pleading, holding up her hands.

Mom got shot right through her palm in front of her *crybaby* face.

From the entrance to the food court he surveyed his kingdom of Hell.

Purple smoke thicker at the far end where red letters glowed EXIT and that was a lie, *nowhere to go, suckers.* BOOM he shot that cloud. Some guy charged him throwing coins, made the shooter flinch BOOM cut down that coin-thrower with a shotgun blast that also shattered a window facing the front parking lot.

Crashing glass: he liked the sound so much he blasted out three more windows.

Cool air and sunlight streamed into the purple-smoked debris of the food court.

He wondered who'd discovered that he'd chained the rear doors shut.

Ringing: a smoke detector in BURGER BONAZA as the meat abandoned on the hot grill crackled out black smoke. Theme music as he surveyed the food court.

Moms draped over their kids. Travelers cowered behind metal tables. Dead guy on the floor—must be a bonus score from the first burst sent through the windows. Pools and dribbles of darkness on the red floor tiles, blood from somebody who'd crawled or been carried away, he'd find them in good time.

For a moment he thought about swinging up his wireless tablet to set off the other bombs he'd planted by the roads in and out of this rest stop so he could watch the judging-eyes people in here scramble and scream and break cover trying to escape.

Naw, stick to the plan.

Save the bombs for the wanna-be heroes, cops, and firemen who figure a way around the traffic back ups and road spikes for their red lights and sirens.

You gotta do the walk, man.

He switched from the could-be-empty shotgun—in all the excitement, he kind of lost count of his shots. Slapped a fresh magazine into the assault rifle.

Stepped out among them, knowing their desperate hopes that he was looking for someone in particular, specific, for somebody who was the *why*, for someone *not me*.

Everybody thinking: *I don't deserve this!*

Walk your purple smoke ringing glory and what do you see.

A cash flow corridor of factory food for cubicle fools awaiting coffins.

TVs by the ceiling show talking heads who never say your name.

A lotto screen displays winning numbers for luck you never get.

An ATM machine holds money it won't ever give you.

Two guys hide behind a condiments counter, not so *high school cool* now.

Bald guy, white shirt, tie, nametag, hands in the air, so who's the boss?

College girl, on the floor like a dog, *yeah*, what do you got to say now, bitch?

Black leather biker with a gut wound by the wall, who's scared today?

Somebody praying to the big empty that never cares.

So who gets to play this next round of—

"YOU'RE A BIG BOOGER-HEAD!"

He heard it above the smoke detector ringing.

From outside. Through the shot-out windows. The parking lot. A . . . a kid.

"YOU'RE A SCARED MEANIE!"

Some little girl. Off the bus. Out there hiding amidst the parked cars.

"NOBODY WANTS TO FUCK YOU!"

The shooter cocked his head.

"NOBODY KNOWS WHO YOU ARE!"

He faced that new whine in his skull.

"YOU'RE A TEENY TINY NOBODY!"

Nothing. Just nothing. Just a snotty kid little bitch girl doesn't know nothing.

"AND *YOU'RE* WHO DOESN'T KNOW WHAT FUCK IS!"

He squeezed a burst out the window toward that sound in the parking lot.

Food court fading echo of gunshots ringing smoke detector and STILL he heard:

"NA-NANA-NA-NA YOU CAN'T SHOOT NOTHING!"

The shooter thumbed his assault rifle to Select Fire.

Squeezed three shots in a sweep over the visible car roofs.

"YOU CAN'T GET ME!"

Not from in here.

The black robot whirled left, whirled right.

Fifty-fifty choice.

Either the side EXIT on the left and out alongside the building with its purple smoke cloud still so thick the scavenging seagulls floating overhead couldn't see what they smelled sprawled on the black pavement.

Or back through the main doors to the flat cement slab entryway that would give him a 180 degree-plus field of fire from the purple smoked zone, up to the white gazebo, then the easy sweep all over the whole front parking lot, then toward the right to the distant gas pumps that were destined to be awesome pillars of fire.

Main doors.

He's there. Elbows the shiny steel plate automatic door opener. Rifle up, alert position, gun butt by his shoulder. Just like SWAT guys on TV. Staring over the barrel. Focused. Sliding past the heap of dead men blocking his way down one ramp. Past the Army jacketed meat slumped in a wheelchair nearly blocking the stairs by the top of the second ramp where the shooter had pushed it.

Stairs are tricky while aiming over an assault rifle, so he SWAT glides down the second ramp to the heap of bodies, women on top *fucking bitches.*

"YOU CAN'T FUCK!"

Two quick shots at that *in the parking lot* sound.

The shooter lowered his rifle, the better to see.

Gunshots ringing in his ears, the ringing smoke detector

back in the food court: he doesn't hear the whirr of rubber tires on cement as coming behind him, the wheelchair bearing Army-jacketed meat rolls *rushes* down the ramp.

Splashing hits his left side and back, head, stings his eyes. That splash hit him from off the ground and the heap of dead women.

Stinks, what—

SMACKED in his face with an empty plastic orange bucket pumpkin.

Eyes burning, the blur of some woman swinging a pumpkin to hit him again/*feint*, he knew that was a feint, blocked her true attack kick with the assault rifle and knocked her down *Why do I smell?* His gun barrel sought the *her* to kill.

In the shooter's new *behind him*:

Warren's blood smeared on his forehead.

Warren's Army jacket worn for Trick Or Treat.

Condor launched himself from the rolling wheelchair.

Yelled so the shooter whirled.

Tossed the 'bucks cup full of *wet* into the shooter's face.

Tripped with inertia from his wheelchair leap.

Condor crashed to his knees, heard the *falling on concrete* of that cup.

That paper cup he'd stuck into the stream spewing out of the bullet-punctured steel tank under a car that sheltered him and Malati and a child who wanted to be called Punkin and nodded all the way down into her bones that she *could* she *would* she'd do what she had to do even if she wasn't 'posed to.

The 'bucks cup he'd used to bail that spewing stream into Punkin's pumpkin bucket. Bucket full, he filled the cup to carry with him. Crouched low so the robot shooting inside the rest stop facility couldn't see him as like in some *don't spill* Fourth of July picnic contest, he frog-ran to the level concrete right outside the main doors. Purple smoke mushroomed inside the food court. Condor set the cup down. *Don't spill!* He pulled the Army jacket off Warren. Got his black leather jacket on the dead vet. Smeared blood from Warren's third eye on his own forehead. Grunted the body onto the heap of corpses blocking the other ramp. Plunked himself into the wheelchair.

Malati, careful not to spill the liquid from the pumpkin she carried, fumbled where Condor'd told her, the throat-shot bus driver's shirt pocket— *Got it!*

Tossed a tumbling glint of silver to the man in the wheelchair.

Malati draped herself over the murdered teachers.

Punkin yelled like she was 'posed to.

Death stalked down the ramp.

Got ambush doused with gasoline.

That stinking wet killer jerked Condor off his knees.

Condor pushed the bus driver's open silver cigarette lighter against the shooter and thumbed the wheel.

WHUMP! A fountain of fire engulfed the man who'd come to kill and die BUT NOT LIKE THIS!

Screaming. A human torch blazed the morning.

Dropped between the burning man's wobbling feet, Condor jerked the combat knife from its ankle sheath—slammed the blade up into the crease of shooter's groin.

Blood sprayed Condor, wiped on the Army jacket as he scrambled away.

The burning man staggered.

Collapsed in a flaming heap.

Sickening sweet stench of baking crackling flesh and gasoline.

Condor, hands and knees scrambling up the ramp past the overturned wheelchair to where his black leather jacket clad the body of Warren.

Helicopters.

Chopping the air, racing in low, fast and hard to kill or capture who's crazy.

Whoever's crazy.

"*Remember,*" the soldier who'd had a gun and was named Doug had said: "*We can do anything we want as long as nobody ever knows who we are."*

From his knees, Condor yelled: "Punkin!"

Trashed his way free of the bloody Army jacket.

"Punkin! All clear! FREE BIRD! FREE BIRD!"

There! Running toward the main entrance from between parked cars.

Her face *not gonna cry* and *gonna run, run, RUN!*

Condor—*Vin, my name is Vin*—wiped his face with Warren's jacket, saw the smear of blood, hoped he looked close to whatever survivor's normal was.

The seven-year-old girl with curly brown hair and red-white-and-blue clothes ran toward the silver-haired man who'd revolutionized her *supposed to*'s.

Condor pulled his black leather jacket off Warren.

Maneuvered that dead vet's arms and body enough so Warren wore the gas and blood-stained Army jacket he'd died in.

Shrugged himself into his own black leather jacket with its weight of legends.

Collided with and swept a little girl into his arms.

Swooping *roar* over them as helicopters flew a draw-fire pass.

Malati stumbled toward them.

The package, her responsibility, his arms wrapped tight around the *don't you dare call her a little girl,* that silver-haired Condor told Malati: "You spy, you lie."

Then he held the seven-year-old so they stared into each other's eyes.

"Punkin, I'm so proud of you! You did it! You did everything right! You saved so many people and *us,* you saved you and me and Malati. You're so great! But Punkin: there's one more giant big *'posed to.*"

She nodded with all her heart.

"You can't tell the whole truth. The real truth. You gotta tell the good truth. The guy who you helped, the man who saved you, the guy who got the gas from the shot-up car, rolled over there and did it, the guy who burned and stabbed the bad guy . . .

"It was him." Condor nodded to Warren's body. "The guy in the Army jacket. That's the most anybody else probably saw. That's all you say or tell anybody *ever*. He did it. Got the gas. Tossed it, lit the monster on fire. He rolled his wheelchair away to escape, that bad guy squeezed off a wild shot. Must have hit the Army jacket guy, you don't know. You only know you made it and you did what you were 'posed to."

Every good lie needs a *why*.

"Punkin," said the silver-haired man, "me, Malati, we're spies. No matter what, we've got to be a super secret that nobody but you ever knows. You can only say that we were here with you. Just people who ran and hid and didn't get shot. We're all telling the same story with the true part being what you did. But with the wheelchair guy. You, her, me: we're a *cross our hearts* forever secret."

Punkin nodded her solemn vow.

Must stay secret spies in that rampage of her life made as much sense as anything else anyone ever told her.

She hurled herself back into Condor's arms. He got held tight.

This, he prayed to the meds: *Let me remember this, this.*

Helicopters vibrated the world.

Burnt flesh stench. Shattered glass. Purple smoke swirls. Megaphone commands.

When the three of them sprawled on the sidewalk in front of the shot-to-shit rest stop, before she cell phoned the Panic Line and like a pro triggered the *make sure it holds* cover story of them as *random survivors* not identified in official police reports, named in newspapers, or broadcast by television crews who showed up on their own helicopters while flying ambulances were ferrying out the sobbing wounded, before all that, her face pressed against asphalt, Malati whispered to the silver-haired

man laying beside her:
   "Is it always like this?"
   And he said *yes*.

for Ron Mardigian

CONDOR IN THE STACKS

First published by the Mysterious Bookshop, 2015

"Are you trouble?" asked the man in a blue pinstripe suit sitting at his DC desk on a March Monday morning in the second decade of America's first war in Afghanistan.

"Let's hope not," answered the silver-haired man in the visitor's chair.

They faced each other in the sumptuous office of the Director of Special Projects (DOSP) for the Library of Congress (LOC). Mahogany bookcases filled the walls.

The DOSP fidgeted with a fountain pen.

Watch me stab that pen through your eye, thought his silver-haired visitor.

Such normal thoughts did not worry that silver-haired man in a blue sports jacket, a new maroon shirt and well-worn black jeans.

What worried him was feeling trapped in a gray fog tunnel of numb.

Must be the new pill, the green pill they gave him as they drove him away from CIA headquarters, along the George Washington

Parkway and beneath the route flown by 9/11 hijackers who slammed a jetliner into the Pentagon.

The CIA car ferried him over the Potomac. Past the Lincoln Memorial. Up "the Hill" past three marble fortresses for Congress's House of Representatives where in 1975, he'd tracked a spy from US ally South Korea who was working deep cover penetration of America by posing as a mere member of the messianic Korean cult that provided the last cheerleaders for impeached President Nixon.

The ivory US Capitol glistened across the street from where the CIA car delivered Settlement Specialist Emma and silver-haired *him* to the Library of Congress.

Whose DOSP told him: "I don't care how 'classified' you are. Do this job and don't make trouble or you'll answer to me."

The DOSP set the fountain pen on the desk.

Put his hands on his keyboard: "What's your name?"

"Vin," said the silver-haired stranger.

"Last name?"

Vin told him that lie.

The DOSP typed it. A printer hummed out warm paper forms. He used the fountain pen to sign all the correct lines.

"Come on," he told Vin, tossing that writing technology of the previous century onto his desk. "Let's deliver you to your hole."

He marched toward the office's mahogany door.

Didn't see his pen vanish into Vin's hand.

That mahogany door swung open as the twenty-something receptionist yawned, oblivious to the pistol under her outer office visitor Emma's spring jacket. Emma stood as the door opened, confident she wouldn't need to engage her weapon but with a readiness to let it fill her hand she couldn't shake no matter how long it had been *since*.

The DOSP marched these *disruptions* from another agency through two tunnel-connected, city block-sized library castles to a yellow cinderblock walled basement and a green metal door with a keypad lock guarded by a middle-aged brown bird of a woman.

"This is Miss Doyle," the DOSP told Vin. "One of ours. She's been performing your just-assigned functions with optimal results, *plus* excelling in all her other work."

Brown bird woman told Vin: "Call me Fran."

Fran held up the plastic laminated library staff I.D. card dangling from a lanyard looped around her neck. "We'll use mine to log you in."

She swiped her I.D. card through the lock. Tapped the keypad screen.

"Now enter your password," said Fran.

"*First,*" CIA Emma told the *library-only* staffers, "you two: please face me."

The DOSP and Fran turned their backs to the man at the green metal door.

Vin tapped six letters into the keypad. Hit ENTER.

The green metal door clicked. Let him push it open.

Pale light flooded the heavy-aired room. A government-issue standard metal desk from 1984 waited opposite the open door. An almost as ancient computer monitor filled the desk in front of a wheeled chair. Rough pine boxes big enough to hold a sleeping child were stacked against the back wall.

Like coffins.

"Empty crates in," said Fran, "full crates out. Picked up and dropped off in the hall. It's your job to get them to and from there. Use that flatbed dolly."

She computer clicked to a spreadsheet listing crates dropped off, crates filled, crates taken away: perfectly balanced numbers.

"Maintenance Operations handles data entry, except for when you log a pick-up notice. They drop off the Review Inventory outside in the hall." Fran pointed to a heap of cardboard boxes. "From closing military bases. Embassies. Other . . . secure locations.

"Unpack the books," said Fran. "Check them for security breaches. Like if some Air Force officer down in one of our missile silos forgot and stuck some secret plan in a book from the base library. Or wrote secret notes they weren't supposed to."

Vin said: "What difference would it make? You burn the books anyway."

"*Pulp* them," said the DOSP. "We are in compliance with recycling regulations."

CIA Emma said: "Vin, this is one of those eyeballs-needed, *gotta-do* jobs."

"Sure," said Vin. "And you'll know right where I am while I'm doing it."

The DOSP snapped: "Just do it right. The books go into crates, the crates get hauled away, the books get pulped."

Vin said: "Except for the ones we save."

"*Rescuer* is not in your job description," said the DOSP. "You can send no more than one cart of material *per week* to the Preserve stacks. You're only processing fiction."

The DOSP checked his watch. "A new employee folder is on your desk. We printed it out. Your computer isn't printer or Internet enabled."

"Security policy," said CIA Emma. "Not just for you."

"*Really.*" The DOSP's smile curved like a scimitar. "Well, as your Agency insisted, this is the only library computer that accepts his access code. A bit isolating, I would think, but as long as that's '*security policy*' and not *personal.*"

He and brown bird Fran adjourned down the underground yellow hall.

Vin stood by the steel desk.

Emma stood near the door. Scanned her Reinsertion Subject. "Are you OK?"

"That green pill wiped out whatever OK means."

"I'll report that, but *hey*: you've only been out of the Facility in Maine for—"

"The insane asylum," he interrupted. "The CIA's secret insane asylum."

"Give yourself a break. You've only been released for eleven days, and after what happened in New Jersey while they were driving you down here . . .

"Look," she said, "it's your new job, first day. Late lunch. Let's walk to one of those cafés we saw when we moved you into your house. Remember how to get home?"

"Do you have kids?"

Her stare told him *no*.

"This is like dropping your kid off for kindergarten," said Vin. "Go."

Emma said: "You set the door lock to your codename?"

"Yeah," he said. "*Condor.*"

His smile was wistful: "Can't ever get away from that."

"Call you Vin, call you Condor, at least you have a name. Got my number?"

He held up his outdated flip-phone programmed by an Agency tech.

She left him alone in that subterranean cave.

Call him Vin. Call him Condor.

Ugly light. The toad of an old computer squatting on a gray steel desk. A heap of sagging cardboard boxes. The wall behind him stacked with wooden crates—*coffins*.

Thick heavy air smelled like . . . basement rot, paper, stones, old insulation, cardboard, tired metal, steam heat. A whiff of the coffins' unvarnished pine.

He rode the office chair in a spin across the room. Rumbled back in front of the desktop computer monitor glowing with the spreadsheet showing nine cases—*pinewood coffins*—nine cases delivered to this Review Center. He clicked the monitor into a dark screen that showed his reflection with seven coffins stacked behind him.

Only dust waited in the drawers on each side of the desk's well. The employee manual urged library staffers to hide in their desk wells during terrorist or psycho attacks. *Like the atom bomb doomsday drills when I was a—*

And *he remembered!* His CIA-prescribed handful of daily pills didn't work perfectly: he could *kind of* remember!

Tell no one.

He slid open the middle desk drawer. Found three paperclips and one penny.

From the side pocket of the blue sports jacket he fetched the stolen fountain pen.

Sometimes you gotta do what you do just to be you.

He stashed the stolen pen in his middle desk drawer.

Noticed the monitor's reflection of seven coffins.

WAIT.

Am I crazy?

YES was the truth but not the answer.

He turned around and counted the coffins stacked against the back wall: *Seven.*

Clicked open the computer's spreadsheet to check the inventory delivery: *Nine.*

Why are two coffins missing?

The CIA's cell phone sat on his desk.

This is your job now. No job, no freedom.

Condor put the cell phone in his shirt pocket over his heart.

Suddenly he didn't want to be there because *there* was where *they* brought him, *transporting* him like a boxcar of doomed books. He counted the coffins: *still seven.* Walked out the door, pulling it shut with a click as he switched out the light.

The wide yellow-bricked hall telescoped away into distant darkness to his left. To his right, the tunnel ran about thirty steps until it T'ed at a brick wall.

He turned left, the longest route that let him look back and see where he'd been. Floated each stepping foot out in front of him empty of weight like Victor'd taught him in the insane asylum: aesthetically correct *T'ai chi* plus a martial arts technique that foiled foot-sweeping ninjas and saved you if the floor beneath your stepping shoe vanished.

Footsteps! Walking down that intersecting tunnel.

He hurried after those sounds of someone to ask for directions.

The footsteps quickened.

Don't scare anybody: cough so they know you're here.

The footsteps ran.

Pulled Condor into running, his heart jack hammering his chest.

Go right—*no left,* twenty steps until the next juncture of tunnels.

Whirr of sliding-open doors.

Dashing around a yellow brick walled corner—

Elevator—doors *closing!* He thrust his left arm into the doors' chomp—they bounced open and tumbled him into the bright metal cage.

FIST!

Without thought, with the awareness of ten thousand practices, his right forearm met the fist's arm, not to block but to blend with that force and divert it from its target.

The fist belonged to a woman.

And in the instant she struggled to recover her *diverted* balance, the palm of Condor's left hand rocketed her up and back so she bounced off the rear wall of the elevator as those metal doors closed behind him.

The cage groaned toward the surface.

"Leave me alone!" she yelled.

"You punched me!"

His attacker glared at him through black-framed glasses. Short dark hair. A thin silver loop pierced the right corner of her lower lip. Black coat. Hands clenched at her sides, not up in an on-guard position. She had the guts to fight but not the know-how.

"You chased me in here!" she yelled. "Don't deny it! I finally caught you! Stop it! You keep watching me! Doing things!"

"I don't do things!"

"Always lurking. Hiding. Sneaking. Straightening my reading room desk. KNOCK IT OFF! Weeks you've been at this—not gonna take it next time I'll punch—"

"*Weeks?*" he interrupted. "I've been doing *whatever* for weeks? Here?"

The elevator jerked to a stop.

Doors behind Condor slid open.

He loomed between the glaring woman and the only way out of this cage.

The elevator doors whirred shut.

The cage rumbled upwards.

He sent his right hand inside his sports jacket and she let it go there, confirming she was no trained killer. Pulled out his Library of Congress I.D. Showed it to her.

"Activation Date is today, my first day here. I can't be the one who's been stalking you."

The elevator jerked to a stop.

The doors behind Condor slid open.

"*Oh.*" She nodded to the open elevator doors. He backed out the cage. She followed him into a smooth walled hall as the elevator doors closed. "*Um,* sorry."

"No. You did what you could to be *not* sorry. Smart."

"Why were you chasing me?"

"I'm trying to find an exit."

"This is a way out," she said and led him through the castle. "I'm Kim."

He told her he was Vin.

"You must think I'm nuts."

"We all have our own roads through Crazytown."

She laughed at what she thought was a joke, but couldn't hold on to happy.

"I don't know what to do," said Kim. "Sometimes I think I'm imagining it all. I feel somebody watching me, but when I whirl around, nobody's there."

"Chinese martial arts say eyes have weight," Vin told her.

"I'm from Nebraska," she said. "Not China."

Kim looked at him, *really looked* at him.

"You're probably a great father." She sighed. "I miss my dad and back home, though I wouldn't want to live there."

"But why live here?"

"Are you kidding? Here I get to be part of what people can use to make things better, have better lives, be more than who they were stuck being born."

She frowned: "Why do you live here?"

"I'm not ready to die," he said. "Here or anywhere."

"You're a funny guy, Vin. Not funny *ha-ha*, but not *uh-oh* funny either."

They walked past a blue-shirted cop at the metal detector arch by the entrance. The cop wore a holstered pistol of a make Vin knew he once knew.

Just past the security line waited a plastic tub beneath an earnest hand-inked sign:

OLD CELLPHONES FOR CHARITY!

Funny guy Vin pictured himself tossing the CIA's flip-phone into that plastic bin. A glance at the dozen cellphones awaiting charitable recycling told him that would be cruel: His flip-phone was so uncool ancient that all the other phones would pick on it.

Condor and *not* his daughter stepped out into March's blue sky chill.

She buttoned her black cloth coat. "Would you do me a favor? You're new, so you can't be *whoever* it is. Come by my desk in the Adams reading room around noon tomorrow. Go with me to my office. See what I'm talking about, even if it's not there."

Standing in that chilly sunshine on a Capitol Hill street, Condor heard an echo from the DOSP: "Rescuer is not in your job description."

Sometimes you gotta do what you do just to be you.

"OK," said Condor.

Kim gave him her LOC business card, thanked him and said goodbye, walked away into the DC streets full of people headed somewhere they seemed to want to go.

"Remember how to get home?" Emma'd said.

An eleven-minute walk past the red brick Eastern Market barn where J. Edgar Hoover worked as a delivery boy a century before. Condor strolled past stalls selling fresh fruit and aged cheese, slabs of fish and red meat, flowers. He found himself in line at the market grill, got a crab cake sandwich and a lemonade, ate at one of the tall tables and watched the flow of mid-day shoppers, stay-home parents and nannies, twenty-somethings who worked freelance laptop gigs to pay for bananas and butchered chickens.

Where he lived was a blue brick townhouse on Eleventh Street, N.E., a narrow five rooms, one-and-a-half baths rental. No one ambushed him when he stepped into the living room. No one had broken the dental floss he'd strung across the stairs leading up to the bed he surfed in dreams. A flat screen TV reflected him as he plopped on the couch, caught his breath in this new life where nothing, *nothing* was wrong.

At 8:57 the next morning, he snapped on the lights in his work cave.

Counted the coffins: *Seven.*

Checked the computer's spreadsheet: *Nine.*

Crazy or not, that's still the count.

Sometimes crazy is the way to go.

Or so he told himself when he'd flushed the green pills down the blue townhouse's toilet at dawn. Emma'd report his adverse reaction, so probably there'd be no Code Two Alert when that medication wasn't seen in Condor's next urine test.

His thirteen other pills lined up on his kitchen counter like soldiers.

Condor held his cooking knife that looked like the legend Jim Bowie carried at the Alamo. Felt himself drop into a deep stance, his arms curving in front of his chest. The Bowie knife twirled until the spine of the blade pressed against the inside of his right forearm and the razor sharp cutting edge leered out like he'd been taught decades before by a Navy SEAL in a lower East Side of Manhattan black site.

Condor exhaled into his here-and-now, used the knife to shave powder off five pills prescribed to protect him from himself, from seeing or feeling or thinking that isn't part of officially approved *sensible* reality. Told himself that a shade of unapproved crazy might be the smart way to go, because standing in his office cave on the second morning of work, it didn't make sense that the approved coffin count was (still) off by two.

He muscled a cardboard box full of books onto a waist-high, brown metal cart, rolled the burdened cart over to the seven empty coffins and lost his virginity.

His very first one. The first book he pulled from that box bulging with books recycled from a closed US air base near a city once decimated by Nazi purification squads and then shattered by Allied bombers. The first volume whose fate he decided: *The List of Adrian Messenger* by Philip MacDonald.

Frank Sinatra played a gypsy in the black and white movie.

That had to make it worth saving, *right*? He leafed through the novel. Noted only official stamps on the pages. Put that volume on the cart for the Preserve stacks.

Book number two was even easier to save: a ragged paperback. Blue ink cursive scrawl from a reader on the title page: "You never know where you really are." That didn't seem like a code and wasn't a secret, so no security breach. The book was Kurt Vonnegut's *Slaughterhouse Five*. Sure, gotta save that on the cart.

And so it went. He found a bathroom outside his cave, a trip he would have made more often if he'd also found coffee. Books he pulled out of shipping boxes got shaken, flipped through and skimmed until the Preserve cart could hold no more.

All seven pine wood crates were still empty, coffins waiting for their dead.

Can't meet Kim without dooming—*recycling*—at least one book.

The black plastic bag yielded a hefty novel by an author who'd gone to a famous graduate school MFA program and been swooned over by critics. That book had bored Condor. He plunked it into a blond pine coffin. Told himself he was just doing his job.

Got out of there.

Stood in the yellow cinderblock hall outside his locked office.

If I were a spy, I'd have maps in my cell phone. I'd have a Plan with a Fallback Plan and some Get Out of Dodge *go-to*. If I were a spy, an agent, an operative, somebody's asset, my activation would matter to someone who cared about me, someone besides the *targets* and the *rip-you-ups* and the *oppo*(sition), none of whom should know I'm real and alive and *on them*. If I were still a spy, I'd have a mission.

Feels like forty years since I was just me.

Terrifying.

No wonder I'm crazy.

Outside where it would rain, the three castles of the Library of Congress rose across open streets from Congress's Capitol Dome and the pillars of the Supreme Court because knowledge is clearly vital to how we create laws and dispense justice.

And *yes*, the swooping art decco John Adams castle where Condor worked is magnificent with murals and bronze doors and owls as art everywhere.

And *true*, the high-tech concert hall James Madison LOC castle that looms across the street from the oldest fortress of the House of Representatives once barely kept its expensively-customized-for-LOC-use edifice out of the grasp of turf hungry Congressmen who tried to disguise their grab for office space as *fiscally responsible*.

But *really*, the gem of the LOC empire with its half-billion dollar global budget and 3,201 employees is the LOC's Thomas Jefferson building: gray marble columns rising hundreds of feet into the air to where its green metal cupola holds the "Torch of Learning" copper statue and cups a mosaic sky over the castle full of grand marble staircases, wondrous murals and paintings, golden gilt and dark wood, chandeliers, a main reading room as glorious as a cathedral, and everywhere, *everywhere*, books, the words of men and women written on the ephemera of dead trees.

Down in the castles' sub-basement of yellow tunnels, Condor walked beneath pipes and electrical conduits and wires, past locked doors and lockers. He rode the first elevator he found up until the steel cage dinged and left him in a cavern of stacks—row after row of shelves stuffed with books, books in boxes in the aisles, books everywhere.

He drifted through the musty stacks, books brushing the backs of both his hands, his eyes blurred by the lines of volumes, each with a number, each with a name, an identity, a purpose. He circled around one set of stacks and saw *him* standing there.

Tom Joad. Battered hat, sun-baked lean Okie face, shirt missing a button, stained pants, scruffy shoes covered with the sweat dust of decades.

"Where you been?" whispered Condor.

"Been looking. How 'bout you?"

"Been trying," said Condor.

A black woman wearing a swirl of color blouse under a blue LOC smock stepped into the aisle where she saw only Condor and said: "Were you talking to me?"

The silver-haired man smiled something away. "Guess I was talking to myself."

"Sugar," she said, "everybody talks to somebody."

He walked off like he knew what he was doing and where he was going, saw a door at the end of another aisle of books, stepped through it—

BAM!

Collision hits Condor's thighs, *heavy* runs over *hurts* his toes—*Cart!*

A metal steel cart loaded with books slams into Condor as it's being pushed by . . .

Brown bird Fran. Pushing a metal cart covered by a blue LOC smock.

"Oh, my Lord, I'm so sorry!" Fran hovered as Condor winced. "I didn't see you there! I didn't expect anybody!"

She blinked back to her balance, sank back to her core. Her eyes drilled his chest.

"*Vin*, isn't it? Why aren't you wearing your I.D.? LOC policy requires visible issued I.D. The DOSP will not be pleased."

She leaned closer: "I won't tell him we saw each other if you won't."

"Sure," he said. *And thus is a conspiracy born.*

"That's better." She straightened the blue smock over the books it covered on her cart. "You should wear it anyway. If you're showing your I.D., you can go anywhere and do darn near anything. For your job, I mean."

He fished his I.D. from inside the *blah* blue sports jacket issued him by a CIA *dust master* who costumed America's spies. Asked her how to get to the reading room.

"Oh, my: you're a floor too high. There's a gallery above that reading room back the direction I came. You can't miss it." She tried to hook him with a smile. "How soon will you out-process the next shipment of inventory?"

"You mean pack books in the coffins to be pulped? It's only my second day."

"Oh, dear. You really must keep on schedule and up to speed. There are needs to be met. The DOSP has expectations."

"Must be nice," said Condor. "Having expectations."

He thanked her and headed the direction she said she'd come. Went through the door labeled "Gallery."

That door opened to a row of taller-than-him bookshelves he followed to one of six narrow slots for human passage to the guardrail circling above the reading room with its quaint twentieth century card catalog and research desks.

Nice spot for recon. Sneak down any slot. Charlie Sugar (Counter Surveillance) won't know which slot you'll use. Good optics. Target needs to crank his or her head to look up. Odds are, you spot that move in time to fade the half-step back to not be there.

Condor moved closer to the balcony guardrail. His view widened with each step.

Kim sat at a research desk taking notes with an iPad as she studied a tan book published before a man in goggles flew at Kitty Hawk. Kim wore a red cardigan sweater. Black glasses. Silver lip loop. A glow of purpose and focus. She raised her head to—

Condor eased back to where he could not see her and thus she did not see him. He walked behind bookshelves, found the top of a spiral steel staircase.

You gotta love a spiral steel staircase.

That steel rail slid through his hand as the world he saw turned around the axis of his spiraling descent. The reading room. Researchers at desks. Kim bent over her work. A street op named Quiller from a novel Condor'd saved loitered by the card catalog with a bespectacled mole hunter named Smiley. The stairs spiraled Condor toward a mural, circled him around, but those two Brits were gone when he stepped off the last stair.

Kim urged him close: "He's here! I just felt him watching me!"

"That was me."

"Are you sure?"

"Two tactical choices," he answered. Her anxious face acquired a new curiosity at this silver-haired man's choice of words. "Maintain status or initiate change."

"Change how?"

Condor felt the cool sun of Kabul envelop him, an outdoor marketplace café where what was supposed to happen hadn't. Said: "We could move."

Kim led him into the depths of the Adams building and a snack bar nook with vending machines, a service counter, a bowl of apples. They bought coffee in giant paper cups with snapped on lids, sat where they could both watch the open doorway.

"Oh, my God," whispered Kim. "That could be him!"

Walking into the snack bar came a man older and a whiff shorter than her, a stocky man with shaggy brown hair and a mustache, a sports jacket, and shined shoes.

"I don't know his name," whispered Kim. "I think he tried to ask me out once! And maybe he goes out of his way to walk past where I am! When I feel eyes on me, he's not there, nobody is, but it could be, *it must be* him."

The counterwoman poured hot coffee into a white paper cup for Mustache Man. He sat at an empty table facing the yogurt display case. At the angle he chose, the refrigerated case's glass door reflected blurred images of Condor and Kim.

Life or luck or tradecraft?

Condor told her: "Walk out. Go to your office. Wait for my call."

"What if something happens?"

"Something always happens. Don't look back."

Kim marched out of the snack nook.

Mustache Man didn't follow her.

Call him Vin. Call him Condor.

He thumb-popped the plastic lid loose on his cup of hot coffee.

Slowed time as he inhaled from his heels. Exhaled a fine line. Unfolded his legs to rise away from the table without a sound, without his chair scooting on the tiled floor.

Condor carried the loose-lid cup of hot coffee out in front of him like a pistol.

Mustache Man was *five, four, three* steps away, his head bent over a book.

Condor "lurched"—jostled the coffee cup he held.

The loose lid popped off the cup. Hot coffee flew out to splash Mustache Man.

He and the stranger who splashed him yelped like startled dogs. Mustache Man jumped to his feet, reached to help *some older gentleman* who'd obviously tripped.

"Are you all right?" said Mustache Man as the silver-haired stranger stood steady with his right hand *lightly* resting on the ribs over Mustache Man's startled heart.

"I'm sorry!" lied Condor.

"*No, no*: it was probably my fault."

Vin blinked: "Just sitting there and it was your fault?"

"I probably moved and threw you off or something."

"Or something." The man's face matched the I.D. card dangling around his neck.

Mustache Man used a napkin to sponge dark splotches on his book. "It's OK. It's mine, not the library's."

"You bring your own book to where you can get any book in the world?"

"I don't want to bother Circulation."

Vin turned the book so he could read the title.

Mustache Man let this total stranger take such control without a blink, said: "Li Po is my absolute favorite Chinese poet."

"I wonder if they read him in Nebraska."

Now came a blink: "Why Nebraska?"

"Why not?" said Condor.

The other man shrugged. "I'm from Missouri."

"There are two kinds of people," said Condor. "Those who want to tell you their story and those who never will."

"Really?"

"No," said Vin. "We're all our own kind. I didn't get your name."

"I'm Rich Bechtel."

Condor told Mustache Man/Rich Bechtel—same name on his I.D.—that he was new, didn't know the way back to his office.

"Let me show you," volunteered Rich, right on cue.

They went outside the snack nook where long corridors ran left and right.

"Either way," Rich told the silver-haired man whose name he still hadn't asked.

"Your choice," said Condor.

"Sorry, I work at CRS." *CRS: the Congressional Research Service that is and does as it's named.* "I'm used to finding options, letting someone else decide."

"This is one of those times you're in charge," lied Condor.

He controlled their pace through subterranean tunnels. By the time they reached Condor's office, he knew where Rich *said* he lived, how long he'd been in Washington, that he loved biking. Loved his work, too, though as a supervisor of environmental specialists, "seeing what they deal with can make it hard to keep your good mood."

"Is it rough on your wife and kids?" asked Condor.

"Not married. No family." He shrugged. "She said *no*."

"Does that make you mad?"

"I'm still looking, if that's what you mean. But *mad*: How would that work?"

"You tell me." He stuck out his right hand. Got a return grip with strength Rich didn't try to prove. "My name is Vin. Just in case, could I have one of your cards?"

That card went into Vin's shirt pocket to nestle beside Kim's that Condor fished out as soon as he was inside his soundproof cave. He cell-phoned her office.

Heard the click of *answered call.* No human voice.

Said: "This is—"

"Please!" Kim's voice: "Please, *please* come here, see what— *Help me!*"

Condor snapped the old phone shut. Grabbed the building map off his desk.

Couldn't help himself: counted the stacked coffins.

Still seven where there should be nine.

Time compressed. Blurred. Rushing through tunnels and hallways. Stairs. An elevator. Her office in a corridor of research lairs. Don't try the doorknob: that'll spook her more. Should be locked anyway. His knock rattled her door's clouded glass.

Kim clacked the locks and opened the door, reached to pull him in but grabbed only air as he slid past, put his back against the wall while he scanned her office.

No ambusher. Window too small for any ninja. Posters on the walls: a National Gallery print of French countryside, a Smithsonian photo of blue globed earth, a full-face wispy color portrait of Marilyn Monroe with a crimson lipped smile and honesty in her eyes. Kim's computer glowed. A framed black-and-white photo of a Marine patrolling some jungle stood on her desk: *Father? Grandfather? Vietnam?*

"Thought I was safe," babbled Kim. "Everything cool, you out there dealing with it and I unlocked the office door. It was locked—swear it was locked! Looked around and . . . My middle desk drawer was open. Just a smidge."

Kim's white finger aimed like a lance at a now wide-open desk drawer.

Where inside on its flat-bottomed wood, Condor saw:

HARLOT

Red lipstick smeared, gouged-out letters in a scrawl bigger than his hand.

Kim whispered: "How did he get in here? Do that? Weren't you with him?"

"Not before. And you weren't here then either."

A tube of lipstick lay in desk drawer near the graffiti, fake gold metal polished and showing no fingerprints. Condor pointed to the tube: "Yours?"

She looked straight into his eyes. "Who I am sometimes wears lipstick."

"So he didn't bring it and he didn't take it. But that's not what matters."

"Look under the lipstick," he said. "Carved letters. Library rules don't let anybody bring in a knife, so somebody who does is serious about his blade."

"I'm going to throw up."

But she didn't.

"Call the cops," said Condor.

"And tell them what? Somebody I don't know, can't be sure it's him, he somehow got into my locked office and . . . and did *that*? They'll think I'm crazy!"

"Could be worse. Call the cops."

"OK, they'll come, they'll care, they'll keep an eye on me until there's no more nothing they'll have the time to see and they'll go and *then what*? Then more of this?"

She shook her head. "I'm an analytic researcher. That's what I do. First we need to find *more* to verify what we say for the cops to show we're not crazy!"

"First call the cops. Then worry about verifying. Crazy doesn't mean wrong."

"What else you got?" Her look scanned his scars.

"Grab what you need," he said. "Work where I found you, the reading room, in public, not alone. I don't know about afterwards when you go home."

"Nothing's ever . . . felt wrong there. Plus I've got a roommate."

"So did the heroine in *Terminator*."

"Life isn't science fiction."

"Really?" Condor rapped his knuckles on her computer monitor.

Made her take cell phone pictures of HARLOT and email them to herself before he shut that desk drawer. "Got a boyfriend or husband or any kind of ex?"

"The last somebody I had was in San Francisco and he dumped me. No husband, ever. Probably won't be. Evidently all I attract are psycho creeps. Or maybe that's all that's out there. Why can't I find a nice guy who doesn't know that's special?"

"Do you like mustaches?"

"Hey, I wear a lip ring."

"Have you ever mentioned mustaches to anybody?"

She shook her head *no*.

"Then maybe he's had it for a long time."

Kim shuddered.

He escorted her back to the same reading room desk.

Left her there where her fellow LOC employees could hear her scream.

Took the spiral steel staircase up and went out the Gallery door, walked back the way he first came, through the stacks, row after row of shelved books. Down one aisle, he spotted a shamus wearing a Dashiell Hammett trenchcoat and looking like Humphrey Bogart before he knew his dream was Lauren Bacall.

Condor called out: "What's my move?"

The shamus gave him the long look. Said: "You got a job, you do a job."

His job.

Back in the sub-basement cave. Alone with the *still only seven* coffins. Alone with the cart piled high with the few books he could save from *the DOSP's expectations.*

Anger gripped him. Frenzy. Cramming books into the coffins. Filling all seven pine crates, plopping them on the dolly, wheeling it out of his office, stacking the coffins against the yellow cinderblock wall, pushing the empty dolly back into his cave, logging PICK UP in the computer, snapping off the lights, locking the door, home before five with a day's job done and the shakes of not knowing what to do.

Shakes that had him walking back to work before dawn. His I.D. got him inside past cops and metal detectors, down the elevator to the subterranean glow around the corner from his office and into the unexpected rumble of rolling wheels.

Condor hurried around the corner . . .

. . . and coming toward him was a dolly of pinewood coffins pushed by a barbell-muscled man with military short blond hair and a narrow shaved face. The blond muscle man wore an I.D. lanyard and had deep blue eyes.

"Wait!" yelled Condor.

The coffin-heavy dolly shuddered to a jerked stop.

"What are you doing?" said Condor. "These are my coffins—crates."

Couldn't stop himself from whispering: "*Nine.*"

Looked down the hall to where yesterday he'd stacked *seven* coffins.

The barbell blonde said: "You must be the new guy. I heard you were weird."

"My name is Vin, and you're . . . ?"

The blue-eyed barbell blonde said: "*Like*, Jeremy."

"Jeremy, you got it right, I'm new, but I got an idea that, *like*, helps both of us."

Rush the grift so Jeremy doesn't have time to, like, make a wrong reply.

"I screwed up, *sorry*, stuck the wrong book in a crate, so what we need to do, what *I* need to do, is take them all back in my cave, open 'em up, and find the book that belongs on the rescue cart. Then you can take the crates away."

"I'm doing that now. That's my job. And I say *when.*"

"That's why this works out for us. Because you're who says *when.* And while I'm fixing the mistake, you go to the snack bar, get us both—I don't know about you, but I need a cup of coffee. I buy, you bring, and by then I'll be done with the crates."

"Snack bar isn't open this early. Only vending machines."

Don't say anything. Wait. Create space for the idea to fall into.

"Needing coffee is weak," said Jeremy.

"When you get to my age, weak comes easy."

Jeremy smiled. "They might have hot chocolate."

"I think they do." Vin fished the last few dollar bills from the release allowance out of his black jeans. "If they got a button for cream, push it for me, would you?"

Jeremy took the money. Disappeared down the yellow cinderblock hall.

Vin rolled the dolly into his cave. Unlatched the first coffin, found a frenzied jumble of books, one with ripped cover so the only words left above the author's name were: ". . . LAY DYING"

Remember that, I remember that.

The second crate contained another jumble that felt familiar, all novels, some with stamps from some island, Paris Island. *Yeah, this is another one I packed, one of the seven.* So was the third crate he opened, and the fourth.

But not number five.

Neatly stacked books filled that pinewood box. Seventy or more books.

But only three titles.

Delta of Venus by Anais Nin. *Never read it, maybe a third of this coffin's books.*

The rest of the renegade coffin's books were editions of *The Carpetbaggers* by Harold Robbins, many with the jacket painting of a blond woman in a lush pink gown and the grip of a fur stole draped round her shoulders as some man towered behind her.

I remember it! A *roman à clef* about whacky billionaire Howard Hughes who bought Las Vegas from the Mob, but what Vin remembered most about the book was waiting until his parents were out of the house, then leafing to *those pages.*

Now, that morning in his locked cave in a basement of the Library of Congress in Washington, DC, Vin rifled through the coffin of discarded volumes of *The Carpetbaggers* and found nothing but those books, stamped properties of public libraries from New Mexico to New Jersey, nothing hidden in them, nothing hidden under them in the pinewood crates, nothing about them that . . .

What smells?

Like a bloodhound, Vin sniffed all through that coffin of doomed novels.

Smells like . . . Almonds.

He skidded a random copy of each book across the concrete floor to under his desk and closed the lid on the coffin from which they came.

The sixth crate contained his chaos of crammed-in books, but crate number seven revealed the same precise packing as crate five, more copies of Anais Nin and *The Carpetbaggers*, plus copies of two other novels: *The Caretakers* that keyed more memories of furtive page turning and three copies of *Call Me Sinner* by Alan Marshall that Vin had never heard of. Plus the scent of almonds. He shut that crate. The last two coffins held books he'd sent to their doom and smelled only of pine.

Roll the dolly piled high with coffins back out to the hall.

This is what you know:

Unlike the books that filled seven of the *there-all-along* coffins, the volumes in *where'd-they-come-from* two coffins were precisely packed, alphabetically and thus systematically clustered C and D titles, and all, *well*, erotic.

And smelled like almonds.

Remember, I can't remember what that means.

Jeremy handed Condor a cup of vending machine coffee. "You find what you were looking for?"

"Yeah," said Condor, a truth full of lies.

Jeremy crumpled his chocolate stained paper cup, tossed it on top of the crates.

"I'll come with you." Vin fell in step beside the man pushing the heavy dolly.

"You are weird. Push the button for that elevator."

A metal cage slowly carried the two men and the coffin dolly up, up.

"Do you see many weird people down here?" asked Condor.

"Some people use this way as a shortcut out to get lunch or better coffee."

Rolling wheels made the only sounds for the rest of their journey to the loading dock. Jeremy keyed his code into the dock's doors, rolled the dolly outside onto a loading dock near a parked pickup truck.

An LOC cop with a cyber tablet came over, glanced at the crates, opened one and saw the bodies of books, as specified on the manifest. He looked at Condor.

"The old guy's with me," said Jeremy.

The cop nodded, walked away.

The sky pinked. Jeremy lifted nine crates—*nine*, not *seven*—dropped them into the pickup truck's rear end cargo box for the drive to the recycling dump.

"This is as far as you go," Jeremy told the weird older guy.

Condor walked back inside through the loading dock door.

The rattling metal grate lowered its wall of steel.

Luminous hands on his black Navy SEAL watch ticked past seven a.m. Condor stalked back the way he'd come, as if retracing geography would let him remake time, go back to *when* and do it right. When got to the stacks where he'd been lost before, down the gap between two book-packed rows, he spotted a mouse named Stuart driving a tiny motorcar away in search of the north that would lead him to true love.

Condor whispered: "Good luck, man."

Voice behind you! "Are—"

Whirl hands up and out sensing guard stacks spinning—

Woman brown clothes eyes widening—

Fran, sputtering: "I was just going to say '*Are you talking to yourself?*'"

Condor let his arms float down as he faded out of a combat stance.

"Something like that."

"Sorry to have interrupted." She smiled like a woman at a Methodist church social his mother once took him to. Or like the shaved-head, maroon-robed Buddhist nun he'd seen in Saigon after that city changed its name. "But nice to see you."

Condor frowned. "Wherever I go, there you are."

"Oh, my goodness," twittered Fran. "Doesn't that just seem so? And good for you being here now. The early bird gets the worm. Believe you me, there are worms. Worms everywhere."

Flick—a flick of motion, something—*somebody* ducking back behind a shelf in an aisle between those stacks way down where Stuart drove.

"By the way," he heard Fran say: "Good job. The DOSP will be pleased."

"What?"

"Your first clearance transfer."

"How did you know I was sending out a load of coffins?"

Her smile widened. "Must have been Jeremy."

Amidst the canyons of shelves crammed with books, Condor strained to hear creeping feet beyond the twittering brown bird of a woman.

"Just walking by his shop in the basement, door must have been open, I mean, I used to have your job working with him."

Prickling skin: Something—*someone*—hidden from their eyes in the canyons of stacks moved the air.

"Vin, are you feeling OK?"

"—just distracted."

"Ah." Fran marched away, exited through a door alone.

Alone, Condor telepathed to whoever hid in this cavern of canyons made by rows of shelved books. Just you and me now. All alone.

Somewhere waited a knife.

Walk between close walls of bookshelves crammed with volumes of transcribed RAF radio transmissions, 1939–1941. He could hear the call signs, airmen's chatter, planes' throbbing engines, bombs, and the clattering machineguns of yesterday.

Today is what you got. And what's got you.

What got him, he never knew—a sound, a tingling, a corner-of-his-eye motion, *whatever*: he whirled left to that wall of shelved books, slammed his palms against half a dozen volumes so they shot back off their shelf and knocked away the books shelved in the next aisle, a gap blasted in walls of books through which he saw . . .

Mustached and eyes startled wide Rich Bechtel.

"Oops!" yelled Condor. "Guess I stumbled *again*."

He flowed around the shelf, a combat ballet swooped into the aisle where Rich—suit, tie, mustache—stood by a jumble of pushed-to-the-floor books.

Condor smiled: "Surprised to see me here?"

"Surprised, why . . . ?"

"Yes, *why* are you here?"

The mustached man shrugged. "It's a cut-through to go get good coffee."

"Did you cut through past the balcony of the reading room?"

"Well, sure, that's a door you can take."

"So why were you hiding back here?" said Condor.

Rich shrugged. "I was avoiding *call me* Fran."

Confession without challenge: *As if we were friends*, thought Condor.

"A while back," continued Rich, "I was over here in Adams working on a Congressional study of public policy management approaches. One of the books I had on my desk was a rare early translation of the *Dao De Jing*, you know, the . . ."

"The Chinese Machiavelli."

"More than that, but *yes*, a *how power works* manual that Ronald Reagan quoted. Fran mistook it for something like the Koran.

She walked by my research desk, spotted the title and went off on me about how dare I foster such thought. Things got out of hand. She might have pushed my books off the desk, could have been an accident, but . . ."

"But what?"

"I walked away. When I see her now, I keep walking. Or try not to be seen."

Condor said: "Nobody could make up that story."

The caught man frowned. "Why would I make up any story?"

"We all make up stories. And sometimes we put real people in the stories in our heads. That can be . . . confusing."

"I'm already confused enough." Rich laughed. "What are you doing?"

"Leaving. Which way are you headed?"

Rich pointed the way Condor'd come, left with a wave and a smile.

The *chug chug chug* of a train.

One aisle over, between walls of books, railroad tracks ran through a lush green somewhere east of Eden, steel rails under a coming this way freight train and sitting huddled on top of one metal car rode troubled James Dean.

Condor left that cavern of stacks, walked to the Gallery where he could see the empty researchers' desks on the floor of the reading room below. Checked his watch. Hoped he wouldn't need to pee. Some surveillances mean no milk cartons.

What does it mean when you smell almonds?

Don't think about that. Fade into the stacks. Be part of what people never notice.

On schedule, Kim with her silver lip loop and a woman wearing a boring professional suit walked in to the reading room. The roommate left. Kim settled at her desk. He gave the counter-surveillance twenty more minutes, went to his office. No coffins waited outside against the yellow wall from a delivery by Jeremy: *Watch for that.*

So Condor left his office door open.

Sank into his desk chair.

Footsteps: outside the open door in the hall, hard shoes on the concrete floor of the yellow underground tunnel. Footsteps clacking louder as they came closer, closer . . .

She glides past his open door in three firm strides, strong legs and a royal blue coat. Silver-lined dyed blond hair floats on her shoulders, lush mouth, high cheekbones. Cosmic gravity pulls his bones and then she's gone, her *click click click* of high heels turning the basement corner, maybe to the elevator and out for mid-morning coffee.

Don't write some random wondrous woman into your story.

Don't be a stalker.

But he wasn't, wouldn't, he only looked, ached to look more, had no time to think about her, about how maybe her name was Lulu, how maybe she wore musk—

Almonds.

Up from behind his desk, out the lock-it door and *gone*, up the stairs two at a time, past the guards on the door to outside, in the street, dialing *that number* with the CIA cell phone. A neutral voice answered, waltzed Condor to the hang-up. He made it into his blue townhouse, stared at his closed turquoise door for nineteen minutes until that soft knock.

Opened his door to three bullet-eyed *jacket men*.

Emma showed up an hour later, dismissed them.

Sat on a chair across from where Condor slumped on the couch.

Said: "What did you do?"

"I called the cops," answered the silver-haired man who was her responsibility.

"Your old CIA Panic Line number. Because you say you found C4 plastic explosives. But you don't know where. You just smelled it, the almond smell."

"In the Library of Congress."

"That's a lot of *where*. And C4's not as popular as it used to be."

"Still works. Big time boom. Hell of a kill zone."

"If you know how to get it or make it and what you're doing."

"You ever hear of this thing called the Internet?"

She threw him a change-up: "Tell me about the dirty books."

"You know everything I know because I told those *jacket men*, they told you. Sounds crazy, right? And since I'm crazy, that's just about right. Or am I wrong?"

Emma watched his face.

"They aren't going to do anything, are they? CIA. Homeland Security."

"Oh, they're going to do something," said Emma. "No more Level Five, they're going to monitor you Level Three. Increase your surprise random home visits. Watch me watching you in case I mess up and go soft and don't recommend a Recommit in time to avoid any embarrassments."

"How did you keep them from taking me away now?"

"I told them you might have imbibed early and contra-indicated with your meds."

"Imbibed?"

"Tomorrow's St. Patrick's day." She shook her head. "I believe *you believe*. But you're trying to be who you were then. And that guy's gone into who you are now."

"Vin," he said. "Not Condor."

"Both, but in the right perspective."

"Ah," said Condor. "Perspective."

"What's yours? You've been free for a while now. How is it out here?"

"Full of answers and afraid of questions."

She softened. "How are the hallucinations?"

"They don't interfere with—"

"—with you functioning in the real world?"

"*The real world.*" He smiled. "I'll watch for it. What about Kim's stalker?"

"If there's a stalker, you're right. She should call the cops."

"Yeah. Just like I did. That'll solve everything."

"This is what we got," said Emma.

"One more thing we got," said Vin. "At work, I can't take it, packing coffins."

"Is it your back?" said Emma. "Do you need—"

"I need more carts to go to Preserve. I need to be able to save more books."

Emma probed. Therapist. Monitor. *Maybe friend.* "Those aren't just books to you. The ones at work. The novels."

Condor shrugged. "Short stories, too."

"They're things going to the end they would go to without you. You act like you're a Nazi working a book-burning bonfire. You're not. Why do you care so much?"

"We sell our souls to the stories we know," said Condor. "The more kinds of stories, the bigger we are. The better or truer or cooler the story . . ."

His shrug played out the logic in her skull.

"I'll see what I can do," said Emma. "About the cart."

"Carts," corrected Condor.

"Only if we're lucky."

She walked out of his rented house.

Left him sitting there.

Alone.

Sometimes you gotta do what you do just to be you.

Next morning, he dressed for war.

Black shoes good for running. Loose black jeans not likely to bind a kick. His Oxford blue shirt might rip if grabbed. He ditched the *dust master*'s sports coat for the black leather zip-up jacket he bought back when an ex-CIA cocaine cowboy shot him in Kentucky. The black leather jacket let him move, plus it gave the illusion of protection from a slashing knife or exploding bomb.

Besides, he thought when he saw his rock 'n' roll reflection walking in the glass of the Adams building door, *if I'm going down, I'm going down looking like me.*

Seven pine wood crates waited stacked against the yellow wall outside his cave.

Condor caressed the coffins like a vampire. Inhaled their essence. Lifted their lids to reveal their big box of *empty*: smooth walls, carpentered bottoms of reinforcing slats making a bed of rectangular grooves for books to lay on and die. His face hoovered each of those seven empty coffins, but only in one caught a whiff of almonds.

He tore through his office. The computer said nine coffins waited outside against his wall. Desk drawers: still empty, no weapons. The DOSP's fountain pen filled his eyes. *Use what you got.* He stuck the pen in his black leather jacket.

Two women working a table outside the Adams building reading room spotted a silver-haired man coming their way. They wore green sweaters. The younger one's left cheek sported a painted-on green shamrock. She smiled herself into Condor's path.

"Happy St. Patrick's Day! You need some holiday green. Want to donate a dollar to the Library and get a shamrock tattoo? Good luck *and* keeps you from getting pinched. How about one on your hand? Unless you want to go wild. Cheek or—"

The silver-haired stranger pressed his trigger finger to the middle of his forehead.

"Oh, cool! Like a third eye!"

"Or a bullet hole."

Her smile wilted.

He stalked into the reading room. Clerks behind the counter. Scholars at research desks. *There*, at her usual place, sat Kim.

She kept her cool. Kept her eyes on an old book. Kept her cell phone visible on her desk, an easy grab and a *no contact necessary* signal. He kept a casual distance between where he walked and where she sat, headed to the bottom of a spiral staircase.

Playing the old man let him take his time climbing those silver steel steps, a spiraling ascent that turned him through circles to the sky. His first curve toward the reading room let him surveil the head tops of strangers, any of whom could be the oppo. The stairs curved him toward the rear wall that disappeared into a black and white Alabama night where a six-year-old girl in a small town street turns to look back at her family home as a voice calls "*Scout.*" Condor's steel stairs path to the sky curved . . .

Fran.

Standing on the far side of the reading room. Condor felt the crush of her fingers gripping the push handle of a blue smock covered cart. Saw her burning face.

As she raged across the room at silver lip-ringed Kim.

You know crazy when you see it. When crazy keeps being where crazy happened.

Obsession. Call it lust that Fran dared not name. Call it fearful loathing of all that. Call it outrage at Kim's silver lip loop and how Kim represented an effrontery to The Way Things Are Supposed to Be. Call it envy or anger because that damn still young woman with soft curves Fran would never be asked to touch got to do things Fran never did. Or could. Or would. Got to feel things, have things, be things. Lust, envy, hate: complications beyond calculation fused into raging obsession and made Fran not a twittering brown bird, made her a jackal drooling for flesh and blood.

For Kim.

Kim sat at her desk between where Fran seethed and where Condor stood on spiral silver stairs to the sky. Kim turned a page in her book.

Fran's eyes flicked from her obsession—spotted Vin. Saw him see the real her. Snarled, whirled the cart around and drove hard toward the reading room's main doors.

Cut her off! You got nothing! She's got a knife!

Condor clattered down the spiral steel stairs, hurried across the reading room. He had no proof. No justifiable right to scream "HALT!" or call the cops—and any cops would trigger *jacket men* to snatch him away to the secret Maine hospital's padded cell or to that suburban Virginia crematorium where no honest soul would see or smell his smoke swirling away into the night sky.

He caught his breath at Kim's desk: "Not a mustache, a her!"

Kim looked to the main door where he'd pointed, but all she saw beyond Vin charging there was the shape of someone pushing a cart into the elevator.

Vin ran to the elevator, saw its glowing arrow: ↓

Over there, race down those stairs, hit the basement level—

He heard *rolling wheels* from around that corner.

Rammed at Condor came the blue smocked cart.

That he caught with both hands—pulled more. Jerked Fran off balance. Pushed the book cart harder than he'd ever pushed the blocking sled in high school football. Slammed her spine against a yellow cinderblock wall. Pinned her there: *Stalker had a knife and a woman like Fran with knife-tipped shoes once almost killed James Bond.*

Condor yelled: "Why Kim?"

"She doesn't get to be her! Me, should be her, have her, stop her!"

The fought-over cart shook between them. Its covering blue smock slid off.

Books tumbled off the cart. Books summoned from heartland libraries to our biggest cultural repository where they disappeared on *official business*. Condor registered a dozen versions of the same title banned in high schools across America *because*.

"You filled the coffins! Tricked libraries all over the country into sending their copies of certain titles here to the mothership of libraries! You murdered those books!" Condor twisted the cart to keep Fran rammed against the wall. "You're a purger, too!"

"Books put filth in people's heads! Ideas!"

"Our heads can have any ideas they want!"

"Not in my world!" Fran twisted and leveraged the cart up and out from under Condor's push. The cart crashed on its side. He flopped off his feet, fell over it.

Wild punches hit him and he whirled to his feet, knocked her away.

Yelled: "Where are the coffins?! Where's the C4?!"

"I see you!" She yelled as the book she threw hit his nose.

Pain flash! He sensed her kick, closed his thighs but her shoe still slammed his groin. He staggered, hit the stone wall, hands snapping up to thwart her attack—

That didn't come.

Gone. Jackal Fran was gone, running down the basement tunnel.

Cell phone, pull out your cell phone.

"Kim!" he gasped to the woman who answered his call. "Watch out, woman my age Fran and she's not a brown bird, she's the jackal after you!

"Don't talk! Reading room, right? Stay in plain sight but get to the check-out counter . . . Yes . . . The library computer . . . Search employee data base— No, not Fran *anybody,* search for Jeremy *somebody!*"

A ghost of Fran whispered: *"I used to have your job working with him."*

Over the phone came intel: an office/shop door number, some castle hole.

The DOSP's pen tattooed that number on the back of his left hand.

He hung up and staggered through the underground tunnel.

Scan the numbers on the closed doors, looking for numbers with an SB prefix whatever that— *Sub-basement! Like my office!* One more level down.

At a stairwell, he flipped open his ancient phone and dialed another number: "Rich it's Vin, you gotta go help somebody right now! Protect her. Tell her I sent you. In Adams Reading Room, named Kim, silver lip loop . . . I thought you'd noticed her! And that's all right, you just . . . OK, but when you couldn't find the right words you walked on, right? Go now! . . . Don't worry, nobody knows everything. Play it with what you've got."

He jogged through yellow tunnels like he was a rat running a maze, *I'm too old for this,* staggering to a closed brown metal door, its top half fogged glass.

Condor caught his breath outside that door. The door handle wouldn't turn. He saw a doorbell, trigger-fingered its button, heard it buzz.

The click of a magnetic lock. The door swings open.

Come on in.

Jeremy stands ten steps into this underground lair beside a workbench and holding a remote control wand. The door slams shut behind Condor.

"What do you want?" said a caretaker of this government castle.

Caretaker, like in the novel Fran tried to murder, some story about sex and an insane asylum and who was crazy. *Stick to what's sane.* Condor said: "The coffins."

"They're here already?"

Scan the workshop: no sign of the two missing coffins. A refrigerator. Wall sink. Trash tub of empty plastic water bottles. The back of an open laptop faced Condor from the workbench where the tech wizard of this cave stood. Jeremy tossed the remote control beside an iPhone cabled to the laptop.

"Oh," said Jeremy. "You meant the crates for the books."

He took a step closer. "Why do you care?"

"There's something you don't know you know."

"I know enough."

Off to Jeremy's left waited the clear plastic roller tub holding half a dozen cell phones and its color printer sign proclaiming OLD TELEPHONES FOR CHARITY!

One heartbeat. Two.

"I didn't know you were the one collecting charity phones."

"What do you know?" Jeremy eased another step closer.

Sometimes crazy is the way to go.

Jeremy's blue eyes narrowed, his hands were fists.

Feel the vibe. See the movie.

Sunny blue sky behind the white dome of the US Capitol. Across the street rises a castle with a green metal top and giant gray concrete walls of columns and grand staircases, windows behind which people work, a fountain out front where bronze green statues of Greek gods flirt and pose their indomitable will.

Tremble/rumble! The Library of Congress's Jefferson building shudders sprays out exploded concrete dust like 9/11, like Oklahoma City. Fireballs nova through castle rooms of wood panels, wood shelves, books that no one would see again. Those walls crumble to rubble. The last moment of the castle's cohesion is a cacophony of screams.

You'll never make it to the door. Locked anyway. And he's between you and its remote control on the workbench by the computer umbilical chorded to an ultra phone.

Make it real: "You and Fran."

"She's just a woman," said Jeremy. "More useful than a donkey, not as trainable. Like, deluded. Like all women in this Babylon where they don't know their place."

"Oh, I like all the places they will go," said Condor, quoting the book he'd heard read a million billion times to a frightened child traveling beside his mother on a bus through a dark Texas night. "Where'd Fran take those two coffins—*crates* that you and her use to smuggle in C4?"

"Somewhere for her stupid crusade."

For *her* stupid crusade. Not *our.*

A lot of roads run through Crazytown.

Jeremy took a step closer.

Condor flowed to walk a martial arts *Bagua* circle around him.

Almonds, a strong whiff in the air of what had been stockpiled down here.

"She even bribed you," guessed Condor as Jeremy turned to keep the silver-haired man from circling behind him.

"She funded the will of God."

"Fran thought the only God she was funding was hers. Didn't know about yours."

"My God is the only God."

"That's what all you people say."

Why is there a floppy flat empty red rubber water bottle on the floor?

Condor feinted. Jeremy flinched: he's a puncher, maybe from a shopping mall *dojo* or hours watching YouTubes of Jihad stars showing their wannabe homegrown brothers out there the throat-cutting ways of Holy warriors.

"Slats!" said Condor. "On the inside bottom of the crates. Reinforcing slats, they make a narrow trough. Somewhere outside, after you dump the books, you mold C4 into those slats—cream color, looks like glue on the wood if the guard outside checks. Odds are the guard won't check all the crates every time, you only use two, and even if somebody checks, nobody notices.

"Fran paid you to cut her out a couple crates before you delivered them. That gave you time with the crates in here to peel out what you hid, pass them on to her, she gives them back full of what you don't care about to fold back into the coffin count."

"Way to go, cowboy." Jeremy had that flat accent born in Ohio near the river. "You get to witness the destruction of the Great Satan's temple of heretical thought."

"Wow, did they email you a script?"

"You think I'd be so careless as to let the NSA catch me contacting my true brothers in the Middle East before I proved myself—"

Lunge, Jeremy lunged and Condor whirled left—whirled right—snake-struck in a three-beat *Hsing-i* counter-charge to—

Pepper spray burned Condor's face.

Breathe can't breathe eyes on fire!

The Holy warrior slammed his other fist into the silver-haired man's guts.

Condor was already gasping for air and flooding tears because of pepper spray. The barbell muscled punch buckled and bent him over, knocked him toward the workbench, teetering, stumbling—crashing to the floor.

Get up! Get up! Get to your knees—

The blue-eyed fanatic slapped Vin, a blow more for disrespect than destruction.

Condor saw himself flopping in slow motion. Kneeling gasping on the hard floor. His arms waving at his sides couldn't fly him away or fight his killer.

White cable connects the laptop to iPhone: Jeremy rips that chord free.

Whips its garrote around the kneeling man's neck.

Gurgling clawing at the chord cutting off blood to brain air to lungs, pepper-sprayed eyes blurring, a roar, a whooshing in his ears, can't—

BZZZZ!

That doorbell buzz startles the strangler, loosens his pull.

Blood rush to the brain, air!

BZZZZ!

Strangler jerks his garrote tight.

GLASS RATTLES as someone outside bangs on that door.

Can't scream gagging here in here help me in here get in here!

Jeremy spun Condor around and slammed him chest-first into the workbench.

Hands, your hands on the workbench, claw at—

Seven seconds before blackout, he *saw.*

The remote for the door. Wobbling on the workbench. *Flop reach grab—*

The jihad warrior whirled the gurgling apostate away from the high tech gear.

Thumb the remote.

The door buzzes—springs open.

Fran.

Screaming charging rushing *IN!*

Jeremy knees Condor, throws him to the floor and the garrote—

The garrote goes loose around Condor's neck *but won't unwrap itself from the strangler's hands*, holds his arms trapped low.

"Stop it!" Fran screams at the treasonous pawn who's trying to steal her destiny. "He's mine to kill!"

Down from heaven stabs her gray metal spring-blade knife confiscated from a tourist, salvaged from storage by an LOC staffer who could steal any of the castles' keys.

Fran drove her stolen blade into Jeremy's throat.

Gasping grabbing his hands to his neck/what sticks out of there.

Wide eyed, his hands grab GOT HER weakness percolates up from his feet by the prone Vin, up Jeremy's legs, he's falling holding on to Fran, death grips her blouse that rips open as the force of his pull multiplied by his fall jerks her forward—

Fran trips over sprawled Condor.

Swan dives through the air over the crumpling man she stabbed.

Crashes *cracks* her skull on the workbench's sharp corner.

Spasms falls flat across the man she stabbed whose body pins Condor to the floor.

Silence. Silence.

Crawl out from under the dead.

Hands, elbows, and knees pushing on the concrete floor, straining, pulling . . .

Free. Alive. Face down on the floor, gasping scents of cement and dust, sweat and the warm ham and cabbage smell of savaged flesh. A whiff of almonds.

Jackhammer in his chest:

No heart attack, not after all this. Come on: a little justice.

Condor flopped over onto his back.

Saw only the castle's flat ceiling.

Propped himself up on his elbows. Sat. Dizzy. Sore from punches, getting kneed, strangled. Pepper-spray, tears, floor dirt, sweat: his face was caked. Must look like hell.

Nobody will let you walk away from this.

Almonds, C4: where's the C4?

The workbench, the laptop, glowing screen full of . . .

A floor plan. The LOC jewel, the main castle Jefferson Building.

A pop-ad flashed over the map, a smiling salesman above a flow of words:

"Congratulations on your new cell phone basic business plan. Now consider moving beyond mere networked teleconferencing to—"

The white computer chord garrote lay on the floor like a dead snake.

A snake that once connected the laptop computer to an iPhone.

An iPhone capable of activating all cell phones on its conferenced network.

A *for charity* tub that gobbles up donated old cell phones from our better souls.

The iPhone screen glowed with the LOC castle map and its user-entered red dots.

Dizzy: he staggered toward the wall sink, splashed water on his face, empty plastic water bottles in a tub right by that weird red rubber bag that doesn't belong here.

Vision: Jeremy smiling his Ohio smile, walking through the metal detectors with the baggy crotch of his pants hiding a red rubber bottle full of goo that's not water.

Grab the roller tub for donated cell phones. Close the laptop, put it in the tub beside the iPhone. The phone glowed the map of the castle.

The crisscrossed corpses on the floor kept still.

How long before anyone finds you?

Thumb the remote, the door swings open. Push the plastic tub on wheels into the hall. Condor pulled his blue shirt out of his waistband, used it to polish his fingerprints off the remote, then toss it back through the closing door into the basement shop, plastic skidding along the concrete floor to where the dead lay.

Go!

Race the rumbling plastic tub on wheels through the tunnels of the Adams building to the main castle of Jefferson, down into its bowels and follow the map on the iPhone screen to a mammoth water pipe. Gray duct taped on the inflow water pipe's far side: a cellphone wired as a detonator into a tan book-sized gob of goo.

Boom and no water for automatic sprinklers to fight fire.

Boom and water floods an American castle.

Pull the wires out of the gob of C4. Pull them from the phone. Pull the phone's battery. Toss the dead electronics into the tub.

What do you do with a handful of C4?

A shot bullet won't set it off. And C4 burns. Only electricity makes it go *Boom!*

Squeeze the C4 into a goo ball, shove it into your black jacket's pocket.

Condor charged the plastic tub on wheels to the next map number on the iPhone: bomb against a concrete weight-bearing wall. The iPhone led him to three more bombs. Each time he ripped away the electronics and squeezed the goo into a shape he could hide in his jacket pockets, and when they were full, he stuffed C4 goo inside his underpants.

Boom.

Run, catch that elevator, roll in with the tub. A man and a woman ride with you. He's a gaudy green St. Patrick's Day tie. She looks tired. Neither of them cares about you, about what happens in your crotch if the elevator somehow sparks static electricity.

Next floor plan in the iPhone.

Stacks, row after row of wooden shelves and burnable books and *there*, under a bookshelf, another cell phone wired goo ball. Rubber bands bind this apparatus to a clear plastic water bottle full of a gray gel that a bomb will burst into a fireball.

Lay the bottle of napalm atop the cell phones in the wheeled tub.

Your underpants are full.

Cinch the rubber bands from that bomb around the ankles of your pants. Feed a snake of C4 down alongside your naked leg in the black jeans.

Roll on *oh so slowly.*

Hours, it takes him hours, slowed more by every load of C4 he stuffs in his pants, inside his blue shirt, in the sleeves of his black leather jacket.

Hours, he rolls through the Jefferson building for hours following iPhone maps made by an obsessed fanatic. Rolls past tours of ordinary citizens, past men and women with lanyard I.D. Rumbles down office corridors, through the main reading room with its gilded dome ceiling, until the final red X on the last swooped-to page of the iPhone's uploaded maps represents only another pulled apart bomb.

In an office corridor, a door: MEN'S ROOM.

Cradle all the napalm water bottles in your arms.

The restroom is bright and mirrored, a storm of lemon ammonia.

And empty.

Lay screwed open water bottles in the sink so they *gluck gluck* down that drain.

One bottle won't fit. Shuffle it into the silver metal stall.

Can't stop, exhausted, drained, slide down that stall wall, slump to sitting on the floor, hugging the toilet like some *two beers too many* teenager.

The C4 padding his body makes it hard to move, but he drains the last non-recyclable water bottle into the toilet. That silver handle pushes down with a *whoosh*.

The world does not explode.

He crawled out of the stall. Made sure the water bottles in the sink were empty. Left them there. Left the tub of cellphones and wires in the hall for janitors to puzzle over. Dumped Jeremy's laptop in a litter barrel. Waddled to an elevator, a hall, down corridors and down the tunnel slope to the Adams building toward his own office.

Kept going.

Up, main floor, the blonde went this way, there's the door to the street, you can—

Man's voice behind Condor yells: "You!"

The blue pinstripe suit DOSP. Who blinks. Leans back from the smell of sweat and some kind of nuts, back from the haggard wild-eyed man in the black leather jacket.

"Are you quite all right, Mister . . . *Vin*?"

"Does that matter?" says this pitiful excuse for a government employee foisted on the DOSP by another agency.

Who then unzips his black leather jacket, fumbles inside it, pulls out—

A fountain pen Vin hands to the DOSP, saying: "'Guess I'm a sword guy.'"

Vin waddled away from his stricken silent LOC boss.

Stepped out into twilight town.

They'll never let you get away with this.

Capitol Hill sidewalk. Suit and ties with briefcases and work-stuffed backpacks, kids on scooters. That woman's walking a dog. The cool air promises spring. An umbrella of night cups the marble city. Some guy outside a bar over on Pennsylvania Avenue sings *Danny Boy*. Budding trees along the curb make a canopy against the streetlights' shine and *just keep going, one foot in front of the other*.

Go slow so nothing shakes out of your clothes.

Talking heads blather from an unseen TV, insist *this*, know *that*, sell *whatever*.

Waves of light dance on that three-story-high townhouse alley wall. Music in the air from the alley courtyard's flowing light. Laughter.

Barbecue and green beer inspired the St. Paddy's Day party thrown by the *not-yet-thirty* men and women in that group house. They did their due diligence, reassured their neighbors, *come on over*, we're getting a couple of kegs, buckets of ice for Cokes and white wine, craft or foreign beers for palates that had become pickier since college. There was a table for munchies. Texted invites blasted out at 4:20 before "everybody" headed out to the holiday bars after work. Zack rigged his laptop and speakers, played DJ so any woman who wanted a song had to talk to him and his wingman who was a whiz at voter precinct analyses but could never read a curl of lipstick.

Bodies packed the alley.

Everybody worked their look, the *cool* stance, the way to turn your face to scan the crowd, the right smile. Lots of cheap suits and work ensembles, khakis and sports jackets, jeans that fit better than Condor's bulging pants. Cyber screens glow in the crowd like the stars of a universe centered by whoever holds the cellphone. Hormones and testosterone amidst smoke from the two troughs made from a fifty-gallon drum sliced lengthwise by a long gone tenant of yore. Those two barbecue barrels started out the evening filled by charcoal briquettes and a *Whump!* of lighter fluid. By the time Condor'd eased his way to the center of the churning crowd, a couple guys from a townhouse up the street had tossed firewood onto the coals so flames leapt high and danced shadows on the alley courtyard's walls.

The crowd surged as Zack turned up the volume on a headbanger song from the wild daze of their parents.

Who were Condor's age.

Or younger.

Hate that song, he thought.

He reached the inner edge of the crowd who amidst the flickering light tried not to see the *getting there* debts pressing down on them or the pollution from the barrel fires trapping tomorrow's sun. They'd made it here to this city, this place, this idea. They worked for the hero who'd brought them to town, for Congress *of course that would matter*, so would the group/the project/the committee/the caucus/the association/the website they staffed, the Administration circus ring that let them parade lions or tigers or bears, *oh my*, the downtown for dollars firm that pulled levers, the Agency or Department they powered with their sweat and so they could, *they should* sweat here, now, in the flickering fire light of an alley courtyard. Swaying. Looking. Hoping for a connection—heart, mind, flesh, community: get what you can, if nothing else a contact, a move toward more. The music surged. An American beat they all knew pulsed this crowd who were white and black, Hispanic and Asian, men and women and maybe more, who came from purple mountains' majesty and fruited plains to claim the capital city for this dream or that, to punch a ticket for their career, to get something done or get a deal, *to do* or *to be*—that is this city's true question and they, *oh they*, they were the answer *now*.

Near the burning barrels, a dozen couples jumped and jived to their generation's music blaring out of the speakers. Glowing cellphones and green dotted the crowd—bowlers, top hats. Over there was a woman in green foil boa. That woman blew a noise-maker as she shuffled and danced solo—not alone, no, she was not alone, don't anyone dare think that she was alone. She saw him, a guy old enough to be her father, all battered face lost in space, heard herself yell the question you always ask in Washington: *"What do you do?"*

He felt the heat of the flames.

"Hey old guy!" yelled Zack, DJ earphones cupped around his neck like the hands of a strangler. "This one's for you. My dad loves it."

Zack keyboarded a YouTubed live concert, Bruce Springsteen blasting *Badlands.*

Cranked up the volume as elsewhere in this empire city night, silver lip looped Kim shyly thanked a man with a mustache for being the knight by her side, for dinner, for *sure,* coffee at work tomorrow morning, for however much more they might have.

But in that alley, in that pounding drums and crashing guitars night, lovers like that became just part of the intensity of it all, like individual books in the library stacks of stories stretching into our savage forever.

Call him Vin. Call him Condor.

His arms shot toward the heaven in that black smoked night and he shuffled to the music's blare, arms waving, feet sliding into the dancing crowd.

A roar seized the revelers. A roar that pulled other arms toward heaven, a roar that became the whole crowd bopping with the beat, the hard driving invisible anthem.

"Go old guy!" shouts someone.

A silver-haired frenzy in black leather and jeans rocks through the younger crowd to the burning barrels, to the fire itself, reaches inside his jacket, throws something into those flames, something that lands with a shower of sparks and a sizzle and crackles and on, on he dances, pulling more of that magic fuel out of his jacket, out of its sleeves, out his— *Oh My God! He's pulling stuff out of his pants and throwing it on the fire!* Every throw makes him lighter, wilder, then he's dancing hands free in the air, stomping feet with the crowd bouncing around him. "Old guy! Old guy!" Cop cruisers cut the night with red and blue spinning lights. The crowd throbs. "Old guy! Old Guy!" Burning almonds and fireplace wood, barbecue and *come hither* perfume, a reckless whiff of rebel herb that will become legal and corporate by the decade's end. "Old guy! Old Guy!" There are bodies in a basement, mysteries to be found, questions clean of his fingerprints, books to be treasured. There are lovers sharing moments, dreamers dancing in the night, madmen in our marble city, and amidst those who are not his children, through the fog of his crazy, the swirl of his ghosts, the weight of his locked-up years, surging in Condor is the certainty that this *oh this,* this is *the real world.*

for Harlan Ellison

RUSSIAN ROULETTE OF THE CONDOR

CHAMBER ONE
Will You Still Need Me

Silver-haired, blue-eyed Vin held an empty white coffee mug as he stood at the kitchen sink. He looked through the window to the outside world where across the road came a stranger carrying a black cane and walking without a limp.

Satellite radio filled this house inside Washington, DC's Beltway that Thursday morning in April 2016, savvy rock songs curated by a human being, not an algorithm. Amidst the music, Vin heard Merle in the dining room whimpering *goodbye* to the changing of the guard.

This two-story house rose from a grass lawn and was set back from a curved suburban road just over the Maryland border from America's white marble capital city, a gothic dwelling surrounded by a black iron bars fence tall enough to keep out casual interlopers but short enough to not look like a prison or a fortress or their inevitable fusion.

Vin looked away from the kitchen window.

Poured his attention into the empty white coffee mug.

Today I'll work how the globe spins, he thought, *yet now I'm standing here, showered and dressed after T'ai chi, then coffee at the dining room table with Merle and her insisted-on actual paper copies of the day's* New York Times *and* Washington Post—

—and I'm vacillating over whether to microwave a third cup from the glass pot of cold coffee. Whether to boil the tea kettle, make a fresh pot. Whether to go no more coffee today, stick my mug in the dishwasher.

He set the empty white coffee mug on the kitchen counter.

Glanced out the window, but black cane man was gone.

Vin filled the tea kettle, put it on the stove's burner, *whumped* on that blue flame.

The man with the black cane didn't limp.

"Bonnie," said Vin: "Scan perimeter."

A.I. Bonnie filled the three screens on the kitchen wall with images: Ms. Night Shift driving away. The curved tree line bordering the back yard. Middleclass homes seen through the black pole fence and across the two-lane old highway/commuter road.

Those screens scrolled: Sensors Track No Intrusion.

Vin turned his back on the open door to the dining room. Grabbed a glass jar filled with coffee beans. Heard shoes stepping on the wooden floor and turned around to see Mr. Day Shift enter the kitchen carrying his black medical bag.

"Hey, Justin. Everything OK?"

"Why wouldn't it be?" Justin put his black medical bag on the kitchen table. "She seems pretty good this morning. Moving fine. Almost a smile. Might be the new meds."

"Might be."

"Speaking of new meds," said Justin, "orders sent some for you."

"How many pills can one person take?"

"This is just a new version of the nose spray to counter the side effects of that prostate med."

Justin flicked the first snap on his medical bag.

The tea kettle on the stove rumbled with heating water.

Vin shook coffee beans into the grinder, pushed its lid down for a whine that drowned out the music and all other sounds in the kitchen until Vin stopped the grind.

Heard the rumbling tea kettle generate a soft toot.

Heard the *Snap!* of a plastic medical glove.

Vin turned.

Saw *why wearing medical gloves* Justin pull a blue cap off a white plastic, thumb pump nasal spray bottle. Justin set the blue cap onto the kitchen table, his face a tense smile as he marched toward Vin holding the ready nose spray out like it was a hypodermic needle.

"Easy now," said Justin, "might as well get it over with."

Black cane man didn't limp.

Vin threw the coffee grinder at Justin but its cord plugged into a counter socket jerked the grinder short and flipped it over. Coffee perfumed brown powder dusted the kitchen.

Justin boxer-shuffled forward, thrusting the spray bottle at Vin.

The tea kettle whistled a cloud of steam.

The radio played the pounding drums opening riff of *Mystery Achievement*, Chrissy Hynde and The Pretenders' breakout song from Vin's Seventies & Eighties cocaine mission daze.

Vin dodged a stab of the nasal spray.

Lunged toward the tea kettle crying on the stove—

—evaded Justin's stab and grabbed toward a black cast iron fry pan.

Justin charged but Vin rolled back. His right arm stroked the killer's stabbing arm, flowed with that force while redirecting it. In the blink after Justin controlled his stagger, sank/bounced up in his shoes, Vin dropped deeper into his own root and with his left hand on Justin's ribcage directed their resultant upward surge of energy into rocketing already-rising Justin off his feet, popping him back toward the open door to the dining room . . .

. . . where into kitchen with its *stop me whistling* tea kettle came Merle.

Her thick widow's peak hair never went back to blond after what happened silvered it from roots to shoulder length tips. She'd kept her high cheekbones, clean jawline. Even though chronic trembles and psychiatrist-sanctioned yoga kept her thin, mature breasts strained the bland tan blouse she wore that morning and round hips mooned her black slacks.

Her sapphire eyes nova'd as Justin crashed into her and knocked her on her ass.

Justin stabbed the nose spray toward where Merle'd been—

—whirled back and hooked a stab at Vin . . .

. . . who diverted that thrust upwards: the nasal spray stabbed Justin's throat *pssst!*

The nasal spray bottle hit the kitchen floor.

Vin kicked Justin who staggered to the kitchen counter with terror-widening eyes and a quarter-sized wet spot glistening on his throat.

Justin's gloved hands frantically wiped the wet spot trickling down his flesh as his eyes went bloodshot. He collapsed onto his back.

Vin yelled: "Why?"

Justin's red blotched face tightened into a skeletal leer. For the seven months he'd been detailed to the day shift, Justin had bitched about the radio always tuned to *"somebody singing about their own shit like it matters."* Now his bloodshot eyes revealed rage as he hissed from one song he'd heard that made sense: "Money changes everything!"

Those stretched tight lips spit—

—Vin dodged that toxic gob as convulsions shook Justin . . . let him go.

The tea kettle whistled.

The radio's song changed.

Vin grabbed trembling Merle: "Are you OK? Did spray hit—no, we'd know by now."

"You said *no*," cried Merle. "You said *no more. Never again.* Everything was . . . *no!*"

"Merle listen, *listen*! We've got to move now!

"Bonnie!" yelled Vin. "Lockdown!"

That A.I. female voice called out: "Lockdown initiated. What alert protocol, Condor?"

Justin was inside. A penetration agent. If there's one . . . A black cane back-up killer . . .

"Protocol Pearl Harbor!" yelled Vin/Condor to the A.I.'s ears and see-all screens.

He pulled Merle out of the kitchen, through the dining room covered with actual meat world newspapers proclaiming: *Clinton, Trump Win Big In Primaries. Life Expectancy For White Females In America Down. What's Next For Bernie Sanders? National Archives Hosts Screening of 'Elvis & Nixon' Documentary.* He felt Merle shrink into herself, but she gave him no resistance as he hustled her up the stairs.

"Merle, you're OK, but we've gotta evac'! Your Go Bag. In your closet. Grab it and meet me right back here."

Condor encouraged her with a soft shove. Scurried into The Office with its glass table where three giant screens faced a keyboard and the black executive office chair on wheels.

"Bonnie: Replay fast-forward perimeter scans last seven—no, eight minutes."

Scenes outside this house filled the screens . . .

. . . with nothing unusual. With no image of a black cane man.

"What the fuck?"

Either the V's been hacked or I'm crazy.

Condor knew both scenarios were true.

He jerked open the closet door—

—no roaring-out Frankenstein monster.

Condor grabbed a messenger bag holding a shoulder-holstered upgraded 1911 .45 automatic he strapped over his long-sleeved maroon shirt. Clipped a belt holstered .45 onto his right hip. He bent—cursed the stiffening of his six decades—strapped a sheathed combat knife onto his right ankle under his washed-out black jeans. Made sure his black sneaker-like shoes were tied. Glanced at his bag's gear: the dopp kit with toothbrush and paste, razor, five cycles of daily meds; ammo mags; three burner phones and charge cords; an envelope with $2,000 in cash; three passports and driver's licenses; three wallets packed with identity-back-up "pocket litter" and credit cards; a thick packet of lilac-scented baby wipes.

He pulled on a faded black leather bomber jacket that covered his guns.

He shoved his cellphone, wallet and keys into jacket pockets, glanced at the computer screens: Screen One waterfalled data, flashed PROTOCOL PEARL HARBOR. Screen Two flashed images from inside the house—the kitchen with its corpse, the living room, the bed in the next room where he woke up with Merle. Those views kept glitching. Blackness jarred by intermittent lightning flashes commanded Screen Three.

He looped the messenger bag across his chest—made it hard to grab the shoulder-holstered .45, but the gun on his right hip was still a clear draw.

Condor met Merle in the hall. Her Go Bag hung like a heavy purse from her shoulder.

A secret underground emergency escape tunnel ran from the basement to the trees behind the house and beyond the black iron poles fence, its entrance covered by covert cameras, but based on the screens Condor'd just checked, those cameras couldn't be accessed or trusted.

Plus, Justin knew that escape route. The NSA tech/security/medical aides knew little about the V they'd been detailed to via Top Secret/Code Word Access bureaucratic machinations, but they knew their deployment's emergency protocols—they had to. Since Justin knew about the tunnel, whoever *money changes* flipped him into a traitor also probably knew, logically would post a backup strike option for Justin failing and his targets following Evac Procedures.

But watchers outside the house might think that Justin hadn't taken his chance yet. That he was operational.

Condor strained to sense everything as he hurried Merle down the stairs.

No sounds from an attacking breach team. No dead bang grenades. Scents of his and Merle's sweat. Her pine shampoo. Their fear.

Bottom of the stairs, he made her look at him: "One chance."

"Good chance," he lied. "They don't know we know. Our car's parked in the driveway, facing toward the gate to the street. Don't run. Get in, seatbelt. We clear the gate like we're going to the grocery store but we're in the wind."

"You should have let me die last time—was your fault then, too. You're Condor and you always bring death."

"I give what I get. Let's go."

He stepped out the front door into the sunlit morning first, braced for a bullet . . .

. . . that didn't come.

Condor dawdled between Merle and the world as she scurried around the back of the red Ford, dove into the front seat, slammed the car's door. He slid behind the steering wheel, used a twentieth-century key to turn on the engine, raised the gate-opening wand—

Cracking glass!

A bullet punched a coin-sized hole through the driver's side window just beyond his face.

Punched a fist-sized hole through the front passenger window—a trajectory Merle's head had bent out of as she curled in her seat to click her seatbelt.

Condor slammed the gearshift into Drive.

Aimed the security wand at the gate—

—*nothing*: the iron barred, electronically secured system stayed shut.

He punched the gas and the Ford surged toward the locked gate.

A bullet zinged off the car roof.

Condor cranked the steering wheel. The Ford shot off the brick paved driveway and onto the green lawn in a loop that aimed it back at the gothic house.

Merle screamed: *"What are you doing?"*

He stomped on the brakes. Tires gouged living earth.

Condor slammed the gearshift into reverse. Lined up the iron gate between the Ford's side mirrors just like he had driving truck in *pay for college* summers. Stomped on the gas.

The Ford slammed its backend into the iron bars gate at 39 mph. As Condor'd gambled, the air bags didn't deploy. The collision knocked the gates open. Knocked one gate free so it spun off the Ford's red roof as Condor punched the gas, the road *outta here* in his windshield.

"We could have been killed!" yelled Merle.

"Any time, any day!" Condor swerved through a yellow light.

"Are they following us?"

He checked his mirrors: "Who the fuck knows."

The red Ford sped down Georgia Avenue, past Fort Stevens where a Union General once yelled to top-hatted, front line-observing Abraham Lincoln to *'get down you fool'* so Confederate snipers wouldn't nail the President. Condor went right onto Military Road, a multi-lane divided road cutting across the top of DC Military Road narrowed into a city street. The Ford went left on Nebraska. Cut around a black Jeep turning into the alley behind Politics & Prose bookstore.

Merle whispered: "Are you going to Homeland Security?"

Headquarters for that post-9/11 cobble waited 2.3 miles from where they were.

Clear city street ahead—

—Condor stomped on the brakes. The red Ford shuddered. Drew rubber lines on the gray pavement. Lurched to a stop crossways on Nebraska Avenue, blocking both lanes.

"Get out!" he yelled to Merle. "Grab your Go Bag!"

Then he was sneakers on the street as approaching traffic from both directions screeched to halt at the roadblock red Ford. Car horns blared through morning air.

They raced along the sidewalk the direction they'd been going. Cut away from a triangle patch of grass proclaimed by a white on brown sign to be Jeff Stein Park, scurried up the slope of a high school soccer field, made it to the backend of a block of stores.

Condor looked back to the car horns' cacophony.

No determined strangers charged after them.

Merle gasped: "Gotta, can't, let me catch—"

"Watch behind us, walk backwards, hold onto me: I'll walk us to Wisconsin Avenue."

Condor pulled his cellphone from his shirt pocket, swiped and tapped a Facetime call.

Second ring and a visual filled his cellphone screen.

She wore her dyed red hair long enough for a feminine curve below her clean jaw and short enough to be acceptable for combat. The Edward Hopper print of silent souls at a nighthawks' diner counter that Condor'd gifted her hung behind her on the wall of an apartment that could have been in Washington, could have been in Warsaw.

She said: "Are you clear?"

"Unknown," said Condor. "You?"

"Processing but probably cool. Janitors found a USB stick in your downstairs computer. We're tearing it apart, but odds are, kitchen guy stuck it in there before . . .

"Glad to see you," she said.

Gave Condor a smile he told himself was almost like a daughter's.

He said: "Can you hear me?"

"Maybe we all can," said the redhead. "Is your companion clear?"

"On the team. What's happening?"

"Somebody must not like you. Or us. Or both. We've contained the USB stick's hack. Sophisticated. Nation state, not a cartel or private player, but not our level."

The red-haired woman's face blanked. "You need a new tea kettle."

"Bring us in," said Condor.

"Where?"

Condor stopped at the subway on Wisconsin Avenue's busy and big bucks' street.

"Chris Harvie's ground. We're downbound."

His cellphone showed the red-haired woman blink. Nod. "ETA?"

"Maybe 20, 25. Work for you?"

"It better," she said.

Ended the Facetime connection and left him staring at his reflection in a black screen.

On that Washington street, Merle whispered to him: "Chris Harvie's dead. You . . . We were . . . She loved him, Faye loved him."

They heard a subway rumbling into the station at the bottom of a nearby escalator.

Condor spotted an orange sedan with black lettering on its door cruising up Wisconsin Avenue toward them while an unmarked SUV pulled up so a cellphone-waving woman could open its backdoor and climb in. Condor beckoned the orange sedan to the curb.

The Middle Eastern–looking driver whirred down the front passenger window: "Yes sir! Taxi sir! Anywhere you want!"

Condor pushed Merle into the orange taxi, climbed in and told the driver: "Just go!"

He looked back to the sidewalk where they'd been: saw no one *who.*

Looked to the taxi's rearview mirror. Found the driver's eyes.

Said: "First intersection, take a left. Go one block, left again, then one block and left. Take a right, head back down Wisconsin Avenue."

"Right turns or even a U would be easier."

"Easier's not always the way to go."

Condor stared into the rearview mirror. The side mirrors. Turned to look behind them.

No car obviously followed the orange taxi.

He let himself sink into the backseat beside trembling Merle.

"Take Massachusetts Avenue," said Condor. "Go to Capitol Hill, by Union Station."

"Whatever you want, Sir," said the taxi driver. "And thank you for using one of us professionals and not some loner who gets to you through your cellphone."

The orange taxi slid through traffic, rolled past the gray stone Washington Cathedral, motored down Massachusetts Avenue through the neighborhood known as Embassy Row for its mansions housing foreign ambassadors and their staffs. They drove past a statue of WW II hero Winston Churchill holding his hand up to make his trademark V.

Condor sighed as the orange taxi curved around one of Washington's traffic circles where on a beautiful September Tuesday morning in America's Bicentennial Year of 1976, assassins for the US-backed right wing Chilean military dictatorship used a car bomb to blow up and murder a Chilean diplomat from the overthrown leftist regime who had political asylum in America. Condor'd been working his unrelated fifth Op, walking four blocks away. He heard the *boom.*

Merle said: "Why did you sigh? What's wrong? What's—"

He lied. He told the truth.

"I always wanted to kiss a girl in a taxi."

Merle shook her head. "Where were you going with that taxi kiss?"

"Where it would be better than this," he said.

They rode in the back seat, stared out their own windows.

"Up ahead," said Condor. "There's a small park between the Capitol Dome and Union Station. Let us out there."

Condor dropped two $20 bills on the front seat. Slammed the door on the driver's *thank you*'s. Led Merle onto turf where seventeen months before, along with Faye, they watched California-blond Senate staff lawyer Chris Harvie catch a bullet in the head because of knowing them. Condor scanned *business suits*: men and women quick-walking through the shortcut of the park. Some there for *position*, some for *policy*, some for *profit*, some for *power*, and all of them who worked for the taxpayers—and perhaps even the Wall Street and labor union lobbyists—all their shoulders carried slivers of some American dream. But none of them knew Chris Harvie's name, or if they did, he was just another tragic street shooting, not a KIA from a spy war.

Condor led Merle through the half-square block park.

Turned this way. Turned that. Walked a slow circle as if in gung fu's *bagua*.

"She's not here," he whispered. "They're not here. No cover team. No exfilt team."

He and Merle stood still in an unseeing crowd on Thursday morning a rifle shot away from the white icing dome of the US Capitol.

An anonymous car pulled to the curb across the park from where they stood.

Out of the front passenger door climbed a man with a black cane.

"Run!" yelled Condor. He wanted to rocket Merle safe. Wanted to wave his hands *Help police!* Wanted to draw a .45 and blast killers who only he in the crowd recognized.

The anonymous car was to their left, driving to the curb where they were headed.

"We gotta make it across the street!" said Condor. "Get to Union Station!"

The anonymous car slammed to a halt in the traffic lane in front of them.

Condor glimpsed the driver—a stout bald man with giant bushy eyebrows.

HONK!—a city bus controlled its angry surge at the anonymous car's rear bumper.

Condor ran Merle behind the bus, waved and begged *crazy old man jaywalking*. The bus screened them from the park, honked again as they ran toward the gray stone castle of Union Station. From behind them came the hiss of brakes *released*, the *grrr* of a bus engine.

Condor's legs hurt. His lower back hurt. His chest heaved and his lungs burned.

Don't let my sore heart be my killer!

He kept his right hand free, wrapped his left arm around Merle. Staggered them past the subway entrance where there would be no escape if a train didn't come at exactly the right second. Hustled them into Union Station, to a corridor toward the train yard tracks.

Saw no white shirted, blue uniformed Amtrak employees

Slammed into a door's EMERGENCY ONLY push handle.

He pulled Merle through the door after him.

No one on the tracks. Rows of parked—and empty—passenger trains.

He grabbed her hand, hurried them around the front end of a silver dragon Amtrak passenger train. Around a second such train's rear car.

A gliding bird watched a man and woman flee over gray stones between empty trains.

Ahead, *far ahead*, Condor saw the curved roof and brick walls of a tube building for shared work spaces, cubicles full of dreamers, quants, drones, and desperation housed in a renovated sports coliseum where back in the Cold War's *Apocalypse Any Second* era, The Beatles played their first ever American concert to screaming fans.

Merle gasped as they'd staggered alongside an empty passenger train. "You . . . you've run us into a funnel! We're trapped!"

The round yellow light atop a dormant signal arm five feet to Condor's left *exploded*.

Came a male voice from behind Condor: "If I want to shoot you now . . . *dead*."

Condor held his hands out from his sides.

Turned to face that voice.

Black Cane Man strode toward them, a silencer-equipped automatic pistol pointed at them from his right hand, the black cane carried like it was nothing in his left.

"One shot for the sniper cane, *yes*? But we have much more than one shot now."

Black Cane Man stopped out lunging range.

Condor doubted he still had any such fight left in him.

"This could be quick. Professional. She could even be let to run away. After all, she's already officially crazy and no one believes her.

"Our mutual friend," said Black Cane Man.

"Not professional enough," said Condor. "Not good at *mokroye delo*."

Black Cane Man didn't flinch at "*wet work*" and thus validated Condor's guess.

"Dead?" Black Cane Man shrugged. "He was a good buy. Full of stories about the crazy old woman who still looked like a good fuck and how him and others like him came every day to take care of her while the strange man of the house, a man who even though he's *so old*, still he trolls Internet for the CIA like a commanding *Surfer Joe* who they'll miss *big time*."

"I'm not CIA," said Condor.

"So, *what then*? Tell me. Mercy doesn't come cheap. NSA out of Fort Meade? That's where our friend was stationed."

Condor shook his head *no*.

"The Pentagon? Homeland Security? FBI? Surely not the State Department."

The pistol staring at Condor shifted its gaze toward trembling Merle.

"Your value is an already established trigger squeeze. But her, the woman you take away from your work to care for, the woman you stare at with moon eyes when she's not looking—or not see-ing—she is optional. Our optional. My optional. You must—"

A red mist flowered the gunman's head.

He crashed to the ground.

Red-haired Faye walked toward them. Her *no ring* left hand dangled a pistol.

"I knew he was tracking your cell phones," said Faye. "Like us. Like we did to him, once NSA tech broke the USB stick's coding and back-hacked it."

An approaching engine hummed behind Condor: a motorized Amtrak golf cart raced their way filled with men wearing hard hats and fluorescent yellow official vests, looked back to Faye and her face told them that faux work crew belonged to the V.

"We didn't have much time to set up," said Faye. "Lucky I live on the Hill."

"Lucky you're great solo," said Condor.

Merle shook her head: "How . . . here . . . how . . ."

Faye fought her still-pounding pulse to send a reassuring smile to the older woman.

"First mentioned '*ground*' rendezvous is the O.Z., the Obser-vation Zone. Second set is the real destination. Commo'd in descriptors only a few know, like '*downbound*' from the song 'Downbound Train' meaning roughly here."

"Shit," whispered Merle.

Faye looked at the body on the gray cinders. "Wish we could have taken him alive."

"It's the Russians," said Condor.

"Again?" said Faye.

Condor shook his head: "Still."

Looked at the train yard world under Washington, DC's gray sky.

Said: "*Why?*"

CHAMBER TWO
A Walk in the Sun

FBI Special Assistant to the Associate Assistant Director for Counter-Intelligence Rick Applegate sat behind his desk in Washington, DC's J. Edgar Hoover headquarters at 10:07 on that Thursday, May 5, 2016, morning reading a *no wireless connection* computer tablet display of an inter-agency report on China's Ministry of State Security's penetrations of a five billion dollar international corporation when his outer office aide Hargesheimer yelled: "*Oh, shit!*

"No!" blurted Hargesheimer. "Sorry, Sir, I . . ."

"That's alright, son," said a man's deep voice Rick *maybe* recognized. "Understandable reaction. Tell your boss the Marines have landed."

Rick reached the outer office in two heartbeats.

There stood Marine Corps Major General David Wood, six-foot-three of packed muscle with two stars on the shoulders of his uniform, which held half the medals he deserved.

"Hey, Rick," said the unexpected Marine. "Good to see you again."

"You, too, Sir."

They'd talked a few times five months before at a joint Marines-FBI Task Force on securing Corps bases against mass shooters and/or domestic-based terrorist attacks. Plus, after

Rick's promotion to Headquarters, they'd nodded at a couple formal receptions, Washington *show up because* affairs that Rick—and he was pretty sure the General—hated.

"'One of *those* days," said General Wood. "Left the Barracks up on 8th, headed west for a stop on the Hill where everybody loves the uniform and nobody likes to listen to what it's got to say, rolled down here for a quick check in Upstairs with *you know who* to let him know his rear is covered on this and that, figured: *Why not pop in and see one of my favorite Marines?*"

"I'm honored," said former First Lieutenant, USMC, Rick Applegate.

"Let me get you to throw a little help," said the General.

"Whatever I can," said Rick.

The General angled his head to Rick as Hargeshemeir watched and listened. "My plumbing says I'm not the young man you are. I'm wondering if you can escort me to the nearest men's room so I won't be fidgety when I go Upstairs. We got time."

"Ah . . . sure, Sir. It's just down the hall. Let me grab my suitcoat—"

"You're fine as you are, son. I only want to take your time that's absolutely necessary."

The General nodded to Hargesheimer, led Rick out of his office and into the hall.

Ridiculous to feel like I need my gun, thought Rick who unclipped it from his belt and locked it in his DC desk after he arrived at headquarters every regular morning.

The General—and Rick couldn't even imagine this verb until they were almost there—*prattled* on and on about many things Washington mixed with everything Grampa mixed with some things Corps, non-stop talking as he pushed open the men's room door . . .

. . . still loudly prattling the everything of nothing in this tiled echo chamber as he marched past the three silver metal commode stalls, pushing open their doors to reveal *empty*.

General Wood gestured to three side-by-side urinals. "You could use this step-up, too."

The General claimed the middle urinal.

His upper body was visible above the aluminum privacy divide.

Rick heard the General unzip even as that Marine nodded the order for Rick to claim the urinal beside him. The General kept tapping his chest above his heart while glaring at Rick's.

Blink, and Rick tapped his blue shirt's pocket that held a cellphone.

Still talking—something about the good old days of Ronald Reagan when cops with machineguns didn't patrol the streets outside Congressional office buildings—General Wood nodded, both an affirmation and an appreciation that Rick *got it*.

"Sorry, son. It's probably gonna take a bit for me to get things going."

Then at Rick's eye level on the tiled wall they faced beyond their urinals, General Wood's hand slapped and held there a white piece of paper with hand-inked black letters:

No notes. No records. ORCON. No report to any Bureau
boss including Director and Attrny. Gen. No e-entries
any kind. No verbal anything. Stay shut the fuck up.
White House level T. Secret. Tomorrow. 2:33 p.m.
Meet unknown to you Old Man. Bring NO CELL PHONE or
electronics. At top Lincoln Memorial. Deep cover. Fullest
authority. My full vouch personal & Corps. He'll say:
"Have you been to the Wall?" Recognition code
response you: "Trying to stay off there." GO SOLO.
Tell nobody nothing forever!

The General kept talking about nothing *relevant*—baseball, a Congressman caught pawing female staffers, why classic boxing was more aesthetic than modern mixed martial arts.

Rick burned the note into his memory.

"ORCON"—*Originator Controlled.* "Tell nobody nothing forever!" FBI speak *plus* punch you in the balls *do-or-die* Drill Instructor fury.

Wasn't the lemon-scented antiseptic air conditioning that chilled Rick to his bones.

He nodded to the General.

Who crumpled the note in his hand.

The sound of General Wood peeing echoed through this tiled bathroom.

Prompted Rick to need to and do the same.

All the while over the sounds of water trickling onto white porcelain, the General kept talking. Kept talking as he flushed his urinal. Filled their there and then with audible verification.

Rick finished and zipped, flushed.

The prattling General stepped into a stall, dropped the crumpled note in the toilet bowl's water, proclaimed: "Don't you hate it when other people don't flush?"

Then he practiced what he'd preached.

The stall's toilet whooshed and gurgled, whined to silent.

The water in the bowl held nothing but vanishing trembles.

"Persistent little turd," said General Wood and flushed that toilet again.

Told Rick: "Let's wash up and get the Hell out of here. We each got big shit to do."

Side-by-side at the sinks, General Wood said: "How's your family, wife, and three kids?"

Electricity tightened Rick as he washed his hands.

No reason the General would know shit about Bess and their kids.

"All fine . . . *Sir*," Rick said to the *he bleeds, too* mere mortal man standing beside him.

Met the General's stare in the bathroom mirror with his own eyes of steel.

They were done talking.

Until in the hall outside the bathroom, the General reached out his hand Rick didn't hesitate to shake as the General said: "I'm proud of you, son. All great luck. And *Semper fi.*"

Rick got home at 6:52 that night—not late, not early. Such scheduled definitions were more common since he'd left his Special Agent in Charge post at an Ohio field office and joined *the Hoover.* He unlocked the front door to his suburban Virginia family home, walked to his chattering family in the open kitchen.

Didn't take off his gun.

Bess sat on a stool at the open kitchen's counter, her laptop screen showing the photo of a black bird—*a crow,* she'd corrected him: *"You've got to learn the true names of the birds"* then shook her thick, shoulder-trimmed midnight hair in mock shock that most married couples would recognize. The crow photo—a black bird spreading his wings to take off, his beak open to caw—was one of nine of her photos picked for a gallery's "Emerging Artists" show in three weeks.

She started emerging since long before I knew her, thought Rick. He smiled at a memory from their wedding—a man who'd known her and her siblings in college, *"the fabulous Wong sisters."* Rick felt proud that Bess was finally getting the world to see the full glory of her.

Seeing the glory of their teenage daughter Thel scared the hell out of Rick. She was smarter than everyone else in the family, a poet, a long and lean cross-country racer who let her glistening black hair ripple behind her as she ran not for medals that she won, but *because.*

Rick loved her with limitless pride and joy.

Shook with the anger and terror of knowing how the world could—*might*—treat her.

"Don't worry, Dad," Thel'd told him one day out of the blue as if she read his mind. "I'll run hard and make it all rhyme even if I can't make it all make sense."

Eleven-year-old Bo sat at the kitchen table with his second-grade brother Nate, telling him how it was time to set Pokemon aside and concentrate on the Marvel Superheroes universe—and history, *of course*, added Bo when he saw *Dad's home.*

They all saw it in him.

Bess spotted it first and he felt her heart settle its dread deep in her *dantian*, but Rick couldn't tell if Thel read the vibe of Mom or the coil of Dad that told her *oh-oh, step up strong*. Everyone saw Bo send his kid brother Nate the *It's gonna be OK* smile.

They sat around the kitchen table and ate dinner, fresh rainbow trout marinated in raspberry vinegar and green beans that had never tasted so good and so useless. Rick felt himself falling away from the kitchen's perfect yellow glow illuminating everything he had to lose.

The kids went to their bedrooms early without quarrel or complaint. All of them hugged Dad *goodnight*. None of them mentioned how long they all held on.

Bess waited until their bedroom door was closed.

Until he'd closed his bedside table drawer on his stashed gun.

Waited until they brushed their teeth with mint toothpaste and wore what they slept in and lay in their bed held by the darkness that still let them discern each other's shape in the glow streaming through their second-floor windows from stars, from whatever moon was out there, from the house lights of neighbors who never knew.

Bess lay her head on the bones caging his heart.

"This promotion meant you were supposed to be done with things like . . . *whatever*."

"I am," he told her.

"Can you tell me why it doesn't feel that way to me or the kids?"

"No."

"You're not in the field now. You're a top boss. The buck stops with you, not bullets."

"This isn't—might not be like that at all. Not about bullets. That you can see."

The woman he loved whispered in the dark: "All I care about seeing is you."

"And our kids. And the world we make them live in. And everybody else's kids."

Bess tried to smile as she said: "Why did I have to fall in love with a good man?"

"If I am, you made me that way."

Bess curled on top of him, her leg slid up over both of his as she folded herself into the straddling, her loins pressing down on his. He cupped her face in bedroom darkness that cloaked her brown eyes from his yearning even as he felt glistenings on the soft warm of her cheeks.

Gray clouds threatening rain and chilly air made the next morning, but Rick decided not wearing a topcoat was a more justifiable risk than putting another layer of clothing over his weapon's access. He chose not to wear his ballistic vest—that would cause questions and any question increased risk. The news in his cell phone told him about President Obama getting an outpouring of emotion when he visited Flint, Michigan, and drank the local water that had been poisoning the town's children with lead for years because of corruption. Headlines screamed *Hillary Clinton Email Probe* and *Trump Takes GOP's Reins.*

"Long lunch," Rick told Hargesheimer when he left the office at high noon. Left his personal and Bureau cellphones locked in his desk drawer, the former an isolation of his heart, the latter a direct and actionable violation of Procedure.

Rick left his issued BuCar parked in Hoover's underground garage.

Walked the city blocks around FBI headquarters that when Nixon was President, held burlesque houses and strip bars starring legends like Tempest Storm, and that like the porno movie theater then two blocks from the White House, laundered cash to the Mafia.

Brick agent savvy shaped his steps. Even in his dread of this day he felt the *welcome back* surge of that knowing, this doing, a tingle of schooled savagery he knew most Americans never owned and with good luck would never need.

By 12:44 he'd zig-zagged through streets of lawyers and lobbyists, chroniclers and cops of badges or bureaucracies. Walked amidst convincers and crusaders and *come along for the ride* women and men wearing suits of power for charming and coddling, channeling and challenging this city's marbleized air. He reached Metro Center in its canyon of flat faced office buildings regulated to be shorter than the towering white stone obelisk of the Washington Monument. If some cover team was on him, they were far better than any he'd run or run from.

He joined a line at a food truck that sold him *energy for* as a meat 'n' tomatoes sandwich, tasted nothing and washed it down with a bottle of water. If he'd been *naked deep cover*, he'd have gone to a museum with metal detector security screenings that had public bathrooms for him to use, benches for him to sit on while he pretended to study the art on the walls instead of seeking any art stalking him in those halls, but *yeah*, he had an iron on his hip.

That's why God and Seattle gave us coffee shops, he told himself. As long as he bought, he could sit with what he got and rest through the tick-tock to *when*.

Rick flagged down a blue taxi at 1:49. Had the black driver who was old enough to be his father drop him on *the big money's* K Street, walked two blocks, flagged down a cab that took him to the Mall—the once-open turf of visual freedom now getting choked by pressure groups' deserving monuments stretching through the city from the white icing Capitol Dome, past the long Reflecting Pool to the wise, sad eyes of Abraham Lincoln's marble statue.

Rick gauged how long it would take him to walk from where he stood in the trees by the Korean War Memorial's larger than life stone statues of grim-faced American soldiers on patrol, get to the Lincoln Memorial's steps, climb them to where a black opera singer denied the venue of the lily white Daughters of the American Revolution once stood and sang free for everyone.

Semper fi haunted Rick. *Fidelity Bravery Integrity*. Honor. Duty. The rule of law. The way things should be. The way they are. Oaths he swore. Promises made. Proper Procedures. What was right. What was wrong. What to do with what came along.

He marched out of the trees, along the Reflecting Pool, up the levels of white marble stairs to the entryway columns of the open front stone cavern honoring a man who gave his life for freedom, justice and country only to get gunned down in an ambush.

Rick unbuttoned his suitcoat as he climbed those steps.

Was a slow day for tourists. Rick estimated the Monument hosted maybe a hundred visitors. A group of senior citizens nervously staring at the heart-pounding stairs they'd have to climb to say *been there, seen that*. Two handfuls of middle-aged family and friends—one speaking Japanese, one with men wearing Kansas City Chiefs jackets.

As Rick reached the second long and wide flat stone landing before the final set of stairs, giggling elementary school children dashed up the stone steps. St. Paul, Minnesota, senior class trippers slouched and swaggered and *OMG*-d as like teenagers everywhere, they ignored a tag-wearing woman while that obvious chaperone gazed upon history. Her hair the color of the raspberries in the vinegar from his dinner last night caught Rick's eyes, but he had more important things to see.

At 2:29, four minutes from contact, Rick was fourteen steps from where Abe Lincoln loomed and the three walls boxing him in were carved with his words about truth, justice, patriotism, compassion. A dozen paces to Rick's right on a marble step stood a bald man scanning the Mall with binoculars, seemingly oblivious to what Rick thought when he saw that squat man's face with a new stubble mustache and shaved off eyebrows.

Rick crossed the threshold and entered the cavernous gray stone chamber.

Figure thirty, thirty-five people wandering around in here. Multiple *possible*'s. Multiple innocent collateral casualties, far more than that New Jersey night when he soft clothes sat at the bar waiting for some connected moke named Seba who claimed he was ready to flip so he could dodge his clip. Rick's partner that night—Harry Gossett, good Bureau—sat with a stevedore's beer in his hands as his corner chair leaned against the wall and his eyes scanned everything.

You've got no backup now, Rick told himself as he scanned this Op Zone.

Where are the Harry Gossett's of the world when you need them?

Oh yeah, that's who I'm supposed to be.

Am, motherfucker.

And like that . . . *there he was.*

Has to be him, thought Rick. *Half a dozen "unknown to you Old Man" possible's, but this guy, this silver-haired citizen has the edge, plus he's walking toward me soft pad like a mountain lion. The paws I've got to watch are his hands stuck "innocently" where I can't see them in the side pockets of his faded black leather bomber jacket.*

That silver-haired man smiled.

Stood just out of striking range. Nodded to Rick. Turned like a tourist to stare out of Memorial at the long Reflecting Pool. The Washington Monument's hard and rising obelisk. The horizon glisten off the Capitol's white dome. Flapping American flags.

The silver-haired man said: "Hell of a sight, huh?"

Not the recognition code!

Rick just said: "Yeah."

"I wasn't supposed to be here today," said the silver-haired *still could be.* He turned from what world waited outside and put his blue eyes on Rick's face. "How about you?"

Rick shrugged. Saw nobody else who might be the contact. Saw nobody paying them any mind. Nobody standing in earshot.

"Odd how free will compels us through the circumstances we can't choose," said the old *maybe innocent and just lonely* guy. "Life's such a mixture of *gotta* and *oughta* and *wanna.*"

"'Least it is here," said Rick: *Break contact or let it ride?*

"Ah, *here.*" The old man smiled. Turned to face the outer world. "Like *here* is so real."

"It's what we've got."

"Unless what we've got is a multiverse."

"You sound like one of my sons."

"Which one—Bo or Nathan?"

Don't shoot don't grab him don't jam your pistol under his jaw until he talks just DON'T!

Don't let the motherfucker even *think* he's got you rattled.

Let him come out to play.

"Our *here* could be one of infinity's jokes," said the old man. "Scientists who took us to the moon talk about how our *real* might just be one version. That perhaps hundreds more versions of *all this* exist in a swirl of dimensions, a multiverse where each verse is different. Timelines and what happened become different versions of themselves. Many of the same people and things *here* are *there* and *there* and *there*, too. What you 'know' is real, but what if there are different versions of real that are equally true?"

The silver-haired Unknown Hostile smiled: "Your boys would say that's how and why we have superheroes."

Give him *nothing.*

"Then, of course," said the old man, "a butterfly you never see flaps its wings and all your everything changes. Your scene starts with the same elements then . . ."

Hands! He's pulling his hands out of black leather jacket pocket . . . empty.

"... the butterfly routinely flaps its wings and everything from then on changes."

The silver-haired man watched his right hand float up to eye level between them.

"Maybe it's not the butterfly's fault. Maybe 'fault' isn't the right word. That's both an intent and an outcome-based word. And maybe it's not the butterfly. Maybe you're the butterfly. Something insignificant that you do. Maybe choose to do. Free will and all that."

The old man fixated on his brown dotted, pale-skinned right hand as it slowly turned this way and that, like it had a life and will of its own.

"Maybe you do one small thing with your hand one Thursday morning, and that ripples out through everything and every second thereafter."

"So where are we now?" said Rick. *Open the door, let him walk in to you.*

"How the fuck should I know," said the old man. "Have you been to the Wall?"

Make the beat between long. Let him know not to fuck with you like that.

"I try to stay off of there," said Rick.

The old man said: "Let's take a walk in the sun."

"Mind your step," he added as they marched outside to the glow.

They walked side by side in a scattered crowd. Grade schoolers. High schoolers. Tourists with cellphone cameras. No one walked close enough to hear their low spoken words.

"Who are you?" said Rick.

"You want a name?" said the old man whose rock 'n' rolled ears seemed to work just fine.

"A name is nothing. I want your number."

"I've spent a lifetime resisting being a number."

"Are you from over the river and through the woods?" *Langley. CIA.*

"I'm the V," said the old guy. "Or the V is me. Or both. And now you."

"What the hell is the V?"

"*Virtual.* Not what you see around us. We exist and operate in and from the Internet. Online. No there *there.* There is no *us.* We're not trolls or cyberwarfare sharks, we're swimmers who use the data seas to run Ops with nobody noticing.

"No payrolls or offices other than where you have your screens—though sometimes that can become what it was never supposed to be, a place you always need to work out of, and that place can become an acquired target of whatever oppo' buys a mistaken glimpse.

"Picture it this way: When what we do requires a plane to take X from Y to Z, zapping through some military group or even a private airline comes an order in their own data flood. If you're a V chasing a bad guy in Phoenix and need some unwitting help, the Marshall's Service scrambles, experts at the manhunting job they don't know started and ends outside their chain of command. Need an extract of a C.O.—*Conscious Operative*—need to get him and what he's done home, and a nearby otherwise deployed Special Ops team in Niger hits the silk.

"There's not many C.O.'s. Mostly the V are Actors—components of the V who work for other power centers, who feed the V and when necessary, give hands-on support. And it's all kept humming by a hive of Handlers."

"With you as the Queen Bee."

"I'm Control Function, yeah. Conceptualized the program, too. Way back when."

Rick shook his head *NO*: "This is now and I've never bought the whole '*super-secret intelligence apparatus, deep cover command, phantom agents*' bullshit."

"America's almost always had *secret phantom spy* groups. In Vietnam, we had MACV-SOG. The Phoenix Program. Then phantoms emerged from 'Nam, like the Intelligence Support Activity that now has a garrison at Fort Belvoir. Or Blue Light, the 1970s *nobody saw it out there* 'anti-terrorism' Special Forces group that became Delta Force. Or Task Force 157 that ran from 1966 until a black ops crook blew its cover in 1977. And of course, we had the Plumbers back in Watergate."

"Oh, *please*: don't give that '*deep state*' bullshit that's just started up again," said Rick.

"I'd laugh," said Condor, "but the joke is on us. That '*everything happens for a human planned and controlled reason*,' is narcissistic, conceited, self-flattering bullshit. The closest thing America's got to a 'deep state' is Washington's crowd of 30,000 lawyers and 12,000 lobbyists and big political donors who pay to play and whoever's out there kicking back at them, plus the hordes of *got-a-cause* crusaders."

"And you say you're legit," said Rick.

His silver-haired companion said: "Do you think *the General* would serve anything that wasn't known by him to be righteous?"

"Hell of a voucher," agreed Rick.

"Just for you. He was the best Actor to get you."

"You mean recruit me."

"This is the twenty-first century. Don't think *recruit*—think *link*. The ultimate way to overcome bureaucratic walls and tunnel vision bullshit and to be invisible to everyone."

"Not enough for me," said Rick. "Beyond verification I confirm, I need to know, to have, something about you *from* you. Like what to call you."

The silver-haired man stopped.

So did Rick on that step, meeting that hard blue-eyed gaze as the stranger said:

"Call me Condor."

They turned together to walk down toward the next white stone level. Rick remembered: *"You've got to learn the true names of the birds."* Took no notice of bald binocular man walking ahead of them and off to the left like he was a leaf blown by their wind.

Condor told the decades-younger man beside him: "The V needs you. To be an Actor."

"Why me?" said Rick.

"Rising star for Bureau counter-intelligence. Former SAC in the heartland. Brick agent. Worked O.C. when *The Godfather's* mob became just one of the killer packs in our streets and corporate suites. *Semper fi* with a combat Silver Star. Guts. Savvy, smart, schooled. Not some data cruncher or legal eagle or bean counter: a philosophy M.A. that muscles you up so you can visualize beyond data plus all its *how's* and *why's* and *oh-oh's*."

They reached the sidewalk in front of the steps leading back to where they'd been. Rick let his companion casually drift to the left so they headed toward the Wall, just like most tourists. The raspberry-headed chaperone drifted behind them.

Condor said: "It's the Russians."

"I've been working the Chinese."

"They're out there, too, but their game is long and they're already sure they're going to win. Absorb us like a billion grains of sands on the global beach, each of them different as they let us sink into them. Classic soft style *gung fu*: yield, turn, *dah*.

"The Russians are more hard style Western history minded, overwhelming force, punch you in the face or stab you in the back, gut you with a smile.

"Threw their first getting *to know how* e-punches back in 2007. Hit the former Soviet Union satellite, now *wants to be free from Mother Russia* country of Estonia with cyber hacks and attacks. Hit their Parliament, media, banks, Internet providers.

"Iran cyber attacked us in 2011, the Russians leveled up in June, 2014. The 'Trolls From Ogino.' *Kremlebots*. Officially the Internet Research Agency. Your FBI missed it a'coming, but *kremlebots* and their parallel cadres keep getting bigger and 'better' and nastier.

"*Dezinformatsiya*—disinformation. Call it *deza*—actual fake news. Not *'Go Russia!'* propaganda, but flooding Americans' consciousness with lies credited to a fake source so all sounds plausible. Or even just *'people are saying'* or *'everyone knows'* or *'there's just no question that.'* Half-lies and twists, omitted or nonfacts. Escalated that data flooding with hacks that co-opted our own First Amendment with disclosures designed not to reveal truths but to smear it into *deza*.

"All of it's part of the biggest ever in history use of classic Russian *aktivniye meropriyatiya*—Active Measures. Don't outright oppose or attack your enemy: make them fall apart by disrupting them internally. Generate distrust. Anger. Blind and thus stupid rage. Capitalize on and compound cynicism or bigotry and ignorance that's already there. Get your enemy fighting amongst themselves, citizen vs. citizen. *'Oh, yeah?'* vs *'Un-unh.'* Pour hate and fear like gas amidst your enemies and let them light the matches."

Rick shook his head *NO*: "Like you said, this is 'in history.' *Active Measures* have been around a long time under other names. Hell, Condor: we did them in Vietnam and Chile and other places when you were probably just starting out at whatever spy game you say you run. Britain had a whole covert influence campaign run out of some building in New York to get America to come in to World War II on their side—we would have anyway, *but.*"

"*But,*" said Condor. "That was then and this is now, where *but* creates an overwhelming new universe because of the Internet. Everybody's connected. Everybody's reachable. Everybody's a *but* and it's all online, all the time. Facebook and all the social media. Websites pop up in your e-mail from a name you don't really know—and then you forward or pass on that connection to real people who you do know, so your credibility sells their lies.

"The Russians have troll farms the size of Detroit factories with armies of keyboarding techs flooding US social media sites and cyber streets with *provokatsiya*—provocation. They're doing Madison Avenue proud.

"Hell, the supposedly best minds and best paid bodies of *us* have been selling lies and scams and shams for dollars to *regular Americans* ever since the first newspaper full of ads rolled off the presses and the first county fair carnival barker stepped on stage. Now it's hard to tell the sales pitches from programming we haven't turned off since the first radio clicked on.

"You can't go into a gas station or convenience store in America without hearing the drone of some TV *all talk all the time* and *of course*, that's all *true*. You can't go to the grocery store without seeing newspaper tabloid headlines with absurd OMG reports and celebrity gossip. Now those *'I Married A Gill Man'* tabloids sell a political twist from whoever the publisher is.

"The Nazis' Joseph Goebbels back in World War II called it *'The Big Lie.'* If you shout it loud enough and long enough and everywhere all the time, even if people don't believe the details, the roar numbs their brains and shapes what else they hear and see. All that *plus* dumbed-down education designed only to get kids a drone job *plus* our obsession with mirrors *plus* celebrity worship turned Americans into the *perfect* target to get hit with Active Measures via the Internet that defines the multiverse version we call *the way things are.*"

"*So what?*" said Rick as they drifted closer to the start of the cobblestone walkway that sloped in front of the Wall, that black mirror that honors 58,318 killed in the Vietnam War, Americans as names, not statistics, a memorial that initially officially horrified and outraged flag-waving conservatives. "Why have you dragged me out here on a sunny day? Put me on a line where everything I've pledge my life to is in jeopardy because this walk is some *do or die* secret? Hit me with some 'recruiting pitch' that's a classic counter-intelligence red flag?"

Neither man looked behind them.

Condor stopped in front of a black mirror wall panel.

Faced his own reflection amidst line after line after line of names who never got to be as old as he was that sunny afternoon.

The old man trailed his fingers over a name carved in black mirror stone.

Whispered: "Hey, Mike."

Walked on.

Waited until they were off the path and away from the Wall to answer Rick.

"The Russians leveled up the black e-ops they've been doing, then leveled up again and again. They think for Russia and its billionaires to rise, America and our middle class have to crash or fall apart, become jokes, suckers, and slaves to some new multiverse. They're attacking our democracy at a level and with power this multiverse has never seen. They aren't *primarily targeting* the government. They get that in America, government is at least nominally *of* the people and *by* the people. So that's who the Russians are really attacking now: the people, Americans as free individuals, *us*.

"Even your Bureau knows that," Condor told Rick as the drifted through the trees alongside the Mall. "The Russian Active Measures, the *deza*, the Facebook and Internet campaigns: At first they worked willy-nilly, whatever chaos they could cause. They backed whatever home-grown disruptions and disrupters were doing, didn't matter if the politics were Left or Right, whacko or *Me Me Me*.

"This February, your colleagues in the Justice Department found out that Russian spy executives ordered their trolls on social media to '*use any opportunity to criticize Hillary and the rest except Sanders and Trump*'. The Russians support those two because they're the biggest disrupters out there in American politics, no matter what they believe or push. The trolls hacked the Democrats and the Republicans. They created fake *deza*

Twitter accounts like @TEN_GOP that has 100,000 duped fol-
lowers, attacked guys like John McCain. They ran online ads like:
*'You know, a great number of black people support us saying that
#HillaryClintonIsNotMyPresident'* and *'#Hillary4Prison.'* Doesn't
matter that she's got her own real problems and what looks like
a hollow high school campaign approach to politics. The trolls'
chaos multiplies errors and drives everybody crazy, suspicious,
pissed off so they walk away from being good, conscientious, sort
of free citizens."

Condor shook his head: "All that puts the FBI and our whole
government in a *lose-lose* gunfight. By law and by conscience,
they can't come in and fuck with an election, come down or
appear to come down attacking one partisan side or supporting
the other—even though as they keep digging to fight crime and
find truth, besides the biggest threat Russians, they're gonna also
find a couple Arab Oil Empires and drug cartels' attacks and big
dollars.

"Plus," he said.

"Plus what?"

"Plus too many people believe that stupid cliché that *'My
enemy's enemy is my friend.'* No: your enemy's enemy is who *he*
is and he's out for himself. We keep forgetting that. Some people
in politics reach out to get any help they can, the hell with what
it costs or who it comes from, winning is everything. Winning
is where and when all the goodies flow. And corrupt people are
easy to corrupt further and fool.

"So there are a lot of lines that have been crossed that might
equal collusion and corruption, maybe even treason—if you
guys chase and get the evidence."

FBI Special Agent Rick frowned: "If the people who benefit-
ted the most from Russia's Active Measures, who maybe crossed
the lines into corruption—where some of them already were, I
know things about *both* of the big teams—if what happens is *bol-
stered by foreign spies* bad guys take charge of our government,

no matter how moral they want to be, self-preservation is the first rule of Jungleland. That means being in the Bureau, carrying any badge or wearing any sworn-to-protect-America uniform, anybody trying to follow the law and the evidence under the command of and with their new legally sworn in bosses . . . All that could get real sticky."

"Y'a think?" Condor shook his head. "Let's just hope that the sticky is sweat and tears, no blood."

Paused, said: "No more blood."

Told Rick: "But they will come after you. After the crime hunters in the Bureau."

"Who *they?*" said the FBI Agent.

"Yeah," said Condor.

They walked on without answers.

Condor told Rick: "That's why we need you as an *aware* Actor in place. Not only do you have to fight against all that we can't see now, you have to keep the system working strong so whatever *fight other bad guys* Ops the V needs to do won't get blocked by the Russians."

"If I had more about what the Russians have going on, I'd be more likely to believe you."

Condor turned to face Rick—

—and probably scan to be sure no one is close behind me, thought Rick.

"There's a secret FBI Op about that now, a human target chase. Nobody at your level knows about it. Hell, because of what we've been talking about, the Bureau's keeping this secret from damn near everybody."

Rick said: "Except you."

"Well," said Condor, "we are the V."

And suddenly Rick knew that was true. Knew he'd stepped over some line.

Condor said: "The codename for your Bureau's Op is *Crossfire Hurricane.*"

"What?"

"*Crossfire Hurricane*," said Condor. "That's a lyric from a song by the Rolling Stones."

"You are fucking shitting me! The FBI—my Bureau, *fucking J. Edgar Hoover's FBI,* adopting a codename from the fucking Rolling Stones!"

Condor smiled: "There isn't a fiction author out there who could make that up."

Rick shook his head.

"Plus there's a dossier," said Condor. "Ex-spies. Brits. Our guys."

"So I've heard," said Rick.

"I don't know what's in it," said Condor. "There may *or may not* be what we used to call *'a smoking gun'* proving Russia's Active Measures stepping over the line into an act of war. Could be proof of compromise or corruption equaling treason. But if the dossier is real, it'll be like most of *'the take'* in spy games: facts and Sherlock Holmes deductions and *maybe's* and *sources who,* all of which requires faith, a gut check, trust in what history's taught us, what we know about people's souls, know about the bloody hands and black hearts of nations."

"The election is long from over," said Rick.

"But the politics have already been re-shaped. America's been changed forever. Is still being changed, but not by the forces of democracy or truth, justice, and the American way."

Condor smiled: "Your boys and their superheroes know more about *what's what* than many 'official political experts' who get all the press and the big bucks TV contracts."

"Not enough," whispered Rick. "All that—all this is not enough."

They'd circled back. Stood between the Reflecting Pool and the levels of stairs leading up to the Lincoln Memorial. They stood in the sunshine of that Friday afternoon where anyone could see them but never really know.

"Why now? Why me? Why all this? Just *fucking* WHY?"

"Because the Russians just leveled up again and went to wet work."

FBI Special Agent Rick Applegate stared at the man he'd just met, put *street cop* in his tone: "You telling me—a sworn lawman with a badge and gun—that there've been violent criminal incidents on US soil? In FBI jurisdiction?"

"Yes. But the bad guys lost. So far. That's all you need to know—for now."

Rick shook his head and his anger came out.

"Who the hell are you—*really*?" said Rick. "What's your legal authority and chain of command? Accountability, checks and balances?"

"That's there," said Condor. "And you'll see it *when*. But it comes down to each of us in the V. To you. And that's who we *really* are: *you*.

"This is life," he said. "You need to trust. Maybe you trust what you can see, what you can touch—but where did it come from and what is it at its core? So you choose to trust yourself and ideas, beliefs that let you get through life without screaming every time your heart beats.

"This is your life. You've been asked to trust an old man who comes out of nowhere and says *this is this* but you can't touch any of that and it's not listed in any reality or any multiverse you know. It's person to person, gut to gut, even with the General vouching for it. It's the V, and now you're part of it, one way or the other."

Rick loosened his right hand to draw his gun.

Said: "What '*other*'?"

"You walk away, that's OK. Your call. The V life in this multiverse can't be lived by everyone—and that's not like a challenge of an elite team like the Marines or the Bureau. It just is. You walk away, you're the same Bureau star you are and were always going to be.

"You break ORCON, tell anybody—*anybody*—anything about any of this . . . .No one will believe you. And the V will know. And that necessitates an Op to contain and control the damage we risked here by reaching out to you."

A seagull flew overhead.

Rick flat-out told Condor: "Don't miss."

"We won't because we won't have to. You're a good man, all the way down."

"Now what?"

"Time for you to choose what's right, what's good," said Condor. "What are the costs of doing nothing and so being wrong versus the chances of taking a leap of faith to do some good?"

"The road to hell is paved with *leaps of faith to do some good*."

"And tarred by being wrong and doing nothing."

The wind swayed the trees around them.

"I've got *won'ts*," said Rick. "And that means you and your V—"

"*Our* V," said Condor.

"You've got *don'ts*. You better have. "Better know I'll be locked on those lines."

"*Do's* and *don'ts* are the nature of the game," said Condor. "You choose from what you're given and what you get. Everybody has to. You look out at the world, take a stand, pick a path."

"So what am I supposed to do if I'm an Actor in your V?"

"Your already sworn duty. Your conscience. Your savvy and true. Your job and calling for the FBI. But more. Beyond. When you can, how you can, steer the fight in the Bureau to beat the Russians and beat them hard. However that can happen."

"*Yeah*," said Rick, "and *no*."

Condor blinked.

"You wouldn't have gone to all this trouble. Brought me out here just to *link* me."

"You are *so* the right pick for this Op, for the V," said Condor.

He closed his eyes and took a deep breath of afternoon sunshine.

"We had to be seen together," he said. "A message had to be sent."

Rick's shoes to run or charge pressed white stone slabs by the rippling Reflecting Pool. He controlled his urge to whirl this way and that, looking, searching. Said: "Who?"

"You'll have his photo and file in your V activation."

They walked a half dozen steps as the breeze swayed the trees, flowed around the marble statues of the best their country could be—*had to be*. Condor heard the man beside him rise out of a deep sigh, and they both knew Rick had accepted this new universe.

And Rick said: "What's the message of me?"

"That we know. That we're connected. Geared up. That we won't back down."

They walked a half dozen steps as the breeze swayed the trees.

"We the V or—"

"They don't know that much, but we know that they don't know, and what they do know made them target the unknown. Now they know the unknown is linked to the F . . . B . . . I."

"Shadows pushing shadows."

Condor smiled: "Crazy, huh?"

CHAMBER THREE
Will You Still Please Me

Silver-haired, blue-eyed Vin held an empty white coffee mug as he stood at the kitchen sink. He looked through the window to the outside world where across the road came a stranger carrying a black cane and walking without a limp.

Satellite radio filled this house inside Washington, DC's Beltway that Thursday morning in April 2016, savvy rock songs.

Vin heard Merle in the dining room whimpering *goodbye* to the changing of the guard.

Vin looked away from the kitchen window.

Rinsed out the empty white coffee mug.

Left it in the sink.

Looked back out the window.

An unleashed chocolate brown dog loped through his neighborhood.

Black cane man was gone.

Vin filled the tea kettle. Put it on the stove's burner. *Whumped* on blue flame.

The man with the black cane didn't limp.

"Bonnie," said Vin. "Initiate perimeter check."

Three screens on the kitchen wall filled with images: Ms. Night Shift driving away. The curved tree line bordering the back yard. Real citizens' homes seen through the black pole fence and across the two-lane old highway/commuter road. The loping chocolate brown dog.

No black cane man.

Those screens scrolled: Sensors Track No Intrusion.

Vin turned his back on the open door to the dining room. Grabbed the coffee bean jar. Heard shoes hit the wooden floor. Turned. Saw Mr. Day Shift enter the kitchen.

"Hey, Justin. You doing OK?"

"Same-*same*." Justin put his black medical bag on the kitchen table. "She seems fine this morning. Moving good. More engaged. A smile. The new meds?"

"Might be."

"Speaking of new meds," said Justin, "got a new nose spray for you."

Justin's medical bag clicked.

The tea kettle on the stove rumbled with about-to-boil water.

Vin shook coffee beans into the grinder, pushed its lid down for a *scree* that drowned all other sounds until he stopped.

Heard the rumbling tea kettle generate a tentative toot.

Heard a plastic medical glove being pulled on *Snap!*

Turned to see Justin wore medical gloves. Held a white plastic, thumb pump nasal spray bottle with a still-on blue cap. He marched toward Vin. Held the capped nose spray.

"Let's do this," said Justin.

Black cane man didn't limp.

Vin threw the coffee grinder at Justin. Its cord plugged into a counter socket jerked the grinder short—flipped it over. Coffee perfumed brown powder dusted the kitchen.

Justin ducked and pulled back—

—as Vin flowed after the attacker, dead-certain he had to keep that blue cap on, stop that medicine dispenser from spraying him. He *t'l fang/fa chin* pushed through Justin's arm as the killer reached to pull off the spray bottle's blue cap.

Justin staggered backward.

Vin dove like a high school football tackler—got caught.

In a standing variation of wrestling's full nelson, Justin had leverage against Vin's trapped and tortured crucifix arms. Justin bent back Vin's arms to reach and pull off the blue cap for the nasal spray clutched in his right fingers.

Vin flashed on Frank Sinatra in the black and white movie *The Manchurian Candidate* surprise battling for his life in a New York apartment against the North Korean mole who'd infiltrated American presidential politics as part of a Communist puppet master team.

The tea kettle whistled.

The radio blasted the crashing guitars/piano/drum opening of Warren Zevon's *Lawyers, Guns and Money* from when Vin was hunting the poison pellet shooting Umbrella Assassin who murdered fiction author and anti-Soviet exile Georgi Markov in the streets of London.

Justin twisted to reach the spray's blue cap without losing his grip on the man he wanted to kill. Vin shoved with that twist and they spun through the kitchen.

Vin ducked and Justin rolled across/over/off his back, stumbling backwards—

—crashing into the *come to stop the tea kettle whistling* Merle.

Her silvered thick widow's peak hair'd never went back to blond *after*. Her thick breasts strained her bland tan blouse and her black slacks hips curved like the moon.

Merle's ass hit the floor.

Justin slammed near her on his back.

The blue capped nasal spray popped out of Justin's grip. Rolled toward the stove.

Vin tumbled over the kitchen table. Ended up tangled on the floor with a wooden chair.

Justin jackknifed onto his hands and knees. Crawled toward the stove.

Toward the blue capped nasal spray gently rocking after its roll.

Vin tried to hit Justin with the chair—missed/slammed it into the kitchen counter and knocked its weapon from his grip. He stomped a dragon kick at the crawling killer—missed.

Justin grabbed the nasal spray, staggered to his feet.

Merle leapt on his back.

Justin spun her off. Blocked Vin's punch and hooked one back at him with his nasal spray holding fist. Vin ducked as Justin reached for the blue cap.

Merle grabbed him. He threw her into the kitchen stove. The collision knocked the tea kettle half-off the burner but it kept screaming. That attack stretched Justin's spray bottle holding arm over the burner's exposed blue flames.

Justin yelled—jerked his arm away from fire, dropped the blue capped nasal spray onto the silver metal stovetop. He kicked Vin, grabbed for—

Merle *whumped* Justin in the head with a black iron frying pan.

Dropped Justin to his knees.

"Hit him again!" yelled Vin.

But she froze as Justin oozed up the front of the stove, his face above the aluminum stovetop by the blue flames so he could see as he reached for the blue cap nasal spray—

—that his fingers accidentally knocked into the blue flames.

Vin saw the white plastic *mushroom melt* POP out a mist that the blue flames exploded like a Fourth Of July pink starburst.

Fear triggered Justin's gasping inhale.

He gagged. Pushed away from the stove.

Breath-holding Vin leapt past him, dragged Merle far from the stove, his hand cupped over her nose and mouth.

From the dining room doorway, they watched Justin stagger. His face flowered blotches. Tightened into a skeletal leer. His eyes went bloodshot. *"But I got the money!"*

Justin collapsed on the floor.

The radio played.

The tea kettle whistled.

Blue flames burnt clean the pinked air.

Merle sobbed to Vin: "You said *no!* You said *no more. Never again.* Everything was . . . *no!* Now I'm a killer, too! Just like you! Just like you always do!"

Vin yelled: "Bonnie! Initiate Lockdown!"

That A.I. female voice called out: "Lockdown initiated. What alert protocol, Condor?"

"Protocol Pearl Harbor!"

Condor pulled Merle out of the kitchen, through the dining room covered with actual newspapers proclaiming the official realities of that day. *Clinton, Trump Win Big In Primaries. National Archives Hosts Screening of 'Elvis & Nixon' Documentary. Panama Papers Expose Tax Dodging & Criminal Activities Of World's Wealthy.* Merle let him hustle her up the stairs.

"We gotta get out of this place!" said Condor. "Get your Go Bag!"

Merle hurried to the bedroom as he scurried into The Office with its glass table where three giant screens faced a keyboard.

"Bonnie: Replay fast-forward perimeter scans, last seven minutes."

Scenes outside this house filled the screens . . .

. . . with nothing unusual. But no brown dog. No man with black cane.

Like the replay was a loop of some other day.

"What the fuck?"

He jerked open the closet door—

—to no *"Hy-yah!"* screaming murderous ninja.

Condor grabbed a messenger bag. Strapped his shoulder-holstered .45 automatic over his long-sleeved maroon shirt. Clipped a belt-holstered .45 on his right hip. Glanced at his Go Bag's gear: A dopp kit with toothbrush and paste. Razor. Five cycles of daily meds. Ammo mags. Three burner phones and charge cords. An envelope with $2,000 in cash. Three passports and driver's licenses. Three wallets packed with identity-back up "pocket litter" and credit cards. A packet of lilac-scented baby wipes.

He pulled on a faded black leather bomber jacket that covered his guns.

Cellphone, wallet, and keys scooped off the office's glass table, shoved into jacket pockets. He looped the messenger bag across his chest: 'made it hard to grab the shoulder-holstered .45, but the gun on his left hip was still a clear draw.

Condor found Merle in the hall. Her Go Bag hung from her shoulder.

Forget the underground emergency escape tunnel that ran from the basement's Cold War Armageddon bomb shelter to the trees behind the house and beyond the black iron fence.

Whoever flipped Justin also probably knew about the tunnel and had posted an ambush team.

But watchers outside the house might think that Justin still rocked.

Condor hurried Merle down the stairs.

"We're going to Skorzeny it," he told her, citing the World

War II German commando genius she didn't have time to Google. "Defy reality. Bluff bold. Our car's in the driveway, facing the gate to the street. Be cool. Don't run. Get in, seatbelt. We clear the gate like we're going to the grocery store and fly in the wind."

"You should have let me die last time. You're Condor. You're all about death."

"I try to rock the flipside. Come on."

They opened the *clearly-not-safe* house's shiny black front door.

Condor tried to screen Merle from snipers as they *innocently* scurried to the red Ford parked facing out in their driveway. She beat him to *buckled-up* by nine slamming heartbeats. He gunned the engine to life.

The black iron pole gates securing the driveway from the road . . .

. . . yawned open toward them.

Merle yelled: "What the Hell? You didn't use the wand to—"

Condor slammed the gearshift into DRIVE. Punched the gas.

The red Ford surged toward the slowly opening gates.

A purple van swung onto the driveway.

"No!" screamed Merle as the purple van telescoped in the red Ford's windshield.

The purple van's driver cranked his steering wheel. The van still charged ahead but now desperately angled off the collision city driveway toward the green lawn.

Six tons of machine welded steel in purple and red packages slammed past each other at a combined speed of 49 mph. The red Ford scraped along the purple van, the Ford's windows so low that all Condor could see was a grape wall grinding his car door, ripping off the side mirror. Merle's side scraped the opening steel gate.

The red Ford . . . popped free of the squeeze, clattered away on this commuter road.

Merle screamed: "You're crazy!"

"Yeah!"

Whoosh past the city bus pulling away from the curb.

"Are they following us?" said Merle.

"How the fuck should I know!"

Condor glanced toward where the driver's side mirror wasn't. Toward the side mirror on the bent-in door beside Merle where now he saw only the sidewalks flying past the car. He flicked his eyes to the rearview mirror. The colliding squeeze had knocked it asunder.

He punched the gas to shoot the red Ford through a yellow light.

Fucking bicyclist on a ten-speed, white helmet won't—

The red Ford blared its horn and the woman pedaling her way to work swayed curbside in the lane the law let her claim for herself as some asshole in a red car sped past her.

Condor picked a lane in the workday traffic.

Whirled to look at Merle—still here, still alive, still alert, still not crashed back to a *needs more meds* hollow passenger. "Grab my cellphone! Inside my jacket! Heart pocket!"

Merle leaned—jerked back by her seat belt.

"Come on!" he yelled to Merle.

She unbuckled. Reached toward the surging car's driver. Thrust her right hand inside his unzipped black leather jacket. Her fingers and palm slid across the sweat-soaked maroon shirt covering his pounding heart. He felt a tug and—

Merle slumped back in her seat, eyes widening as her hand lifted in front of her face—

—the black steel .45 automatic from Condor's shoulder holster.

"What the hell are you doing!"

She whirled to face him and the .45 whirled so it's bore—

"Point it straight up!"

A mom driving a white minivan beside them glanced left, saw *no fucking way* HELP—

—but the beat up old red car shot past her and Mom was too shaken, too *Did I have too many glasses of white wine last night after I put the kids to bed?* to catch the red car's license plate number or push the button on her Bluetooth steering wheel to call 911.

"Point it down!"

"It's going to shoot!"

"*No!* The grip safety's still on and got to be squeezed and you've got to thumb back that hammer spur. Stick it somewhere!"

Took Merle three *whomps* of her closed fist to get the Ford's jammed glove compartment to pop open. Took two punches to slam the glove compartment closed with the .45 inside.

"My phone!" yelled Condor.

Caught a green light!

This time she pulled that communication device from his jacket. "Now what?"

"Swipe to my contacts! Tap on F-Stop! Tap Facetime!"

Calling *bzzt*'s came from the cellphone Merle held as the car raced through city streets.

Condor spotted a white-on-green street corner sign. Careened a hard right onto North Capitol street going down the posted address numbers.

"Hold the phone so I can see the screen!"

Bzzt! Bz—

The black screen filled with a woman's face. Mussed rust hair. High cheekbones. Clean jaw. Wide lips. She told the image of a man in her cellphone: "We cool?"

"Hellhounds on my trail," said Condor. "You?"

"Unknown but eyes wide open. Janitors found a USB stick in your downstairs computer. Odds are, kitchen killer's move, fuck him and fucking him now. Glad to see you're gone."

Gave Condor a smile he told himself was almost like a daughter's.

He said: "Can you hear me?"

"Maybe we all can," said the redhead. "Status your partner."

Merle turned the cellphone to broadcast her face; turned it back to Condor.

The redhead said: "You need a new tea kettle."

Frowned: "What's all that noise?"

Then Merle and Condor also heard what they'd ignored: *Ding! Ding! Ding!* Merle's unfastened seat belt.

A garble of guitars and voices as who the fuck cares what song wailed out of the car radio popped on by the collision back at the gate.

Merle tried to turn the battered radio off. Couldn't. Condor sent her a *forget it* shake of his head. She fastened her seatbelt *click* and stopped the dings.

Condor told the redhead: "We're coming in!"

"Where?"

"Chris Harvie's turf. A dump and jump."

"ETA?"

"Maybe 10, maybe 15. Work for you?"

"It's what we got," she said.

Killed the Facetime connection.

Left him staring at his reflection in a rough road bouncing black screen.

Merle whispered: "Chris Harvie's dead. You . . . We . . . She loved him, Faye loved him."

Condor swerved to pass an empty school bus.

Nodded to the windshield: "There!"

North Capitol stretched straight ahead beyond the red Ford, a four-lane divided thoroughfare clogged with near bumper to bumper traffic. Way beyond those lines of crawling steel, way down on the horizon, Condor and Merle saw the dime-sized glistening curve of the white icing US Capitol Dome.

Condor told her: "Bail out as soon as I stop the car. We race across that Park, look for Faye cruising past for a fast pick up and—"

Starburst hole crackin' bustin' out of the red Ford's windshield!

The twisted vertical rear view mirror filled with a purple van *closer, surging closer.*

"The passenger!" yelled Merle who was one, too. "He's shooting us with a black stick!"

The scraped and dented purple van surged closer . . .

Ramming—van is going to ram . . .

Condor stomped on the brakes as the red Ford zoomed into a major intersection, cranked the steering wheel hard left.

Crying tires. The Ford shuddering leaning on its two right wheels. Oncoming traffic veering away from the crazy left-hand turning Ford. Merle screaming. Blaring horns.

The purple van brakes screeching as it wobbled side to side—

—its front grill and bumper punched the right rear corner of the red Ford, a collision that pushed the Ford further into its sliding-sideways left turn. Condor jammed down on the gas and the red Ford shot off North Capitol street into a DC residential neighborhood.

The van careened down North Capitol street perpendicular to where the Ford raced.

Blocks of row houses behind curbs of parked family cars flashed by the wobbling Ford.

A giant high school loomed ahead two blocks on the right.

Condor turned left.

"Where are you going?"

"I know a cemetery!"

"*No,*" she moaned. "*No.*"

Condor glanced at her face. Saw it shrinking away from fear—from all emotion.

"Stay with me!" he told the woman strapped into the speeding car beside him.

The clattering car. The wobble of broken steering. The smell of burnt rubber.

Who knows what song the radio played.

Through the cracked windshield came a vision of the road rising to a silhouette of tall trees off to the left, their limbs reaching to the blue sky. Another black pole steel fence surrounded the crest of that hill, far bigger ornate steel pole gates opened for a well-paved turn off from the city that ran under an arc of metal letters:

EVERWOOD CEMETERY

The red Ford shot under that steel arc. Past a sign on the side of the fence:

WE PROSECUTE ALL TRESPASSERS

Like that fucking matters.

But Condor braked and slowed to the posted 10 mph speed limit for the one lane road gracefully circling through a square mile of family plots, gravestones dating back to the 1800s, trumpet blowing stone angels, vases of fading flowers, white marble Madonnas with forgiving arms stretched down to lift sinners up.

A giant dump truck blocked the red Ford's path. The idling truck's cargo box angled up so its load of environmental advocates' approved natural fertilizer could slide down to where three men on the graveyard crew filled their shovels and walked through the tombstones scattering sustenance for life with success only for the grass, the planted flowers, the trees.

Vin braked the Ford, backed up in an angled turn, stopped before he hit gravestones, cranked his steering wheel left and curved a clattering but tight turn to go back—

Purple van, stopped dead, blocking the road, front bumper dangling, headlight smashed, red paint lines with dents on the door swinging open to let the front passenger flop out, stout with bushy black eyebrows and none of the paratrooper smoothness of the horseshoe bald man leaping out of the driver's side who Vin'd last—and first—seen walking with a black cane.

What he held in his right hand now puffed smoke and flashed the *pow! pow! pow!* of gunfire recognized by everyone in the cemetery who heard it: after all, this was America, 2016.

The three graveyard workers ducked and ran and scattered amidst the sheltering stones.

Bullets crashed into the grill of the red Ford. Steam hissed into the Thursday morning air. Smells of gas. A popped front tire lurched the Ford down. But the radio didn't die.

"Get out!" Condor yelled as he popped open first Merle's seatbelt, then his own. "Run and hide in the gravestones! Get out of here! They'll come after me!"

She tumble-stumbled out her door, falling scrambling running toward the dump truck.

Condor rolled out of the Ford just as a quirky bullet crashed into the car.

Airbags popped open and filled the Ford's front seat with vision-blocking white balloons.

Condor rolled up, slipped, the hip-holstered .45 filling his right hand for two quick shots, one bullet wildly missing black cane man, the other whistling past Mr. Eyebrows.

Who turned and ran back toward the *get-the-fuck-outta-here* open cemetery gate.

His partner squeezed two shots.

Zing! a bullet ricocheted off the dump truck *Zang!* bounced off the red Ford.

Condor scrambled around the front of the idling dump truck, fired at the blur he saw beyond his gunsight as it rushed bigger, closer, spitting fire and smoke and whines.

He eased down the driver's side of the dump truck—whirl this way, whirl that.

Combat spin around the back of the dump truck: nothing but gravestones as far as he could see. He Weaver stance shuffled along the dump truck's upraised box—weight on his bent shuffling forward left leg, right leg bent and out at a bracing angle, arms extended, left hand supporting his right fist full of the .45 that showed Condor the world over its black barrel.

Breathe, breathe in the air you need that smells of shit.

From the dead or at least dying red Ford still came the blare of the broken radio, Foster The People singing *". . . run, better run, faster than my bullet . . ."* from "Pumped Up Kicks," their hit song back in 2010 when Condor was still locked up in the CIA's secret insane asylum.

He whirled around the back of the truck.

Roar and a bullet zinged past his head.

His trigger squeezed from training BANG! rocked him and he spun back behind the truck knowing that he'd missed the charging closer horseshoe bald/black cane man.

BANG! Condor fired a shot into the gravestones to make his attacker think twice about leaping around the back end of the truck.

RUMBLE ROAR!

Condor whirled to see the truck's bed lift up to dump its mountain of shit sliding down toward him. He got *one*, got *two* sprinter's steps away and leapt before the avalanche of brown crashed into him, swept him forward, slid him face down in the grass.

Gasping, coughing, covered in shit brown, crawling—

Where's my gun? Where's my gun? Where's—

BANG!

Brown *call-it-earth* burst up from the grass in front of his eyes.

A man's voice behind where sprawled: "Such an easy shot you are!"

Look it straight on.

Condor slowly turned until he lay on his back, his arms propping him off the grass.

The horseshoe bald man stood five feet from Condor, smiling down at him over the barrel of an automatic pistol Condor didn't recognize, as if that fucking mattered.

"Black cane has one sniper shot," said the man who used it. He raised the pistol in his hand. "But now we have plenty more bullets. "I pulled the lever handle." Horseshoe Bald Man angled his head toward the now fully raised bed dump truck but never took his eyes off Condor. "We're pulling all your levers. But you were brave, troll man. You and your crazy woman."

Horseshoe Bald Man angled his head back toward the cemetery gate.

"Not like the big-talking but gutless *wanna be* slug they gave me for backup. Ran at your first shot—good shot by the way, not like most of you only video games trolls."

"I'm not a troll."

"Sure you are. Justin sold us that. He saw you all the time Top Secret castle *clickety-clicking* like the head troll, the boss of all your trolls out there trying to click louder than ours."

Go down fighting. Trying. Spying.

Condor said: "All this is too much for just *provokatsiya*."

Horseshoe Bald Man's lips curled down in appreciation. "You know us."

And *thus*, Condor did.

"So," said the man who would kill him: "You're not just a troll?"

Condor ignored the question: "So if not provocation . . . what, a failed attempt to take out your counterpart threat?"

"Does all this look—does it *smell* like failure?"

BANG! *Zing* of heavy bullet.

Before Condor and Horseshoe Bald Man finished flinching—

—Merle yelled: "Stop!"

Condor saw her standing there—behind and beyond the Russian, her hands wildly shaking with the Ford's glove compartment heavy .45.

The Russian stood frozen with his gun locked on Condor.

Who yelled the big lie: "She's a great shot and I'm expendable!"

Whining closer from down in the city came police sirens.

"And you're out of time," yelled Condor. "All alone in a graveyard."

"Am I out of options?"

The faint low *whump whump whump* of a closing-in helicopter.

Condor stood but the man who felt Merle's gunsights moved not. Condor spotted his .45 on a sprawl of manure, picked it up, wiped it off, did what he probably technically didn't need to do, racked the slide—out jumped a bullet, clack of metal on metal.

BAM! Condor blasted a .45 slug into the stinking soil.

Merle flinched.

Condor faced the other man whose pistol was not aimed at the ground.

"You give us everything you got in exchange for not ending up here."

"My name is Fydor. And first I give you that big eyebrows coward fuck who ran away and left me here. But I won't trade anything if all it does is let me live. No prison safe house where I get tortured with *talk talk talk*, bad phone, no friends, nothing cool, and no cash to do, no women. A boss troll like you gets a woman, why not Fydor after I give you everything from this graveyard? SVR agent no more. I give and I get."

"You don't inherit the sweet life from *here*, you earn it *for* us and *from* us out *there*."

Fydor shrugged.

Nodded.

Thumbed his gun so the ammo mag dropped out of the pistol handle and hit the dirt.

Put the gun on the ground.

Faye ran down the grassy slope of the graveyard toward them, gun in her hand as her mouth moved frantically for the Bluetooth earpiece under her dyed red hair.

A dark blue helicopter roared over their heads and stuck a landing back by the gate. Out leapt eight blue jumpsuited, body armored, combat helmeted, assault rifle pointing gunners who had been on Standby Backup for the primary duty White House Secret Service Tactical React Team. They set about securing the area as ordered by whoever issued orders.

White, red, and blue striped, sirens-wailing DC police cars charged through cemetery gates, stopped and held cover position for active shooter alert via the graveyard crews' cell phones. They held their positions waiting for backup that got cancelled until the Feds released the scene where some random feuding gangbangers accidentally charged into a previously-scheduled undercover law enforcement operatives' street training session amidst a graveyard work crew whose schedule had been screwed up by computer error, somehow.

The next day's *Washington Post* carried a four-paragraph story about this Marx Brothers debacle with no reported casualties, no arrests, investigation on-going on Page C3 of the Metro section on that A Section news day about pop star Prince dying and Texas flood waters rising.

Faye eased the pistol out of Merle's wildly waving hands. Tucked it in her belt under the blue nylon windbreaker with bold gold letters on the back proclaiming "FEDERAL POLICE," the anonymous identification that by 2016 had become a common sight in America.

Merle let Faye give her a hug as warriors' shouts came closer.

Faye stepped away. Kept her face toward Condor. Kept her eyes on Fydor.

Said: "Holster your gun, I got him."

Condor did.

Faye told him: "We killed his phones minutes ago so he couldn't hear and track you, so now they can't hear us."

Then she yelled: "Heads up! That third man is with us!"

The SWAT team threw a perimeter around these federal agents they'd come to rescue.

Merle leaned back from Condor's stench as the SWAT team hustled their three protectees to the *whump whump whumping* helicopter, told him: "You need a shower."

CHAMBER FOUR
Secret Heart of Lonely

She walked down the concrete steps' narrow passageway, past the bouncer at the door, into the beer and bricks scented underground tavern, claimed a Sundown Service barstool and ordered *whiskey* from Molly, who gave her *welcome* without giving her a smile, reached toward the bottle-fronted mirror for that night's bar pour—

—got stopped by the newcomer with dyed red hair: "Give me something good."

Molly flowed her tattoo-sleeved, night-worker pale arm to the top shelf like a ballerina.

And *yeah*, he saw all that unfold as he was racking glasses behind the bar and watching Molly for any signals of need she might make. Not that Molly needed anything, brass hair and cobalt eyes that missed nothing, steel nose stud, ruby lips, a clean jaw, strong under her Quarry House Tavern T-shirt topped by a snap button, brocaded cowboy shirt that across the back read:

BEAT IT
CREEP

Then the bar got slammed and he didn't pay any more attention to the red-haired stranger until the night she sat the bar arguing with some random dude who motioned him over, said: "You're P.V., the guy who loves old movies, right?"

"Right enough," he answered.

Figured Random Dude remembered him because he was one of the few men of the Quarry House crew who wore no beard on his clean-jawed, high cheekbones face. He wore his dark brown hair in a brushed down buzz cut above indigo eyes.

"Yeah, whatever." Random Dude leaned across the bar to make his point and not let P.V. slip away. "Faye here says the best black and white horror movie was *The Thing*."

That *Faye* looked straight at P.V. as he said: "She's right."

Random Dude said: "Better than the newer one, all color and shit?"

"Yes. No. Different."

Redhead Faye said: "I like different."

"That's why you come here, right?" said Random Dude on the stool beside her at the bar, his hand sweeping them together as one with a gesture that took in the whole—

—or *hole*—

—of where they were.

Could have been anywhere in real America, but wasn't, was here in downtown Silver Spring, Merry-land, mark it six blocks north of the border with De-See—few miles and many light years from the white marble castles and monuments to heroes who mostly nobody remembers and factories for making the *do's and don't*s of this *here and now* democracy.

Back in June 2016 before that *then and there* slipped into the river of gone, Silver Spring still ranked as out of the loop with the rest of the Beltway burgs that the *never was a "sleepy Southern town"* capital city had already consumed.

True, giant praying mantis construction cranes lined the sky every which way you looked, but the half square mile-plus of *downtown* still held streets full of American Everybodies. Ethiopian one-time refugees, now owners of cafés and hookah bars. Hard workers who spoke Spanish with accents from all over South of the Border. Elegant ebony Africans arguing in flawless

French. Italians and Jews and Greeks who'd run this turf after the 1968 riots' white flight from Washington. Vietnamese-Chinese-Thai-Lao-Japanese and others with visible roots in their corner of the world now dealing with ignorant eyes that saw *same-same*. American blacks of all shades. Two women in hajibs walking out of the Halal grocery store. Plus a river of *who knows what they are* besides white skins flowing with crowd. Was somebody from everybody if you stood still and watched long enough.

They all had cellphones.

What else you'd see was a *going-going-almost-gone* American Dreams town. Pawn shops. Barbershops. Nail salons. A gun store. A corset store with a double-front wide full window display of the goods on sale and none of those foundation garments were about *eros*. A car rental office. Health food store. A rare coin shop. An artist supplies store. Christians with pamphlets. The thrown-out, strung-out, left-out. Most weekend nights meant Hare Krishna's a-chanting and a-dancing and a-bonging drums when the four block outside pedestrian mall was packed with moms and dads and grammas and OMG teenagers and Millennials like P.V. and Molly who he trusted and the dyed redhead named Faye. Most of the outdoor mall walkers were movie going or late shopping or bar hopping, data blasting them from forty-foot-tall searing screens selling shit. For those flesh and blood souls there in Touchable Town, there was a craft brew beer house and a sports bar and a wine bar run by an ex-Marine and maybe twenty-five other places that sold booze with food but none of them—

—*none of them*—

—none of them were underground like Quarry House Tavern. Oh yeah. Even after fire and flood, same as before.

Underground.

One way in, one way out. Down the concrete stairs on the corner alongside a white tablecloth Indian restaurant, a diagonal shaft to a brown door, through it to facing the L-shaped bar

Molly rocked most nights and P.V.'s *whatever* job kept him hopping and bopping and making sure everything was fine with her, plus being a service soldier working the painted cement floor.

A third of the walls had 1950ish basement rec room wood paneling, a third were exposed but sealed brick, and a third of the walls were rippling slabs of stone painted shiny neon red.

The customer mix tallied techs and quants and admins from two giant multinational cyber corporations hq'd in Silver Spring, plus refugees from DC marble, space scientists from NASA, weather worriers from the within walking distance fortress for the National Oceanic and Atmospheric Administration, or NOAA—as in *Noah's arc.*

Don't get them started on the vanishing glaciers.

Families came to Quarry House—rents and runts of all ages, like the night when five-year-old Frances and her three-year-old brother, Alban, took over the floor by their parents' table and gordo danced to whatever was on the jukebox while Molly and P.V. kept servers and customers out of their way. Molly and he couldn't stop grinning as two kids from parents who were their age rocked out.

Many of the bar's usual crowd nested in one of the dozen humongous blockish apartment and condo towers that burst out of Silver Spring's sleepy pavement starting back when the second Bush was President. QHT gave them all a taste of *real* they thought they'd once had and since lost, especially the heavily represented Baby Boomers fifty-five-plus crowd who grew up with a jukebox that was the bar's only mass media—not a fucking sports game or taking head TV screen in the whole place.

The whole place was shaped like a square-cornered U, with the door being in the top right corner while the left corner held the "for everybody" bathroom with graffiti like: "CALL YOU'RE MOTHER!" "YOU call her, I alreaDy did & she said yEs." Penis drawings. A nice sketch of a grinning duck. *"Je ne suis pas comment je peux vive"*—graffiti Faye told P.V. meant *I am not how I can live,* and when he told that to Molly, she said: "No shit."

Walk in and the bar is dead ahead, then as you go through the main room, you pass the bar on your right where Molly might see you as she rimmed a glass with salt, tossed a pinch over her left shoulder while the jukebox blared crashing guitars from The Dead Kennedy's, head-banger punk rock music from before Molly was born.

Molly and the QHT crew passed out fried food menus, poured shots and pulls of fifty-plus beers and sometimes made mixed drinks, sometimes not: *bartender's call,* this was no fancy place with blenders and cutesy concoctions. You want that, climb the stairs and go back into DC for Hipsterville or Dealtown joints. Drive over to big bucks Bethesda or cross the river into Virginia where you can find respectable and reasonable crowds at their drinking and doing spots with windows to the street so everything inside can be seen and envied.

None of that in this underground dive bar.

Was there with its aromas of flesh, beer, and whiskey, fry grease floating from the kitchen and lingered smoke from the nicotine junkies, was there that it took him three, four nights of red-haired Faye drinking at the bar and catching him for snatches of repartee about movies and novels and philosophies that mattered, was *there* after a surprising amount of *then*'s that he noticed the musk of Faye's perfume.

Molly rolled her eyes when she saw that happen.

With Faye, it wasn't that he hadn't *noticed her* noticed her. As a woman. As hot. Which, *oh,* she was. Like him and Molly, somewhere between the *starting out twenties* and the *settling situation forties.* Faye's rust-colored hair cupped her face and her face, *wow*: the eyes, the cheekbones, the lips, a trim body with all the right curves, sleek legs in the black slacks she usually wore. Just the kind of woman who he never stood a chance with back when it was OK for him to think he could and maybe take a shot.

A shot.

Yeah, he once *"took a shot."*

Faye's lips glistened.

She leaned close when she talked to him. And not because of the bar noise or jukebox.

Was on that slow biz Monday night of June 13, 2016. Newspapers screamed stories about the crazy loner who'd sprayed his hates and fears as rapid fire bullets through an Orlando, Florida, gay nightclub, killed forty-nine people, wounded more than fifty. Every time the Quarry House door opened, everyone swiveled to look, to see, to hope, all of them thinking *it can't happen here, it can't happen to me,* but gut sick that they might be wrong. Long about eight, waiter Marco accidentally flipped over his metal tray—the clatter made everyone flinch. After that, the crowd really thinned out, nobody saying why they were making it an early night, nobody needing to. Faye'd been in for a couple hours, left before the place felt like a ghost town.

Come midnight, P.V. cut himself to save the bar his payout for work that wasn't there for him to do. Broke house rules, hit the marijuana vape pen he had a Maryland medical card for—would have shared it with Molly, but she wasn't there. Climbed those concrete stairs.

The moon was up. Newly under construction behemoth buildings loomed all around where he emerged, security lights on their girder-revealing *way up there* roofs and skeletal giant praying mantis cranes rising into the misty darkness. Felt like everything was slipping into *Blade Runner,* a sci fi vision gone mad.

A pair of headlights snapped on half a block down and across the deserted street, two yellow hunter's eyes parked in front of the gun shop, the car's red taillights pointing at him.

The car pulled away from the curb and rolled a 180 so those yellow eyes caught him standing alone on the corner.

He heard a car window whir down. A dark form loomed behind the steering wheel.

Faye's voice called to him from inside the car: "We're both still alive. I got nowhere to go and no one there when I do."

Her engine grumbled in the night.

"You've got no better choice either," she said. "You know that's true. Let's go."

He heard himself say: "Go where?"

"Your place. Probably closer. Your car's parked somewhere around here. Drive you to it."

He got in her dark blue car. Closed the door with a thump that couldn't be any louder than his slamming heart. *God, the smell of her, the closeness!*

"We haven't even kissed," he said.

"When we do," she said, "I'm not gonna stop."

She drove him to the county's all night public parking aboveground pancake garage four blocks away, the level where he stashed his ordinary and thus invisible gray Datsun.

Got out, got in, turned the Datsun's key. It didn't blow up. She didn't race away.

He leaned out and called back to her: "Follow me."

"That's the plan."

The settlement money after they let him go covered the down payment on his three-story, two-unit townhouse just over the DC line, nine minutes from the bar. Since he didn't have a family (yet), he lived in the bottom unit under his fifth set of tenants. The housing shortage in the nation's capital meant the rent he got covered his mortgage, *plus.*

Middle-class in spite of.

Molly owned a smaller, further out, thus cheaper duplex house, the same *make-it* plan she'd inspired in him, get set up so you can be free of the shift life.

As if.

He parked at the curb in front of his house that first night.

Waved Faye's sleek dark blue car into his driveway.

She sashayed past him without a word, without a touch, to his front door. His hand trembled and repeatedly stabbed his door key at the lock.

Until she put her velvet warm hand around his, said: "I got this."

Slid his key into the lock of his door, opened it and let him lead the way inside.

Pulled the door shut behind her. Locked the deadbolt.

She flipped on the overhead light to illuminate his living room/bedroom/kitchen home swollen with no one else there. Like she'd never seen them before, her eyes took in racks of DVD's and VHS tapes from the closed video store where he first worked after they'd let him go. Shelves of novels and short story anthologies. His silver laptop that he used for playing DVDs, for video games, for his Quarry House shift scheduler gig, for checking Facebook to be sure distant cousins were alive and Molly was OK, to surf and search for what wasn't there to be seen.

Faye's gaze drilled him down to his bones.

"So you're an old tech freak? A collector?"

"It's not the tech."

"But the movies. Get them online. You don't have to own them."

From his bones: "Books, movies, keeping them; it's honoring the stories."

She took her time, flowed to him.

Touched her blood-colored fingernails to his forehead: "The stories are in here."

Let her fingers trail softly down his check. Touch his pounding heart: "And in here."

Her fingers stayed on his heart, gentle firmness that kept his *here* a reach away from her.

"We're both here," she told him. "And I don't even know your real name, *P.V.*"

What came out of him was the *now* truth: "Paul. Paul Vineyard."

"That's a start," she whispered.

He fell through the musk of her perfume to their kiss.

Paul felt himself in a movie, a ballet to his bedroom. Everything worked, their mouths learning each other, the tingling velvet fire of her tongue on his, the rose shampoo of her dyed red hair, the perfumed musk warmth of her flesh, her soft firm curves in the palms of his hands.

She stepped back, told him it had been two years and three *clear* physicals *since*. He told her he carried even more untouched and certified clean time. They both bought that as true.

Her smile said: "What about Molly?"

Paul said: "We're just friends. Nothing about her."

"Good," said Faye. Somehow her blouse fell away. She wore a black bra.

Unfastened it from the front between the reveal of pear breasts.

Said: "Want to see it all?"

Seeing yet not *believing* even as he danced their embrace into his bedroom, his shirt, his unsnapped jeans, his kicked off shoes and socks left behind before they bumped against his unmade bed. She touched her toes to pull off her black slacks plus everything underneath, then on her rising back up stretch, pulled his boxers down and off and filled her hand with his eagerness, pushed her thumb in a spot *just so* that sent control back into the rest of him.

Oh, and he took what she gave him, devoured her with his kisses, his mouth, his caressing hands, and *of course* he went down on her, her eyes closing and her back arching her swollen breasts up to the night sky ceiling as he knelt before her on the side of the bed *Ohh!* and she pulled him up, let him press his back on the cool sheets over the firm mattress like it was where he'd been heading all along and she straddled him, the rhythm of their flesh and her moans and cries, his gasps, and he was sure that she seized his coming with her own spasm of true.

Second time, they held each other like intertwined sitting

stars of an *art noveau* movie from back in his parents' daze when sex was still shocking.

The third time was slow and easy as she held him on top of her in the last of the moonlight.

Morning meant high noon, the nightshift clock.

Wondering woke him and she was still there.

How they had sex then doesn't matter.

Faye said: "Do you have coffee?"

A few individual serving packets he'd taken from a roadside motel during a week's refresher course in Nacogdoches, Texas, six months before when Quarry House had still been closed from the fire and the flood. He heated water in a tea kettle he'd salvaged from a rummage sale after someone had let it boil dry.

"How do you take it?" he asked her after he dropped an instant coffee packet in the steaming cup he'd carry to where she lay on his bed checking her cellphone with its news alert stories about Russian hackers breaking into the Democratic National Committee.

"How I can get it," she said.

Slow-sipped away half her cup of wake up, smiled, said: "You're good with silence."

"Have to be."

"Not even The Washington Question: '*What do you?*' so you know my rank in this town."

"That's not important. Or defining."

"*Really.* Does how I make money to live not interest you?"

"I'm more interested in how you live to make money."

"What movie is that line from?" she said.

"The one we're in now."

"*Make this a movie.*" She frowned in thought. Smiled in conclusion. "*Yeah.* That might work. Keep all this from getting . . . complicated."

"Ah," he said. "Complicated. Like a job, a career."

"A career can let you be who you were meant to be."

"Do you like your career?"

"Treasure hunter," she said. "A woman who works her own hours scouring the Internet and estate or yard sales and back-roads looking for what's cheap that the people who can afford lots more don't have time to find. It's a *me* I like fine. Or at least enough."

She stretched out on the bed, rose on her right elbow, the fullness of her front facing him as he did the same pose but left elbow down.

Faye said: "What do you want?

"And I don't mean here," she added, her fingers brushing across the wrinkled sheets, touching his chest with tenderness and *stay* at the same time. "I mean: *What do you want?*"

"To be happy. To matter. To have love that's *more than* but *still* me."

"You might have to settle. One out of three ain't bad. Throw in some kind of two, not so shabby of a life."

"They're not choose-one-or the-other things. They're a triad, a whole."

"Yeah, well, you go down holes, you disappear."

"So what do you want?" he said.

Felt her pull back up and away from where she lay in front of him.

She answered: "Clarity."

They breathed the air between them.

Neither rolled away, hid their naked front.

He said: "What color do you call your hair?"

"Which batch?"

"You know what I mean. What the world sees when you walk by."

"I call it *me*," she said. "Chose it, made it, walking it right at you."

"I like *crimson*," he said.

She blinked.

Saw his interest rising beyond words, checked her cellphone on the bedside table, said: "Gotta go—your shower work?"

"Yeah."

"Is it big enough for two?"

Was, and afterwards standing on the bathmat as she dried him off and his towel lingered here and there on her flesh, she smiled down at what she saw, sank to her knees, opened her smile and leaned toward—

The man named Paul pulled her up to her bare feet.

"*You've got to be kidding!*" Puzzlement lined her forehead beneath her damp dyed red hair. "You've got to be the only man in the known universe to turn down a blow job."

"I, *ah*, that . . ."

Faye frowned: "Bad memory? Or saving the special *from* or *for* true love?"

"Nothing like you'd ever believe."

"So, just like that, *never mind*?"

She saw his eyes harden. He backed her out of the bathroom and she let him scoop her off her feet, carry her, drop her on the bed to loom above her and all she said was: "Your shower better not run out of hot water."

After that, she edged herself into his routine at Quarry House or showing up at his house when got off work while most of DC slept. They never went to her place.

Molly knew the first shift she shared with him *after*.

Shook her head. But worked an honest smile to him as she bumped his fist.

"It's OK to *not* know what you're doing," Molly told him, "but don't do it *stupid*."

"You always know what you're doing," he said.

"And just look at me, here I am, standing tall."

"But her?" said Molly as she wiped the bar and Paul stacked the glasses. "She's got a whole lot going on she ain't showing and you ain't touching—don't give me that look."

Paul told Molly: "I'm the one who's job it is to tell *you* to be careful, watch out."

"We aren't working that shift now," said Molly, who he knew to be working *tough enough* and *toughen up* and *move on* after having just dumped the latest asshole who'd been lucky to get some level of her *yes*.

"You're an *all the way* kind of guy," she said. "You'd drive all night and then back again, just so your girl wouldn't need to take the bus."

"I've never gotten that far," he said.

"Big scary if you did," said Molly. "But know that this *Faye* wants to take you to *her* version of *far* and she's driving the bus, whether you want that or not."

Molly turned away to check the jungle of bottles by the cash register and he turned away to make sure the bar had stash glasses full of clean metal forks and knives.

Went on like that until the night he came in for his shift only to find Zane clattering the set-ups behind the bar. Paul made the Quarry House shifts schedule in a shared-user online app. Zane wasn't posted as working that night: this was Paul's shift, he'd programmed it that way.

Faye sat at the bar in slinky stylish dress.

Leaned across that polished wood.

Made sure Paul heard her say to Molly: "I told you he wouldn't run."

Faye spun on the barstool away from Molly's silent eyes.

Twirled in seemingly slow motion, crimson hair floating in the underground air as she slid off the bar stool, didn't miss a sway or a step as she smiled up to him, sent her heart side hand around the back of his head to cup/trap his skull and said for everyone nearby to hear:

"I'm *so* glad you picked tonight to meet my folks! They're waiting in the back room."

She kissed his unresponsive lips, tenderly slid her perfumed cheek alongside his and whispered in his ear: "*We know who you are, Condor.*"

He watched her hips sway as she walked away to where he knew he had to go.

There's one short concrete step up from QHT's main service area, a red stone archway with the fabled jukebox off to the left as you step into the red-walled back room, two rows of tables split by a wide service aisle that ends at the *for everybody* bathroom just after the last round barstool table, where that night sat Random Dude who'd introduced Paul to Faye.

Paul knew that he was truly, deeply fucked.

Knew it wasn't Random Dude who really mattered.

—wasn't the three tables of real customers—two sets of regulars and one pair of Tinder date newbies—who counted as only more innocent bystander casualties *if*. The regulars sent P.V. smiles. The Tinder couple were too nervous about getting caught ranking each other to see what else might be happening.

Wasn't crimson Faye who mattered.

Was the four-top table near the back she led him to, no other customers seated close by.

The four-top table where *they might have been somebody's parents* sat.

Sat with their backs against the cushioned bench red wall.

Sat with *pay for their presence* mugs of golden beer and a basket of tatter tots.

Don't call her Mom's shoulder-length hair showed silvering from blond that Molly could expect if she lived that long. This older woman wore a sparkling gold jump suit. Vacant eyes.

Who sat against the wall beside her mattered.

Could have been her husband. Cut short, thinning silver hair. Steel-blue eyes. A black hoodie he didn't need on this warm summer night, but a guy his age could sell wearing that as him being sensitive to air conditioning. His lips widened in *call it a smile*.

Faye pulled out the chair across the table from that older man.

Held it for the man she'd fucked.

"You first," Paul told her.

"No, all this is all about you."

Random Dude watched with no expression.

He who'd been tricked sat in the chair Faye commanded. She sat on his right.

The old man told his guest: "I've been dying to meet you."

"Who are you?" said Paul.

"I'm you."

The jukebox vibrated the Rolling Stones' *Sympathy For The Devil*.

The old man smiled. "I'm Condor. Number One to your Number Two. Or rather, your Number Three. The CIA gave one of the Watergate burglars our codename before he did what made him famous. Then they rotated it to me. Then from me to you after I got locked up in their secret loony bin. Then I got out and you—"

"Got out."

The old woman with silvered blond hair said: "You don't need me anymore. I came and did visual verify for your cover. Let me . . ."

She smiled sincere but *oh so not there*: "Let me ride the lemony with happy, not this."

Old Condor nodded—as much to Faye as to the woman he'd come with, who slid from behind the table, drifted to the jukebox. Paul felt her strain against the leash she'd obey *but*.

"That's Merle," said Old Condor.

"She's stoned."

"The lemon drop THC edible is the least of it. The best of it. She . . . requires meds."

"Bet that's all because of you."

"We all have our accidental casualties."

"You need to remember that," added Faye. "You really do."

Merle stroked the curved glass dome over the jukebox.

A hand-black-inked, white paper sign Scotch-taped to that glass read:

FREE TONIGHT—
BE NICE & LIMIT TO
5 TRACKS PER PLAY

Merle flipped the levers to display CD's and their set lists, selections from Buddy Holly and Bruce to Southern rock and Patsy Cline, Otis Redding and Sam Cooke and The Supremes, CD's heavy on the Searing Seventies Sounds from one of the bar owner's youth.

Old Condor said: "After lunch one ordinary day, I came back to work at our CIA black site up on Capitol Hill and everyone else was dead. Silenced machineguns.

"You," he said to the younger man who shared his codename, "you and your cyber team the CIA detailed to Homeland Sec', office in a different part of this same city, went out for morning coffee, you went to the bathroom and everyone died. Silenced machinegun, yes?"

"Does that *how* matter?"

"Not now."

"This *now* isn't *contact procedure* as set by the Agency and Homeland. Why this?"

"Because we need you."

"Who the hell are '*we*'?"

Old Condor told him about the V.

At the jukebox, stoned Merle pushed buttons. Over the years he'd worked Quarry House, Paul had heard all the hard to replace jukebox CD's, recognized within three guitar chords coming over the bar's speakers that Merle had chosen the CD called "Silver Poets—Vol. 7," John Fogerty wanting to know *who'll stop the rain?*

"What do you want?" said Paul.

"For you to be who you are," said Old Condor.

Leaned forward. His brow wrinkled like was truly concerned: "How are you?"

"You mean your spy here hasn't given you a full download?"

Faye's soft voice: "I told him this was the right thing, the right time, now or never."

"Believe me," said Old Condor. "I know how rough surviving the massacre was. Then being on the run. Chased by everybody. But I can barely imagine the courage it took for you to pull the trigger on the traitor who lay on top of you, who slid her mouth around your gun barrel and dared you. You were right. She'd have beaten you every other move you could have done. Killed you. You pulling that trigger saved that Delta Force raid from being a horrorshow."

"Yeah. And it only took the Agency two months of interrogations and investigations and isolations to believe me. Another three months to let me go."

"But they did their best for you then. Therapy. Sent you to Texas to learn hand-to-hand combat to help you fight off your paranoia. Set you up with a settlement, let you . . ."

The old man smiled: "Let you fly away, Condor."

"Don't call me that. That's who you are."

"*We* are. Who we got made. Who we choose to be. Who we can't escape. And I know that's true for you, too, because of Texas."

"What?"

"You went back six months ago. A refresher course on hand to hand combat. How to drop someone trying to kill you. Like you were expecting to need it *again*. Like that need was still inside of you. Like you knew this day would have to come. Like you were preparing for it. Wanted it, even. Not paranoia: a sense of purpose that mattered."

"Why the hell would I have—would I want a 'purpose' like that?"

Old Condor told him about the Russians.

The jukebox played Faye's next selection, a song by Richard Thompson who rocked wanting to ride some wall of death *one more time.* Faye swayed in front of the jukebox, her arms floating the waves of wonder, her face gone to bliss beyond this underground dive bar, a golden soul lost in forever like she was an actor in a surreal *noir* movie like *Blue Velvet.*

A trio of customers filled the arch into the back room, saw a silver-haired woman wearing sparkling gold waving her hands and weirdo dancing. The trio turned back to find a table in the main room or barstools in front of Molly. Nobody wants to mix it up with old and crazy.

Is Merle's dancing a target zone access strategy? wondered Paul.

Took Old Condor all that Richard Thompson song and the next one—Johnny River's *Secret Agent Man*—to tell his tale of the Russians.

A Nobel Prize For Literature winner announced *they're selling postcards of the hanging.*

Paul said: "That's why you did this? Sent Faye? What this is all about? The Russians?"

"No."

"But you said—"

"Past, Present, Future. Yesterday, Today, Tomorrow. The Russians and all this . . ."

Old Condor's hand took in everything: Random Dude, crimson Faye, the golden woman swaying with her arms in the waves, the underground lair with its red walls and old jukebox and Molly unseen behind the bar.

". . . all this is *today.* What's crashed us together here and now is *tomorrow.*"

Paul said: "What happens tomorrow?"

"I'm going to die."

Merle swayed as Roy Orbison sang for the lonely.

The old man's face stayed calm, almost—but not quite—Buddhist serene.

"Are you . . . have they . . ."

"No one's put a personal clock it," said Old Condor. "No

diagnosis or *dead by*, and the last wet boy who tried to make it so . . . made it so for him. But we're all on the *tick-tock* to *when*."

He shrugged his shoulders inside his black hoodie.

"Makes sense," he said. "My age, all I've done and all that's been done to me, could be tomorrow or could be in twenty years, but it's the *could be* that *will be*."

"So . . ."

"I need you to become me."

"*What?*"

"You already *were* me, came up *just like* me, so it's totally logical. Poetic.

"And vital. Not for me. For the V. For our country, fucked up as it is and will continue to be, it's what we got and what we love."

His eyes went to glittering golden Merle swaying with music maybe only she heard.

"Or what we love in part so we can hope for a touchable love that's real and true, even if what we get is not the true and real we thought we'd know."

Faye chimed in: "We take what we can get. We all do. You knew that before us showing up. We give what we can to get what we can. Even if. Even though."

The man she'd fucked said: "So our *touchable* was an operational *if though*."

"You were more than an assignment."

"*Gee*, thanks, I get it."

Faye said: "I hope so. I really hope so. I wish it weren't so."

"*Us*," Old Condor told he who could have been his son. "This is about *us*."

"Why me?"

"Because just like me, Condor is who you are, who you need to be. 9/11 inspired you into the CIA for all the right and good reasons. You became one of their programmers or analysts or tech trackers, quants. But you saw beyond data. You sensed. And you did something about it. Took all the right risks and when you got betrayed, you fought until you won."

"Does this look like winning?" said the younger man in that dive bar.

"For your yesterdays, *yes*," said Old Condor. "Here—all this— it's another reason you're perfect to become me. Who you were meant to be. Who you fought to be before here. Here is real. Here is something true, even with all its own bullshit and poses and poseurs and games. You had the brains and balls and bucks to go anywhere, but you gravitated to here. Sank to the roots of where real people look for love and joy and connection. Here lets you experience all that without the finery and finesse and façade of *public policy* and *who's who* and *very important* and *bottom lines* that are actually lids."

"And I thought people just came here for beers and burgers, whiskey and music, maybe a chance to make out or have the guy on the next stool listen to you."

"What else is there?"

Old Condor shook his head, told who he saw when he looked in tomorrow's mirror: "But all this gritty *real*, you're *in* it, not *of* it. Life took that away from you."

The jukebox stopped playing, yet still Merle swayed.

The man who brought her here kept talking.

"You beat a CIA-trained killer and traitor. Fought al Qaeda. You busted one of the new Nazis out of here one night. Now you know about the Russians of today. And you can envision the shape shifters coming at America tomorrow. You're a rebel who doesn't want to rule. You care enough to put yourself on the line. You go for what other people can't or won't or don't see. Have the guts to pull the trigger."

"*I get to choose!*"

"Yes," said the old man, "and I'm sorry about that, sorry you have to, just . . . sorry."

"Our scars carve us," said she who'd seen more than all of his flesh.

"It's not today," said the old man, "it's tomorrow. If you don't bring your *see it with movies and novels and short story eyes* into the V, then going forward, we gotta rely on regular eyes, people who are smart and good but who sometimes miss this universe's surreal."

"I work in a bar."

"No," said Old Condor. "Even as we talk—just *because* we talked—your consciousness shifted. This is your *used to be's*.

"I got a lot of used-to-be's." The silver-haired man nodded to where golden Merle swayed in front of the jukebox. "Like the songs she's been playing, true and real and feeling *now* but out of gone yesterdays. That's the thing about our *used to be's*. We can carry them around like dead weight, or we can use them to light the way—even if we've got them wrong.

"When I was first learning to be me—was a song on the radio, *Heart Full Of Soul*, the Yardbirds. Took thirty years before I realized I had the lyrics wrong: not '*secret heart of lonely*,' but '*sick at heart and lonely*.' Sometimes we hear what is more our *true* than what's being sung."

Old Condor nodded to the jukebox.

"The songs Merle's been playing are already *oldy-goldy* memories. The street spies who made those songs are passengers on the tick-tock train headed to the junction of Gone & Forgotten. And hell, sometimes the people they sang to couldn't even get the words right.

"Happens to all the secret agents of storytelling. The authors who make you go *wow*. The directors and actors and screenwriters who reveal you in their flickering light. The spies like us who politicians won't or can't or dare not hear the songs we're singing.

"But spies try to touch and tell some truth. That means something—moves something, like being a butterfly who chooses *why* to flap his wings. Maybe *fighting to get things right* creates *meaning* in all the universes, our ripple into forever."

Old Condor pointed to the jukebox.

"You've been listening to all that, moving with the music like you're just like everyone else. But you're not. You have a secret heart. You hear and see deeper true, even though it makes you lonely. And if you ignore that, who's going to watch out for them? Protect them?

"You've got to be the spy in the machine."

Paul felt the red walls of the Quarry House. The smells. The crowds. The customers and crew. Gordo dancing children. Molly.

Faye put a consoling hand on his: "Sometimes if it could have, it would have."

"You have to decide," said Old Condor. "You have to choose."

Faye shook her head. "You can have . . . different places, different people, but the conditions are so jaggedly different that trying to transfer your yesterday *who*'s . . ."

Merle danced to music Paul knew only he and the others at the table heard.

"What you and I did," said Faye, "shows *yes you can*, with other people, the right people. The right rules."

"You won't be alone," said Old Condor. "You'll have us and the V."

"Fuck you," said Paul.

"Yeah," said the old man. "Yeah."

He edged out from behind the table, bent and unbent his way to standing.

Old Condor said: "All best, kid."

Dropped $90 on the table for $40 dollar tab.

Walked out with his arm leading Merle.

Walking shadow for them came Random Dude.

Faye stood.

Leaned down and pressed a soft kiss to Paul's skull.

Left.

Some customer walked to the jukebox. Pushed buttons.

No one heard Paul whisper: "*Je ne suis pas comment je peux vive.*"

He got to his feet.

Left the backroom.

Molly waited behind the bar. Her eyes took him in. She reached under the company wood, opened a cabinet, pulled out the bottle of "her" whiskey.

She poured him a generous shot.

He sipped it once. Sipped it twice. Tried to make it last but couldn't stop himself from knocking it back in one *get it over with* gulp.

Set the tumbler on the bar soft and slow and silent.

Stared through the shimmers in his eyes at Molly staring back at him.

Said: "I gotta go."

And he did, out the door, up the stairs, into that night.

Molly watched the closed door.

Picked up the tumbler. Washed it once. Washed it twice. Washed it three times. Rubbed it dry, then dryer still. Lifted the tumbler toward the shelves stacked with all the others—

—threw it at the distant garbage can.

The sound of a breaking glass.

CHAMBER FIVE
"... and taken away your name."

On that Saturday morning, October 8, 2016, when the news he read to see What's Officially Happening told of Hurricane Mathew charging toward Florida *plus* America's spy czar and its head of Homeland Security jointly announcing that Russia had *indeed* attacked US citizens and political organizations *plus* The Great Reveal, Sasha drank coffee instead of tea as he sat at his desk in the cottage at an Undisclosed Location in the exurbs of Washington, DC.

He drank that coffee to fuel his old heart for the coming drive. Of course, the coffee would probably make him need to pull off near the Beltway and find a place that would let him pee for, *perhaps*, the cost of a cup of coffee to repeat the cycle.

But that was as life is.

Besides, he'd love getting out of the car to breath deep autumn's gold leaves, to hear the whooshing tires of people going somewhere.

Coffee smell filled his cottage with no one but him to savor its perfume.

He loved perfume. How it evoked the choice of dreams over drudgery.

Nine months after he'd been moved in and was pretty sure he could get away with it, he *casually* added to his shopping cart three vials of women's perfume from the grocery store's beauty aisle, one a smell of musk and midnights, one a delightful aroma of flowers and sunshine, one scent seductive beyond name or comparison. The checkout clerk who'd graduated from the local high school and once traveled all the way to Atlantic City paid no attention to the old man's purchases beyond scanning their bar codes for the *ding ding ding*. Sasha secreted the vials in his sock drawer. Sometimes he'd bring out a vial, sniff once or twice to savor lost dreams.

He sipped that morning's black coffee.

Set its mug back on the flat white wood desk beside the black journal he'd bought at an airport on his last trip for them, a purchase that probably didn't even make his escort's report.

The black moleskin journal gave him blank, soft cream pages that were easy on his eyes.

Pages welcoming indigo ink from the fountain pen Jesse had given him.

What Sasha wrote that morning:

Are we ever who we think we are?

The line lay there on the page for anyone to see, to confiscate, to burn.

But now the line *was*.

No *they* could take that away.

He finished his coffee. Put the journal and carefully capped fountain pen back where they lived and would hope for his safe return. Washed his cup in the kitchen sink, who knows what difference that made in the cosmos. Chose the thin gray jacket that some who'd never known true cold might say was not enough to wear on this autumn day.

With a smile, decided *yes, of course* he would wear his cowboy hat. Jesse'd given it to him as a welcome present way back when Putin was not yet who he'd become. The cowboy hat fit Sasha's gray stubbled head with room to spare. *"For your skull as it gets to grow,"* Jesse'd said and they'd laughed. Sasha'd worn it to Jesse's funeral at Arlington Cemetery the year before: How could he not wear it now? The hat was black leather, flat top and narrow rims. Jesse'd called it "gambler's style."

The hat was cool, even though he couldn't wear it in the car when he was driving.

Nothing would happen in the car anyway, *da?*

He thought about going upstairs, opening his sock drawer, selecting a sniff. Just in case.

But *no*: he'd gambled on the positive, would not jinx his choice.

The drive to Washington, DC, took him seventy-seven minutes, and *yes*, part of that was not one but *two* stops to pee.

What are you, Sasha? Nervous?

That made him laugh as he listened to *the woman who wasn't*, her voice coming through his cellphone in the dashboard holder telling him which way to turn and when.

How many of the voices that tell us what to do are real?

Even with traffic, he was *of course* early. Spent twenty-three minutes ignoring relentless redirections of the woman's voice as

he turned this way and that to drive past the beautiful buildings of America's government on Capitol Hill, the three Senate
office buildings and the three sprawling House of Representatives office buildings across the invisible border splitting that city
in two and running like a bullet shot beneath the exact middle
of the white marble Capitol Dome, an image known to everyone
in world except perhaps for 109 million or so of life's forgotten,
flogged, lost, or ignored souls.

Sasha loved the glistening white Capitol Dome. So pure. So
symbolic. Trying so hard to be regal enough for an empire. The
machinegun police barricades were down that morning, so he
drove past the gray Supreme Court where high above the Corin-
thian columns of its somber flat front, etched in stone were not
the words "Equal Justice Under The Five To Four Decision" but
rather some less precise motto.

He followed First Street downhill to the traffic circle in front
of Union Station, followed PARKING GARAGE signs into a
giant structure of concrete pancakes fused on the back of the
train station. Up one level, fairly crowded with parked vehicles.
Up two, half empty. Up three, 70 percent empty. Up four to the
pancake-layered parking structure's top floor, a vast gray concrete lot under only a dome of curved gray open sky.

Why choose a lid to be over you?

Sasha drove onto the top parking lot. No other cars were
parked there.

He drove into a yellow-striped parking space against a
high concrete wall facing the Capitol Dome. From behind his
steering wheel, over that wall, he could see the whole dome
through the windshield of his Jeep that yearned for blizzards,
but when he got out—when he was just a man standing on
the cement—the concrete suicide prevention wall only let him
see the dome's curved white marble top beneath the feet of
a bronze green, armor-clad, sword-carrying woman named
Freedom.

Sasha took the parking ticket with him on the off-chance he'd find some validation.

Put on his black leather cowboy hat.

Took nearly half a minute to walk across the gray concrete parking lot.

Rode the first escalator down.

Rode the second down.

Rode the third down and halfway through that ride, turned to look back over his left shoulder, out through a gap of the parking structure's pancake levels:

Rows of empty parked trains on dozens of tracks.

Bottom of that third escalator was the Alternate Transport level, where you could catch a whiff of urine bus to Manhattan. Sasha saw backpack-heavy young people and white-haired citizens who he might have gone to high school with in Anywhere, America, except he didn't.

He walked the length of the bus level to yet another *going down* escalator, then to a set of motionless concrete steps leading down into Union Station. He pushed through glass doors and was *there*, in the Station on the red-tiled platform above the main floor with its waiting areas for passengers hoping to catch a train to where they prayed to go.

Saturday is a slow day for train travel out of Union Station, a day when you're expected to already be there, wherever that is, having left on Friday for Sunday's or even dawn Monday's return so you had most of the weekend where you were going to be.

Workweek days at Union Station meant cramped waiting areas and long lines eager for the "ATTENTION PLEASE— NOW BOARDING" loudspeaker announcements to become true. Some students, families, senior citizens, tourists, but the workweek DC/New York trains mainly carry suit-and-tie *apparatchiks* shuttling between Castle Corridors and Wall Street.

Sasha rode one last escalator down to the station's main floor.

A lone gray-blue pigeon flapped past his face and swooped over the shuffling crowds.

You're trapped inside a cavern that your fellow creatures keep leaving, thought Sasha. At least in here, food is dropped on the floor and predators have but two legs and zero wings.

Unless there truly are angels among us.

He walked away from the wall cubicles of coffee sellers—*no more, thank you*. Past the cards and spearmint gum and candy plus magazines and books and newspapers shop. Past the hole in the wall for what used to be called donuts but now had fancier names borrowed from the French and Cajuns. Past a hamburger shop with *billions and billions* sold.

Sasha walked past a trio of blue-uniformed, ballistic-vested cops, one holding the leash of a bomb sniffing dog: none of them paid the ruddy-skinned old man wearing a black cowboy hat any mind. He had no *threat profile* as he strode past with the weird sway he'd never healed from after they broke both his legs as a joke to remind him he couldn't even escape into the white howling wind outside the prison housing his window-less, fingernails-scarred cinderblock cell with its smooth door of black steel.

A curved dome, gray stone and gold inlaid ceiling five stories tall, caps the vast main hall of Union Station that along its walls hosts restaurants and shops for everything from suitcases to ballpoint pens to sports jackets you hadn't spilled food on when the train wobbled and the slinky yet tasteful little black dress for tonight's Congressional reception that you forgot to pack.

On second floor landings and balconies surrounding the main hall stand an army of thirty-six *Beaux-Arts*, larger than life stone statues of Roman centurions—helmets, armor, swords, and posed in front of them, shields. These gray stone sentinels gaze down on the vast main hall where the black and white tiled floor provides dark mahogany wood benches for the weary, the waiting, the watching. On a round bench sitting all by himself, Sasha spotted a younger but still silver-haired man wearing a black leather jacket that complimented Sasha's cowboy hat.

Sasha sat down next to the black leather jacket man.

Side by side.

Shoulder to shoulder.

Staring out to the world passing by them.

Or is it "passing them by"? wondered Sasha.

The man in the black leather jacket said: "Howdy, Cowboy."

They laughed.

Kept each other in their peripheral vision as they watched the world swirl.

"Is that what you call me—*cowboy*?"

"Hell, I never know what to call you. *Volkov*, your last name—"

"Jesse, he like many in Moscow, he liked to call me *Volk*. Means wolf."

"Oh, great! Bad enough you're *Alexander* but your friends call you *Sasha* and your family name is both *Volkov* and *wolf*," said the black leather jacket man. "What bugs me about Russian novels is how everybody's got at least two names."

"We can't help it if you Americans limit yourselves." The Russian smiled. "Besides, you are a man with two names. You've just forgotten one of them."

"Wish I could."

"The Relocation Therapists urged me to listen to American music so I could learn your English better. I used the computer to search for songs about spies. Some Johnny Rivers—"

"He had two names, too," said Condor. "A long, easy to forget Italian family name."

"He threw away his family name so he could be famous?"

"No," said Condor. "So he could be heard. So people would remember him, his songs."

"Ah," said Sasha. "To be heard, *yes*, what we all want—as long as it doesn't get us locked up in prison. Or maybe especially if it does.

"The Johnny Rivers song," he continued, circling the conversation as old men do, "*Secret Agent Man*—as if women aren't on the pavements, too. You know that. Know they are so much more than sparrows. One might even head your CIA someday. The song says people like us, you and me—women, too, yes? Says that they—we all know some *they*, yes?—song says they give us numbers, take our names."

They sat side by side in silence, staring out at the world.

Until the Russian said: "So . . . I am *cowboy*?"

They chuckled.

"Sure," said the silver-haired American, "why the fuck not, *Cowboy*."

"Why the fuck are we here, *Condor*?"

Struggling past them came a mother pulling a giant red roller bag piled high with three smaller suitcases, one bag dangling a battered and chewed cloth brown monkey. Mom made her little girl and little boy hold tight to the red roller bag, and nobody would accuse them of easing the weight Mom rolled toward the station door.

After the family had passed, Condor said: "Aren't we friends anymore?"

"Friends, *yes*, even though what you did for Jesse and me was insane."

"You were jammed. I was in town."

"Paris, *oui*, but you set the rooftop door to our escape on fire."

"It was locked. You two were trapped inside that apartment building. GRU goons surrounding the place to bust or bullet you, the unknown mole in the KGB and his CIA handler."

"Because of *fucking right in your CIA* Ames. Fucking traitor."

"Happens," said Condor. "Look at you."

"Yes, but I was yours."

"Still are. That's why I'm here."

"*Ahh*," said Sasha. "But I thought you weren't CIA."

"You told them *no*," said Condor.

They sat on a round wooden bench in the vast main hall of DC's Union Station.

Two men, one wearing a black cowboy hat, one in a black leather bomber jacket.

Both invisible to all the innocent eyes around them. They were just *old* men.

Sasha said: "How much did you pay him?"

Condor frowned: "Who?"

"The shopkeeper with the googly eyes on *Passage del la Main d'or*. We rush in on him from his alley fire escape and you start babbling your terrible French—"

"*Hey!*"

"—pushing a wad of francs into his hand." Sasha shook his head: "Ah, *francs*. I loved the sense of them back then in 1984."

"Never thought you'd call the Soviet Union era *the good old days*."

"Not good days for Mother Russia, but for other places, not so bad."

Condor said: "We're here about today."

"You still haven't told me," said Sasha.

"What?"

"How much you paid that shopkeeper. How many francs you shoved into his hand."

"Enough."

"What brilliant madness you are," Sasha told the American sitting beside him. "Out of nowhere, three men burst into the back of his shop. We didn't even know what it was, but you see, you *saw*. You stuff him full of francs. And *he*, he himself paints us up, white faces and that horrible lipstick. Darker red than blood. He even finds black pants that mostly fit, white and black striped shirts—mine was too tight, my muscles."

"*Sure*. Your *muscles.*"

"Black berets, like we are commandos, *mais no*: you made us into fucking *mimes*."

"Got us out of there."

"But you make us do the ridiculous! The mimes! Fire engines—*wee—ooo, wee-ooo*."

"The GRU goons busted into the burning safe house. Found out you were gone."

"*Wee-ooo, wee-ooo*." The black cowboy hat shook from side to side. "Goons everywhere. We can't run even if the goons can't tell who we are *because we're mimes*. Remember that brick wall by the outdoor café? We see two of those French policemen—"

"*Gendarmes*."

"And you put your white-gloved hands straight out, fall against the brick wall like you've been ordered to be searched by the cops! Jesse, he knew, he falls in line right beside you, hands on the wall and what was I supposed to do?"

"You knew what to do." Condor smiled. "I wanted to yell, '*Up against the wall, motherfucker!*' But, you know: my terrible French. English would have blown our cover."

"We were mimes! We could not talk! Three mimes, spread eagled against the bricks. The streets full of GRU goons looking for us."

"Those two the CIA got pictures of later, they stalked right behind us, remember?"

"You peel off the wall. Do the mime *waving the hands* shuffle behind Jesse and me. Then go *up against the wall, motherfucker* a-gain! Right beside me. Jesse, he knows to do it next, and I'm number three. All the way down the cobblestone street, we go like that. Jesse called it leapfrogging. The corner and three mimes turn and go down the next street."

Sasha shook his black cowboy hat. "That taxi driver didn't want to be in our circus."

"But he still took the last of my francs. Got us to the safe house."

"You left us there. With phone for CIA scoop up team to get

Jesse safe. Get me to where trusted KGB officer is supposed to be so I can still be your spy. *Until.*"

"Wasn't my Op. I was just in town. You were in a jam."

"*Now* tell me," said Sasha. "Last year—week after Jesse's funeral. You show up unannounced. Nobody else. We drink the good Scotch you brought, but you only have one."

"The rest belonged to you and him."

"I drink it still. One small sip on nights *when.*"

Sasha said: "You never told me what happened *when* you left us. Tell me *now.*"

"Not your Op."

"Is my *life.* Names or numbers, is what we've got. *My life.* I paid for it. Tell me."

Condor said: "I got lost."

"What?"

"I'm a mime in the streets of Paris with terrible French and no more francs. And I'm lost. And it's getting dark."

Condor shook his head.

"Took me almost an hour of bad miming to earn enough to ride the subway. Cars packed with people leaving work, museums. To cafés to meet people they love. Homes where children laugh. Trains whoosh through tunnels under the city. I'm a mime sitting alone in a subway car. And I can't say anything. Ask anybody for directions. Because I'm a deep cover spy and don't dare cause a scene. Because I'm a mime. Because my French is terrible and when they hear that, they'll think I'm an American making fun of their culture.

"Must have spent an hour crisscrossing Paris underground, hoping to realize I'm in a station I know with time to jump off the train."

"How?" said Sasha.

"Not *how,*" said Condor. "*Her.*"

A fashionably dressed, gray bouffant hair, stout but shapely woman wearing sturdy low heels that still gave that certain sway clicked her way over Union Station's black andwhite tiles, strode past a wooden bench where two men from her (real) age demographic sat, but a glance told her they were too much trouble and too damaged to be on any train she wanted to ride. She had no more time to waste on obvious disasters.

"Paris subway. I'm lost and alone and trapped as a fucking mime. Pull into an underground station. Doors *ding*. People get off . . .

"*Et voila*: she pops into the car. The perfect woman mime. Wild eyes and white glove gestures. That dark red lipstick we're wearing, hers is not even smeared. Her white face makeup is smooth, black beret on her chestnut hair."

Sasha said: "*Chest*-nut?"

"Dark brown, but richer.

"She spots me. Makes her eyes go wide. Claps her white gloves to her face.

"What I could I do? I clap my hands to my cheeks.

"The subway doors close. The train surges forward. She bats her eyes. Swirls her head to look away so everyone sees she's totally watching me.

"The other passengers on the subway love it—or at least give us a grudging *humph*. Figure it's our act. Two lost souls meeting on a train beneath the heart of the city.

"She swirls around a subway pole. I swoop up—"

"*You?*" said Sasha with a cock of his black cowboy hat. "*Swooping?*"

"*Hey!* You'd just run across the rooftops of Paris with me and Jesse. Back then, I was in my thirties. Swooping happened.

"My big move? I glide past her in the subway car aisle. Sidle up to an older—*Jesus, remember when people in their fifties were older?* Older woman, bouquet of flowers in her hand. I do an elaborate feint so the crowd sees. Pluck a flower from the bouquet like I'm stealing it."

"You were stealing it."

"Yeah, but for . . . for art. For love. Or at least love's pantomime.

"I swoop, *motherfucker*, I sway. I sidle up to where she's batting her black makeup eyes pretending to pretend she's not enthralled. Present the flower.

"She takes it. *Oh so shy* eyes-batting thrilled. Trails the flower over my chest. Over my heart. Swoops back to bouquet lady. Like a fencer, slips that flower back into the bouquet. Doesn't knock off a petal. Mimes *merci*. Flutters down the aisle backwards toward me—

"—whirls around and suddenly, she's *the vixen mime*. Slow stalking. Sly smiling. One. Long. Leg. Step. After. Another. She's at the pole where I'm holding on . . .

"The subway pulls into a station. The doors *ding* open.

"Her white gloves beckon me as she walks backwards off the train. I'm swaying and coming with her like a lucky fish on a line.

"Over the platform. Through the crowd. Riding the up escalator. Never breaking character. Getting it—getting each other. Knowing what the other person means and making what you mean into motion. Creating the script. She flirts. I glide closer. She turns away coy. Turns back *come on*. Dances like she's in a ballet.

"On the sidewalk. A Paris night. There's the Eiffel Tower. A curved bridge over the Seine. People are out strolling and it's like they'd expected us. Mimes. Two people hiding behind white makeup, caught up in their own drama for you to see or walk on by.

"We do the mime flutter. The chase. The come-together. Standing there. Smiling for real under our makeup. She is who she is and she's who she wants to be. Thirty-something. Like me. She's seen and been and done and kept going. Like me. And we haven't, we don't touch.

"She does this grand gesture to a sidewalk café. Strings of colored lights and clatters. Soft yellow glow. Outdoor tables. Her brow furrows. She smiles the ask.

"And I realize—*oh man do I realize*—I'm starving."

Sasha smiled. "*Starving*, yes? Not just *hungry*."

Condor said: "I frown. Sad. Shrug. Pull out the empty pockets of my black pants.

"Her white gloves press her cheeks in shock. She shakes her finger at me, scolding—then turns it into a beckoning *come with me*.

"Mime. The whole time we mime. The maître de. Unflappable. Works with our miming like *of course, why not*. Seats us. The waiter shows up. Nobody bats an eye. The mime who saved me takes a menu. Shows it to me—*like I can read French!* I shrug with both my white gloves up and out—but smile. She points to this, points to that. A carafe of red wine. The waiter pours. We dramatically toast. Drink.

"We left the same smear of red lipstick on our glasses.

"Not a word. She mimes that she's some kind of actress. I lie, mime that I'm a writer. That red lipstick is all smiles on us. Two strangers in the same greasepaint."

"Any couple, anytime, anywhere."

"But we were two mimes sitting in a sidewalk café, at night, in Paris.

"Dinner was beyond belief. Some kind of chicken in wine sauce. I don't remember eating. I'll never forget how delicious.

"Afterwards we're standing alone on the sidewalk after the café. Traffic whizzing past. She cocks her head. Waits for me to fill the stillness.

"The frown pulled my whole face down. Sad clown. I tap where I don't have a wristwatch. Grimace and rock from side to side, urgency. Use both hands, my wiggling fingers trailing tears down my cheeks. Shrug and lift my hands up. Helpless."

"Hopeless," said Sasha.

"She gestures about my pockets. I shrug."

"But the CIA has its Panic Line. All you needed—"

"*I fucking know what I needed!*"

Sasha forced himself to relax so the man sitting shoulder to shoulder with him on the Union Station bench would feel and follow that softening.

"She reaches out," said Condor. "Our first touch. Takes my left hand, white gloves over our flesh. Puts the last of her francs in my open palm. Closes my fist.

"She swirls away. Flags down a taxi. Opens the back door.

"I slouch. Face her. Press my white-gloved hand over my heart.

"She presses two fingertips to her dark red lips. Presses them to mine.

"The taxi driver yells *Allons! Allons!* I'm in the back seat. The door slams. He starts to pull away, but there's time, there's still time, there's fucking time for me to press my white-gloved hands against the glass of the back window, stare out it at her staring back at the cab *leaving*."

"What happened then?" said Sasha.

"You went back to Moscow. Ames betrayed you. Jesse got you out in a spy swap."

"*No*, we all know what happened to me. What happened to you? What did you do?"

"Told the taxi driver the address of another safe house. My real Op. Then *this* and *that* and some other things. I came up with the idea for the V. Got it up and running, which meant I wasn't a '*company man*' anymore. Then the CIA locked me up in their secret insane asylum."

"No wonder."

The two old men laughed.

"And here we are," said Sasha. "Where you still haven't told me *why*."

Condor said: "They're going to kill you."

All sound in the bustling train station fell away from Sasha.

Condor rode the silence.

Sasha said: "Why? Or better, why now?"

"Have you read the news today?"

"Sadly. The Big Reveal: *'Grab 'em by the pussy.'* That is the news in America today. And tomorrow. And all your brilliant poll-taking and mirror watching political poofers—"

"Poofers?" said Condor.

"They talk. They fill up the TV, the newspaper. But all their *we know what's real* goes *poof* because they only hear themselves. They will say *'grab the pussy'* is the end of him, is beyond what people will accept. Is like a horror movie clown gone crazy. But they'll be wrong.

"They don't get it because he doesn't look like who they see in their mirrors. And they're right about that, he isn't like them. That's why people like him. People trust clowns to be clowns who must be somebody under their makeup. Better than someone who pretends he wears no makeup: We all know it's there. Clown you at least trust to be lying to you. Like reality TV."

"They're coming for you, Sasha. And you know that. All the way back to Trotsky—"

"—with an ice ax in Mexico," interrupted Sasha, who'd spent hundreds of hours of playing board games like *Clue* with CIA babysitters who kept him company in a Colorado safe house for the first year of his swapped-out life.

"I know the CIA read you the hit list since Russia started up revenge whacks again after the lull when the Berlin Wall fell. Poison pellet in the park. A bullet in an alley. A car accident. Suicide flying out a fourth-story hotel window."

"We were better at it in my day," said the wolf.

"Now is now, and you, you tell the CIA *no*. Don't let them move you to their witness protection. You don't take them up on their *expensive as hell* fallback offer to set you up with babysitters at your cottage, let you live the life you say you won't give up so it doesn't get ripped from you by your old crew. And to top all that off, you tell them that you'll burn any *without your permission* protection team you catch."

"I've been in enough prisons."

Condor leaned forward on his folded thighs.

Sasha looked down at the black leather jacket back of this man who'd saved his life once.

"Why are you here, Condor?"

"You know your old colleagues in Russia. The uniforms change. The job doesn't."

The former Russian spy said: "They are looking for *polenzi durak. Useful fool.* You have a lot of them in American politics. Almost better than an actual compromised leader. Control is difficult in any politics, anytime, anywhere, anyway, so why not just make your enemy more out of control than you? Hell, control is difficult in any intelligence operation, look at us. Come to think of it, look at everybody."

"Right now," said Condor. "I'm looking at you. For Jesse. For me. If I can't get you to be smart, I better try and stop you from being stupid."

Sarcasm edged through Sasha's words: "You're too nice to me."

"We all have our failings."

"Just don't fail to see the real Russia, *yes*? We—

"—*they*," Sasha corrected himself, "are only 144 million people and America has 325 million, but Russia is born of Stalingrad, the stupid communists, *yes*, but also *one million* of us died refusing to give up to the Germans. Fighting in the streets of the city. Starving. Dying in the snow. Now they will be *finally* be number one. No one is going to conquer Russia."

"I don't think anyone wants to," said Condor. "*Well*, China . . ."

"But more," said Sasha. "We all want more, yes? You. Me. That waiter bussing the table. Russia. The oligarchs who are Russia, now not needing to sneak and pretend and fight communist fools in the government. Whatever else, Russia is now more like the days of glory when we were an empire in this world. Respected. So the people love the man who gave them that dream of back when things were great, they love Putin."

Condor said *see*.

"*See* what?" said Sasha.

"Not *see*, not that word."

"What then? You are speaking Spanish now—*si*?"

"I said '*c*.' Like in A, B, C."

Alexander Volkov *aka* Volk *aka* Wolf *aka* Sasha blinked.

Said: "You are talking to someone I can't see."

"I can't see her either."

"But she can see us? Hacked into the Station's security cameras?"

"They don't work well enough." The born in the USA spy frowned: "You agreed to meet me. But only here. Why?"

"Does this train station mean something special to you, Condor?"

"These days, any place I get to be is special to me. But why here for you now?"

"Well . . . public place where just in case you come with a pick-up team, I have better fighting chance. Witnesses are problems for you Americans."

"I don't fuck with my friends."

"But your friends fuck with anybody," said Sasha.

"You should see what my enemies do."

"I have. I was."

"No other reason to come here to Union Station?" said Condor.

"Ice cream afterwards. Food court in the basement. I've been here before. Plenty of parking. Easy to find even if the woman in my cellphone wasn't talking to me."

"You had your cell phone on," deadpanned Condor.

Sasha said nothing.

"Why?" said Condor.

The man in the black cowboy hat said: "Sometimes you have to walk out on the line. Just to see. Verify. You can't always trust weathermen."

"*Fuck.*"

"Are we still friends?"

"We passed being friends running across the rooftops of Paris." Condor shook his head. "The CIA said your whack is scheduled for next week. Not now."

"So what? Are you saying they were wrong again? And now my old but new colleagues spotted the unexpected, us two birds with one stone? Stalingrad taught *seize the chance you see.*"

Sasha's eyes traveled up to the second-floor balcony. To the stone statues of Roman Centurions. He scanned every nook and cranny as he said:

"Is it true that the shields those statues stand behind were put up *after* the statues were installed? That your religious leaders and the politicians who they owned insisted on hiding the statues' genitals that were probably only some codpiece flower thing? That they wanted to hide any hint of sex from American citizens' eyes?"

"Public decency and morality."

"And private what? *Grab 'em by the pussy?*"

Condor said: "We have to move."

Cowboy hat and black jacket stood as one, walked side by side across chessboard tiles.

Sasha said: "Are you heavy?"

"This is America," said Condor.

Two old men shuffling through Union Station collided as they turned face to face. Luckily, their crash into each other became like a mutual hug, the cowboy reaching deep inside his buddy's unzipped black leather jacket, no doubt checking to be sure that old guy's heart was still beating. They parted. Adjusted their clothing and walked on.

Shoulder to shoulder.

Side by side.

Hands empty and free.

"Your invisible woman," said Sasha. "Is she nearby? Perhaps with friends or relatives?"

"No. You said come alone. I knew you'd catch me in even any well-intentioned lie."

"How does your *she* know anything about what's going on here?"

"You aren't the only one with a turned-on cellphone."

"*Ahh*," said Sasha. "You are already deep in this Op."

"Not by choice. And your part was CIA. Until you told them no, *my friend*."

"Sorry—not about telling the CIA *no*, but about getting you here in this now."

"What were you thinking?"

"That they wouldn't want to kill me with the CIA right here."

"*I'm not CIA!*"

"Well *now* I believe you."

They'd strolled a circle along the walls of shops in the main hall like two old men walking the circle of a big clock from seven up to eleven and past twelve. No one else seemed to be walking the clock behind or ahead of them on this tick-tock.

They strolled past the front wall of double doors filled with sunlight.

Stayed on the tick-tock circle.

Sasha said: "What does your telephone 'c' mean?"

"Call the cavalry."

"Are they coming?"

"I've got one op' who's a tough street angel. She's running the keyboard but out of the combat zone. And I've got a newbie. All the right scars but not enough street time beyond them, young guy, just like I was. He's near. But I gave him orders about any kind of *if*. He's to stay close, watch and learn, but stay clear."

"He means something to you."

"He's gotta be tomorrow."

"Let's hope not starting today," said Sasha.

"So," he said as they curved toward the passageways leading

from main hall to the waiting areas and gates for trains. "No cavalry?"

"Probably not in time."

"How many falcons?"

"Now the pings analyze out as fourteen, probably more. Every door covered."

"Will they come in?" said Sasha.

"Let's not wait and see. No more collateral casualties. Sorry, Chris Harvie." Condor frowned. "Where did you park?"

"That's the last place we should go! They probably setup there as soon as they could! It's a perfect kill zone." Then Sasha's grim line grin said *got it*. His mouth said: "Come on."

Black cowboy–hatted Sasha led Condor to the escalator running up from the passengers waiting areas and gates to trains. He took the lead, the first to step on those rising stairs.

Fluttering shot past them, a pigeon desperately trying to get the hell out of there.

The two old men reached the flat, red-tiled entrance level.

Condor said: "I think we can skip the parking validation machine."

"OK," said Sasha as they pushed their way through the EXIT doors into the sunlight for the parking structures, pancake layers, "but does this mean no ice cream?"

The stepped into the crisp chilly air.

Neither man zipped up his jacket.

No bullets cut them down as they walked past clusters of waiting bus customers.

Up the first escalator.

Sasha rode top, eyes scanning where they were going, what they were passing.

Condor rode drag facing backwards.

A few people whose faces and hands did nothing suspicious rode down past them.

What looked like a snippy married couple got on the UP escalator below Condor's gaze.

Second level, Condor walking out from being in a straight line behind Sasha until they were both on the next UP escalator.

The snippy married couple turned and walked into the pancake parking's second level.

Condor and Sasha rode the third escalator up. Rode it alone. Rode it ready.

The fourth and final escalator carried them up into the top level's entrance.

"How do you want to do this?" said Sasha.

"Give them a choice," said Condor.

"They wouldn't do—they haven't done that for us."

"*Us* isn't *them*. And if we are, we're already dead."

Sasha and Condor pushed open the glass doors. Stepped outside.

Their right hands hung chosen empty by their sides.

That vast concrete field.

A seeming thousand steps away, in the concrete field's left corner: Sasha's parked car.

A line of five men waited perhaps fifteen paces from the car, faced the two old men.

Condor and Sasha stepped forward as one.

Black leather–jacketed Condor and black cowboy-hatted Sasha stopped a first down in American football away from that skirmish line of five still empty-handed, *cautious* hunters.

One those hunters, a bushy eyebrows man, yelled in clear English: "*Bonus!*"

Before that shout echoed off the suicide wall around this vast concrete wasteland of yellow-striped slots came the blare of a disembodied electronic woman's voice blasted at full volume through all present cyber devices: "*Stoy!*"

This whole cast of killers froze.

Like a shot, knew they were not alone. Knew they were known.

Sasha translated: "*Halt.*"

From far off, those on the cement parking lot roof/floor heard the sound of a helicopter.

Coming closer.

Bushy-eyebrows man shouted at his comrades: "*Trakhat' ikh!*"

Condor flowed like he was half his age, swooped into the Weaver stance. His left hand cupped his right and the .45 1911 automatic pistol created for American soldiers to stop fanatical religious terrorists. His eyes—

BAM! BAM! BAM!

Slug two knocked Bushy Eyebrows backwards and slammed him onto the cement.

Gunshots echoes going *gone* as the chopping sound of a helicopter grew louder.

Condor lowered his gun arm and through the ringing in his ears yelled: "*Stalingrad!*"

The four men facing the two spies they'd come to kill stood absolutely still, but Condor sensed that his shouted word had moved them, moved Sasha.

The chopping sounds of a helicopter.

Slowly, his eyes on the four men standing by their sprawled boss, Condor walked a curve around the Russians and toward the Jeep. Sasha traveled with him.

The four Russians had been to the ballet. Moved as one. On the escalator down, *gone* as the October Saturday shook with the sound of a helicopter.

Condor stood beside Sasha, with him between his car and the sprawled corpse.

"*Fuck them,*" said Sasha. "*Trakhat' ikh.* That's what he yelled."

"Oh."

"Mutual Assured Destruction," said Sasha. "The old Cold War. That's what you wanted them to know."

"No," said Condor. "*Stalingrad*. No retreat. No surrender. No fucking around."

A helicopter roared over their heads.

Condor told Sasha: "You'll have to stay now."

"No longer than it takes for you who aren't CIA to clear me to go."

The helicopter landed on the far side of the cement roof/top level of Union Station's pancake levels parking structure. A SWAT team hopped out and hustled a *tactical advance*, assault rifles aimed and ready, orders streaming into their helmets' earpieces.

The two old men glanced at Sasha's Jeep.

Slugs one and three had punched holes through the driver's door.

Sasha shook his head. "I'm going home."

"But you," said this man in the black cowboy hat: "Where are you going, Condor?"

CHAMBER SIX
Runaway American Dream

'Twas the day after Christmas and nothing was stirring in this suburban Washington, DC, neighborhood, not even at the Martin's old house that odd couple bought in September. Of course, there must have been something going on *somewhere!* After all, 2016 had been quite a year: the Chicago Cubs broke the 108-year-old curse and won the World Series.

They—the odd couple, not the Cubs—they were nice people, of that everyone in the neighborhood was sure, though no one had ever done much more that exchange *polites* with them and feel an odd chill that wasn't from the gold leafed October air when they moved in. The new people kept to themselves—except for the visitors—but that was understandable given *her conditions* that their real estate broker accidentally let slip into neighborhood ears.

She seemed fine when you drove by the house and spotted her.

Actually, she looked great, though all the men in the neighborhood, no matter their age, were careful *not* to say so to their wives—who knew anyway, who could read that look on their *better not* husbands' faces. She'd dyed her shoulder-length silvered hair to a more treasured golden blond. The way it suited her, maybe way back before she'd turned at least fifty-five—most said sixty or more—maybe she'd been a natural blonde. She looked strong, trim, though Lisa Calhoun, the brilliant rocket scientist who worked at NASA and lived next door, said the woman's hands sometimes trembled.

Probably from her conditions.

Zoophobia. Fear of animals.

Especially big animals. Like deer. Or snarling dogs straining the leashes of their poop bag carrying owners on the way to the park that ran beyond the stream behind the houses for everyone on the Calhoun's side of Shelby Road. Good thing that the new folks' renovator found that medical-needs exception buried in the county home construction zoning code *and then* found those like-new lengths of black metal pole fences salvaged from a warehouse fire up in Baltimore. What a work crew! Like the Army Corps of Engineers dropped into a combat zone. Only took them three days to ring the house with a chest high black steel pole fence. But some people in the neighborhood were not convinced that even that high of a fence could stop the leaping deer that had become like garden plundering rats in the suburbs of DC.

2016 was the year Bambi went berserk.

The (dyed) golden woman of that house also suffered from *agoraphobia*, not so much fear of leaving her home as fear of new people and new places, of any *strange*.

That's why the workman replaced the glass insert front door with a *can't-see-through-it* thick slab of black wood that looked like it could stop a cannonball.

Went oddly well with the brick house and the new windows

that seemed double insulated for winter with some kind of fila-ments running through them, probably for heat.

The rehab construction started on the day when hurricane weather was hitting the East Coast and bombs were falling on Syria and GOP Presidential Candidate Trump said that Russia's President Putin "has been a leader far more than our president has."

They moved in on an October day when the polls showed Hillary Clinton increasing her lead over Donald Trump in the Presidential race.

They must have been busy unpacking when the newspapers talked about a census report that said 41 million people in Amer-ica lived in poverty, 12 percent of the population and rising, one in three of them being children, the highest *kids in poverty* rate in the industrialized world.

And somewhere in their unpacking of boxes padded by crumpled newspapers, that new couple might have spotted a dif-ferent news story that said 5 percent of Americans in 2016 had crossed the line into being millionaires—*yay!*

Of course, most of the people on Shelby Road were in the *everybody else* category, what the numbers crunchers called median income folks, and when those keyboard clickers ran the *Who's Number One?* by percentage for those lucky middle chunk of winners, America ranked twenty steps down from the top slot of all the countries in the world.

Nobody in the neighborhood could quite figure where the new couple fell in life's deal of dollars. Sure, like everyone else around them, they (probably with some mortgage collecting bank) owned their house—*Goodbye, Martins!*—but beyond all that, two months after they joined the neighborhood, the new odd couple were still strangers.

Everyone in the neighborhood was probably a stranger to them, too, right?

Like, there's no way they could have known about the

second-mortgaged Mignaults at the top of Shelby Road, how Peter was losing to throat cancer from cigarettes all the *deza* had sold him, sitting in his home waiting while his twenty-nine-year-old, lived-there-too son stole his pain meds to feed his Oxy addiction as poor Mary's boss struggled to keep her on the payroll so she wouldn't lose the family health insurance that covered nearly 19 percent of their medical costs.

And the newcomers couldn't have known about Annie and Sheila's eight-year-old who tested as *on the spectrum* for autism that no public school could accommodate.

Or how Hank three doors up from the newcomers was in line to be the new Special Assistant to the Assistant Director for Interagency Synergy in the Department.

Or who was staring at their walls, staring out their windows.

Or who would joyously dance around her empty house with the music in her ear buds.

Was the election on November 8 that let the street learn the new neighbors' names.

The next morning, way early when most everyone was *what the hell happened to the pollsters always being right*, Isabel Calhoun, the bright red-haired sprite who was taking an after high school gap year, just back from Ghana and teaching in a town where no one had indoor plumbing, now living back at home with her mom, that *after-the-election* morning sprite Isabel went up and down Shelby Road putting single red rose on the doorstops of her neighbors to remind everyone of the beauty in this world.

And somehow, almost like he had camera eyes on the street or something, the new man of the Martin's old house, a silver-haired guy who could have been Isabel's lonely grandfather, he saw her on her secret mission. Unlocked the steel bars gate, stepped out into the street with her for a chat. To find out *why*. To say *thank you*.

Told Isabel he was *Vin*.

And that the blond woman he lived with was *Merle.*

Might have said they were married, Isabel couldn't remember. Did remember that he told her that he was a "reclusive" science fiction writer and that Merle ran an Internet-based art business that accounted for frequent visitors who were much younger than them.

Plus Merle had "home visit nurse check-ins" for her conditions.

Some of those people must have brought in groceries, because you never saw Merle or Vin at the local stores, or out much in nearby downtown Silver Spring.

Though there was that one odd time where a clean-cut young man driving a New York license plate car spent several nights with the older couple. A few neighbors saw him going in and out of the house, and everyone winced when they saw a scabby scar on his left check.

One of those nights, Jim Kerry, who lived up the block and retired from being a White House reporter, Jim saw that New York car parked on the downtown street with the gun shop. The scarred man sat behind the steering wheel staring out the windshield toward nothing but the Construction/Destruction skyline and the door down to a dive bar called the Quarry House.

That young guy sat there the whole time Jim was picking up carryout dinner from the Jamaican café for him and his wife, Louise, who back then kept hoping that the three suicides of students in the public high school where she taught represented coincidence, not contagion. Jim saw that scarred man just sitting in that New York car, looking out the windshield, watching the void or maybe what he couldn't or wouldn't get out to go see.

Maggie from down the block, who liked to know what was going on and sure could tell you about it, Maggie just happened to be walking past that house uphill from hers one of those days when we all had our black bagged trash and our recycling's blue bins out in the street for weekly pickup, and *wouldn't you know it*: the silver-haired new home owner was taking out his trash at that very moment. Maggie launched into it—why not just skip over any *polites* and get to the heart of things. Said that nice young man who'd been parked in the driveway inside their property's bars, was he your son?

Weirded Maggie out, what happened then.

Remember, that was still when nobody knew his name was *Vin*, so Maggie called him *that silver-haired guy behind the bars around his house*. She said he looked at her—he'd been looking at her since he spotted her hustling up the street, but until she said *son*, he'd been looking at her like some kind of hawk. Then, said Maggie, kind of like hangdog came over him, and it must have been a big dog, because he couldn't speak, could only shake his head *no*.

Hope Vin never let Merle know about that dog, what with her fear of animals.

After that, everyone thought that even though the young man with the scar wasn't anybody's son, a bunch of people figured that woman who dyed her hair red, a few folks wondered if Ms. Redhead 2016 might not be the new neighbors' daughter.

Nobody ever got a chance to ask her, though she often visited Vin and Merle.

Like on that day after Christmas in 2016 when $6.5 *billion* in easily *trackable* money had been spent deciding America's Congressional and Presidential elections. In the DC suburbs of Virginia, the once hippest mall of upscale retail stores inside the Beltway was a ghost town where the iconic American department store Macy's, its signs still hanging on the mall's vast walls, became a homeless shelter for hundreds of American families, sanctioned by its new owner, a corporation named for dead billionaire Howard Hughes who'd dazzled air travel, Hollywood and Las Vegas, and even worked with the CIA.

From behind his desk in his third-story loft office, Condor

watched his screens show bundled-up Faye get out of her car, lock it as the iron gates clanged shut behind her.

Inside the house, Merle worked the security code to open the black front door for Faye.

Once that black door closed, Condor let whatever those two women were doing go unmonitored as he went back to helping a Handler in Saigon (OK: *Ho Chi Minh City*) maneuver a Conscious Operative out of Burma (OK: *Myanmar*) who was rescuing two political dissidents marked for death by the 90 percent Buddhist government in their persecution of the Rohingya minority. Satellite photos of that sealed country showed government security forces had burned down five towns. CIA *Credible High* intelligence reports told of thousands of Rohingya murdered, epidemic gang rapes, infanticide, and refugees on the run.

Condor forced himself to face the music—or rather, to not turn off the satellite radio playing in the background as he worked, the gravely bass voice of poet Leonard Cohen, who'd died from a fall the day before the 2016 election, singing: "*You Want It Darker.*"

C.O./Saigon (*Un-unh: forget it*) signaled no more backup needed.

Condor heard footsteps climbing the stairs to the second-level bedroom/guard posts.

Heard a knock on the closed door for the stairs up to his V work lair.

Didn't check the monitors to see *who.*

Didn't think twice before yelling: "OK!"

He swiveled his chair away from three monitors on his desk as up the stairs came Faye.

That redhead smiled like a daughter he never got to have: "Merry Christmas. I guess."

"And Happy New Year," said Condor.

"*Ya think?*" she said, mimicking him.

"I hope," he told Faye. "You know about Moscow?"

"I saw a CIA alert," said Faye.

"Oleg Erovinkin. A general in both the KGB and then its re-branded FSB internal spying and secret police agency. Linked as a possible source in the ex-British spy's dossier about our Pres-ident-elect and the Russians, the oligarchs and Putin and their spies. Erovinkin is—was—sixty-one, good health, vibrant, and *today* he was found dead in the back of his car in Moscow. The FSB is investigating and already saying it was *of course* just a heart attack."

"Happens with old guys," said Faye.

"Like me," said Condor.

"Let's hope not. You're fine, right? The medical team says so."

"How do you know what our medical team says?"

Faye blushed. "Part of my job is backup and security. For Merle, mostly, who they say seems to be doing fine, even great. Like a long dark cloud's been lifted off her."

"Nice recovery."

They both knew he wasn't talking about Merle. He pushed that *medical team knowledge* issue no further. Why should he?

Faye said: "Are you, *are we* working that Erovinkin hit?"

"Not a V op."

"Even after what happened at your last nest?"

"That was the Russians making a mistake. *Yeah*, we had to play it and play it out. But they still don't know what they penetrated with their killer spy Justin. The Russians think they attacked and wounded a troll operation. Minimal data plus mistaken mirror reasoning."

"Even after *Stalingrad*?"

"You trigger killers, killing comes back at you. They probably expected, *accepted* that."

"Iffy."

"What isn't *iffy* in this life?"

"This life *us*, or—"

"Any life," said Condor.

The radio in the background played some song they both knew, didn't care to name.

"What about your friend Sasha?" said Faye.

"He knew Erovinkin—or at least of him. The Agency let him know. Sasha still won't relocate from his cottage. I gave him a call. He wanted to talk about bare trees in winter."

"*Russians*," said Faye.

They sat there in that secret loft and just breathed.

Until Condor said: "What about our guy?"

Faye didn't break eye contact. "We don't talk much."

She shrugged. "When you aren't running him on an op', he's up in Brooklyn. He doesn't fit—where do any of us fit—but up there, nobody notices."

"He needs to see as much of himself as he can."

"Yeah," said Faye. About something.

"Do you two . . . ?"

She looked out the loft windows, past the winter bare trees to the suburban gray horizon.

He let it go.

Said: "He's done good in the field. He levels up to Handler next week."

"I figured you just up him all the way to replace you as Control Function."

"No," said Condor. "That will be you."

Faye blinked.

"It's all in place. You'll run the V *when*."

"I . . . I . . ."

"There's no better choice," said Condor. "For anybody."

"What if I don't want that. Don't want to be . . . You said *he* was going to be *you*."

"He will. When you say he's ready. When you want to . . . to be whoever you want to be."

"When does anybody ever get that?"

Red-haired Faye drilled him with her eyes. "Are you . . ."

Softened it with a grin: "Are you *v*-aporizing?"

"I don't know. I don't want to log off until I do. But doing *me* means being ready."

"I have a thousand questions."

"I have zero answers."

The radio sang about breaking this trap.

"You missed lunch," said Condor. "It's coming up on dinner: Want to stay?"

"*No!* I mean, *no*," she said. "Thanks, but . . . "

"Sure."

"What do you think will happen?" said Faye. "With the Russians? Their attacks on us?"

"What do *you* think?" said Condor.

"I think it's all fucked up."

"What brave new world has come 'round." He shrugged. "Our *on the way out* President is putting sanctions on Russia for interfering in our election. We'll see how long that lasts and works. The Pentagon is beefing up its cybersecurity. Supposedly there's going to be a new $300 million bill in the coming Congress to help states gear up their polling and electoral security."

Faye shook her head.

"All that's fine and good, but it doesn't hit the heart of the beast. The social media frauds. The *active measures'* campaign of big lies and black money manipulations and compromises and attacks. The mauling of the minds and hearts of all of us out there in our American screens. None of it touches *the big obvious* of how big money driving elections is inherently corrupt. And even if the Russians stop doing what they did *that worked*, there's still drug cartels, big oil countries, China, small dictators who've got big tech and dirty dollars. They all want to fuck with us to grab more power."

"People forget," said Condor, "even though that kills them. Most voters don't remember what they used to know or didn't get taught, so most of them don't know enough about their own lives. Most voters probably think Tammany Hall is a country and western singer."

"Or a reality TV star," said Faye.

"Like you said," Condor told her: "Fucked up."

The radio played some new song.

"Happy New Year," whispered Faye.

"To us all."

She flowed to her feet with *gung fu* grace.

He followed his guest's lead with the cautious stiffness that now owned him.

"I should get going," said Faye, "because . . . well, *you know*."

"Sure," he said, without a clue as to what she meant, but being polite, social.

They stood staring at each other, that awkward moment when what the occasion calls for is unclear and what you want to do and should do are equal mysteries.

"Don't want you to be yet another man in *Me, too* trouble," said Faye, so she hugged him.

Almost like a daughter.

Who he had to let go.

All daughters and sons are let go.

"Anyway," said Faye—

—and grinned in a way he couldn't *grok*: "Really, have a *hell* of a happy new year."

Then she walked down the stairs toward tomorrows' best kiss.

Condor sat at his desk.

Looked beyond the three monitors, through the loft windows to the graying light.

Checked his watch: only 4:33, but *hey*: it was the afternoon after Christmas, he could—

The door at the bottom of his stairs opened.

Footsteps clunked up—

—bringing Merle into the office holding a plate and a glass of water in her hands.

Her (dyed) golden hair seemed thicker and more flowing than usual. Condor remembered *not* listening to the sounds of her downstairs in the shower while he'd been engaged in that murderous Buddhists op'. She must have washed her hair, her closed eyes face upturned into the rain of warm water, her fingers sudsing her thick *back-to-blond* hair, her pale shoulders slick with wet that flowed down her body, down her wrinkled back to the hanging low round moon of her ass, down her chest to where her breasts sagged, down between her flabby legs, water flowing down into the shower's drain.

His mind knew that's how she must have looked. His heart saw her differently.

Now as she walked through the fading afternoon in the office lair that shaped his life, Merle wore a baggy gray hoodie and a pair of stained black sweat pants with worn out sneakers that padded across the carpet toward him.

"I brought you a sandwich for dinner," she said of the plate she carried.

"I was going to quit work and—"

"No."

Condor blinked.

"You never quit work," said Merle. "Today's not over. Stay up here. Eat. I already have."

"We never do this. If Techs haven't dropped off dinner, usually it's me who heats up the leftovers or burns some poor dead cow."

"Haven't you heard? Haven't you noticed? It's like I'm a new old me."

He faced her from his desk chair as she stopped in front of his knees.

"Here I am," she said.

Put the plate with a sandwich on his desk.

Picked a thick gray football pill off the plate and held it out to him.

Said: "And here you go."

All of him went cold.

"Relax," said Merle. "It's not nose spray."

"What made you think of that?"

"It's not me who jumped to that," said Merle. "It's you, Condor."

"You don't have to call me that."

"It's grown on me," said Merle. "Take your pill.

"What's the matter?" she said as he stared up at her. "After all we've been through, don't you trust me?"

There it is.

There it always is.

Like he told Rick Applegate. Like he told the other Condor. Like Sasha knew.

Trust.

At some point, we all have to pull that trigger.

He took the pill from her (!) polished blood-red fingers.

Popped it into his mouth, took a drink of odd tasting water from the glass she gave him.

Swallowed it all.

He opened his mouth wide like a convict to a skeptical guard: "Did it. What does it do?"

"How the hell should I know?" said Merle. "It's the brand new superhero."

She looked out the windows.

"About an hour of daylight left. Have Bonnie tell me when you're ten minutes from coming down, or she'll tell you when to come. Wait for a trace of pink in the sky."

Merle reached under her gray sweatshirt . . .

. . . pulled out a medical marijuana vape pen.

Set it on the desk by the plate.

"Eat first," she said. "Save that for sign off. Then go in the bathroom there before you come downstairs. Brush your teeth. You don't want to get busted for bad breath."

She clumped down the stairs and never once looked back.

Was a turkey and tomato sandwich. Mayo and some kind of lettuce, too. Chunks of dark meat left over from what they hadn't eaten from the dropped-off as an extended hospitality from Techs who'd invited the two of them to Christmas dinner outside the bars.

Merle hadn't felt up to going.

Or so she'd said.

Bad for security and command protocols.

Or so he'd said.

He stared through and beyond the screens to all that he could do with them, past the killing and the conning and the spying of the V and with it into wherever he wanted to go from the comfort of his desk chair. Like the Russians, he could download a data profile of anybody, hack the Facebook and other social media domains of ex-lovers, of friends from college or high school, but what was the point? He saw them as they needed to be with his mind's eye.

Best not to meet the ghosts in your machine.

Wunk: the monitor screen showing images of inside this house went dark.

The outside monitors showed no threats beyond the steel fence's black bars.

Shelby Road, quiet and still.

Only bare trees in the woods out back, no one in the gaps between him and his neighbors.

Sensors indicated no stirrings, not even a mouse.

Black screen. Had to be a command given Bonnie or through a keypad, both options control-coded to his voice or retinal scan.

Or to Merle.

She'd needed that power to command some small reality of privacy.

Was only right. Only fair. After all, she'd been trapped everywhere with him since . . .

Well, since Chris Harvie was shot dead.

Condor could override Merle's orders, *but* . . .

The radio played. Two of his three screens glowed with images and data.

Condor sat at his desk and in his choice as the sky outside darkened.

Told himself the pounding of his heart and the tightening of his mind and spine were only nerves or some side effect of whatever drug Merle'd fed him.

He'd been drugged before.

Laughed at the thought of his spy agency *V* as *vape*. Or maybe *V* for *Vin*.

He hit the marijuana vape pen. Coughed and choked and wheezed.

Walked into his lair's bathroom and minty-flavor brushed his teeth.

Walked out and announced: "Bonnie, tell Merle I'm on my way."

Than rather than wait Merle's "suggested" ten minutes, he told Bonnie to activate off duty protocols, seized control of the tick-tock and walked down the stairs.

Opened the door.

Fire! This place is on—

Candles. Flickering candles.

Their soft flickering glows softening the darkness in his—*their*—bedroom.

Acting as sentinels lighting the stairs down to this house's main level.

Thick, long candles. Probably could burn for hours. Dozens and dozens of candles.

He closed the door up to the V's office lair.

That *click* activated Bonnie to turn on music downstairs in the dining room.

Gravely-voiced, dead John Stewart singing the song he wrote that others made famous:

Daydream Believer.

Last time I heard that, thought Condor, was in a therapy session with Merle, a "confrontation release" treatment where the Top Secret cleared shrink had him rattle off songs he thought should be played at his funeral in an attempt to get Merle to articulate and go beyond her PTSD and angry trembles and terrors.

What session am I in now? thought Condor as candles flickered and that song played.

Was it a random *clong*—one of those moments when you're in the street and what you see and what's been haunting you crash together with their perfect soundtrack you hear playing in some radio or device?

Was it an algorithm-driven selection made by A.I. Bonnie who controlled so many of his breaths and who *of course* could be trusted?

Or is this something Merle set up?

Like the candles. Like the sandwich. Like the vape. Like the mystery pill.

Nowhere to go except down the candlelit stairs to where the music played.

The invisible smoke of those dozens of flames smelled like vanilla, like flowers.

Merle stood in the dining room, her back to Condor as she lit the last candles that warmed where they were into a comfort cave with a locked black front door and painting covered walls and a row of back windows filled with that dark night.

That day after Christmas, her hair she'd dyed blond in November cascaded in soft waves. Her sapphire eyes glistened, brushed blush brought life to her pale, high-boned cheeks. She smiled as he entered the dining room, her wide lips painted a slick glowing red he was sure matched Marilyn Monroe's in a photograph he and Merle saw when he'd urged her to read a magazine article revealing movie star Marilyn as an intellectual, philosophical, feminist star.

"See?" Condor'd told Merle who told him that her own M.M. initials for Merle Mardigian sometimes triggered thoughts of that suicided—or was it murdered?—mistress of politicians. *"We can be more than who we're trapped as."*

Merle wore a dress Condor'd never seen.

Her dress wasn't white like Marilyn's, was a darker red than blood, shoulder straps sliding down to a deep V between her breasts bound by no bra, the dress flaring out so she could spin and flash her bare legs and then he noticed not sneakers but angels' well-heeled red shoes.

She let his eyes take in the all of her in as she stood beside the bare white wood rectangular dining room table, a scene lit well by flickering candles.

Merle said: "Is this who you wanted?"

"What?"

"Way before all the bullets. After you got out of the CIA's crazy house. When you used to watch me come into the Starbucks up on Capitol Hill. When you saw some dream of *us* before you hijacked my life to fight off your death. Was this who you wanted me to be?"

"I wanted you to be you."

She cocked her head with a grin that said *Really?*

"I want to find the *you* who was all the *you* I ever wanted *you* to be."

"And this," she said, take a step closer to him. "This what you get. What you spies call *the take*. And you took it. Get to take it. Are stuck with it."

"This isn't you," said Condor.

"This isn't who I was. Who I've been for the last, *what*, seems like eternity. That one good night *before* when I thought *maybe*. Then all the nights after Chris Harvie when clinging to you and doing what I could that you wanted me to do was all I could do and it was never enough for either of us, though you faked it pretty well."

She took a step closer and he could smell musk perfume she'd never worn before.

And he realized the secret identity of the new superhero pill.

As the vape mushroomed through him like she knew it would.

He couldn't log what songs were playing over the pounding of his own heart.

"So," she whispered as she stood before him with no more than a thin novel between the press of their clothed flesh. "Here I am. You're Control Function. What are you going to do?"

He trapped her face in the cup of his hands, his mouth found hers and felt her sticky lips surprisingly not hesitate as they opened and slid him into the velvet tongue of her kiss.

She pushed herself against him from his thighs to his heart, her faced turned up to his and his hands spread wide on her back, *careful* not to presumptuously/offensively slide where they wanted to go. She took his left hand, kissed his palm, leaned back so she could fill his grasp with the flesh of her right breast below her silky thin red dress.

Said: "Come with me."

She led him out of the dining room, up the stairs but ahead and above him by two steps so the entire focus of his life locked onto the tremulous sway of her moon flesh inside the red dress.

Flickering candles lit their journey into the bedroom they shared.

Paled shadows of flowered light waved on the bedroom's blue walls.

The bed was turned down to its white sheets and fluffed pillows.

Merle trailed her hands down his chest, stepped back, grinned: "Your socks are still on."

Standing on one leg, then the other with speed and balance meant maybe his decades of practicing *T'ai chi* hadn't been for mere enlightened survival after all. Not only did his socks fly off, his shoes were gone, too, then quickly went his faded black jeans, his maroon flannel shirt and the long-sleeved blue winter hiking underwear top. Part of him realized the heat must have been turned up beyond the thermostat's normal setting and all of him burned.

"See?" she said, looking at him. "I told you. Superhero."

They crashed together, mouths on each other, red lipstick smearing both their skins.

His right hand stroked down her spine, looking for the dress's zipper . . .

"Pull it off," she whispered.

Straps jerked down her shoulders, trapping her arms at her sides, freeing *oh* freeing her breasts and he couldn't help from caressing their tipped flesh, squeezing ever so gently as Merle's shoulders and chest heaved her breaths and he took first one, then her other nipple into his suck.

Condor jerked the dress all the way down, over her *oh* her hips, down her thighs as he dropped onto the carpet with both knees and *oh yes* discovered she wore nothing under that garment but her pride and the scents, *oh* the scent of her that filled his nostrils and nuzzling and kisses. "*There!*" she cried, opened herself to him until a scream jerked her back from the intensity, pulling him but he was kissing the backs of her thighs, kissing the wondrous roundness and secrets of her ass, kissing up her spine and wrapping his arms around her to pull her warmth against his, kissing her neck, her cheek, his hands full of her breasts. She turned to see his face over her left shoulder and before she strained to kiss him, before they stumbled to the bed, she filled her eyes with his ache, whispered: "*Want, do what you want!*"

And he did and then after a miracle short while, she made him do so again.

The man who'd become Condor lay with his face pressed on the bones of M.M.'s warm chest, tried to hear the beat of her heart.

"Are your pulse and blood pressure back down to normal yet?" she asked him.

"Everything's back down to normal," he said.

"We'll see."

She pulled herself out from under his weight.

Walked through the flickers of light to the bathroom beyond the foot of the bed.

Clicked on that light. Stood staring into the sink's mirror.

Soaked a washcloth with steaming water, wrang it out, wiped it over her loins, between her legs, under her arms, rinsed it and wiped her closed eyes face. Pulled a towel off the shower bar, dried herself, hung the towel back up and . . .

Picked up a gold tube of lipstick. From where he lay on the bed, Condor watched her turn that metal tube and slide a dark red tip into the world.

She turned and caught him staring at her but unlike ever before, she grinned.

Slammed the bathroom door shut.

Must have been five, might have been ten minutes.

Laying there alone on the rumpled bed, staring at the white closed bathroom door, Condor heard the toilet flush. Heard the sink run.

The bathroom door flew open.

Merle stood there. Naked. Silhouetted by the small room's light.

Her hair looked perfect and even in the dim, he saw the darkened thickness of her lips.

She threw—*tossed*—the hot damp washcloth at—*to*—him.

"You're turn," she said as he got off the bed. "Do all you gotta do to do it all right."

She'd have heard the toilet flush, the sink run again as he worked the bathroom.

"Come," she said when he joined her, and naked like her, he followed.

I can have Bonnie delete the security footage of what we did, thought Condor.

Or not.

They each held onto the railing as they walked down the stairs.

He glanced at the closed black slab front door as he followed her into the candlelit dining room: *Of course the black door was still solid and locked, secure.*

Their bare feet padded them to the kitchen island.

Merle pulled open the junk drawer, lifted out another vape pen, offered it to him.

Condor shook his head no: "I think I'm fine."

"That's your first mistake."

Merle twirled the vape pen in her fingers like a wand.

Slid its tip between her scarlet lips, sucked longer than the recommended two seconds.

What about her other drugs—I mean, meds? thought Condor.

Spasms of coughing and choking shook her body but she never lost her red smile.

Held the V pen out to him.

"You're not going to make me go there alone, are you?" said Merle.

He hit the pen, then let the chocking shake through him and remembered the good old days of illegal water pipes that sent you smooth.

Wasn't that he couldn't stand straight or mistakenly thought it was OK for him to drive, was that being how he was then meant being in the *wow.* The dizzy high of stoned.

She took the pen back and set it on the counter.

"Bonnie," ordered Merle. "Kill the music."

The house that was their fortress and their prison fell silent.

"My turn," she said.

"What are we doing?"

"You've got no complaints so far tonight."

Her hand floated up in front of her grinning face, her fingers beckoned him to follow.

Of course he did—bumped into the dining room table but made it to the far end of the table and the cushioned dining room chair she sat him in and scooted him up to that ten-foot-long white rectangle. The wall of windows to the night rose on his heartside. His forward gaze held the kitchen and the stairs up. The locked black door *in and out* of *then and there* was unseen but logically where it had been moments before.

He watched her walk away.

Sit in the dining room chair opposite him on the far end of the table.

A naked man and a naked woman sitting across a white plane from each other.

His head in the clouds, Condor smiled at her.

Her lips so red, Merle smiled at him.

Her right hand *blink* holding/aiming at him a pistol.

Roaring rushing realization.

The pistol in her right hand—now also braced by her left hand—the gun was a revolver.

A revolver evolved from the Colt six shooters carried by cowboys of yore and lore.

The black bore of that revolver stared at Condor.

The gun close enough for him to see all the chambers looked loaded.

They should be: after all the *after's*, Security Protocols stashed handguns all over this new house, weapons easy to use after a quick grab, and since—no denying it—Condor was not as young as he used to be, and since Merle's firearms training after they'd survived Justin's attack consisted of two range sessions he'd barely coaxed her through, logic dictated that the weapons stashed for quick grabs should be as easy to use as possible.

Hence the revolver in a holster clipped under the dining room table.

No safety. No complications of cock the hammer first, then fire—though you could, and a cocked hammer made it easier to lock the gun bore on its target. The revolver Merle held was the model issued to millions of American cops before the late twentieth-century dawn of *everybody's armed* with rapid fire, high capacity killing machines.

Six chambers. Six bullets. One would be enough. Especially at close range.

She grinned: *"Surprise!"*

A naked old man and a naked old woman. Sagging skin with brown age spots. Muscles flat. Bones weary. Smelling of. Sitting at the dining room table in a house on Shelby Road, night after Christmas 2016. Staring into each other's eyes over the barrel of a revolver.

In her hands.

"My turn," she said again.

Condor's aged heart slammed against his ribs, but he kept his voice calm.

Said: "Your turn for what?"

"To be the game master—*mistress*, actually. After all, life is a game, yes?"

"No. Life is what we've got and what we make it."

"*Ah.*" The revolver in Merle's hand waved in a gesture to take in all of that night after Christmas. "Which of those is what's going on here?"

"You tell me. You've got the gun."

She waggled the revolver in her hand: "Oh, yes I do."

"But it's not enough."

"Still, like you said," smiled Merle with her blood red lips, "it's what I've got."

She leaned forward over the white table, the gun wandering this way and that but always less than a blink from dead zero on Condor. "Don't you want to know why?"

"Right now, I'd rather know *what*. I can guess a lot of your ghosts of *why*."

"Don't you wonder about the ghosts to come?"

He sat there. Waiting.

The woman initialed M.M. said: "All I wanted was a shot to be free to be me."

She stared at the revolver. "But—looks like this is the gun I got.

"You gave it to me," she said. "You and your V and all this."

"And all that's out there, too," said Condor, nodding to the windows. "Don't forget that."

"But it was your gravity, your momentum that brought me here."

"I can't apologize any more than the thousand times I already have."

"Who the fuck believes your apologies? You won. You got what you wanted." She waved the gun toward the stairs leading up to where they'd just been. "*Remember?*"

"Your choice, too."

"*Really.* Choosing from what the guns give you isn't being free, it's guessing how you can stand to be fucked."

"What are you going to do," he said, knew she rightly heard it as both question and creed.

"Fuck it," she said.

Stabbed the revolver at him, that black steel wobbling in her fist.

Screamed: "*FUCK IT!*"

Even A.I. Bonnie knew better than to react.

Burning red rage flowed from Merle's face. She settled back in her dining room chair.

The revolver calmed. Heavy in her hand, she rested the butt on the table. Kept the barrel pointed at him. Kept her finger on the trigger.

"Was this last time," she said, "what made me *get it* to get us here was the Russians."

She waved the revolver: "Don't you get it yet?"

Her right finger came off the trigger but stayed in the gun's steel trigger loop.

Her left hand swooped her palm along the revolver's cylinder of bullets wheel.

Whirring clicking of bullets spun through the firing line.

"Saw that in a movie," said Merle.

The gun barrel pointed at him as her words fired the *what* of their *here and now*:

"Russian Roulette. Six chambers of fun. Six bullets in the gun. What a game."

Merle aimed the gun at Condor, said: *"Pow!"*

Pressed the gun barrel to her own skull: "Or *Pow!"*

"One shot," she said, "don't you always say we only get one shot at this life?"

"This isn't how Russian Roulette works," said Condor. "There's supposed to be only one bullet in the six chambers. You take turns spinning. You get a *click*—empty chamber, you live. You pass the revolver, maybe that person gets to spin the cylinder to give them back the odds of one-in-six, maybe they don't. And if they don't, if they get a *click*, you don't get to spin either when it's your turn to pull the trigger. That's Russian Roulette."

"So call this is *American Roulette*," said Merle. "All our chambers are loaded.

"Or are they? Are some chambers filled with those dummy rounds you made me use to practice loading? Those dummy rounds, in the *snapped shut* cylinder and from where you're sitting, they'd look totally real."

She pointed the gun with its full chambers cylinder at Condor: "Is what you see real? Or are you just stoned?"

She laughed at him, laughed and laughed and laughed. At him. At them. At this.

Condor waited until her laughter had to breathe.

Said: "If you've got six full chambers of *real*, there's a lot of ways this could go *bang*."

Raised his right hand in the shape of a pistol with his thumb cocked straight up.

Pointed his barrel forefinger at the woman who pointed a revolver at him.

Condor fired his finger gun: *"Bang!"*

Pointed his finger gun at his own skull: *"Bang!"*

Aimed back at Merle *"Bang!"* double-tapped the finger gun back to his skull *"Bang!"*

Held his finger gun out trembling and shaking so it would miss target her: *"Bang!"*

Pointed his finger gun to the ceiling and the night's starlit sky beyond: *"Bang!"*

"Plus," said Condor, "not every shot is a killer."

"Aren't you going to say we should just walk away like this never happened?"

"We can walk away, but not into that lie. That would be fake news."

"What's real?"

"Nobody knows the whole of what's real, we just know the hole we're in.

"Like the chamber of a gun." Merle lifted her revolver-heavy hand: *"American Roulette.* We all gotta play. The only thing you don't know is where the bullet is going to go."

The room breathed deep.

Condor said: *"Take your shot."*

ACKNOWLEDGMENTS

A fact's a fact and that is that, but in 2016, *that* became more important than ever, so to underscore reality, plus to honor, recognize and credit sources and inspirations for this *of course fictional* story, thanks to: Henry Allen, Anne Applebaum, Matt Apuzzo, Devlin Barrett, Charles Blow, The Beatles, Kate Campagna, Lou Campbell, Michael Carlisle, Richard Condon, David Corn, Elvis Costello, Philip K. Dick, Jackson Diehl, John Dos Passos, Elizabeth Dwoskin, Bob Dylan, Nicholas Fandos, Henry J. Farrell, Adam Goldman, Amy Goldman, Bonnie Goldstein, Joseph Goldstein, Mathew Goldstein, Harry Gossett, Nathan Grady, Tom Gray, *The Guardian*, Ben Guarino, Jeanne Guyon, Maggie Haberman, *Harpers*, Rob Hart, Michael V. Hayden, Daniel Hoffman, Sari Horwitz, Stephen Hunter, Aldos Huxley, Michael Isikoff, Andrew Kramer, Walter Kirn, Joe Lansdale, David Lynch, Kristen Mallette, Ron Mardigian, Michael McFaul, Louise Mensch, *Mother Jones*, *Newsweek*, *The New Yorker*, *The New York Times*, Roy Orbison, George Orwell, Evan Osnos, Kathleen Parker, Otto Penzler, Rick Perlstein, John "Jack" Platt, *Politico*, Quarry House Tavern owners and managers and staff,

David Remnick, Johnny Rivers, Tony Romm, Matthew Rosenberg, Vladimir Sakharov, Michael S. Schmidt, Michael Schwirtz, Scott Shane, David Hale Smith, Bruce Springsteen, Jeff Stein, John Stewart, The Rolling Stones, Richard Thompson, Anton Troianovski, Karen Tumulty, Kenneth P. Vogel, *The Washington Post*, Tim Weiner, Joshua Yaffa, *Yahoo! News*, The Yardbirds, Warren Zevon.

ABOUT THE AUTHOR

James Grady (b. 1949) is the author of screenplays, articles, and over a dozen critically acclaimed thrillers. Born in Shelby, Montana, Grady worked a variety of odd jobs, from hay bucker to gravedigger, before graduating from the University of Montana with a degree in journalism. In 1973, after years of acquiring rejection slips for short stories and poems, Grady sold his first novel: *Six Days of the Condor*, a sensational bestseller that was eventually adapted into a film starring Robert Redford.

After moving to Washington, DC, Grady worked for a syndicated columnist, investigating everything from espionage to drug trafficking. He quit after four years to focus on his own writing, and has spent the last three decades composing thrillers and screenplays. His body of work has won him France's Grand Prix du Roman Noir, Italy's Raymond Chandler Award, and Japan's Baka-Misu literary prize. Grady's most recent novel is *Last Days of the Condor* (2015). He and his wife live in a suburb of Washington, DC.

JAMES GRADY

FROM MYSTERIOUSPRESS.COM
AND OPEN ROAD MEDIA

MYSTERIOUSPRESS.COM

Otto Penzler, owner of the Mysterious Bookshop in Manhattan, founded the Mysterious Press in 1975. Penzler quickly became known for his outstanding selection of mystery, crime, and suspense books, both from his imprint and in his store. The imprint was devoted to printing the best books in these genres, using fine paper and top dust-jacket artists, as well as offering many limited, signed editions.

Now the Mysterious Press has gone digital, publishing ebooks through **MysteriousPress.com**.

MysteriousPress.com offers readers essential noir and suspense fiction, hard-boiled crime novels, and the latest thrillers from both debut authors and mystery masters. Discover classics and new voices, all from one legendary source.

FIND OUT MORE AT

WWW.MYSTERIOUSPRESS.COM

FOLLOW US:

@emysteries and Facebook.com/MysteriousPressCom

MysteriousPress.com is one of a select group of publishing partners of Open Road Integrated Media, Inc.

THE MYSTERIOUS BOOKSHOP, founded in 1979, is located in Manhattan's Tribeca neighborhood. It is the oldest and largest mystery-specialty bookstore in America.

The shop stocks the finest selection of new mystery hardcovers, paperbacks, and periodicals. It also features a superb collection of signed modern first editions, rare and collectable works, and Sherlock Holmes titles. The bookshop issues a free monthly newsletter highlighting its book clubs, new releases, events, and recently acquired books.

58 Warren Street
info@mysteriousbookshop.com
(212) 587-1011
Monday through Saturday
11:00 a.m. to 7:00 p.m.

FIND OUT MORE AT:

www.mysteriousbookshop.com

FOLLOW US:

@TheMysterious and Facebook.com/MysteriousBookshop

CPSIA information can be obtained
at www.ICGtesting.com
Printed in the USA
BVHW030755270219
541194BV00003B/1/P